Pel tugged at the magic flowing through and around the chamber, causing the fetch's chest to close. It healed almost instantly. The wizard Athelstan fell back, startled, in a most graceless and unwizardly fashion.

Though the fetch was technically dead, Pel could see that the pattern in its heart kept it alive. The network that ran through the rest of its body, like a miniature of the matrix itself, let it move and function. But there was a break in the pattern, a discontinuity. Where the pattern found in normal living creatures continued down into fractal complexity, the fetch's energies simply flattened out and looped back upon themselves; Pel wondered if Athelstan had seen it.

Excited by this discovery, without thinking what it might do, Pel reached out and repaired the flaw.

The fetch sat up. It opened its eyes and looked about.

Then it started screaming.

By Lawrence Watt-Evans
Published by Ballantine Books:

The Three Worlds Trilogy:
OUT OF THIS WORLD
IN THE EMPIRE OF SHADOW
THE REIGN OF THE BROWN MAGICIAN

Legends of Ethshar:
THE MISENCHANTED SWORD
WITH A SINGLE SPELL
THE UNWILLING WARLORD
THE BLOOD OF A DRAGON
TAKING FLIGHT
THE SPELL OF THE BLACK DAGGER

The Lords of Dûs:
THE LURE OF THE BASILISK
THE SEVEN ALTARS OF DÛSARRA
THE SWORD OF BHELEU
THE BOOK OF SILENCE

THE CYBORG AND THE SORCERERS
THE WIZARD AND THE WAR MACHINE

NIGHTSIDE CITY
CROSSTIME TRAFFIC

THE REIGN OF THE BROWN MAGICIAN

Volume Three of
The Three Worlds Trilogy

Lawrence Watt-Evans

A Del Rey® Book
BALLANTINE BOOKS • NEW YORK

A Del Rey® Book
Published by Ballantine Books

http://www.randomhouse.com

Library of Congress Catalog Card Number: 95-96247

ISBN 0-345-37247-6

Manufactured in the United States of America

First Edition: May 1996

10 9 8 7 6 5 4 3 2 1

For Julie
of course

CHAPTER 1

*H*er car was gone. *Amy Jewell had looked out the front* door and seen that the curb was empty, and had stepped back inside and closed the door.

Her car was gone.

That had come as a shock at first, but it shouldn't have. After all, she had left it out front months ago.

It was hard to realize that it had really been months, that it hadn't all been a dream, that they hadn't somehow returned to the moment they had left.

But it had been real, and it had been months ago that she had parked her car out front of Pel and Nancy Brown's house in the expectation of being safely back home and in bed by midnight. She and her lawyer had come here to find out why there was a nonfunctional spaceship in her backyard; she hadn't planned on anything more than an evening of explanations.

She certainly hadn't planned on spending months going through hell in two other universes.

But then, just to see if the stories she had been told were true, she and the others had stepped through a magical portal in the basement wall into a universe she called Faerie, where Shadow ruled—and after that she had been caught up, unable to return, until now.

She had fled from Shadow's monsters into the third universe, dominated by the Galactic Empire, where she had been captured by pirates and sold into slavery; she had spent weeks as a slave before the Empire had rescued her from her master, Walter, and his helper Beth.

1

At least she'd survived—Nancy Brown had been killed by the pirates, Nancy's daughter Rachel by her master. Walter had killed a slave once, but he hadn't killed Amy.

She was pregnant by that son of a bitch, though. Not that she intended to stay that way. The Empire had hanged Walter and Beth both, and she intended to abort Walter's child and be rid of it, as well. She'd never managed to have any children when she was married, not even before she had found out what a bastard Stan really was and divorced him. She wasn't about to start now with *Walter's* kid.

After the rescue she had spent boring weeks at Base One, the home of the Imperial Fleet, and then she had been sent back into Faerie as part of a raiding party that was meant to assassinate Shadow.

She hadn't intended to really attempt anything that stupid; she'd intended to use the Faerie magic to go home the minute the Empire's troops weren't watching her. But then the wizard who knew the portal spell had been killed, and she and the others had been stranded again.

So they'd gone on with the plan to assassinate Shadow, knowing it was suicidal.

And it *was* suicidal—most of the party had either died or deserted.

But the most amazing thing in the whole adventure was that they had actually managed it, eventually—Pel Brown and Prossie Thorpe had killed Shadow. Proserpine Thorpe, Registered Master Telepath, who had rebelled against the Galactic Empire and was now a refugee here on Earth with Amy, had shot a powerless Shadow dead.

And Pellinore Brown, a marketing consultant from Germantown, Maryland, had set it up. He now controlled all the power, the magical matrix, that Shadow had held.

He had sent Amy, and Prossie, and his lawyer Ted Deranian safely back through the portal in the Browns' basement, and here they were, but Pel hadn't been able to do anything about all the time that had passed while they were going through hell in those other realities.

So of course the car was gone, after so long.

Amy did wonder what had happened to it, though; had it been towed, or stolen, or repossessed, or what?

She realized then that she didn't have her keys, so she couldn't have started it anyway. She didn't have her driver's license, or any money, or anything else—her purse, if it still existed at all, was back on Zeta Leo III, where she'd been Walter's household slave, in that other universe where the Galactic Empire ruled hundreds of planets.

Ted's car was gone from out front, as well.

Pel's and Nancy's were in the garage; Amy checked, and found them both sitting there, somewhat dusty but apparently intact.

That didn't help much, though; even if she hadn't been bothered by the idea of stealing one of them, she didn't know where any keys were. She supposed one set was still in Nancy's stolen purse—and that was probably on Zeta Leo III, like her own. As for any other set, well, who knew where Pel kept his keys?

She wondered if Ted might know—or if not, whether he might know how to hot-wire an ignition.

Ted, however, was firmly settled in the family room, in front of the TV, watching CNN "Headline News," trying to catch up on what he'd missed, and to convince himself . . .

Well, to convince himself of something, but Amy wasn't sure just what. That he'd imagined the whole adventure? That it was all real? That whatever had happened, everything was normal now? For all she knew, he was checking to see whether this was really Earth, and not some twisted alternate version.

Whatever he was doing, he had ignored her ever since he found out that the TV worked and that the power and TV cable hadn't yet been cut off for nonpayment.

Prossie seemed to be wavering between the two of them; she was fascinated by the TV, but she also seemed to consider Amy her lifeline, and whenever Amy stayed out of sight of the family room for more than a few minutes Prossie came looking for her, calling her name quietly into the silent depths of the Browns' house.

It was hardly surprising that Prossie felt out of place—certainly no more surprising than the car's absence. After all, this wasn't Prossie's native world.

Amy paused in the hallway as Prossie caught up; for a moment both women hesitated, but neither spoke, and at last Amy led the way.

She wasn't really going anywhere in particular, just looking around; she didn't want to settle down the way Ted had, she wanted to keep moving, to get on home to her own house up in Goshen, but her car was gone and she didn't have any money or identification or credit cards, and she was wearing only the filthy, tattered remains of Imperial military-issue pants and T-shirt. She couldn't catch a bus or call a cab.

She might be able to find something she could wear in Pel and Nancy's closet. She and Nancy hadn't been the same size at all—Nancy had been smaller—but there would surely be something, one of Pel's shirts maybe. She didn't like taking things without permission, but this was an emergency, and she'd only be borrowing it until she could get home.

And besides, it wasn't as if Nancy would ever need her clothes again.

But Amy still didn't have money for a bus or a cab.

If the phone still worked she could call a friend for a ride, but she needed to think things through first. Who would she call? What would she say? What had happened all those weeks she was gone? Was the wreck of I.S.S. *Ruthless* still lying in her backyard?

She wished that thing had never fallen out of the sky onto her land; that had been what got her involved in all this in the first place. The Empire had been trying to establish contact with Washington and had suddenly discovered, when *Ruthless* popped out of a space warp over Amy's backyard, that their antigravity drive didn't work in Earth's universe.

And no one had believed it was real, so the crew had been thrown in jail down in Rockville, and Ted had bailed them out because Pel had been contacted by people from Faerie who wanted to talk to the Imperials, and then they'd all stepped through the portal in Pel's basement for a quick look, just to see if it was real . . .

Well, they were back now, and Amy wanted to go home, but what about Ted, and Prossie? What would become of them, if Amy left? Prossie had nowhere to go, and Ted seemed so out of touch with reality that Amy wasn't at all sure he could take care of himself.

There were hundreds of questions. She needed to think, and she thought best when she was moving, when she was looking at things. So she rambled through the Browns' empty house, looking around and trying to think, while Prossie followed along, saying nothing.

Amy thought Prossie probably had at least as many questions of her own, and it was really very thoughtful of her to not ask them yet.

She looked in the master bedroom, but did not explore the closets or dressers—she wasn't ready for that yet. Going through the Browns' clothes would be a little too intimate.

She would get to it, but first she just wanted to look.

Roaming from room to room with another woman tagging after her seemed so very familiar and comfortable that she wasn't sure whether to laugh or cry; it was just like looking over a prospective client's home with the client a step behind. And the Browns could certainly have used an interior decorator—or maybe just a good cleaning crew. The house was a mess.

It wasn't just the dust and general air of abandonment, either. Things were out of place, drawers left open, books stacked in front of empty shelves. Amy couldn't be certain, but she thought the house had been searched. She didn't remember any such disarray when she had been here before; true, that had only been for a few hours, months ago, and she hadn't seen most of the house, but she was fairly certain things were different.

The house hadn't been burgled; the TV and stereo and other valuables were all still there.

Someone, she guessed, must have reported the Browns missing. The police had probably gone through the place, looking for clues—and maybe not just the police, if someone had made the connection to the crashed spaceship. The FAA and the Air Force had been interested in it.

She smiled wryly at the thought as she stood in the door of poor little Rachel's bedroom. Somehow, she doubted the police or the Air Force would ever have figured out that everyone in the house had magically walked through a solid concrete wall in the basement and emerged in another universe, caught up in the conflict between the Galactic Empire and an all-powerful wizard named Shadow.

The smile vanished as she stepped into the bedroom and looked about. Toys were strewn across the floor; a floppy green-and-red plush alligator lay on the bed, gaping foolishly at her.

Poor little Rachel Brown, six years old, had been sold into slavery and then murdered. There wasn't anything funny about that.

Rachel's mother had been raped and killed by pirates—not storybook pirates with eye patches and peglegs, but serious, workmanlike pirates with guns and a spaceship. Rachel's father had survived, but he was back there in Shadow's place, mourning them both, with some crazy idea that he could bring them back from the dead.

Six Earthpeople had walked through that basement wall, and only two had come back—Pel was still in Faerie, and Nancy and Rachel and Susan, Amy's lawyer Susan Nguyen, whom she had dragged along, were all dead.

And the Faerie folk who had created the portal were *all* dead—Raven of Stormcrack Keep, and the wizards Valadrakul and Elani, and Squire Donald . . .

No, not quite all, she corrected herself; Stoddard might not be dead—he'd deserted, and might be safe somewhere in Faerie. He was gone, though, and the others were dead.

So were at least a dozen of the Imperials who had been involved.

There wasn't anything funny about any of it.

"I want to go home," Amy said suddenly. "Did you see a phone anywhere?"

Prossie blinked at her. "What's a phone?"

"Proserpine Thorpe is definitely on Earth now," the telepath said, standing at attention and staring straight ahead.

Undersecretary for Interdimensional Affairs John Bascombe leaned back in his desk chair and looked up at Carrie Hall's face.

Thorpe was the rogue telepath, the one who had gone into Shadow's universe with that barbarian Raven and the Earthpeople and that idiot Colonel Carson who'd got himself killed. She was the one who had started refusing orders, or making up her own—crimes that would have gotten her, or any other telepath, hanged or shot within hours, anywhere in the Empire. The Empire couldn't tolerate disobedience in the mind-reading mutants.

She was also Carrie Hall's cousin—all the telepaths, all four hundred and sixteen of them, were a single extended family, scattered across the Empire.

But Thorpe had been in Shadow's universe. Bascombe himself, along with General Hart, had sent her there after she and most of the crew of *Ruthless* had managed to get home to Base One.

Earth wasn't in Shadow's universe.

There were times Bascombe regretted that he had wangled himself this job. It had *looked* like an easy road to advancement, and it definitely had promise, but he kept stumbling across all these complications.

"Earth," he said.

"Yes, sir," Carrie answered, her gaze fixed on the wall behind him.

"You're absolutely sure she's on Earth, Hall? Not on some backwater like her last appearance, or some obscure part of the Shadow reality we haven't seen before, or some other planet in Earth's universe? Or on Terra? I'm told that Earth and Terra are very similar."

"Yes, sir. I'm sure. She's on Earth."

"Do you have any idea what she's doing there?"

Carrie hesitated.

"No, sir," she said.

"You can't read her mind?"

Carrie hesitated even longer this time.

"Sir, it's ... it's difficult, when she's on Earth," she explained, "especially since she isn't just ignoring me, she's actively trying to shut me out, and even without the use of her own telepathic abilities she knows how to make it difficult for me."

"So you haven't been able to read *anything*, telepath?" The doubt was plain in Bascombe's tone.

"Just ... just glimpses, sir. It's hard to describe."

"Try."

"I really wouldn't know where to begin, sir. There's a memory of a gunfight in a meadow somewhere, and something about blinding colored lights, and thoughts of death, and the image of a machine showing colored moving pictures, like a miniature movie."

"You can't do any better than that?"

She didn't answer, but he could see the unhappiness on her face.

Bascombe took his time watching that unhappiness before he said, "This renegade, I am told by you telepaths, has popped into real space twice in the past sixty hours. You tell me that these two appearances were over a hundred light-years apart, even though there's no sign of a spaceship involved. At considerable expense we've sent expeditions to both supposed locations, each one with a telepath along. And now you come in here and tell me that she's on Earth. Do you expect us to send another expedition *there*? Do I need to remind you what happened to *Ruthless*?"

"No, sir." Carrie's face was blank again.

"Then what *do* you expect, telepath?"

"Nothing, sir," Carrie said. "I just thought it was my duty to inform you."

Bascombe nodded.

"It was. You did. Now get the hell out of here—and I want you to write up a report on everything you can read from Proserpine Thorpe's mind, and keep on writing it from now until I tell you to stop, and send a copy of the new material to me once a day."

"Yes, sir." Carrie turned and fled.

When she was gone, Bascombe stared at the door.

For decades the Imperial government had relied on those damned mind-reading mutants for much of their intelligence gathering and long-distance communication. Thorpe wasn't the first one to go bad, and she probably wouldn't be the last, but each time anything like this happened, Bascombe worried; someday they might *all* go bad.

And this time it was all mixed up with the two known alternate universes, with the thing called Shadow that had been sending its spies and monsters into the Empire for the past seven years, and with the party of troublemakers Bascombe and his political rival General Hart had sent to their deaths. And now there was this thing about near-instantaneous travel across deep space.

At least, the telepaths *said* Thorpe had somehow crossed all those light-years in a day or so, without a ship. If that was true, if hopping between universes could provide near-instantaneous interstellar travel, that could mean that space-warp technology, Bascombe's own little bailiwick in the Department of Science, might be even more important than he had thought.

And if it wasn't true, it could mean that the telepaths had *already* gone bad.

Near the end of the row of gargoyles that drained the rooftop was one with a broken jaw. Its granite chin was gone, and the rusted end of an iron pipe protruded below the stumps of fangs, a jagged hole in the pipe's underside spilling water in uneven splatters onto the stone of the tower's battlement.

The steady rush of water from the others, pouring out over the side, did not bother Pel Brown at all, but the pattering from the broken pipe sounded like a child's running feet, and that sound tormented him. It was as if Rachel's ghost were running endlessly across the parapet.

He wanted to reach out and grab her, pull her back to safety, away from the edge—but she wasn't there.

Rachel would have adored this place, he thought, with its spires and its gargoyles, its spiral staircases and its secret passages. That she had not lived to see it was still unbearable, despite the weeks that had passed since he was told of her death.

He stood under the overhanging eaves, watching the rain, watching the streams of water pouring out into space, watching the one stream that scattered and fell short, watching the repeating pattern of splashes on the stone.

He had, for the moment, suppressed the visible portion of the aura of magic that surrounded him; to outward appearances he was only a man, but he could still feel the matrix he held, the power that flowed around and through him.

He could stop the sound, of course; any time he wanted to, he could stop it. He could blast the gargoyle into powder, if he chose. He thought that with a little more effort he could repair it, gathering dust from the air around it and healing the carved stone.

He did neither; instead, he drew the power to him, reached out into the web, into the power matrix, and found the lines that led up into the clouds overhead. He shifted them, working by feel in a way he had no words to explain.

The rain stopped, as if someone had shut off a faucet. Almost immediately after the last drops plopped onto the tile roof the steady flow from the other gargoyles slowed, and the spattering fall from the broken pipe changed its rhythm, becoming less even.

And that was worse.

It didn't sound like his daughter anymore; it didn't sound

like anything. It was as if he had erased the last trace of her. The sky was still gray overhead, the water was still dripping from the eaves, the battlement was still glazed with rain, but no invisible child's footsteps pattered on the stone.

Instead, damp air swirled and whispered across the stone, driven not by wind, but by the magical currents of the matrix.

He pulled the power to him, grabbing at it, hauling it in; magic seethed in his mind and his fingers, and the distinction between himself and the matrix he held became vague and uncertain. A red sheen blurred his vision for a second, and then was swept aside in a shower of crimson sparks that danced wildly across the stonework.

He was glowing again; his control of his appearance had slipped, and a halo of shifting colors flickered around him.

He ignored it, looking upward. The clouds hung above him, low and dark, and he sent a broad band of scarlet fire snaking upward, lighting them to the color of blood.

The unnatural glow suffused the landscape; the green forests on the distant hills turned black, the gray marshlands that encircled the fortress were tinged with a rusty life, and the castle itself took on a color that had never been seen in nature, not in this world, nor on Pel's native Earth.

It looked like something out of a horror movie, Pel thought, that eerie sky and the thick clouds and the gargoyles, hovering above him.

That seemed perfectly appropriate. He felt as if he'd fallen into a story, months ago, and been unable to climb back out. Sometimes it was science fiction, as in the Galactic Empire, with their spaceships and blasters; sometimes it was an epic fantasy, as when Shadow had made him into a wizard and he had turned on her and destroyed her. Why shouldn't it be a horror story now?

He released the knot of power he had gathered—not in a spell, as he had thought he would, but in a simple release. The power flowed back into its natural patterns—or at any rate, into a form as natural as the patterns could be while still bound together in the world-spanning matrix that Shadow had created for herself and passed on to Pel.

The rain began falling anew, and Pel turned away.

He had no reason to be up here, really. He had been exploring the fortress for lack of anything better to do—or rather, because he was not sure he knew what he wanted to do.

He knew what he wanted to *have*—he wanted his wife and child back. And he knew that he held a power that could allegedly raise the dead.

But he didn't know what he had to do to make it work. He didn't know how to find out.

Hadn't someone said that knowledge was power? Well, Pel thought, the converse didn't seem to be true. He had all the power he could want, but it hadn't gotten him much in the way of knowledge.

He stepped into the tower, closed the door behind him, and started down the stair. The way was dark and narrow, the slit windows covered by dusty shutters, and Pel had no lantern or torch, but he didn't need one—he carried the mobile focus of all this world's magic with him wherever he went, and its glow brilliantly illuminated the surrounding stone walls.

He didn't need to see at all, though; the matrix also let him sense the shape of the world around him in some more direct way he did not understand.

It was amazing how quickly he had become accustomed to carrying this thing about wherever he went, he thought as he tramped down the steps. Shadow had used something like hypnosis on him, he knew—something that used magic, rather than the simple psychological stunts and suggestions employed by Earthly hypnotists. She had wanted him to learn quickly, not for his own good, but so that he could serve her purposes that much sooner. So he found it possible to accept calmly that his senses were altered and enhanced, that he was bound to a network of mystical force as if it were a part of his body, that he could draw on that seemingly infinite source of energy and therefore no longer grew tired, no matter what he did.

It was mad, really; he was living out an insane power fantasy. Shadow had used this matrix to rule her entire world, and had intended to conquer others, as well; surely, Pel thought, no individual could handle such physical power. It had to be some sort of dream or delusion—a story, not real.

If it was all real, then how could he accept it so calmly?

He paused, and looked about at the shifting glare of colors that shone across rough gray stone.

Was it real?

Of course it was. Poor Ted Deranian had thought he was dreaming, and it had gotten him beaten and abused; Pel wasn't going to make his mistake. This was all real.

But how did he know he hadn't dreamed Ted? And Amy and Prossie, and all the others. None of them were here now to tell him if he was mad or dreaming. He had sent the three of them, Amy and Ted and Prossie, safely back to Earth, and the rest were dead or missing.

He shook his head, and magical currents twisted and writhed around him.

He wasn't dreaming. It was all real. It was as real as anything had ever been; he reached out and touched the nearest wall, felt the cool, hard stone under his fingertips.

It *was* real.

It was real, and he controlled all the magic in this world of magic, and it didn't seem strange at all. It seemed perfectly natural.

He wondered it that was a good thing.

The technician sat up abruptly at the sound of the beep. He blinked at the panel, and his eyes widened as he saw the code number indicating which phone was in use. He reached for his own phone.

"Get me Major Johnston," he said. "We have an outgoing call on the Brown phone."

CHAPTER 2

He could make the fetches obey him.

It wasn't really much of an accomplishment for a person in Pel's position, but it was a start.

He supposed that making living people obey him would probably be easier; he could just threaten to incinerate them, and they would obey out of fear.

Fetches, however, were already dead. To be exact, they were dead people Shadow had revived as her servants; the fortress held dozens of them.

There were *hundreds* of homunculi in the place, if that was the correct term for all the creatures Shadow had created from scratch, rather than just reanimated—everything from artificial insects to the dead dragon at the foot of the grand staircase, and Pel could sense that there were even bigger beasts outside the castle, such as the burrowing behemoth that had attacked Pel's party at Stormcrack, months earlier, or gigantic bat-things like the one Valadrakul of Warricken had slain in the Low Forest of West Sunderland.

Pel had decided to start with the fetches, though; they were all human in appearance, for one thing, and he was more comfortable with that. For another, he was very concerned with the resurrection of the dead. He didn't want Nancy and Rachel to be mere zombies, like the fetches, but he assumed that any spell that could restore his family would be somehow related to whatever Shadow had done to produce fetches.

He had found three of them simply standing in one of the corridors, lifeless and mute. At first he had stared at them, expecting them to notice him; then he had tried ordering them verbally, telling them to walk.

They had stood there, unmoving, as the shifting colors of the matrix had played across them, rich deep blue and honey gold predominating just at that moment.

Then he had used the matrix, used his magic, and had found the little tangle of magic in the heart and spine and brain of each fetch, the magic that, he saw, controlled each one's action. He had poked and prodded at one with immaterial fingers—and the fetch had twitched and shivered and blinked.

He had told it, "Speak," and it had opened its mouth, but no sound came out. He had realized, with shocked disgust, that it wasn't breathing.

"Breathe," he had told it, and the chest expanded; air was sucked into its lungs in a hollow gasp, then expelled in a rasping wheeze.

One breath, and it stopped.

Pel shuddered.

"Never mind that," he had said. "Will you obey me, now?"

The fetch had blinked, then nodded, and suddenly seemed alive again—somber and silent, but alive. He had, he saw, had to establish a link between its internal web and the greater web of the matrix, a link that Shadow must have once had, and must have severed at some point—probably when she first transferred the matrix to Pel.

Having established the link he controlled the fetch entirely, just as he controlled the matrix itself.

And that meant he could make the fetches obey him. He would have servants—or rather, slaves—who could run errands for him, do whatever he needed to have done.

That was a good start, he thought. It was a definite step forward on the road to using the matrix properly, and to learning to resurrect the dead.

"Go to the throne room," he ordered. The fetch sketched a bow, then turned and marched away.

It was only a first step, though. There were things he

needed to know if he was to bring Nancy and Rachel back from the dead, things that he couldn't learn just from ordering fetches around, and while the matrix probably contained all the knowledge he needed, somewhere, somehow, he didn't know how to get at it. He needed someone to talk to about his plans, someone who could teach him.

Someone to teach him magic, he thought, as he watched the fetch march down the passage toward the throne room. Pel's lips tightened, and the aura flickered into harsh reds and smoky browns.

He wanted a wizard.

Shadow had been the last matrix wizard, the only wizard who regularly raised the dead. While Shadow was dead because Pel had sent Prossie Thorpe to kill her, Shadow had not been the only wizard in Faerie.

Even though Shadow had roasted Valadrakul to death, and Shadow's creatures had butchered Elani, Pel thought he knew at least one other wizard who still lived: Taillefer, that fat coward who had refused to open a portal to either Earth or the Empire. After Elani had died, Valadrakul had not known how to open portals to other worlds, so he had summoned Taillefer—and Taillefer had refused to help, for fear of drawing Shadow's attention.

Well, Pel had learned how to open his own portals. And now he could send fetches out to . . . Pel smiled grimly. He could send fetches out to *fetch* Taillefer.

Taillefer might not know how to raise the dead, but he surely could teach Pel *something*.

Pel strode toward the throne room, still smiling.

Amy hung up the phone. "Donna says she'll be here in about twenty minutes," she said. She smiled with relief.

Prossie didn't smile back. "Then what?" she asked.

"Then she'll drive us out to my place," Amy replied. It was such a pleasure to be able to say that, to be able to take cars and telephones for granted, to know what was going on again! "I guess she can drop Ted off on the way, and then we can settle in. I don't know if there'll be much that's fit to eat after all this time, but we can get into some decent clean clothes." She frowned slightly, thinking and planning. "I don't have my keys, but if I have to, I guess I can break a window to get in. Or maybe I should call a locksmith. I'll have to find one who'll take a check; I don't have any cash. The checkbook's gone, too, but I have extra checks at home."

Prossie nodded, though it wasn't a very enthusiastic gesture. Amy didn't really notice. She was on familiar ground after months of living nightmare; she didn't want to think about Prossie's problems yet. There would be time for that later.

"There's canned soup, that'll still be good," Amy said, talking more to herself now than to Prossie. "And I should have something that'll fit you—you're only an inch or so shorter than I am, right?" She sighed. "I wonder if they stopped delivering my mail? I guess if Pel's phone still works, mine will, too, but there must be about three months' bills waiting. And all my clients will have given up on me—I'll have to just about start the business over again."

She paused and glanced at her companion, but Prossie didn't respond.

Amy continued, "I suppose that spaceship is still in the backyard—did you have anything on board? It might still be there, if nobody's gotten in and stolen it. And I'll need to call the doctor and make an appointment as soon as I can." She shuddered slightly. She didn't like to think about getting an abortion, but it had to be done—she couldn't afford a baby, and anyway, her life was quite disrupted enough without bearing the child of a dead rapist from another universe.

And it wouldn't hurt to have a general checkup, after all she had been through.

"Do you think they might have posted guards around the ship?" Prossie asked suddenly.

Amy blinked at her, startled. "Who?" she asked.

"Your government. The ones who arrested us."

Amy put a hand to her mouth, then admitted, "I hadn't

thought of that." Then she lowered the hand and managed an uncertain smile. "But even if they . . . no, they *can't* have guards there; it's private property, and poor Susan had a court order or something. And we haven't done anything wrong."

As she finished her attempt at reassurance Amy realized she could hear sirens; she turned to look out the window. For a moment she stared in disbelief; then she headed for the living room for a better view.

"How did they know?" Prossie asked as she followed Amy. "Do you think they might have telepaths, somehow?"

"No," Amy said, "they don't have any telepaths. They might have the place staked out, though. I didn't think we were that obvious." She paused, then added, "They must have tapped the phone."

Prossie didn't ask what that meant.

A moment later, Amy and Prossie were joined by Ted, and the three of them stood at the front window watching as men in suits and uniforms emerged from the two county police cruisers that had pulled up in front of the Browns' home, and from an official-looking car in the driveway, a sedan that had a government seal of some sort on the driver's door.

Amy realized, annoyed, that she hadn't had a chance to go through Nancy's closet; she was still in her Imperial rags. She doubted these people would let her change.

And her hair was a mess—her last bleach and perm had all grown out long ago, and she hadn't even had a chance to brush it in days.

Ted moaned softly.

"We have a report, sir," the lieutenant said, saluting briskly.

Bascombe put down his pen and glowered at the young man.

"A report from *whom*?" he demanded. "From where? About what?"

"From Registered Master Telepath Bernard Dixon, sir!" the lieutenant said, snapping sharply back to attention.

"Ah," Bascombe said. "And exactly which of our mind-reading freaks is this Dixon?"

"Telepath Dixon is currently serving aboard I.S.S. *Meteor*, sir, investigating the reported reappearance of the renegade, Proserpine Thorpe."

"*Which* reported reappearance?"

"Uh . . . the first one, sir. I think." The lieutenant quivered uncertainly. Bascombe sighed.

"Tell me about it," he said.

"Yes, sir. According to Dixon, he has established, working in cooperation with five other telepaths, the approximate location of Thorpe's reappearance. He reports that there is only one system it could have been in, an unnamed system with no habitable planets—the navigator aboard *Meteor* has the catalog number, but it was not included in the report. Dixon is unable to narrow it down any further; no physical traces have been found, and telepathy, he says, is not sufficiently precise over interstellar distances to be more exact."

"Did he say how he found the system at all?" Bascombe asked.

"Ah . . . that was not included in the report I received, sir," the lieutenant admitted.

"Dismissed," Bascombe said.

"Sir?" The lieutenant blinked.

"I said dismissed. Get out."

The lieutenant almost forgot to salute again as he hurried out.

Bascombe picked up his pen and considered.

He knew how the location was determined; telepaths on a dozen planets had been asked to report which direction Prossie Thorpe had been in, and those were then adjusted by the astronomers to allow for planetary rotation and used as approximate vectors. Where the resulting lines—or rather, cones, since none were narrow enough to be lines—intersected, that was where Thorpe had been.

Meteor had been sent to explore the resulting volume of space; the charts didn't show any inhabited systems there, but the charts could be wrong.

This time, according to Dixon, they weren't. And he'd

checked back with five other stinking mutants to see if his distance felt right.

So Thorpe hadn't appeared on an inhabited planet, or even just a habitable one.

That meant a ship.

And that might explain why her stay there had been so brief, only about a minute—she had delivered something to a ship, and then returned to Shadow's world.

But if she was just a courier, why would Shadow, or Raven, or whoever was behind it, use a telepath? A telepath would stand out like a beacon—Thorpe *had* stood out like a beacon.

Someone had wanted the Empire to know something was going on; someone had wanted to get the Empire's attention—but who? And why?

Was it a distraction, a feint? Or was someone trying to tell them something, a message they weren't receiving?

What about Thorpe's other appearance? That one had been narrowed down to two possible systems, one of them, Upsilon Ceti, home to the Imperial colony of Beckett; I.S.S. *Wasp* was scheduled to arrive at Beckett Spaceport in a matter of hours.

If there had been a telepath on Beckett in the first place, maybe life would have been a bit simpler—but four hundred telepaths couldn't cover three thousand Imperial planets, and Thorpe had only appeared in the Beckett area briefly. It wasn't quite as fast as the other, about five minutes instead of one, but it was brief.

Was that a message of some kind? Why Beckett, which was a quiet little backwater?

And now Thorpe was supposed to be on Earth, the only human-inhabited planet in the third universe, and this time she was staying there. What did *that* mean?

Did it mean *anything*? Or were all the telepaths lying? Had Thorpe ever really been in any of those places? Carrie Hall's reports hadn't started arriving yet, but he was fairly certain that when they did, they'd be useless.

Something was definitely going on, but whether the

enemy was Shadow, or Raven's band of revolutionaries, or some faction within the Empire, or the telepaths themselves, Bascombe didn't know.

But he intended to find out.

He almost called for a telepath, but then he caught himself; he rose and stepped to the door, and called to his receptionist, "Miss Miller, have a messenger sent to Special Branch; I want orders sent to *Meteor* to stay where they are and search carefully for any signs of activity—ships, gravity fields, lights, whatever."

"Yes, Mr. Bascombe."

He nodded, and retreated back into his office.

The message would be sent by telepath, of course; there was no other way to reach *Meteor* except through Dixon. Sending it downstairs to Special Branch on paper, though, would mean that no telepath would be reading his mind directly.

At least, not legally.

And if telepaths were reading minds illegally, he couldn't stop them in any case—but that way lay madness. Telepaths *could* be listening to any thought, at any moment.

He just hoped they weren't.

"Am I under arrest?" Amy demanded, folding her arms across her chest and glaring up at the man in the blue uniform who seemed to be in charge of the whole business.

They hadn't let her change her clothes, and the gesture was as much for the sake of decency as out of annoyance. Her T-shirt was torn on both sides, and she wasn't wearing anything under it.

She tried not to think about that.

Major Johnston sighed. He turned a chair around, sat down, and leaned on the back.

"No, ma'am," he said, "you aren't. However, if that's what it takes to get you to cooperate, it can be arranged."

"On what charge?" Amy protested. "I haven't done anything!"

"I don't know just what charge, ma'am," Johnston said.

"I'm not a lawyer; I work for Air Force Intelligence, so I know something about the laws, but I'm not a lawyer, and in a complicated case like this . . ." He didn't finish the sentence; instead he shrugged and said, "But there's no question we could find something. You were one of sixteen people who disappeared all at once without any rational explanation, and now three of you—*only* three—have turned up again, one of you apparently gone at least temporarily nuts. I think we could get you booked on suspicion of *something*, kidnapping or assault or something. Withholding evidence, if nothing else."

It was Amy's turn to sigh. At least the officer hadn't included indecent exposure in his list. She wished Susan were there—but Susan was dead. Amy had seen her body lying on the floor of Shadow's throne room, back in Faerie.

Amy supposed that she could have called on the surviving members of Dutton, Powell & Hough—Bob Hough must be back from his vacation long since—but how could she explain to *them* what had happened, how Susan Nguyen had died? So she had passed up the chance to call her lawyer when this Johnston had offered it.

She had managed to stall her removal until her friend Donna had arrived, so at least someone knew where she was and more or less what was happening, but Donna wasn't going to get her out of jail if these security people, whoever they were, did decide to arrest her.

"Is Ted okay?" she asked. "He was pretty upset."

"Mr. Deranian is, indeed, upset," Johnston admitted. "While I won't tell you any of the details, he seems to be very unsure of his own grasp on reality. He has asked repeatedly to go home, and we may oblige him in that—we're waiting for an opinion from a psychologist on whether it's safe for him to be alone. We've tried to call his sister to look after him, but she doesn't seem to be available."

"But you won't let *me* go home!" Amy protested.

"You, Ms. Jewell, are not screaming and crying and irrational."

Amy glared at him. Johnston glared back.

"What about Prossie?" Amy asked.

Major Johnston sighed again.

"Your other companion," he said, "tells us that her name is Registered Telepath Proserpine Thorpe, formerly of the Special Branch of the Imperial Intelligence Service. Beyond that, I'd prefer not to say at this time." He hesitated. "*Is* that her name?"

"As far as I know, it is," Amy said.

Johnston stared at her for a moment, then said, "All right. You don't want to talk to us. I don't know why not. This whole bizarre case is jammed full of things I don't know. It's been driving me crazy for months, ever since that damned whatever-it-is fell out of nowhere into your backyard and I got assigned to make sense of it. I've been trying to do that without any real information, but I can't. Now, you could give me real information, and you say you won't—but can't you at least say *why* you won't tell me what's going on?"

"Because you won't believe me. Besides, it isn't any of your business."

"How do you *know* I won't believe you?"

Amy closed her eyes. It wasn't really an unreasonable question. Johnston certainly seemed more reasonable than the soldier who had been questioning her before, who had just kept demanding she tell them where she had been for so long, and who had refused to ever accept "I don't know" as an answer.

"Because," she said, opening her eyes and staring straight at Major Johnston's face, "it's all impossible, so impossible that Ted Deranian doesn't believe it, and he was *there*. That's why he's upset, you know—he thought it was all a dream, and that he'd finally woken up, and then you people came and hauled him away, and that means either it's real, or he's still dreaming." She sighed. "Now, do you expect me to believe that you'll just accept my word for something so incredible that a man who lived through it thinks it was just a nightmare?"

Johnston considered that for a long moment.

"All right," he said, "so maybe I won't believe it. But maybe I will, and what can it hurt to try me?"

"You won't argue?" Amy had visions of trying to tell her story and having every point questioned, every absurdity denied, until nothing made any sense at all.

"I don't know," Johnston admitted, straightening up for a moment. "Try me."

The man's apparent honesty was disarming; Amy shrugged, unfolded her arms, and said, "You ask questions. I'll answer—for now."

Shadow had known how to see through other people's eyes, and hear through other people's ears, Pel reminded himself. She had been able to spy on anyone, anywhere in the entire immense world she ruled. It couldn't be that difficult.

He closed his eyes, clenched his fists on the arms of his throne, and concentrated on the webs of magic that reached out in all directions around him.

He could sense things out there, like tiny sparks caught in the meshes of color and darkness, things that he was fairly sure were people, and he tried to focus in on one specific twinkle, tried to see through it—and nothing happened. He didn't connect; he didn't see anything, through his eyes or anyone else's.

Shadow had known how, but Pel didn't. He could sense the shape of the matrix, all the currents and eddies of magic that flowed through Faerie; he could tell when something disturbed those currents, and he was fairly certain he knew when the disturbance was a wizard stealing a little power, and when it was just some harmless peasant stumbling through a place where the magic ran strong. The wizards seemed to have odd little patterns of their own, sort of like fractal designs within the larger design of the matrix. Pel could see that.

But he couldn't see through other eyes.

He could tell more or less how far out in the network any movement was, yet he couldn't directly match up the matrix with the outside world; he couldn't make any correlation between magical streams and physical ones, couldn't tell where the web lay on land, where on sea—or where it soared through the air or burrowed underground, or even climbed away from the planet into whatever lay beyond the sky in this strange realm. The network he had inherited from Shadow was centered on the fortress where he sat, but it extended, however tenuously, through this entire universe.

He could spot the fetches he had sent out, carrying messages, but though he thought he might be able to transmit a couple of basic commands, such as a signal to return, he couldn't really communicate with them. He could tell which direction they had gone, and could see how far they had progressed in terms of the matrix, but what that translated to in miles he could only estimate, and the farther away they got, the less reliable that estimate was.

Where ordinary people appeared as analogous to white or golden sparks, and wizards seemed to have faint traceries woven inside those sparks, the fetches were something like smoky red embers, and were bound into the matrix itself, rather than being independently existing structures that sometimes impinged upon the net. It seemed as if Pel ought to be able to at least see through *those* eyes—but he couldn't. He didn't know how. He couldn't see where they were or what they were doing.

He opened his eyes, slumped back in the elaborately carved throne, and stared through the glimmering colors at the big open doors at the far end of the room.

He didn't look at the spot where Susan Nguyen's body had lain for so long. At least he'd made a little progress on *that* problem—with the help of the fetches he had had the corpse settled on a spare bed, and had put a preserving spell on it as best he could. He had seen how the meats in the fortress kitchen were preserved, and he had painstakingly built up the same magical structure over poor Susan, and it seemed to be working.

But not much else was. He was fairly certain, now, that he'd sent those fetches out on a fool's errand. He hadn't given them any directions; he'd just told them, "Go find wizards and bring them here."

But he hadn't known what directions to give them. He didn't even have a map. He had never *seen* a map of Shadow's world. He wasn't even sure there *were* maps.

He knew the route he had taken to reach the fortress, from the Low Forest of Sunderland across the Starlinshire Downs and the coastal plain to Shadowmarsh; he had looked across the rift valley called Stormcrack and seen Stormcrack Keep, perched on the other side; but where these fit in their world, where Stormcrack lay in relation to Sunderland or Shadowmarsh, he had no idea at all. He thought he remembered Raven mentioning that Stormcrack lay in the Hither Corydians, while the mountains visible from Sunderland were the Further Corydians, but what that meant he didn't know. He had heard other names, as well, but they were just names.

It wasn't fair. In all the stories the hero knew where everything was. There were always maps. Tolkien's books had had maps all over them. Even the movies had maps sometimes.

If Shadow had had any maps, Pel hadn't found them yet.

How could he find anything, or anyone, without maps, without any means of long-distance communication? And while he could sense fetches and wizards in the matrix, he didn't know how to guide the red embers toward the white snowflakes and golden spiderwebs; how could his fetches find anyone?

He had sent them out, a dozen of them, with orders to find wizards and bring them back—Taillefer in particular, but if they found *any* wizard, that would do. But how could they do that? How would they know where to go?

He hadn't thought this through.

He couldn't even send notes; most people in this world seemed to be illiterate, and those who weren't used a different alphabet from the one he knew. He had told the fetches to summon wizards, but he had left it up to them to figure out how to deliver that summons.

They might not be able to; fetches were pretty limited.

He could go out searching on his own, he supposed—but he wasn't sure just how to best use his magic to travel. Conjuring winds that would blow him around, the way Taillefer did, seemed dangerous and haphazard.

And he wouldn't know where to go. It was a very big planet. The matrix seemed to stretch to infinity.

He would have to get organized about this. As Shadow's heir and master of the matrix, he was, in theory, ruler of all Faerie; he didn't need to run his own errands, or send out all his servants. He could order *other* people to do it all.

And besides, he had told Amy that he intended to be a *benevolent* ruler here, to teach these people how to lead more civilized lives; how could he carry out that promise if he stayed holed up here in his castle, making no contact with the outside world?

It was time to start playing his role properly. He would get this place organized—and that would enable him to fetch wizards who could teach him how to raise the dead.

And if he did some good for the natives in the process, all the better; they could certainly use some help. The towns and villages he had seen on his way to Shadowmarsh hadn't exactly been paradise. He remembered the gibbets in every village, the disemboweled corpses of the people who had offended Shadow—at the very least he could do away with that sort of thing.

He realized that he could start right on his own doorstep—quite literally on his doorstep, where the corpses of half a dozen Imperial soldiers still lay. He hadn't even done anything about them.

Not that he could do very much, but at least he could have them decently buried.

And after that he could send messengers out to the surrounding villages.

He sat up straight, closed his eyes, and sent out a summons to the fetches still in the fortress, and to the handful of homunculi and other creatures over which he had established his control.

CHAPTER 3

"*I don't care if you believe me or not,*" Amy said wearily. "It's over, it's done, and I just want to go home and forget about it."

"What about the spaceship in your backyard?" Major Johnston asked.

Amy sighed.

She had to admit that Johnston had done his best to make it easy on her; he hadn't nagged, hadn't argued, hadn't pushed when she said she didn't know something—but on the other hand, he had this annoying habit of finding questions she didn't want to think about.

"I don't know," she said. "What about it?"

"Are you going to just leave it there?"

"Do I have a choice?"

"Assuming you have a choice."

"I haven't decided. Do *you* want it?"

Johnston hesitated, then admitted, "We haven't decided, either. We might; please let us know before you do anything drastic with it."

"Sure," Amy said. "May I go now?"

"Um . . ." The major hesitated. "Not *quite* yet, I'm afraid."

"We've got the report from Beckett, sir," the lieutenant said.

Bascombe leaned back. "Let's have it, then," he said.

"The formal statement is still being written up, sir, but the gist of it is that several unidentified corpses were found

28

in a field outside Blessingbury that could easily have been the place Thorpe appeared. All but one of the corpses were adult males, in some sort of black livery, carrying swords; the one female wore a gray robe and carried no weapon. All had been killed by blaster fire, but no blasters were found; a more careful search is ongoing."

Bascombe blinked and straightened up.

"Swords?" he said.

"Yes, sir. That's what the telepath *said*, anyway."

"The bodies—were they human?"

The lieutenant hesitated. "Well, yes, sir, so far as I know," he said. "The report calls them dark-haired Nordic males, which would certainly seem to *imply* human. I don't think any autopsies have been done yet, though."

"Dark-haired Nordic?"

"Yes, sir, Nordic is the standard term for any pure-blooded white, you know, it's not just the true . . ."

"Shut up."

Bascombe knew Imperial racial classifications as well as anyone; what he didn't know was why any Imperial citizen, except a few holders of ceremonial titles back on Terra, would be carrying a sword.

Shadow's creatures might well use swords, but most of them didn't seem to be genuine human beings. Even the humanoids often had black skin—not the brown of a Negro, but actual black.

On the other hand, the people of Earth were authentic human beings, so far as Bascombe knew. Of the four who had stayed at Base One for several weeks, three had been white, one Azeatic; Bascombe had never seen a Negro Earthman, but that didn't mean much, since that foursome was hardly a fair sample.

Did Earthpeople still use swords? Earlier reports had indicated that they carried projectile weapons—not blades, but gunpowder-and-bullet firearms. Perhaps this group had been even *more* primitive, though, or had been uncertain their guns would work in Imperial space. Swords always worked. And they never needed reloading.

Still, swords seemed more appropriate to Shadow's world. Shadow itself relied on its superscientific "magic," but its slaves didn't seem to, and in fact much of the "magic" didn't seem to operate in normal space.

Or maybe these had been members of Raven's resistance movement. Bascombe didn't think much of Raven of Stormcrack Keep—the man was obsessive and abysmally ignorant, determined to fight Shadow's science with . . .

With swords.

This was all getting very complicated—Shadow, Earth, and Raven were all possibilities.

If the telepaths hadn't made it all up.

"Lieutenant," Bascombe said, "I want one of those corpses brought here to Base One, as fast as possible. Make sure the sword comes with it, and someone who saw everything as it was first found—*not* a telepath."

"Yes, sir." The messenger turned to go.

"And," Bascombe added loudly, "send the telepath Carrie Hall up here."

Major Reginald Johnston sat at his desk, staring at the fancy silver pen he'd gotten as an award two years before, rolling it between his fingers as he tried to think it all through logically.

Sherlock Holmes always said that when you had eliminated the impossible, whatever remained, however unlikely, had to be the truth—but how did you know what was really impossible?

The three of them were all reasonably consistent in their stories. Details varied, of course, but not to the point of showing any actual contradictions. Deranian insisted that the whole thing was a dream or hallucination, and would only talk about it on those terms, and only with a psychologist; Jewell didn't claim to understand any of it, only to be reporting what she thought she had experienced; but Thorpe, if that was really her name, was the tough one, as she claimed to actually be *from* one of these other universes.

And that should have been easy to disprove, but it wasn't.

So either it was all true, and the United States had blown a chance to make peaceful contact with aliens not just from another planet, but from another universe entirely, or else the whole thing was the most elaborate and inexplicable hoax Johnston had ever heard of.

It didn't make *sense* as a hoax—but a Galactic Empire in another universe? Wizards and castles in a third? If it was a hoax, how did the hoaxers get that spaceship there? Why hadn't anything leaked in the months since it had crashed? Who was Proserpine Thorpe? Where did she and the others come from? Where did they go?

What did Sherlock Holmes say to do after you had eliminated the impossible, and found there was *nothing* left?

For months, ever since that impossible spaceship had fallen out of nowhere and the case had been dumped in his lap, Johnston had been looking for an explanation. He had thought that when he found some of the missing people he would have that explanation.

He supposed he *did* have an explanation now—but he didn't like it, and he didn't want to believe it. All the same, he had to cover the bases. If it *is* true, he asked himself, tapping his fancy silver pen on the worn spot on the blotter, if it *is* true, what do I do about it?

A Galactic Empire. An all-powerful wizard.

Hell, it was simple enough, really; the first thing any commander does is collect information, scout out the territory. Even when the territory was in another universe, that rule still held.

And you pass the information up the chain of command, keep headquarters informed—but how in hell could he tell anyone about this one? If *he* didn't really believe it, how could he convince anyone higher up?

And *that* brought him to the first rule, not of military strategy, but of political strategy: CYA.

He would file the appropriate reports, full of qualifiers and ambiguity, and other than that he wouldn't say a damn thing to anyone until he could provide *proof*. He would investigate the hell out of everything, have the Brown house searched right down to the foundations, have Jewell and Deranian and Thorpe watched every minute, send someone to check out whether there was any research being done on . . . on what? Other dimensions?

The Golden Fleece Award people on that senator's staff might know—research like that would be right up their alley.

He put down the pen and reached for the intercom.

Pel looked over the motley crew he had gathered before his throne. Colored light flickered across black clothing, black leather, glossy black fur—Shadow's color scheme had been pretty limited. Maybe she saw enough colors from the matrix, Pel thought.

He counted nine fetches—kitchen help, mostly, but since Pel could draw all the energy he needed from the matrix, he didn't need to eat, so why should he maintain a kitchen?

There were four hairless, black-skinned homunculi, human in appearance except for their color; three of them, two male and one female, were naked. Pel had no idea what purpose they had served, why Shadow had created them, but he had found them and had been able to make them obey him.

There were about a dozen other creatures, but most of them Pel had no name for; Shadow had apparently been fond of experimenting, and had often been generous with claws, teeth, scales, and tentacles. Two could reasonably be called hounds, and one resembled a panther, but the others weren't so easily classified.

Hundreds of other creatures lived in the fortress—if they were really alive—and there were literally thousands more in the surrounding marsh and the forests beyond, but Pel hadn't yet managed to gain control of all those.

He didn't see much use for the sluglike marsh-monsters, in any case. The dragon might have been nice, but he had killed that—which reminded him, he should incinerate the remains before they began to stink.

Most of the rest of Shadow's creatures he just hadn't gotten to yet. So he had about two dozen obedient servants of various shapes, none of them particularly appealing.

"All right," he said, "I want all of you to go out of this place, and go out to the villages, and bring back people. Alive. Don't hurt them. I want to talk to them. Understand?"

Roughly a score of heads nodded.

Pel hesitated.

"No children," he added. He didn't want to terrorize any kids. "Adults only. For that matter, make it men only." This was a primitive and sexist world he was in; he didn't want to worry about the sexual politics of the situation. He looked at some of the nonhumanoid creatures and asked, "Can you tell men from women?"

The bobbing movements, hissings, and grunts looked and sounded like agreement.

"Good. Okay, then go." He sat back on the throne as his audience turned away.

He didn't know how to send them after anyone in particular, but he figured that out of any random group of men they might bring in there would be someone he could make use of, as a messenger at the very least, maybe as a deputy or more.

And he had to send several of these creatures because he didn't know whether he could trust any one of them to do the job, or how people would react. If he sent only one, as a trial, it might get killed by some panicky peasant, or it might fall in a bog somewhere—he wasn't sure how bright most of the things were.

Besides, he wouldn't mind having enough of a sample of the population to be at least slightly representative. You didn't test a new product on just one potential buyer; he wanted to have a few people brought in.

They might even find poor Tom Sawyer, if he was still alive out there somewhere.

Pel blinked. "Wait," he called.

The pack of monsters paused in the doorway of the throne room; two of the homunculi turned back to face him, but the fetches and most of the rest simply stopped where they were.

Spaceman Sawyer was still out there somewhere, either alive or dead, and Pel had completely forgotten about him until just now.

How could he have been so thoughtless?

He had been busy, he had had other problems to worry about, but it was still unforgivable. He had left an Imperial soldier wandering around in Faerie, trapped in an alien land, when he—Pel—could have sent him home to the Galactic Empire in a matter of minutes.

And not just Sawyer, who had turned back at the fortress gate; there was Ron Wilkins, who had deserted the party days earlier, somewhere in the villages this side of Starlinshire. And there might be other survivors of the Imperial landing party, as well—most had stayed at the ship with Lieutenant Dibbs, and while most of that group had later turned up dead, Pel knew that at least a couple were still unaccounted for.

He could send any of them who were still alive back to their home universe.

And if they hadn't disguised themselves, they'd be easy to spot. They had all been wearing those silly Buck Rogers uniforms the Galactic Empire used.

"Purple," he told his waiting servants. "You find any men wearing purple, you bring them to me. Whatever men you can find, bring them here, but *especially* if they're wearing purple!"

They had even given her her car back; Amy knew she shouldn't complain. They'd provided some sandwiches— soggy and stale, but genuine Earth food, without any of the strange off-tastes of the Empire or Faerie. They'd just been doing their jobs, and Major Johnston had really been very reasonable, given how incredible the whole thing sounded.

But still, she was furious.

They were going to be watching her house every minute, they admitted it. They were tapping her phone. She wasn't to leave the state overnight.

She ought to have a lawyer; this couldn't be constitutional, watching her like this. But Susan was dead.

Should she call Bob Hough?

She looked right as she came to an intersection, and had to lean forward to see past Prossie; that reminded her of the telepath's presence.

Poor Prossie would need help settling in, and having Bob Hough around wouldn't make that any easier. Amy needed to see the doctor, and Bob Hough wouldn't help with *that*, either—in fact, from some remarks he had made during the divorce hearings, Amy didn't think Bob would approve of her getting an abortion, even if he believed her about the father being a rapist and murderer, which he probably wouldn't.

The damn government people would see her going to the doctor, would probably find out all about it—she hadn't mentioned her pregnancy to Major Johnston, since it wasn't anyone's business but her own.

She didn't *want* the government to know about it. What if they decided that the baby was some sort of valuable specimen, living proof that Earthpeople and Imperials could interbreed? Maryland might have legal guarantees of a woman's right to an abortion, but she was pretty sure the feds could find a way around that if they wanted to.

She frowned as she drove on through the intersection. She was making it sound like some trashy late-night movie, thinking about "aliens" breeding with human women—with *her*. This wasn't science fiction, and she wasn't some silly heroine in a tight skirt and heels, who was no use for anything but screaming. And Walter wasn't an alien, he was just a bastard—a dead bastard. She didn't want his kid, and she wasn't going to carry it.

If anyone tried to interfere with that, *then* she'd call a lawyer.

* * *

It was raining again, and Pel was back on the battlement, looking out over the marsh. Wind whistled around the stone of the tower and sprayed water across the wall, and water pattered unevenly from the broken gargoyle.

He didn't let the sound bother him this time, at least not consciously; after all, he was doing everything he could to bring Rachel back. His messengers had gone out into the world of Faerie, and until they returned, what else should he be doing? The dragon had been reduced to ash, Lieutenant Dibbs and the other dead Imperials were buried, and Susan's corpse was as well preserved as he could manage.

All he could do was wait.

He could feel the matrix surging and flowing around him, all that power at his disposal—but he didn't know what to do with it.

Waiting was always hard, especially waiting alone. If he had someone to talk to, he thought, it might not be so bad.

For a moment he considered opening a portal to Earth and sending a messenger to find Amy Jewell and bring her here. She knew his situation, she had been through it all with him; he could talk to her.

So had Ted Deranian, of course, but he had cracked under the strain. And Prossie Thorpe, but she wasn't from Earth, they didn't have a common background. It would have to be Amy or no one, he thought.

It was foolish, though; Amy was probably getting on with her own life, trying to get her decorating business back on track, catching up on everything she had missed while they were all trapped in the Empire and in Faerie. She wouldn't appreciate being dragged away.

Besides, it would take time to find another fetch or homunculus and break it to obedience, time for it to find its way to Amy once it was on Earth, time to bring her back—by then his messengers would probably be returning.

There were still plenty of nonhuman creatures around the fortress—hellbeasts, Raven had called most of them—but those wouldn't do; they couldn't live in nonmagical universes. The ones Shadow had sent into the Galactic Empire had all died within hours, according to everything Pel had seen and heard. Earth's space was different from Imperial space, but Pel didn't think it was any more magical.

Fetches and homunculi were sufficiently human to function in the Empire, and presumably on Earth, but he had used up every cooperative surviving fetch and homunculus he could readily find, sending them all out as messengers.

About a hundred fetches had died—or rather, been destroyed; fetches were *already* dead—in the fight with Shadow. That had left the place somewhat understaffed.

He sensed through the matrix that there were still creatures he had not seen deep in the subterranean depths of the fortress, and some of them were probably homunculi—but it just wasn't worth the trouble of going down there and finding them and enchanting them into obedience, and then sending them to Earth, where they wouldn't know how to drive or use the phone. They'd probably just get run over trying to cross a street.

Besides, what good would it really do to talk to Amy? What did she know about Nancy or Rachel, about losing loved ones? It wasn't as if the two of them had been friends before all this had started; they hadn't even known each other.

And really, Pel and Amy hadn't hit it off all that well while they were traveling together, either. Pel remembered Amy weeping with exhaustion, Amy vomiting by the side of the road, Amy shouting hysterically . . .

He didn't need company *that* badly.

He would wait.

Undersecretary Bascombe looked down at the black-garbed corpse, then over at the sword next to it, and finally up at the soldier accompanying it.

"You were there when they found them?" Bascombe asked.

"Yessir."

"It looked just like this?"

"Ah, well ... not exactly." The soldier hesitated; Bascombe favored him with an inquisitive glare.

"Well, what I mean is, it was fresher; we didn't have anywhere good to put it on ice on the ship here, sir."

"Oh, of course." He looked down again. "But it was dressed like this? Had the blaster wound in the chest? And the sword?"

"Yessir."

Bascombe nodded. He turned to the doctor beside him. "How long's he been dead?"

"Well, Mr. Secretary, that's hard to say ..." The doctor fumbled with the buttons of his white lab coat.

"Try," Bascombe said tartly.

The doctor sighed. "Well, sir," he said, "there are conflicting signs. Some of the evidence of overall decay indicates a death within the past three days, while tissue desiccation would seem to indicate a much earlier demise. Seems to me that despite what the sergeant here says, someone's made partially successful attempts to preserve this fellow's remains. Either that, or he was not at all well for some time before his death."

That figured, Bascombe thought; the entire thing was confusing, so why should even so simple a detail as time of death be any different?

The corpse did prove a few things, though.

First off, it was real—something mysterious *had* happened where the telepaths reported it; it wasn't all a fabrication. Everything the telepaths had reported that could be readily checked on *had* been checked on, and it was all true.

If there *was* some sort of conspiracy or rebellion under way among the telepaths, it was indetectably subtle—and since there was no obvious way the telepaths could have obtained these mysterious corpses, the plotters would also have to have hitherto unseen, unknown resources.

Second, the corpse was dressed in the manner of some of the people who took part in previous incursions made by Shadow, and was armed with a sword; there was nothing to connect it in any way with Earth. No one had ever found any evidence that Earth had interdimensional capabilities; once they knew it was theoretically possible to travel between universes, the Empire's own crash program had taken five years to produce the space-warp generator, and Earth, which had no antigravity, no blasters, and little semblance of the Empire's applied science, had supposedly known of the Empire's existence for no more than a few months.

If Earth was involved, then the Earthpeople had hitherto unseen, unknown resources, and *they* were being indetectably subtle.

In other words, if either the telepaths or the Earthpeople were behind this, the Empire was outmatched—but all the evidence pointed to Shadow.

Shadow was definitely up to something.

The question was, up to *what*?

CHAPTER 4

One man had died of fright.

Pel hadn't expected anything like that; for a few moments guilt closed his throat, and he blinked away tears.

He *should* have expected it—the poor sucker had been abducted without warning, captured by a pair of zombies and dragged off to the fortress of a world-conquering evil power, a power well known for hanging and disemboweling its enemies.

Nobody out there knew that Shadow was dead, that her replacement was one of the good guys—or at least, *tried* to be one of the good guys.

Not that he was very good at it, he thought as he wiped his eyes and tried to swallow. The storybook heroes never made such stupid mistakes, never accidentally killed innocent bystanders.

Maybe, when he had learned how to resurrect the dead, he could bring this poor fellow back, too. "Take him to the kitchen," he told two of the fetches when he could speak.

The other involuntary guests all shuddered, glancing at one another and at the corpse as the fetches carried it away.

Pel silently cursed himself, and his eyes teared up again, this time more with frustration than grief. "That's where it's easiest to preserve him until I can revive him," he explained.

It would take some effort to always remember that these people were accustomed to assuming the worst. Under Shadow, assuming the worst was the only way to avoid disaster.

He looked the survivors over. There were eight, so far,

and more on the way—that was really a pretty promising result. None of them were wizards or Imperials; most of them were scruffy and dirty and looked like peasants, but still, this was a good start.

He looked them over, standing or crouching at the eastern end of the throne room, faces averted or eyes shielded against the glare of the matrix and blinking anyway. They obviously had no idea what was going on.

He had debated waiting for the last few, but he had already kept the first arrivals in suspense for over an hour while this group collected, and the others wouldn't reach the fortress for a while yet; it was time to begin.

"I assume you think that I'm Shadow," he said, and without meaning to he let the matrix amplify his voice so that it boomed and echoed; one man clapped his hands over his ears, and others flinched, but they all turned to listen.

"I'm not," Pel continued. "Shadow is dead. But before she died, she turned her power over to me."

He paused, unsure what to say next; he hadn't gotten that far in preparing a speech. He'd assumed he could just wing it, make it up as he went along—he'd done that often enough in marketing presentations. But now he'd been disconcerted by the one who died, thrown off his pace, and he was struggling to remember what he'd planned to say. He had figured that he would tell these people that the hangings and other executions were to stop, that they were free now—but how did he get to that from the announcement that Shadow was dead?

And if they were free, how could he order them to stop hanging people, or bring him wizards, or do anything else?

And somehow he had pictured himself speaking to a group of well-dressed, dignified village elders, rather than a bunch of terrified farmers who were cowering against the wall in confusion, too scared to speak.

"Shadow is dead," he repeated.

One of them blinked, and ventured a whisper, "Shadow is dead; long live Shadow."

His neighbors turned to stare at him, then quickly looked

back at the blaze of color and light that was all they could see before them.

When Pel, too startled to react immediately, said nothing, about half of the men mumbled, "Shadow is dead, long live Shadow."

Pel slammed a fist onto the arm of his throne, and outside, unheard, magically driven winds whipped around the fortress walls; Pel could sense them through the matrix. Within the throne room his glow shifted toward reds and blues and shadows, away from the lighter and warmer colors. This was so slow and frustrating! These people didn't understand, and he didn't know how to explain it to them.

"No, no," he said. "Shadow is *dead*; there *is* no more Shadow. I am not Shadow!" He fought down the light and color, so that the men could see him. "I'm just a man, a man who has Shadow's magic."

The peasants peered at him through the lessened glare, then glanced at one another, and after a moment one of them called unsteadily, "Who are you, then?"

"My name is Pel Brown."

Feet shuffled. No one spoke.

Pel realized that his name wasn't much of an answer. "I came here from another world," he said. "Shadow wanted me to help her with something, but she lied to me, and . . . and I killed her."

It was surprisingly hard to admit that, and for a moment he wondered whether a trace remained of the geas Shadow had placed on him, the magical compulsion not to harm her.

But it was probably, he knew, just guilt. He didn't like to admit to being a murderer, even if it was justified homicide, even if he hadn't pulled the trigger himself. He'd seen Shadow kill his friends for no reason, so even though he couldn't harm her himself, he had set up a situation where Prossie Thorpe would kill her.

He'd conspired to commit murder, and why *shouldn't* he feel guilty about it? Maybe the heroes in books and movies never had any qualms about the villains they killed, but he wasn't any hero, despite what had happened to him, and even if Shadow had been a murderer many times over and a truly evil person, he wasn't happy about her death.

And the man who had died of terror didn't help any; that wasn't justified, it was just carelessness. He hadn't meant it to happen, but it was still his fault.

The peasants muttered among themselves. If he bothered, he could extend his senses through the matrix and hear every word they said, find out if they were blaming him for their companion's death—but why bother? He let them mutter.

He hoped someone would step forward and speak up, ask questions, turn this into a proper conversation—but no one did. He supposed he shouldn't be surprised; this world's culture seemed pretty authoritarian, not much given to discussion.

So it would have to be a speech.

"I have all Shadow's power," he said, "but not her knowledge, and not her . . . her ambition. I'm not going to hurt any of you. I have no desire to rule your world; in fact, I want you to be free, and happy."

One man managed to work up an almost-hopeful expression at that, but that was countered by looks of dread on other faces; Pel supposed that to most of them, *any* talk of change sounded threatening.

He would just have to work past that.

And he knew where to begin; he remembered his horrific walk to the fortress.

"When I came here," he said. "I came down the road from the Low Forest in Sunderland, and I passed through several of your towns and villages, and in most of them there were dead bodies hanging. Who were they all?"

The peasants looked at one another. No one wanted to be the spokesman, obviously. Pel sighed. "You," he said, pointing, "on the end, in the green. Step forward."

The man hesitated, then stepped forward, placing each foot carefully; it looked as if he was having trouble breathing.

"Who were all those people who got hanged?"

"I . . . I know not, my lord . . . Your Majesty. In . . . in my own village, the last to be hanged was a man named Norbert . . ."

The colors surged up, flickering orange, as Pel momentarily lost control of his emotions, his guilt and grief turning abruptly to anger as frustration got the better of him.

"Not their *names*, idiot!" he shouted, and the walls echoed back a dull, angry roar. "I mean, what were they *hanged* for?"

The men cowered back against the wall; one moved for the door, but Pel twisted at a strand of his web and the doors slammed shut.

Someone moaned, and Pel forced himself to calm down; he didn't want any more deaths. He didn't even want anyone to faint.

But he *did* want answers.

"Why were they hanged?" Pel demanded. "You, why was this Norbert hanged?"

The man in green glanced back at his companions, found no help there, and after a false start and a throat-clearing, managed to say, " 'Twas said he had failed to show the village elders the respect due their station."

Pel glared, though he doubted anyone could see his expression through the magical haze. He had expected something like that, but it was still infuriating. Death for the most trivial wrongs—that had been Shadow's style. No wonder the men were scared. "He didn't kill anybody?"

The man blinked, and made the chopping motion that Pel had learned was the local equivalent of shaking one's head.

"He didn't even *steal* anything?"

Another chop.

All those people, horribly dead for nothing, and it had been deliberate, not accidental like the one the fetches were taking to the kitchen; Pel felt sick. "All right, listen, all of you," he announced. "From now on, you only hang *murderers. Only murderers.* You understand? You can . . . you can beat thieves, or flog them, or throw them in jail, or whatever seems appropriate, but you *can't kill them.* Is that clear?"

Heads bobbed. That gesture was the same here—just another of those annoying situations where things were only *partly* different, just familiar enough to be confusing.

"And you don't disembowel *anyone*, is that clear? Not unless a murderer chops people up with an axe or something, then maybe you can gut him, but *nobody else.*"

"The Elders . . ." someone began.

"To hell with the elders!" Pel shouted. "You go tell them to stop hanging people or they'll answer to me! If they don't believe you, you send 'em here! And look, hey, you can take fetches back with you to prove you were here. I don't want anyone else killed! Shadow's dead, and you don't *do* that stuff anymore!" He was standing in front of the throne now, pointing and yelling; magic swirled and blazed around him, actual flame flaring briefly from the air behind him as his anger sucked energy from the matrix.

The eight men all pressed flat against the wall, hands over their ears, driven back by sheer volume. Seeing them there, Pel's anger suddenly passed, and he flopped back into his chair.

"And you can clean up your villages, too," he said in his normal tones. "Maybe pave the streets. Put in sewers— some of those places stank. There's no reason you can't live decently, can't have indoor plumbing and all the rest of it."

No one answered, though a few risked uncovering their ears.

"You don't know about all that stuff," he said, with a gesture of dismissal. "It can wait. We'll get to it."

"Ah . . . Your Majesty," the man in green said, head down, "if one could be permitted to speak . . ."

Pel slumped back in the throne. "Oh, go ahead and speak," he said. "Stand up straight and tell me all about it."

"Majesty, we . . . I am but a poor cobbler," the man said. "I know naught of governance or law, and would only go about my business. Wherefore, then, am I brought hither? Why speak to me of roads and hangings and the rest? Would it not be better to call upon the councils of the wise, the Elders and those who have a say in such matters?

Or perchance, to send forth your own ministers, an you are displeased with our lords?"

"You don't have a say?" Pel asked.

"Nay, surely not," the cobbler said. "I'm neither prince nor councilor."

"You're a person, aren't you?"

The cobbler blinked. "Aye, but . . ."

"Well, then you have a say," Pel proclaimed. "*Everybody* has a say. It's time you people got rid of your lords and ladies and learned some democracy." Blue streaked through the matrix for a moment. "Listen, all of you," Pel said. "From now on, I want things to be run democratically around here. I want you to elect your leaders, not just let them happen. Vote for 'em."

"Majesty, I understand this not a whit."

"I mean I want you to choose your own leaders by getting everyone to vote—each person says who he wants, and whoever gets the most votes wins."

The men stared at him uncomprehendingly.

"It's simple," Pel insisted. "Look, suppose the eight of you were somewhere together and needed a leader. Each of you would say who you wanted to be the leader, and whoever got five or more votes would win."

"But . . . 'tis all very well, but how to know who shall vote?" the cobbler asked.

"*Everybody* votes!" Pel said, waving his hands to include all the world.

"Let *everyone* have a say?" one of the other men protested. "The fools, the children, women? People bearing grudges?"

The others murmured agreement, and Pel stared at them just as uncomprehendingly as they had stared at him a moment before.

It was at that point that Pel realized he didn't *care*. If they didn't want to be democratic, what business was it of his? If they didn't want to build sewers, why should he care? *He* didn't have to live in their stinking villages.

He didn't really care whether they cleaned up their villages, he discovered. He had told them to stop hanging and disemboweling anyone who argued with the village elders, and they had agreed, and that was the really important change. Death mattered. Death was important. The rest of it, elections and building sewers and aqueducts and so on, that could wait, or they could figure it out for themselves.

He had had an idea, when he sent the others back to Earth but chose to stay here, that he might play the great leader, that he might show the people of this world the way to a more modern, more civilized lifestyle, but if they weren't interested, it wasn't *his* problem.

"Suit yourselves," he said, his hands dropping.

His problem was getting his wife and daughter back.

"All right," he said, "forget all that. But no more hangings, no more eviscerations, no torture—none of that stuff. Be good to each other. Shadow's dead. You tell everyone she's dead, and that Pel Brown is running things now." He hoped that that name would reach Wilkins and Sawyer and other Imperials who were still alive, and they could come and find him and he could send them home. "No hangings, and the name's Pel Brown. You understand?"

Heads nodded.

"And there's something else. Something important."

He could see them tense, he could, through the matrix, hear them drawing quick breaths and holding them; he could sense muscles tightening, pupils dilating.

"I want wizards," he said. "I want every wizard you can find, I want every wizard there *is*. Send word out through all the world—every wizard must come to *me*, here in my fortress." He stood up and pointed nowhere in particular, to emphasize his words. "*All* the wizards. Especially Taillefer. They come here, or they're in deep shit. I can find them if I have to, and they know it." This last wasn't as certainly true as he made it sound; he was sure that he could locate anyone who dared to use magic, since all magic was linked into a single network and he controlled that network, and he thought he could tell someone experienced in wizardry by the patterning in their own tiny bit of matrix, but he did not yet really know how to interpret the data, how to convert a sensation in the matrix into a place in the real world.

But that didn't matter.

The important thing was what *they* believed.

He thought for a moment about telling them to find Imperials, too, but then he dismissed the idea. They didn't seem all that bright, and he wanted to keep it as simple as he possibly could. The creatures he had sent out to fetch this bunch hadn't come across anyone wearing purple; probably Sawyer and Wilkins were hundreds of miles away.

"You find wizards. You tell your village elders, you tell *everybody*. Any wizard doesn't come here might as well cut his own throat and be done with it, you understand?"

They were cowering back against the wall, and Pel realized that intangible clouds of dark gray were rolling around the throne room, interspersed with gouts of flame and vivid flashes of crimson—the matrix was picking up his insistence and interpreting it. His guests, or captives, or whatever they were, were probably scared half to death.

He dropped his pointing finger and calmed the roiling currents of magic.

"You get the idea," he said. "No more hangings, and find wizards, and send them here. Now, get out of here, go home, tell everyone." He made the twist in the web of power that would link him to the fetches, and ordered them, "You go with these men, you make sure people believe them about the hangings and the wizards. Take a week, that should do it, then come back here." He waved in dismissal. "Get out of here, all of you."

He slumped back into the throne and watched as the eight men fled, the fetches trudging stolidly after them.

He hoped none of them tripped and fell down the stairs on the way out.

Johnston peered warily down the basement stairs.

Except for being unusually dusty, which came from being shut up and neglected all summer, the place looked per-

fectly ordinary. It was hard to believe that the doorway to
another universe had appeared in this house.

Well, maybe it hadn't—but the house didn't look much
like part of an incredibly elaborate hoax, either.

Carefully, he trudged down the steps. Behind him came
a heavily loaded Air Force lieutenant, struggling to maneuver two cases of equipment safely.

"You'll want to change those lightbulbs," Johnston said,
pointing. "The Jewell woman says they're burnt out."

"Yes, sir," the lieutenant agreed, looking up.

"That's the wall, right there, according to the description
both the women gave," Johnston said, indicating the bare
concrete. "Poke at it if you like, do anything you want that
won't damage it—take pictures, measure it, whatever."

"Yes, sir."

"Set the radio up first."

"Yes, sir."

"We don't really expect anything to happen, you understand—but if it *does*, it could be anything, any time."

"Yes, sir." The lieutenant set the cases on the basement
floor.

"Any questions?"

The lieutenant looked around, then shrugged. "No, sir."

Johnston nodded. "Your relief will be here at eighteen
hundred hours."

"Yes, sir."

Johnston hesitated, then crossed to the blank wall. He
stared at the gray blocks, reached up and tapped one.

Just concrete. His hand didn't vanish into a chilly medieval forest, nor a bare white desert, nor any of the other
places Jewell and Thorpe had described and Deranian had
babbled about.

"Be careful," he said as he turned to go.

There were advantages, Amy decided, to having vanished in
a manner sufficiently mysterious that it attracted the attention
of Air Force Intelligence. They hadn't paid her bills, but at
least they'd collected her mail and kept the post office from

returning it all. Their patrols had scared off burglars. And they'd made sure none of the utilities were shut off.

It was too bad they hadn't bothered to answer her phone or explain to any of her clients what had happened. The tape on the answering machine had filled up the first week, mostly with ever-more-angry complaints from the Fosters.

After calling to make her doctor's appointment she had tried to phone all of her clients. Some, including the Fosters, didn't answer; one had moved; one hung up on her. Prema Chatterji was still interested in a consultation, but the others were pretty clearly a total loss. Being called away without warning on "personal matters" for more than three months was not good business.

And after going through the mountain of mail and matching the unpaid bills against her bank balance and the undeposited checks, she knew she was broke, or nearly so—if nothing bounced and she hadn't missed anything and she could transfer from her savings account, she would wind up with a balance of about eighteen dollars.

That wouldn't even pay for groceries to replace what had gone bad. She sighed.

"Is it bad?" Prossie asked.

"Yeah, but it could certainly be worse," Amy said. She looked up, out the living-room window at the Air Force car parked out front. Those people wouldn't let them starve, she was sure. And they were back on Earth, and alive and well.

"It could be a lot worse," she said.

"I want agents on Earth and on Shadow's world," Bascombe said. "You tell me how to get them there."

The scientist glanced at the telepath, then shrugged. "We can get them through the warp," he said, "but antigravity doesn't work in either of those realities, so getting them down safely is ... well, it's an engineering problem. And getting them *back* is tougher."

The telepath, a man named Brian Hall, Carrie Hall's brother, whom Bascombe had not dealt with before, said,

"You want to use someone who's already there. On Earth, our only possible contacts are Prossie Thorpe and the five we contacted before . . ."

Bascombe interrupted, "I thought there were six."

"Yes, sir; one of them has died."

Bascombe nodded. "Go on," he said.

"Yes, sir. Well, none of those contacts was very satisfactory. Carleton Miletti apparently could only transmit, not receive; though he was aware of our attempts at contact, none of our messages got through. Oram Blaisdell and Ray Aldridge . . . well, frankly, sir, I'm not sure either of them was entirely sane. And the other two, Angela Thompson and Gwenyth—we never got her last name—are both underage females, which limits their usefulness."

"What about Shadow?"

"We can't read Shadow's mind, sir; we tried, and the telepath who made the attempt died. As for other people in Shadow's universe, we've never managed a solid contact; we don't know why."

"What about our people who went there?"

"I don't know, sir."

Bascombe glared at him.

"I mean, sir," Hall said, "I don't know if any of them are still alive, and no attempt has been made to contact any of them. I doubt any attempt at contact will succeed, but I don't *know* that."

"Try it," Bascombe ordered him. "And get your sister going on contacts on Earth." Then he turned back to the scientist. "And I want your department to figure out how we can get agents safely to Earth and Faerie. Don't worry about getting them back yet; we can take care of that when the time comes."

"Yes, sir." The scientist glanced at the telepath; the telepath carefully avoided the man's gaze.

"Go on," Bascombe said. "Both of you. Get on with it."

"Yes, sir."

CHAPTER 5

Pel wondered why he kept coming up to the top of the tower. The rain through the broken gargoyle still sounded like a child's footsteps; it hadn't changed any. He'd heard the rain before, seen the landscape spread out on all sides, drawn the currents of power down from the skies and guided them through the clouds. There was nothing new up here.

But there wasn't anything new elsewhere in the castle, either. There wasn't anything he wanted anywhere in the entire place.

A gust of wind blew dripping rainwater toward him; his aura turned it aside with no conscious command. Pel barely noticed; he just stared out over the marsh.

He knew why he was up here; it was because he was bored. He was bored and miserable, and this place, out in the rain, with its vast and depressing view, was nicely suited to being bored and miserable.

Really, it was rather amazing that he was bored and lonely and unhappy. At least in theory, he was the absolute ruler of an entire world; he was an all-powerful magician, with anything he wanted his for the taking.

Except he didn't want any of it.

What he wanted was his family back. Or even, he thought, and hated himself for thinking it, just to know that they were really, permanently dead, and he could never have them back, because at least then it would be *over*, and he could get on to whatever came next—despair, grief, whatever, and maybe someday, if he lived long enough, building a new life for himself.

But this not knowing, this *possibility* of their resurrection, was driving him crazy. He wasn't thinking straight, hadn't been able to keep his mind properly on anything since he had first heard Nancy was dead.

Shadow had *said* she could raise the dead; she had had her fetches, and even though those weren't much better than zombies, there was no reason to think they were the best the magical matrix could do.

After all, Shadow had wanted servants, not companions; she hadn't been doing anyone any favors with her resurrections.

Pel didn't want servants. He wanted Nancy and Rachel back. He wanted to hear *real* running footsteps on the battlements.

He paused, staring out over the marsh.

On the battlements? Did he want to stay *here*, if he managed to bring his wife and daughter back from the dead?

Probably not. It was lonely here. Controlling the matrix gave him power, it let him move and reshape matter anywhere in this world, and at least in theory it could let him see through the eyes of others, hear through their ears; it made him the unquestioned final authority; but it cut him off from everyone else at the same time. No one had even remembered that his predecessor, Shadow, was human—they'd all called her "it," and treated her as a force of nature.

He didn't think he was at that extreme, but the men he had had dragged in hadn't exactly treated him as another like themselves. He had had the power of life and death over them; when he hadn't made a conscious effort, they hadn't even been able to see him through the seething aura of magical energy that was the visible manifestation of the matrix.

And when they did see him, those peasants in their homespun and leather . . .

He looked down at himself, at the battered purple slacks

he still wore. He remembered Raven of Stormcrack Keep, with his black velvet cloak and high boots; Valadrakul of Warricken, with his braids and knee-length vest; Elani, with her red robes.

He didn't belong here. He belonged back on Earth—but with his wife and daughter, and it was only in *this* world that anyone had the power to revive them.

He had the power.

All he had to do was learn how to use it.

And that, of course . . .

He stopped in midthought, and stared down at the causeway that connected the fortress to drier land to the east of the marsh. He wasn't sure whether he had seen them first with his eyes or through the matrix, and now he needed a moment to convince himself that they were real, and not some damnable illusion the matrix had created.

They were real—there were people approaching the fortress. Six of them—or actually, four people and two fetches.

There was only one explanation, one sort of people who would be coming here.

Wizards!

At last, wizards were coming!

Now maybe he could learn this resurrection business and get *on* with it!

The scientist cleared his throat and glanced nervously at Bascombe.

Bascombe glared back.

"Well, sir, it's simple enough to get people to either of the other universes, really; the space-warp generator is completely functional. The problems arise when you require that they arrive safely and be able to get back . . ."

"I don't *care* if they can get back," Bascombe interrupted. "We don't need to worry about that. Cahn and his men got back, most of them, without any help from us."

"Well, in that case, it's just a matter of landing them safely, and as I understand it, no one was seriously injured in the previous warp transitions . . ."

"I don't want them . . . Wait a minute." Bascombe glowered at the man; the poor twit was almost a caricature of a scientist, probably didn't even like to be called that, wanted to be referred to as a physicist, or an electronician, or something—as if all these arcane distinctions made any difference to anyone normal!

But he had a point; Cahn and Carson had both arrived intact. Bascombe considered their arrivals to be unsatisfactory, but he had to stop and think for a moment to put into words, simple words a scientist could understand, exactly what had been wrong with those landings.

"All right," he said, "I want them to arrive quietly, without throwing away any more ships, without attracting a lot of unwanted attention. Can you do that?"

"Well, sir," the scientist said, "I don't see why we couldn't put them in spacesuits, with a simple antigravity unit to get . . ."

"Antigravity doesn't work there. What else have we got? Isn't there any way to fly without using antigravity?"

The scientist blinked.

"Um," he said.

"Care to be a bit more explicit?" Bascombe let the sarcasm drip from his words.

"Well, we . . . I mean, AG is so cheap and convenient, that we . . . there were experiments, but . . ." His voice trailed off.

Bascombe decided the time was ripe for a suggestion, to get the man thinking positively again. "Why can't we just make the warps come out at ground level?" he asked

"Oh, because . . . well, we were sending ships before, and the control isn't fine enough, and solid matter . . . the interaction . . . it's not *safe*."

"So we have to make these holes in midair, and let our men just fall through?"

"Well, I—" The scientist stopped dead this time, rather than trailing off.

"You what?"

"Well, there's no reason they couldn't *climb* through. With ropes."

"Ropes?" Startled, Bascombe considered the idea.

It seemed very obvious now, so obvious that he wondered how they had missed seeing it sooner. Maybe because it was *too* simple—getting to another universe involved huge machines, vast quantities of energy, super-science of all sorts. Plain old rope didn't fit the image.

They could even have saved most of Carson's group, if they had wanted to.

But then, Bascombe remembered, they hadn't particularly wanted to.

"Ropes," he said.

"At least they didn't cancel my credit cards," Amy said, glancing up as she continued to pull wads of newspaper out of her new purse. "It's a good thing I didn't have all of them with me."

Prossie nodded, then looked down at herself.

Amy had had to guess at the telepath's sizes to some extent, since Imperial standards did not use the same systems as JCPenney, but the clothes seemed to fit fairly well. Prossie didn't look very enthusiastic about the outfit she wore, though.

"Is something wrong?" Amy asked, putting down the purse. She had deliberately gotten something simple and casual for her guest, since Prossie was obviously not ready to go looking for a white-collar job here on Earth, but maybe that had been a mistake.

"It's just so strange," Prossie said. "I've worn a uniform since I was six; except on Zeta Leo Three, I've never seen myself in any color but purple."

Amy shuddered at the mention of the slavers' planet. She asked, "Even off-duty? Didn't you ever have, you know, a furlough or something?"

Prossie stared at her as if she were mad, then apparently caught herself and looked apologetic.

"No, of course not," she said. "I'm a telepath; I had to

wear full uniform at all times, so that people would know I was a Special."

"So this makes you think of when you were a slave, back there?" Amy asked, with a wave at the blue jeans and black sweatshirt.

Prossie hesitated, then glanced at the tattered, filthy remains of her uniform, lying in a heap on the couch.

"I was *always* a slave," she said.

The first wizard through the door prostrated himself, to Pel's surprise; the man dropped to his knees, then flung his arms up over his head and practically fell forward, until his palms were flat on the floor and his nose was at most an inch above the stone.

The others, with only an instant's hesitation, followed their comrade's lead—even Taillefer, who had met Pel before, when Shadow was still alive. Pel was glad to see that Taillefer was one of the group.

He was not glad that Taillefer's familiar face was plastered to the floor. "Oh, get up," Pel said testily, and inadvertently let the matrix amplify his voice into an angry roar.

The four wizards scrambled hastily to their feet.

Pel stared, looking them over—doing so while well aware that they probably couldn't see him through the glare of the matrix. If anyone could see through it, wizards could—but somehow, Pel didn't think these people could.

Physically, they didn't look all that impressive, despite the long robes and fancy embroidery they wore. They were just people, three men and a woman, and not in the best of shape. Taillefer was fat and soft, the woman was bony and unattractive, one of the others had the red scar of an old burn marring one cheek from jaw to eyebrow.

Through the matrix, though, Pel could see that there was a sort of patterning, a power, an inward light and structure to them that the ordinary people he had met did not have. But it was very weak and faint, like a dim copy of a tiny corner of the great matrix.

He could also see that the wizards were able to sense and

touch the matrix in a way no one else had, and he remembered how Valadrakul had been so enthralled by it that he had doomed himself.

None of these four was reacting in quite that way, though they were all certainly fascinated by the flickering tangle of interwoven magic.

"You're wizards?" he asked.

"O great one," the man who had first flung himself down said, "I am Athelstan of Meresham." He bowed deeply and theatrically. "And you, I take it, are Shadow's successor, Pelbrun?"

"Brown," Pel corrected automatically. "Pel Brown."

"Brown Pelbrun, then," Athelstan agreed.

It wasn't worth arguing. "You're a wizard, Athelstan? I know Taillefer, but not you others."

Athelstan cocked his head to the side as if puzzled.

"Aye," he said, "I am a wizard, after a fashion—can you not see as much?"

Pel could see the woman and the unidentified man cringe to hear Athelstan speak so boldly; it certainly was an abrupt change from his first obeisance.

Or had that perhaps been mockery?

"I can see that you can touch magic," Pel said. "But that isn't exactly what I meant."

"Ah." He nodded. "T'truth, O Pelbrun, neither I nor my companions can sense the true patterns, nor shape them; we draw only upon what power we find to hand. Thus, I am neither matrix wizard, nor pattern wizard, but only wizard, plain and simple. Is it this you would have us say?"

"Not exactly," Pel replied. "Look, I *can* use a matrix, obviously—I'm holding the one Shadow built, and I can use it. I have the innate ability that you don't. But I don't know *how* to use it properly, so what I'm asking is not if you have the *talent* of a wizard, but whether you have the *knowledge* of a wizard."

He saw Athelstan glance at the others, who exchanged furtive glances among themselves.

"I know enough to fry you all, though," Pel warned. "Don't think I don't."

"O Brown Magician," Athelstan said, bowing again, "ne'er did I doubt it! An what would we, in any event? As you have said, such as we can touch upon a network, but cannot hold it—were you slain, or in other manner the matrix taken from you, the lot of us could hold it not for the merest instant, but instead would most probably be incinerated in its fiery dissolution. You've naught to fear from us."

"Good," Pel said.

"Indeed, meseems 'twould be very much in our interests to serve you honestly and well," Athelstan continued, "for else how shall we flourish, when all the reins of power are held in your own two hands? Look you upon the pitiful estate of all known wizardry, when only we four can be found of the myriad magicians who once flourished in this realm—and this, merely that Shadow was not pleased others should wield the arts arcane. How, then, shall we not rejoice that Shadow has passed, and that a new overlord is come who, by your profession heretofore, seeks not exclusive dominion?"

By the time Pel had interpreted this speech, and debated with himself how to respond, Athelstan had taken his pause for silent consent.

Pel knew that Athelstan was making at least one wrong assumption; he knew that there were a few other wizards besides these four still scattered about the far corners of Faerie—but only a matrix wizard could have seen that, and it didn't matter anyway. He let Athelstan continue.

"What learning we might have, we place gladly at your disposal, O Brown Magician," the wizard said. "What would you have of us?"

There it was, the question Pel had been waiting for. He took a deep breath.

"I want to learn to raise the dead," he said.

"I want to be useful," Prossie said. "I feel as if I should be doing more, not just sitting here in your house, eating your food and wearing your clothes."

Amy hesitated. "You can't drive a car, though," she said. "You don't have any marketable skills, or any educational record, or anything. I don't know what sort of work you could get. I mean, if I were still in business, I could maybe hire you myself for a while, but right now . . . I mean, I'm going to be job-hunting myself."

"There must be *something*," Prossie said desperately; she was on her feet, standing by the living-room couch, as if, Amy thought, she couldn't bear to stay seated.

"I'm sure there is," Amy agreed, getting up herself. "Maybe working at McDonald's, if nothing else. We'll want to get you a GED, maybe sign you up at Montgomery College or somewhere—maybe those Air Force people could help . . ." At that she glanced out the front window, at the car that waited out on the gravel shoulder of Goshen Road.

It would be nice to get some use out of all this mess, she thought. "Maybe you could sell souvenirs . . ." she began, as she turned to look out through the kitchen, through the glass panel in the back door, at the spaceship that lay in her backyard.

She stopped in midsentence and stared; her mouth fell open.

Prossie asked, "What is it?" She hurried to the kitchen door and looked.

Not realizing at first that Amy was looking out the back, it took her a moment to see what was wrong; she wasted several seconds scanning the kitchen itself, and saw nothing out of the ordinary. At last, though, her gaze reached the window.

"Oh, my . . ." she began.

"Someone better tell the Air Force men," Amy said. She turned and ran for the front door to do just that, leaving Prossie staring wide-eyed out the back, staring at the men in purple spacesuits climbing down a rope ladder that seemed to hang from empty sky.

CHAPTER 6

Samuel Best sometimes wondered whether his name had helped him in his career in Imperial Intelligence. Nobody would admit such a thing, of course, but sometimes he wondered whether, on some level, people expected more of him because of his name, and chose him for tough assignments because he was, after all, the Best.

Not that he necessarily believed he actually *was* the best; to think such a thing could lead to overconfidence, and that could easily be fatal.

He did try to be good at his work, though, and in this case that had resulted in delays that had irritated the hell out of that officious twit, John Bascombe, Undersecretary for Interdimensional Affairs.

Best didn't much care. Bascombe might be an up-and-coming politician, he might be able to ruin Best's life—but screwing up a field assignment could get a man killed. Better to annoy one's superiors and live than to do as one's told and die.

It had just seemed to be common sense to insist on speaking to anyone in the Empire who had actually *been* in this Shadow place, and it wasn't *his* fault if the surviving crewmen of I.S.S. *Ruthless* had been reassigned and scattered.

It was too bad no one from Colonel Carson's squad had made it back alive, but they hadn't; there were only the six men from *Ruthless*.

Not that they had been able to tell him much, in any case; they had only been there for about twenty minutes,

61

and in an area hundreds of miles from his intended point of arrival.

Still, it was useful to know about the heavier gravity, the lower-than-optimum oxygen content of the atmosphere, the blue-shifted sunlight, the pseudoterrestrial ecology, the appearance of a feudal social structure—and the clothing. Best had no desire to be obvious; he wasn't about to go in in uniform.

The squad sent to the *other* universe, the place called Earth, could make their own decisions; he and *his* boys were going in in the closest approximation of local costume they could manage.

This meant that the Earth squad went first, of course—Bascombe hadn't been willing to wait.

That was fine with Best; he wasn't eager to be the first to try this trick of climbing through a space warp on a rope ladder. And the fact that the Empire only had one space-warp generator operational at the moment—though he knew that more were under construction, a fact he was not *supposed* to know—meant that he and his three underlings couldn't go anywhere until the Earth squad was through, and the generator shut down, recalibrated, and restarted.

It seemed to be working, though; having finally approved the preparations, he stood behind Bascombe and to the side, hand shading his eyes, and watched through the thick tinted glass as the four spacesuited figures vanished into the blinding white glare of the space-warp field.

A fifth figure, also suited, emerged from the glare and waved to the control room.

"They're through," one of the engineers said.

"Good," Bascombe said. "Then get this thing shut down and open the warp to Shadow's universe."

"But, sir," someone protested, "If you do that, you'll cut off the men on Earth—the ladder will be sheared off, and we won't be able to retrieve them."

"Roll the damn ladder up," Bascombe said, "and then use it to get Best, here, and his crew, to Shadow's world.

Then you can re-open the warp to Earth. We'll do four-hour shifts hanging that ladder in each universe."

"Give them another hour, sir," Best said. "It'll take me that long to get my men ready."

Bascombe turned to glare at him, looked down at the phony peasant garb Best wore, then shrugged. "Forty minutes," he said. "I want you and your men in the staging area, suited and ready to go, in forty minutes."

"Yes, sir," Best said. He saluted, and stood at attention as Bascombe left the room.

"What an idiot," an engineer muttered when the door had swung shut.

Best didn't bother to reply aloud, but his own opinion was the same.

"It didn't work," Pel said, glaring at the dead dog. It had stopped twitching.

"Well, O Great One," Athelstan said, "did we not say that we knew not the way of it?"

"You said you *thought* you could, if you had enough power," Pel countered.

"Nay, rather, said we that we thought we *might*, had we the power," Athelstan corrected him. " 'Twould seem we were mistaken. Ne'er did we *promise*."

For a moment, Pel just stared at the dog. Then he sighed. "I know you didn't promise," he said. "So you can't do it, you don't know how—but doesn't *anyone* know? *Shadow* knew, right?"

"Yes, it does . . . that is, rather, it *did*." Athelstan stared at the dog as well.

After a moment's silence, the wizard bestirred himself and said, "Hark, then, Master—we know the theory of old, as we told you, handed down from master to apprentice since the earliest years of Shadow's use of fetches. Our knowledge thereof must, we see, be deficient in some wise. Perchance, though, were we to study an ensample of the *practice* of necromantic art, understanding might be gained thereby."

Pel turned and looked at the wizard.

"What?" he said.

Athelstan blinked, then said, speaking slowly and clearly, "O Great One, had we the chance to *study*, and to test, perhaps to destruction, one that had in fact been resurrected from death, might we then gain the understanding we lack?"

Pel stared at him.

"Your fetches, Lord," Athelstan explained, gesturing at the pair that stood guard by the door.

Pel blinked, then glanced at his unmoving servants, then back at Athelstan.

Something twinged, twitched, tickled at him somehow. He paused.

Something felt odd, and slightly wrong, and he wasn't sure what it was or where it was or even whether it was internal or external. Something was *disturbed*, somehow. It might have been somewhere out in the matrix, in the web of magical currents that covered this entire world—or it might have been in his head.

Could it have been a twinge of guilt at the idea of destroying a fetch?

After all, he supposed the fetches had been alive once, free people with their own souls and their own interests and their own rights—but they weren't now; he could see that through the matrix, could see how their magical energies differed from those of real live human beings. Shadow hadn't brought them back that far; she had left them mindless zombies. They were already dead, really; why should he feel guilty about dissecting one, or whatever Athelstan had in mind? He had already killed about a hundred of them himself, one way or another, and didn't feel guilty about it. Letting the wizards kill one more was no problem, not really.

If that was what he had felt, then his subconscious was being silly and unreasonable.

If he'd felt something else, something out there in the

network somewhere, it could wait. Bringing back his family took priority over anything else.

"Sure," he said, "Go to it."

Major Johnston took a final look around the yard, his gaze lingering on the silly-looking purple spaceship. "You're sure no one could be hiding in that thing?" he called.

"Sure as we can be, sir," a lieutenant replied.

Johnston nodded, glanced up at where the rope ladder had disappeared into thin air, then headed back around the side of the house, toward the waiting cars.

There were four of them, lined up by the roadside; he hesitated for an instant, then marched up to the last one in line, an Air Force–blue sedan.

Amy Jewell looked up at him through the closed window. She showed no sign of rolling it down, so he spoke loudly.

"I'm sorry about this, Ms. Jewell," he said. "I'm going to see if we can get you listed as a civilian consultant, and get you some compensation for your time—you and Ms. Thorpe both. We'll provide alternate accommodations for you, if you'd rather not stay here for now. And I'm afraid we may want to buy your house, if these people are going to keep coming."

Amy shrugged, then nodded. "Thanks," she called, her voice barely audible through the glass.

He patted the side of the car, then straightened up.

More cars were arriving, bringing more men—Air Police, so far; Johnston hoped they'd be enough.

After all, next time the Galactic Empire might send an attack force rather than scouts or diplomats. If he had had his way, he'd have had a fully armed squad of Marines here, ready for anything—but he was Air Force, and didn't have the authority to call in the jarheads. A request like that would have to work its way up through channels. He'd started the paperwork, but it would take time.

APs he could do now.

He no longer doubted the existence of the Galactic

Empire; he had arrived just in time to see the rope ladder vanish into thin air. He wished he'd been able to reach the place in less than forty minutes; maybe he could have sent someone back up.

But that might not have been safe. The Imperials had arrived in spacesuits, after all—genuine Buck Rogers spacesuits, bulky purple things with fishbowl helmets, straight out of *Destination Moon*. Maybe they'd needed them at the top of the ladder.

They weren't saying, though.

He glanced at the two civilian cop cars that had been the first things he'd been able to get to the site. Each one had two men in back, spacesuits and equipment removed, but still in their silly-looking Imperial uniforms.

He marched over to the closer one and peered in the open window. "Care to tell me anything?" he asked.

"Lieutenant James Austin, Imperial Service, H-657-R-233-B-708," the purple-uniformed man said, staring straight ahead without so much as glancing at Johnston.

Johnston sighed. He slapped the car roof.

"Take 'em away," he said.

Prossie sat motionless in the back of the groundcar, wishing she could know what the people around her were thinking. Sometimes her mental silence was a blessing, sometimes a curse; right now it was horrible.

The Empire had sent more men—not an envoy this time, no telepaths, but a scouting team, probably, from their actions, Imperial Intelligence.

She wasn't as frightened of the "Smarts" as were most of the people she had known; over the years she had read the minds of several of the dreaded Intelligence agents, and while they generally weren't nice people, they were just people, not the fearsome, emotionless supermen they were reputed to be. She had even worked directly for Intelligence once or twice herself; all the telepaths, the entire Special Branch, were nominally under the joint jurisdiction of Intelligence and the Imperial Messenger Service, always available if the Smarts needed them.

But still, any time Intelligence was involved, matters were serious. The situation was serious *now*.

Especially since she didn't know why they were here.

Especially since one possibility was that they had been sent after *her*.

She knew that the Empire would take a rogue telepath very seriously indeed, if they knew she was here, if they knew she had really, genuinely gone rogue . . .

Otherwise it seemed like quite a coincidence, an Imperial team arriving directly behind the very house she was staying in.

She knew that it wasn't really as much of a coincidence as it first appeared; she had read from the minds of Imperial scientists that something about the shape of space itself made it easier to open a space warp in the same place every time. If the Empire was going to open a warp to Earth anywhere, this would be the natural place; she was here herself because this was where the warp had come out before.

Still, even if it wasn't a coincidence, why were they here? What did they want? She knew, beyond question, that when she had left Base One with Colonel Carson and Raven and the rest, no one at Base One had had any plans for further contact with Earth, with the possible exception of sending Pel and Amy and the rest home someday. John Bascombe had written Earth off as worthless; General Hart had considered it irrelevant.

Why had they changed their minds?

There was one way she might be able to find out; Carrie had tried to contact her several times. Carrie would know what was going on; she wouldn't be able to help it. Maybe Prossie could coax an explanation out of her.

And maybe not. She and Carrie hadn't exactly parted as friends. Prossie had betrayed her family, betrayed all the telepaths in the Empire, by lying to Imperial officers, disobeying orders, and in general breaking any rule she found inconvenient once she was outside Imperial space and cut off from the mental network.

That she had done so because she could now see that she had been oppressed and abused all her life would not matter much to Carrie or the others; they were still there, under the Empire's thumb, subject to summary execution for the slightest infraction of the telepathy laws. Prossie's rebellion could conceivably endanger them all.

And maybe that was why Carrie hadn't done a thing, hadn't lifted a finger or transmitted a thought when Prossie had been utterly at Shadow's mercy and convinced she was about to die.

Prossie was the one who had broken contact, who had been unspeakably rude, who had been refusing to communicate; maybe Carrie would listen, maybe they could make up. They were cousins, bound together by blood and background—surely a little internecine squabble could be patched up.

But Carrie would have to try again before they could talk. Telepathy was impossible in Earth's universe. Prossie couldn't send unless Carrie was listening, couldn't receive unless Carrie was sending.

Carrie or someone, anyway. There were four hundred and fourteen other telepaths in the Empire, at last count. And until one of them tried to reach her, Prossie couldn't talk to any of them.

All she could do was to sit in the groundcar, in the thick silence of her own isolated mind, and wonder whether the Empire wanted her, or wanted Earth.

And whether it really made any difference.

Best brushed aside leaves and peered down at the ground below.

For the most part the earth was thick with dead leaves and moss—nobody lived here, that was obvious.

In one direction, though, the view was different. There was a clearing ahead, and a very strange clearing indeed. It appeared to have been created or enlarged by breaking limbs off trees, where any normal clearing would simply be a place where no trees grew. Most of the clearing was covered by a black mound of something Best couldn't identify; here and there things showed through the black, some of them bones, some of them unidentifiable. At one side, at the very edge of what he could see, something large and purple protruded from beneath the mound, something that Best thought might be I.S.S. *Christopher*.

Most of it was hidden by trees, so he couldn't be sure; he'd have a better look when he reached the surface.

All around the black mound were signs that people had been there—but not that any were there now.

The area looked entirely deserted, in fact.

That was exactly what Best wanted; smiling but still wary he climbed down the rope ladder into the forest.

Athelstan and the woman, Boudicca, were just finishing their dissection when that odd kink in the matrix suddenly vanished.

It hadn't been guilt. Pel had been forcing himself not to think about it, but when it disappeared so abruptly its absence drew his attention. Nothing internal could have done that; he knew it must have been a twist in the currents of magic, not in his subconscious.

That was reassuring.

So it had been caused by something out there in the world somewhere—presumably a wizard, because what else could affect the magical flow? And from the size of the disturbance, big enough to cause him a real twinge, the wizard must be a fairly powerful one.

Another wizard . . . Athelstan and Taillefer and Mahadharma hadn't thought there were any others left alive. Boudicca, more conservative, had refused to venture an opinion. Pel had known there were other people out there who could touch magic but had thought they might all be just beginners or dabblers.

Anyone who could make himself—or herself—felt through the matrix like that wasn't just playing around with fire-lighting spells. If this current batch didn't work out, at least there might be another chance.

"See you," Athelstan said, pointing to the fetch's heart, "how 'tis with this?"

At first Pel thought Athelstan was addressing Boudicca, but then he realized that both wizards were looking in his direction—not quite at his face, because of the haze of magic around him, but in his direction.

"What?" he asked, leaning forward and trying not to be sickened by the sight of the fetch's opened chest.

At first he saw nothing but gore, but then he adjusted his vision, shielding his gaze with a layer of magic—not because it had occurred to him that that would help but just to put something between himself and the exposed organs.

And when he did, he saw the fetch not as a human body, but as a magical structure, and he could see what Athelstan meant: the pattern that kept the heart beating, and that was not at all what they had tried to use on the dog.

"Oh," he said. He studied it for a moment, then said, "I could do that."

"So," Boudicca said, sitting back on her heels. "Thus it is."

"I could do that," Pel repeated.

It was simple, really. Not obvious, but simple.

And judging by what he saw in the fetch, it was stable, self-sustaining. It could be done in anything that had the right general structure to it, it didn't have to be a human heart.

Were the homunculi and the rest done the same way?

If so, no wonder Shadow had made so many of them. It would be easy.

Pel tugged at the magic flowing through and around the chamber, and the fetch's chest closed, healing almost instantly.

Athelstan fell back, startled, in a most graceless and unwizardly fashion. Boudicca merely blinked.

That pattern in its heart kept it alive, Pel could see that, and the network that ran through the rest of its body, like a miniature of the matrix itself, let it move and function.

But there was a break in the pattern, a discontinuity. Where other living creatures continued down into fractal complexity, the fetch's energies simply flattened out and looped back upon themselves; Pel wondered if Athelstan had seen it.

Excited by this discovery, without thinking what it might do, Pel reached out and repaired the flaw.

The fetch sat up. It opened its eyes and looked about.

Then it started screaming.

CHAPTER 7

"*I* know, I know," Johnston said wearily, "*name, rank, and serial number.*" He waved at the prisoners and sat down. He sighed heavily.

"You know," he said, "we aren't at war with the Empire. Right now we aren't at war with anybody, and we'd like to keep it that way. I think I might know a few things you boys don't, things that your superiors would be interested in—but I'm not going to just hand them over if you people insist on acting like prisoners of war. So far, you're just trespassers and illegal aliens . . ." His mouth twitched a little at that phrase, and he had to stop for a few seconds to keep from laughing.

The four of them sat silently as he recovered. The leader, Lieutenant Austin, was glowering at him; one of the others was looking sheepish, a third was staring at his own knees, and the fourth was studying the ceiling.

"You trespassed on Ms. Jewell's land," Johnston said, "and you're in the country without the proper papers, but you aren't felons, you aren't charged with espionage, you aren't considered hostile or prisoners of war. You're maybe subject to a fine and deportation, and that's about it. Now, I'll offer you a deal—you tell us *why* you're here, and we'll take you back and see if we can send you home. If the opening's still there we can send you through by helicopter, maybe, even if the ladder's gone. You keep quiet, and I'll keep you locked up and incommunicado for as long as I possibly can. It's that simple. If your people want to talk, we can talk—not me, I'm Air Force, but we can get the

72

State Department in on it. If you don't want to talk, you stay the hell out of our space. Simple enough?"

The sheepish-looking one shifted his feet.

"We'll give back the suits before you go, too," Johnston added. "No tricks."

The one who had been watching the ceiling tiles threw his superior a glance, but Austin wasn't buying.

It was obvious who needed convincing here.

"Lieutenant Austin," Johnston said, "I'm not asking for much."

"Too much," Austin said.

Johnston sat back and stared at Austin for a moment; the Imperial looked back unflinchingly.

"So what the hell do you want us to do with you?" Johnston shouted suddenly. "You want to rot here?"

Austin shrugged. "You're holding Imperial personnel against their will," he said.

"You're not in Imperial space, you . . ." Johnston bit his words off short; it wouldn't help any to call Austin an idiot.

He obviously *was* an idiot, but it wouldn't help to tell him that.

"Okay, look," he said. "Maybe you think the Empire's going to come in here, blasters blazing, to rescue you—but did they go after the crew of the *Ruthless*? Did they go after the squad that went with Lord Raven? I *know* about all that. I know your blasters don't work here, your ships can't fly here—this is *our* turf. They couldn't save you even if they wanted to, and I'll bet they don't want to."

Austin was unmoved, but the other three were all visibly nervous now.

"Here's what we're going to do, then," Johnston said. "We're going to send *one* of you . . . let's see . . . Hitchcock. We'll send Spaceman Hitchcock back through the space warp, and let him talk to whoever's in charge over there, and tell them that we want to talk, we want answers, and that none of you are going anywhere until we get them."

Hitchcock looked up from his folded hands.

"I know we didn't talk when the *Ruthless* came through, because we didn't know it was for real," Johnston said. "Well, now we know. We want to talk. You just tell 'em that, Hitchcock."

"Yessir," Hitchcock said, smiling nervously.

Austin threw him a look that should have been fatal, and Hitchcock wilted into silence, but Johnston leaned back and smiled.

The formerly dead man—Pel could no longer think of him as a fetch—crouched with his head on Boudicca's chest, shivering silently. He hadn't been eager to answer questions, and Pel hadn't pressed the issue. The man appeared to be unnerved by the memories of spending several years as Shadow's undead servant. Waking up suddenly, with all those memories, had sent him into a screaming fit.

The fit seemed to be past, but Pel still didn't think he wanted to know just what the man was remembering.

The revived dog, on the other hand, seemed perfectly happy with her situation; she sat panting cheerfully as Pel petted her.

" 'Twould seem, O Brown Magician," Athelstan said, "that you now have the knowledge that you sought."

"Yeah," Pel said, scratching the dog behind her ears, relishing the familiar doggy feel of the coarse hair and loose skin. She was a pleasant dog, a mutt, mostly hound—she looked something like a coonhound, only smaller.

He felt pretty pleased with himself just now, and he wanted to bask in it for a moment. He'd fixed the fetch, turned it back into a man. He'd brought a dead dog back to life. He thought he had a good understanding of resurrection, and he could use Susan Nguyen as a final trial, bring her back from the dead to make sure it would work on Earthpeople. Everything was going well.

He didn't expect it to last; he was sure something would go horribly wrong at any minute now, but he wanted to enjoy the feeling of accomplishment while he could.

"Are we then free to go?" Athelstan asked.

Pel frowned as he considered the question.

"I'm afraid not just yet," he said at last. "Not till Susan ... not till I know this works every time. And besides, I don't have the ... the bodies ..." His throat tightened. The pleasant afterglow vanished as he imagined Nancy and little Rachel lying dead. He forced himself to take a deep breath, and asked, "But I can *make* bodies, can't I? Raven said that Shadow could make duplicates of people—do I need a hair or something from the person, to work with?" He thought of the science-fiction stories about cloning people from a single cell, and he thought that it ought to be possible to do something like that with magic.

"Simulacra? Alas, O Great One, I know nothing ..."

Pel's brows lowered, and thunder rumbled somewhere— not outside the fortress, but in the hallway outside the throne-room doors.

Athelstan blanched.

"Perhaps, with some experimentation ..." he said.

"I'm out of this one," General Hart said, shaking his head. "Once you called in Intelligence, I knew enough to get out of the way. It's all yours, Bascombe."

Bascombe, seated comfortably behind his own desk, stared up at the general. "And I suppose you'll deny approving Raven's expedition? We happen to have the paperwork on that one, with your signature all over it."

"Oh, I'll admit to that one, all right," Hart said, leaning back against the gray-painted steel wall. "I did it through the proper channels, you approved it, everything by the book. I sent Major Southern back to Terra with a full report. And that was just a dozen troopers, two officers, a telepath, and a bunch of foreigners—I didn't send any Intelligence agents, Colonel Carson's no loss, and the telepath was authorized higher up. It's not going to look real pretty on my record, but it's not serious."

"Are you suggesting that my follow-up actions *are* a serious mistake?" Bascombe demanded.

"If they aren't," Hart said, straightening up again, "then

why do you want me involved? I can see spreading the blame, but since when would you want to share the credit?"

"I'm just trying to be fair," Bascombe said.

"Oh, of course. You didn't bother to consult me until you heard that the imperial marshal and the secretary of science were on their way here, but then you suddenly wanted to be absolutely *sure* I didn't mind. *What* a coincidence." He put his hands on Bascombe's desk and leaned forward until his face was a foot or so from Bascombe's. "Not a chance, Bascombe. If there's credit to be had here, you can have it. I've had enough of you. *This* one's all yours, and I hope you choke on it."

Best thought he was making good time as he led his little squad through the forest; he just wished he knew where he was going.

Begley, his number-two man, had claimed some expertise in woodlore and had reported finding a track that someone had followed away from that huge pile of rotting flesh that covered the wreck of I.S.S. *Christopher*. Best hoped he was right, and that they were following the right people.

The track became obvious after a point, and now Best was leading the way, with Begley, Poole, and Morcambe following close behind. Morcambe was carrying his knife ready in his hand; the others left theirs sheathed.

Best wished he had thought to bring a bow and arrows—but that assumed one could have been found at Base One, which was doubtful.

This silent forest, with its filtered, scattered sunlight and its thick, rich smells, was getting on his nerves. There could be enemies behind any tree. The *Ruthless* survivors had described monsters that came charging out of the woods at them, that burrowed up out of the ground; the thing that had dropped on I.S.S. *Christopher* looked as if it had had wings before the scavengers and bacteria had started in on it, and that implied that it flew. Monsters could come at them from any direction, from above or below, at any time.

And he didn't want to face monsters with just a knife. A

bow and arrow would have been only slightly better. He wished blasters worked here, and he wondered just what sort of weird place this was that they didn't.

He wanted to get out of the woods, onto open ground. He wanted to find a native to talk to.

The daylight seemed brighter ahead—was that a clearing? Were the trees thinning? He beckoned to the others, muttered, "Come on," and picked up the pace.

"I guess we won't need the chopper," Johnston said, staring at the rope ladder that hung from empty air, swaying in the breeze, its bottom rung bumping gently against the side of the spaceship that covered half of Amy Jewell's backyard. He turned to one side for a moment and said, "There you go, Mr. Hitchcock—your way home. You get up there and tell them that we're ready to talk, and that they don't get their other men back until we do."

Hitchcock nodded, smiling happily as he stepped forward. He already had his spacesuit on. "Will do, Major," he said. He lifted his bubble helmet into place and began securing the seal.

"Major Johnston," someone called.

Johnston turned to locate the speaker.

"Got a call for you." The voice came from the back door of the house, where a lieutenant was leaning out, the receiver of Amy Jewell's phone in one hand.

Johnston blinked, then frowned. "This better be important," he said.

"It's Thorpe," the lieutenant replied.

Hitchcock had his helmet in place; he gave Johnston a questioning look, and the major waved him on toward the ladder.

"I still say we should've suited up some of our own men and sent them along," someone muttered.

Johnston shook his head as he started toward the house. "Too dangerous," he said as he walked. "Could be construed as hostile. Trespassing. Invading. We don't know how rough they play." He took the receiver from the lieutenant. "Ms. Thorpe?" he said. "Johnston here." He turned to watch as Hitchcock started up the ladder.

"Sir," Prossie Thorpe's voice said unsteadily, "I tried to talk to Carrie—to Registered Telepath Carolyn Hall. She contacted me."

"Go on," Johnston said. Hitchcock was moving quickly, but it was a long climb, a good hundred feet at least, probably more.

"She ... she questioned me, but I ..."

The Imperial telepath's tone penetrated Johnston's focus on Hitchcock's ascent. He looked down at the kitchen floor, at the toes of his shoes, and concentrated on the voice in his ear.

"Take your time, Thorpe," he said.

Prossie drew a deep breath and tried to compose herself.

It shouldn't hurt this much, she told herself. She had already *known* she was a rogue, an outlaw; she had already known that Carrie was turned against her. Still, she hadn't *felt* it until she had taken up direct mental contact with Carrie again.

Then she had felt it, all right—that tense loathing and anger, not just from Carrie, but through her from the entire network of telepaths, the entire extended family.

In fact, *most* of it came from the four hundred, not from Carrie—but then, Prossie knew that Carrie hardly had any real existence apart from the network. All her life she'd lived in the family's web of thought and feeling, just the way Prossie had before *Ruthless* came through the warp.

And much of what the family felt they picked up from the normals around them, the nontelepaths. Carrie was working with John Bascombe and General Hart and people who hated and feared telepaths; it was easy for her to direct that fear and hatred at her traitor cousin.

Still, it was a shock to *feel* it. And it was a shock to learn why it was so intense.

Bascombe had sent those men to Earth after *her*.

Carrie hadn't meant to let that slip. She hadn't meant to tell Prossie anything.

And Prossie hadn't meant to tell Carrie as much as she had, either, but any time telepaths communicated directly there would be leakage, there would be things that slipped out. A telepath couldn't completely hide anything without breaking contact.

Hell, even when there was *no* conscious contact, things tended to leak through; telepathy wasn't limited to conscious thought. Anything one telepath knew, they all did, on some level—though they might not all remember it.

Prossie swallowed and gripped the phone, the strange Earthly gadget that was almost like a mechanical telepath, that could transmit voices for hundreds of miles.

"Major Johnston," she said, "I found out what those men were sent after."

"Yes?"

"They think ... they *suspect* that you and your people have joined forces with Shadow, that you're plotting together against the Empire, and that I came here as Shadow's liaison. They came to capture or kill me, and to see whether such an alliance actually exists. I told Carrie that it doesn't, and that Shadow is dead, and she *should* know I wasn't lying, but I can't be sure."

For a moment Prossie heard nothing, and she wondered whether the phone had broken, or whether some part of its mysterious mechanical workings needed extra time to transmit this particular message, but then Johnston asked, "Can you relay to her for us?"

Prossie shook her head before she remembered that Johnston couldn't see her. "No," she said. "She and I ... we can't communicate any more."

"Damn. You're sure?"

Prossie took a deep breath. "Yes, sir."

"Is there anyone *else* she can communicate with, then? Did they send any telepaths with that bunch we have locked up? And please, don't tell me it's Hitchcock, because he's two-thirds of the way up the ladder out here."

"No, sir. Not Hitchcock or any of the others, so far as I know—none of them are telepaths, and I don't *think* any of them can receive." Prossie blinked. "But there are some possibilities, sir—you know, we sort of made contact with some of your own people before *Ruthless* came through. There were six . . . no, five of them, because one died."

She didn't really listen to what Johnston said to her next, because she knew what it was going to be. She closed her eyes and concentrated, remembering.

"Their names . . . there are three men and a young woman, and a little girl. The men are named Oram Blaisdell, and Carleton Miletti, and Ray Aldridge, and the woman is Gwenyth, I don't know her last name, and the little girl's name is Angela Thompson, I talked to her sometimes. I think Carrie's brother Brian was the last one assigned to contact them . . ."

Pel stared at the object in dismay as he wiped blood and bits of fat and skin from his hands. A thick, soapy smell filled the room.

The thing on the table was made of human flesh, or a reasonable approximation. It had the shape of a woman. He thought he could force it to live, if he wanted to.

But it wasn't Nancy.

He had thought he remembered her every feature, every inch, every detail, but the thing he had created, had grown and gathered and shaped into a semblance of humanity, was not Nancy. The face was wrong. The proportions were wrong.

"I was never a sculptor," he said, flinging down his washrag in disgust.

Behind him stood two fetches and three others; two of the others, the two wizards, stirred at his words.

"Your pardon, O Great One," Athelstan said, looking quickly from Pel to the inanimate body and back, "but I see no flaw in this homunculus. Surely, it . . ."

"It's not *Nancy*," Pel shouted at him, wheeling to face

the wizard. The air crackled with anger, and red light blazed from the walls. Boudicca backed away a step.

"Nay, 'tis not," Athelstan admitted hurriedly, "nor did I say it might be. Yet you've created here a woman—is that not a fair start? To make so fine a semblance as you desire, one needs must have better to work from . . ."

"I don't want a *semblance*," Pel barked. "I want *Nancy*. And Rachel. My wife and daughter."

"And surely, with patience, you'll have them," Athelstan said. He gestured at the woman who stood stolidly to the side. "Have you not brought this one back from the dead? Can any doubt that you have the power to wreak whatever you will?"

Pel turned and looked at Susan. She gazed calmly back, and he relaxed slightly. He had brought *her* back without any problem.

But he hadn't had to create a body for her.

"Doesn't look much like Nancy, does it?" he asked her.

Susan looked at the lifeless homunculus. "It's a good try," she said slowly, "but it isn't quite right, no."

Pel turned to Athelstan again. "If we had some of Nancy's hair, would that help?"

"Oh, most assuredly! By the Law of Contagion we derive the Law of Parts, and see thereby that the part can be made equal to the whole—from a single hair, in time, we can surely re-create all the pattern of your wife's flesh."

"Do you know how to do it?"

Athelstan hesitated, then glanced at Boudicca.

"I do," the female wizard said.

"Good," Pel said. He looked at Susan, then away.

If he sent Susan back to Earth, why would she return? It was, perhaps, cruel to keep her here, but so far she hadn't *asked* him to send her home, and it was so good to see her alive again, to have the company of a fellow Earthperson.

Maybe she wasn't sure the magic that had revived her would hold back on Earth—and for that matter, Pel wasn't entirely certain, either, but Shadow's fetches had lived in the Galactic Empire, and Prossie had said simulacra had lived there; why not a revenant on Earth, then? Susan had left Earth alive, and would return alive, and what difference did it make what had happened in between?

But he wanted her *here*.

He would open a portal to Earth, and send someone to bring him back Nancy's hairbrush, and Rachel's, and the bedroom and bathroom wastebaskets, and anything else that might have hairs or fingernail clippings in it.

But he wouldn't send Susan.

"You," he said, pointing at a fetch, "I have an errand for you."

The lieutenant looked up, startled, at the sound of a footstep. He closed his book.

A man was walking across the basement, a pale man dressed in strange black clothes, paying no attention to the lieutenant or anything else. The man was marching directly toward the stairs.

"Hey," the lieutenant said, dropping *Destroyer* novel #82 and getting to his feet. "*Hey!* Hold it, you!"

The man in black paid him no attention whatsoever. He began marching up the stairs, his tread heavy on the wooden steps.

The lieutenant hesitated; should he call in, or stop this guy?

If he took the time to call, the man might get away.

He drew his sidearm. "Stop right there!" he shouted.

The man kept on up the stairs.

The lieutenant cursed; he couldn't shoot in cold blood, not just for ignoring him. The man might be deaf. He shoved the pistol back in its holster and ran after the stranger.

He caught him at the top of the stairs, threw an arm around his neck and pulled him back. The stranger didn't exactly struggle, but he *did* try to keep walking for a moment. When he realized it wasn't working, he stopped.

He let the lieutenant carry him back down to the basement, and did not resist as his arm was twisted up behind his back and held with one hand while the lieutenant used the other to work the radio.

The lieutenant had no idea why the silent stranger was being so cooperative, and he hurried to get his message through while the cooperation lasted.

He didn't know that the fetch had been ordered to bring certain items, and no one had told him to hurry.

"Aldridge and Blaisdell are easy," Johnston told the FBI man, pointing at the list. "Blaisdell's in Tennessee—you people gave us a report on him, which is why we decided to turn the job over to you. That, and we hope you can be less conspicuous about picking them up."

"We'll try," the FBI man said dryly.

Johnston ignored the sarcasm. "Aldridge is in Oakland; he's in the papers. Miletti is supposed to be local, but we don't know which jurisdiction, Virginia or Maryland or the District, and we haven't located him yet. Thompson is trickier—we think she might be in Texas, but that might just be something she was pretending. Thorpe can maybe give you more on that little girl . . ."

The intercom buzzed.

"Damn." Johnston pushed a button. "What is it?" he demanded. He was tempted to add, "This better be good," but he didn't. His people all knew that.

"Sir, there's been an incident at the Brown house . . ." his secretary began.

"Damn," Johnston repeated, releasing the button. He got to his feet and grabbed for his jacket.

"If you can keep up," he told the FBI man on his way to the door, "you can come along."

CHAPTER 8

"*What* the hell is taking so long?" Pel wondered aloud.

No one answered. Taillefer and Mahadharma had both slipped away some time ago, and were probably halfway to their respective homes—Pel thought he could probably locate the wizards' auras, or whatever it was the matrix let him see, but he didn't see any reason to bother. Athelstan was off getting himself something to eat—he'd skipped a meal or two while he tutored Pel in the manufacture of homunculi, and was making up for lost time. Boudicca had stepped out to the privy.

The only people in the room, besides Pel himself, were the revivified Susan Nguyen and a fetch. Fetches generally didn't answer questions, didn't talk at all unless directly ordered to do so, and Susan was keeping her own counsel.

Pel wondered whether the fetch had a name. Obviously it had had one when it was a living man, but did it remember that? Had Shadow given it a new name, perhaps?

It probably didn't need a name, though; fetches didn't seem to have any real sense of identity. They were interchangeable zombies, as far as Pel could see.

Pel supposed he should have asked the dead man he'd revived about it—after all, he'd been a fetch for some time before Pel's experimentation had restored him fully to life. He'd been so distraught, though—Pel had thought it kinder to just let him go home.

Of course, Pel mused, he could just restore *this* fetch and ask him. In fact, he probably should restore all the fetches—and he would, when he had a chance, but for now they were useful and he was busy.

"What's it like, being dead?" he asked Susan.

She stared at him, apparently untroubled by the shifting glare of the matrix. "I don't remember," she said.

"Really?"

"Really. I had shot Shadow, and she turned to face me, and then there was a sudden pain, and then I was lying on the floor and you were standing over me, with Shadow's lights all around you."

"That's all?"

"That's all."

Pel considered Susan for a moment. She was something to think about, to distract him from wondering why that stupid fetch needed half an hour to collect a couple of hairbrushes and wastebaskets. He thought back to that insane, terrible confrontation, here in this very room, just a few days ago, really, when Shadow had killed Raven and Valadrakul and Singer one by one.

"Why'd you try to shoot her?" he asked.

Susan blinked.

"I mean," Pel said, "you were always so good at surviving, at putting up with whatever it took to get through. You didn't fight the pirates who captured *Emerald Princess*, or the slavers on Zeta Leo Three—you just outlasted them. So why'd you try to shoot Shadow?"

"I don't . . ." Susan stopped, obviously struggling to organize her thoughts. She tried again.

"I don't know," she said.

Pel waited, and after a moment she continued, "All my life, I survived by waiting. When I was a little girl I survived the Viet Cong by waiting until my parents saw their chance. Then I survived the Cambodian pirates who sank our boat by not fighting back while they killed my family and raped me, and I survived the refugee camps by never causing trouble, and I survived the racists and sadists all through school and college and law school by just putting up with their abuse. I always played by whatever the rules were, to survive; I became a lawyer so I could have the rules on my side for once. Whoever knows the rules, whoever makes and interprets the rules, comes out on top. So I didn't fight the spaceship pirates or the slavers—they had the rules, and I didn't."

"So why'd you shoot *Shadow*, then? She made whatever rules she wanted!"

"Because I was *tired* of playing by the rules," Susan said. "I was *tired* of being passive; I wanted to finally do something *more* than survive. If Shadow died, we could change the rules any way we wanted."

"But she killed you," Pel said.

"But she killed me," Susan agreed. "It was stupid. I should have just waited, the same as I always have."

Pel hesitated. She'd tried to be a hero, and she'd wound up dead, and Pel figured that that was what always happened to heroes in real life, but here she was. This was real life, but it was like a story, too—the fact that he was alive and Shadow wasn't proved that. "But it's turned out okay," he said. "I mean, you're alive again, and I guess now *I* make the rules, so you're safe."

She stared silently at him.

The room was cool, but Spaceman Hitchcock was sweating visibly.

Bascombe smiled bitterly at that. As if *Hitchcock* had anything to sweat about! He was probably about to be proclaimed a hero for coming back up the ladder alive, as if that was some great accomplishment. Hitchcock was just scared because he was face-to-face with Space Marshal Albright and Secretary Markham—the poor little nobody wasn't used to facing the big brass. Hell, he'd be nervous just facing Undersecretary John Bascombe, and *these* two were probably here to shoot Bascombe's career down in flames.

If he'd had just a little longer Bascombe thought he could have pulled it off, could maybe have moved the Department of Interdimensional Affairs out of the Department of Science and right up to cabinet level.

"Just tell us about it, Spaceman Hitchcock," Secretary Markham said. "Don't worry about the formalities. This Major Johnston offered you a deal?"

"No, sir," Hitchcock said, "He offered the *lieutenant* a deal, and the lieutenant wouldn't take it. Me, they just *told* to come back here and report—I didn't have to do a thing in return."

Markham nodded, and Bascombe frowned.

"And what was it that you were to report, Spaceman?" Marshal Albright asked.

"He said—Major Johnston said to just tell you what happened, and that they want to talk, they aren't hostile. That's all. And that you get the lieutenant and the others back when you agree to talk, and not before."

"And do you think that's the truth?" Albright asked.

Hitchcock blinked. "Do I think what's the truth, sir?"

"That these people aren't hostile."

"*I* don't know, sir. They treated us all right, but . . . well, that doesn't mean much."

"No, it doesn't," Albright agreed. He glanced at the silent figure of his personal telepath, then at the Secretary of Science.

Bascombe wondered how Albright could stand having a telepath with him all the time. It was supposed to be a great honor to have one's own telepath, with one at all hours of the day or night, but that was an honor Bascombe could do without—a damn mutant freak spying on him every second. Bad enough working with them when he was on duty.

Markham had one, as well, of course. Bascombe supposed the telepaths had names and identities of their own, but no one had introduced them; they were just there, part of the background.

That was a drawback to political advancement he had never really considered.

Secretary Markham leaned forward and said, "Spaceman Hitchcock, this Major Johnston is the highest-ranking official we've yet contacted on Earth. Do you think you could go to Terra and tell the Emperor about him?"

Hitchcock went white, and Bascombe winced. In all his years of political jockeying he had never yet had the honor of reporting directly to His Imperial Majesty, and here this poor frightened gee-puller was being offered an audience.

That was an honor Bascombe *did* want—but he wasn't about to get it.

Hitchcock stammered incoherently until Albright finally broke in. "Never mind, Spaceman; I don't think we need to send you to Terra."

Hitchcock relaxed, but at the same time a look of hurt disappointment crossed his face.

"Yet," Albright added. "I'm sure that eventually His Majesty will want to meet you and thank you."

Hitchcock nodded.

Albright and Markham leaned together to confer for a moment, and Albright's telepath leaned in with a word or two as well; then Markham turned and looked straight at Bascombe.

"Mr. Bascombe," he said, "I believe we've heard everything we need from Spaceman Hitchcock for the present, but there are a few things we'd like to ask *you*. If you would be so kind ... ?"

He gestured toward the interrogation chair, where an Imperial guard was guiding Hitchcock to his feet.

Bascombe straightened. Here it was, at last. If he could sell this, he was made.

If not, he was ruined.

He rose and rounded the table, watching the telepaths as he went.

"He doesn't look very healthy," Johnston said, eyeing the pale, black-garbed figure. It was a deliberate understatement; the gaunt stranger looked downright corpselike.

"Doesn't seem to be able to talk, sir," the lieutenant said. "I haven't gotten a sound out of him—not so much as a grunt. He just sits there."

"Do you speak English?" Johnston asked loudly.

The stranger didn't stir; he simply sat, staring straight ahead. A layer of grayish dust covered the family-room sofa, but this mysterious person didn't seem to notice. Johnston looked at the stranger's hands, and at the largely undisturbed dust.

He hadn't touched the couch anywhere except where he now sat.

That didn't seem natural.

An airman stood beside the couch, one hand on the stranger's shoulder. Johnston looked at that, and the lieutenant followed his gaze.

"If we don't physically hold him he starts walking away," the lieutenant explained. "Frankly, sir, I think he's mentally disturbed—autistic, or something. We can't communicate with him at all."

"Then how'd he get into the basement here?" Johnston asked.

"I don't know, sir—I didn't see him arrive. Just all of a sudden he was there."

"We might just let him go and see what he does," Johnston said.

No one answered. The black-clad stranger didn't move.

The fellow looked like a corpse, Johnston thought. It was hard to believe he could move at all.

"Let him go," Johnston said.

The airman hesitated, then lifted his hand. The pale man stood, rising smoothly from the couch without a single wasted motion, and began walking. Johnston, the lieutenant, the FBI man, and one of the three airmen followed; at Johnston's command the other two airmen remained in the family room.

Johnston had expected the stranger to aim for the front door, but instead the silent visitor marched up the stairs and into the master bedroom. There he paused for a moment, scanning the room, then headed for one of the dusty, cluttered dressers. He picked up a hairbrush, then another, and another; clutching the three brushes in one hand he turned and scanned the room again.

"Hairbrushes?" the lieutenant asked incredulously.

The stranger spotted his target, and picked up the pink plastic wastebasket from beside a bureau. He dropped the brushes into it and headed for the door.

The FBI man and the airman stepped quickly aside.

"Major, do you know what's going on here?" the FBI man asked.

Johnston shook his head.

The stranger had to step carefully when he searched Rachel Brown's room—the floor was strewn with toys. Johnston saw him hesitate at the sight of the plush alligator on the girl's empty, unmade bed, the first time the man had acted like a human being, instead of a machine.

Or maybe he was just trying to figure out whether the alligator was a hairbrush. But no, the child's hairbrush was on her bureau, and a wastebasket was at the foot of her bed. The black-clad stranger collected both items and headed back for the stairs, a wastebasket in each hand, hairbrushes in each wastebasket.

"Stop him!" Johnston called to the airmen in the family room.

The pair blocked the foot of the stairs, and the pale stranger stopped and simply stood, as if waiting for them to step aside.

"You aren't going to let him go, sir?" the lieutenant asked.

"I don't think so," Johnston said. "Not yet, anyway. He's got what he came for, I'd say—but why does he want them?"

"Trash, sir?" one of the airmen at the foot of the stairs asked. "He just took the trash?"

"And hairbrushes," the lieutenant said.

"What good would that be to anyone?" asked the airman who had accompanied the officers.

"Maybe he's gonna use voodoo on someone," suggested

the airman who hadn't previously spoken. "Get some hair and nail parings for the voodoo doll, y'know?"

"God knows this guy looks like a zombie!" said the airman beside him.

The others smiled, but Johnston looked at the back of the stranger's head and seriously considered it. It was true, this guy *did* look like a walking corpse.

Jewell and Thorpe had said that there was a universe on the other side of the basement wall where magic, or something one hell of a lot *like* magic, really worked. Maybe this fellow *was* a zombie. Maybe his master *had* sent him after hair and fingernail clippings.

He didn't smell like a corpse; there was an odd, meaty, slightly sweet odor clinging to him, all right, but Johnston had smelled corpses, and this odor was definitely not the stink of a dead body.

Maybe, if he was a zombie, the odor had something to do with the magic that had brought him back from the dead.

"Put him back on the couch," Johnston ordered.

The airmen grabbed the stranger by the arms and hauled him into the family room. He didn't resist, didn't protest, just went along as if it didn't matter in the slightest what he did, or what happened to him.

The lieutenant's theory that the man was autistic did seem to fit—but so did the idea that he was a zombie.

"Come on," Johnston said, "I want to see the basement."

"So that dead woman we found on Beckett was Shadow, and an Earthman is running the show in her world now," Albright said.

"If Hall is right about what she picked up from Thorpe, yes," Bascombe replied.

"But Thorpe's a renegade—we can't trust anything she says," Markham pointed out.

"She's a telepath, and she was talking to another telepath," Albright said. "*I* can't lie to a telepath. Can she?"

"And this doesn't account for Thorpe's brief appearance

in normal space in an unnamed system a hundred light-years from Beckett," Bascombe pointed out.

"That could have been anything," Albright said, waving it away. "It had to be Shadow sending her through, for some reason, and Shadow's dead, so what does it matter?"

"It might," Bascombe said. "Somehow."

"I doubt it," Albright replied.

"Suppose we wait before we leap to conclusions," Markham suggested. "Undersecretary Bascombe has sent a scouting party into Shadow's universe, after all; why don't we wait and see whether this man Best can confirm Shadow's demise?"

"And if Shadow *is* dead?" Albright asked. "What do we do about this Earthman who replaced her?"

"Why don't we just wait until we hear from Best?" Markham answered.

Johnston crossed the basement, ignoring the card table, radio, folding chairs, and video set-up—which, of course, had run out of tape at the crucial moment.

He stared at the bare concrete wall; it appeared perfectly ordinary in the light of the bare bulbs overhead. Johnston glanced up at the lights, then turned his attention back to the wall.

"There's no opening now," he said. "I wonder how he expected to get back?"

"I don't know," the lieutenant said. "I don't know how the hell he got in here in the first place."

"You didn't see any opening here?" Johnston asked, gesturing at the blank wall.

"No, sir—not a thing."

Johnston frowned. He put out a hand, not knowing what he was looking for, and attempted to tap the wall. His hand vanished into seemingly solid concrete.

Astonished, he staggered, thrown off balance. Both hands went out, grabbing at concrete that wasn't there, and he stumbled forward, through the wall.

He caught himself just short of going down on one knee

and stared at the blaze of shimmering, shifting color before him. The cool, dusty air of the Browns' basement was suddenly thin, sharp, clean, crackling with electricity, and redolent of sweat and cold meat. He felt suddenly heavy, the way he sometimes felt the loss of buoyancy upon climbing out of a pool.

He couldn't see anything but colors, as if he were trapped in some incredible light show. None of them, Jewell or Thorpe or Deranian, had mentioned anything like this inside the portals; they'd said the transition was instantaneous. If he'd gone through a portal, shouldn't he have come out somewhere?

"Hello?" he said.

As he settled back on the dark wood of his throne, Pel had the uneasy feeling that there was something Susan was not telling him.

He didn't know what it could be; he believed her when she said she didn't remember being dead, and he believed her explanation of why she had tried to shoot Shadow, but he was sure there was *something* that she wasn't saying about her recent experiences.

Did she know something about why the fetch was taking so long? He didn't see how she could; after all, he was the magician, not her. He was the one who could turn a dead body into a fetch, or bring it back to life entirely. He could sense everything that touched magic, through all the world, and she was just an ordinary human being—a lawyer.

What could she know that he didn't?

He was trying to think of some way to ask her when a man stumbled out of the portal.

Startled, Pel let slip his partial suppression of the matrix's visual manifestations. *He* could still see perfectly well, of course, but anyone else would be blinded by the barrage of light, color, and shadow.

He thought for a moment that the fetch had returned, and wondered why he had been startled, but then he got a better look at the new arrival.

It was a man of medium height, middle-aged, a few pounds overweight, and wearing the uniform of an officer in the United States Air Force. He was unquestionably alive, and not a fetch. He was staring blindly into the matrix glare, eyes watering.

"Hello?" he said.

Pel was in no mood for new complications; for several seconds he considered magically shoving the stranger back through the portal, or even just flash-frying him—burning him to ash would actually be much easier, since it just meant unleashing a little wild energy, where pushing him meant directing controlled energy while maintaining the portal.

But burning him would be murder, and Pel was astonished that it had taken him so long, a good three or four seconds, to realize it.

Besides, this man might know what had become of the fetch, and where the hairbrushes and wastebaskets were.

"Hello," Pel said, letting the matrix amplify and distort his voice into an echoing roar. "Who the hell are you?" he demanded, as he began fighting down the matrix glow.

"Major Reginald Johnston, U.S. Air Force," the stranger said, squinting through the glare. "And you, I take it, are Pellinore Brown?"

CHAPTER 9

"*I want my fetch,*" Pel said. "*And those hairbrushes and stuff.*"

"No problem," Johnston said. "You keep the portal open, and I'll send him right through." He reached inside his uniform jacket. "Let me leave my card—if you or Ms. Nguyen comes back to Earth, I'd appreciate a call."

Pel blinked at him, at the proffered business card—the little white pasteboard rectangle seemed weirdly out of place here in Faerie, in Shadow's throne room, lit by the light of the great matrix.

He accepted it, not with his hand, but with a tendril of magical energy. From Johnston's point of view the card simply sailed through the air to Pel of its own volition, but Pel could see the strands of magic supporting it, the twisted shape of the air that carried it to him.

"And if there's anyone you'd like me to contact—your firm, perhaps, Ms. Nguyen?"

Susan didn't reply; Pel glanced at her sharply as he picked the card out of the air.

"Sure, tell them she's okay," he said.

Pel remembered that he had two sisters, a mother, and some friends back on Earth who might be worrying about him; he was about to mention that when Johnston spoke again.

"While I understand why you're staying here, Mr. Brown," Johnston said, "why is Ms. Nguyen? You aren't holding her against her will, are you?"

"No!" Pel snapped. He frowned and glanced at Susan

again. She wasn't moving; she was just standing there, watching the two men.

"She's free to go," Pel said. "If she wants to go back to Earth, she can." He hesitated, then added, "I admit I enjoy her company here, though."

"Ms. Nguyen?"

Susan shrugged, and Pel felt a surge of anger. Why was she doing this? She was acting like a zombie; this Major Johnston would think that she was drugged, or hypnotized.

"Answer him," Pel said.

"I'm fine, Major," Susan said. "Thank you for your concern."

Johnston was studying her from a few feet away, but then he shrugged, just as she had a moment before. "Whatever you like," he said. "Mr. Brown, thank you for your co-operation. You don't mind if I leave a man stationed in your house until you return to Earth?"

"Not at all," Pel said, not really concerned. That was on Earth; he wasn't going back to Earth until he could bring Nancy and Rachel with him.

"Um . . . if you don't mind my asking . . ."

"Yes, Major?"

"Have you had any contact recently with the Galactic Empire? I mean, since you reached this place?" He gestured at the throne room.

Johnston had explained about the investigation, about questioning Amy and Prossie and poor Ted, but the inquiry still somehow struck Pel as odd—a major in the U.S. Air Force, in uniform and on duty, talking about a Galactic Empire?

Pel had gotten accustomed to the reality of this strange new world he had found himself in, but it still seemed bizarre and somehow wrong that it could interact so freely with the normal, everyday world of Earth. An Air Force officer didn't *belong* in Shadow's fortress, and shouldn't be worrying about the Galactic Empire.

But here Johnston was, with a serious question.

"No," Pel said. "Why do you ask?"

Johnston hesitated. "I'm not sure whether I should be telling you this, but ... what the hell. The Empire sent a scouting party through their space warp recently—four men climbed down a ladder in Ms. Jewell's backyard, and were taken into custody."

"What did they want?" Pel asked, puzzled.

"I don't know," Johnston said. "I'd like to find out."

"They won't say?" Before Johnston could answer, Pel remembered his stay at Base One. "No, they won't, will they? Bunch of pompous idiots."

Johnston smiled.

"Okay, well, I don't know anything about it," Pel said. "It isn't really any of my business unless they come poking around here, but if I find out anything I'll send a message through. This isn't America here, but I'm still a U.S. citizen, I guess—I sure don't owe the Empire any favors!"

Johnston nodded. "Thank you, Mr. Brown, That's all we ask."

"Yeah, well," Pel said, "*I* ask for my fetch back."

Best sighed and leaned back against the tree.

Two hundred miles to Shadow's fortress—that was going to be a damned long walk.

He would have to walk, though—the locals didn't seem to have any other means of transportation. They knew what horses were, but seemed to take his questions about buying one as nonsense—apparently only the hereditary nobility rode on horseback. And oxen were just for plowing, as far as he could see. Oxen would be impossibly slow, in any case.

Well, maybe he wouldn't have to travel the entire distance to find out what was going on; surely, news and rumor would spread. So far he hadn't picked up anything useful, but he and his men were still out in the sticks.

At least, he thought as he looked around at the muddy, malodorous little yard where he'd traded an hour's labor in the fields for a meal and directions, he *hoped* they were still out in the sticks.

* * *

Pel watched as Johnston stepped warily into the portal and vanished, back to Pel's own basement back on Earth.

Someday, when he had Nancy and Rachel back, when he got tired of playing with the matrix magic, got tired of this medieval mess of a world with its stone walls, its goddess worship, its open sewers, Pel would want to step back through just such a portal. He wondered if he could do that with one of his own creation.

Probably not. He'd have to get Taillefer back here and have him do it.

This Johnston seemed like a sensible sort, really—not at all like the assholes running the Galactic Empire, Carson and Southern and the others, and not like the ignorant barbarians who made up most of Pel's own empire.

Or maybe it was just a matter of cultural differences, since after all, Johnston was a fellow American, and whatever else the Imperials and the locals might be, they weren't that. Maybe they weren't really stupid; they'd just grown up with a completely different background. Pel knew that foreigners weren't stupid back on Earth, despite what the bigots might say, and he supposed it must be the same with these people.

In any case, it was good to know something of what was happening back on Earth, good to know that Johnston was there, that there was someone to contact in case of emergency. Pel didn't feel anywhere near as isolated as he had just a few moments before.

Of course, this was all assuming that Johnston had been honest, and Pel would have a more tangible indication of that in just a few minutes, when his fetch either returned or didn't.

Johnston certainly seemed honest enough, and intelligent—he had figured out who Pel was readily enough, and he had asked about the Empire . . .

Pel frowned. What *was* the Empire up to? Why would they send men to Earth? The crew of *Ruthless* had said they were there to make an alliance against Shadow, but this new batch, from Johnston's description, wasn't doing anything like that.

The Empire seemed to be spying on Earth—but it was *Shadow* that had been the enemy. Then wouldn't they be spying on Shadow, as well? Or rather, since Shadow was dead, on *him*?

As that thought struck him he felt a sudden twinge, something in the matrix, somewhere . . . He took a moment to analyze the still-unfamiliar sensations the matrix transmitted.

It was somewhere outside the fortress, somewhere far away, but not *too* far—still on the near side of the world. When he tried, he could sense the world's curvature, could feel the matrix reaching around to meet itself, at the same time stretching up beyond the atmosphere and down deep into the stone below. Compared with all that, this new thing was close by, but he knew it was miles away.

He'd felt it before, he remembered. He had felt the same odd twist in the matrix when Athelstan had first suggested dissecting one of the fetches.

Pel suddenly made a connection.

The Empire probably *was* spying on him—and that's what he felt. He guessed that they'd reopened the space warp out in the forest where *Christopher* had crashed. That's what he'd noticed while he'd been talking with Athelstan—they'd opened it then and sent someone through, and now they'd opened it again—to get a report, maybe?

That was annoying; Pel didn't like the idea of being spied on, and he didn't much want to get involved with the Empire again.

But it didn't matter. If Johnston sent back the fetch, Pel could bring back Nancy and Rachel, and then he wouldn't care what the goddamned Galactic Empire did.

"I say we should send a telepath," Albright said. "This dropping a ladder and waiting for messages is stupid. It's a half-assed, asinine idea, relying on this when we could send a telepath and have instant reports whenever we want them."

"Sir," Bascombe said, "may I respectfully remind you that the only telepath to ever leave Imperial space went rogue, and is still loose? Do we really want to risk the loss of another?"

"Bascombe's right, for once," Markham said. "We don't have enough telepaths to send one along with every single expedition, especially since the freaks can't even read minds once they're there."

"Well, damn it . . ."

"However," Secretary Markham added, cutting off Albright's objection, "I think we might be well advised to see if our mutant friends can pick up a link to Shadow's world. They've read minds there before, haven't they? Have we tried to follow Best's actions from here?" He turned and looked at his own personal telepath.

"I didn't work on that project, sir," the telepath answered, "and I haven't gone over it all consciously, but it's certainly true that some minds in Shadow's world can be read. Not very many, but more than on Earth. As for reading Captain Best's mind, I couldn't say whether it's possible or not. I would suggest that the Halls would be best suited to make the attempt, as Carolyn Hall maintained contact with her cousin Thorpe for some time while Thorpe was in that universe, and Brian Hall has had considerable experience in interdimensional communication."

"Good enough," Albright said. "Get the Halls in here, then."

Pel accepted the wastebaskets and said, "Thanks," before he remembered that he was talking to a fetch.

He paused, startled by his own slip. The fetch had been human once. It wasn't now. Pel could fix that.

He really *ought* to fix that.

After he had Nancy and Rachel back, he promised himself. After that he'd fix *all* the fetches. For now, he had more important things to do.

It was a relief to let the portal to Earth close, finally, and to move on to other things; he collapsed the opening into nothingness, then sent the fetch away with a wave of his hand and stared hungrily into the wastebaskets, at the hairbrushes and the bits of dust and hair.

From that he could grow new bodies—clones, they'd be called in Earth terms; simulacra, they were called here. To the wizards it was a matter of the Law of Parts, of the part containing the whole; Pel tended to think more of the genetic pattern that must be complete in every single cell.

It might be the same thing; he didn't know.

And what's more, he didn't care, so long as it worked.

"Okay, we know one of the players," Johnston said. "Brown and his friends look pretty straight and simple, just the way Ms. Jewell and Ms. Thorpe here said, and he's happy now that he's got his zombie back; as long as he stays on top there I don't think we have to worry, and he currently holds all the strings."

He paused, and looked around at the others—at his staff, the FBI man, Jewell, Thorpe, and the rest of them.

No one spoke.

"This Galactic Empire's another matter," Johnston continued. "They've got the ability to pop through into our reality, and for all we know they can do it anywhere—though the fact that they came through the same place twice might mean it's not that easy for them. They tried to send an embassy first, and we arrested 'em—maybe that's why the second bunch looks like spies, but it might just be they're twisty, and how we treated the first batch didn't matter. They speak English, but that doesn't mean we know how they think."

Thorpe shifted—deliberately, Johnston realized, to remind him of her presence.

"Thorpe, here, *does* know how they think, better than anyone—she grew up there, and she could read minds—so we've got something to work with, but on the other hand, she doesn't understand how *we* think."

Thorpe almost nodded at that.

"They have one big advantage—they can spy on us, with their telepaths and space warps, and we can't get at them at all. So we're going to collect everyone we know they can contact and see if we can open some serious negotiations, and we're going to keep an eye on Ms. Jewell's backyard. But mostly, since we *don't* have any space warps or magical portals or mind readers, we just wait. Unless anyone has a better idea."

This time it was Jewell who got his attention by clearing her throat.

"Was there something you wanted to say, ma'am?" Johnston asked.

She looked around nervously, then shook her head, and he made a note to talk to her privately as soon as possible.

Growing a simulacrum from bits of hair and skin and nail was not the same as creating one from scratch; Pel didn't need to sculpt it, but instead coaxed it along in what seemed a process of unfolding. As he guided the magic through and into it, the little knot of detritus on the workshop table melted together into a little blob, then elongated, expanded, shaped itself.

He had thought that it might grow like a clone, first an embryo, then a fetus, a baby, a child, until Nancy was again a grown woman; he had even idly toyed with the idea of stopping the process a bit early, restoring her to her youthful beauty—not that she wasn't still beautiful, but . . .

But then he'd promised himself he wouldn't do that. He wanted *Nancy*, the way she had been when she was killed, not some close approximation.

And it turned out to be a moot point, because the thing didn't develop that way at all; it didn't acquire any recognizable human features until it was two feet long, and by the time it reached three feet in length and clearly became a person stretched out there on the rough wooden table, it was an adult woman in form, not a child. The familiar breasts were fully developed, in proportion to the still-small body; the hips were as broad, in proportion, as the real Nancy's had been.

He cursed himself for thinking "the real Nancy" that way. This *was* the real Nancy, or at any rate it soon would be. And it was enlarging—*she* was enlarging—quickly, drawing mass from the magical energy Pel poured into her. This wasn't cloning, he reminded himself, this was magic—the laws were different here. Here he really could bring back the dead.

Or at least, he could create a simulacrum . . .

He forced that thought away. He *would* bring Nancy herself back from wherever she was, from wherever her soul had gone. He would have an exact duplicate of her body, grown from her own tissue—wouldn't that be enough?

He hadn't gotten the first simulacrum right, but that was different; that time he'd been trying to re-create her from memory.

This time it would work.

It had to.

"Mr. Blaisdell," the man in the gray suit said, "I'm with the government. It appears that we were, ah . . . a bit hasty in sending you home."

Oram Blaisdell stared at the stranger for a moment. He looked over the blue government sedan parked on the gravel by the road, and around at the surrounding hills. Smoke was rising from the Ballard place down the valley, but he couldn't see any of the neighbors watching.

Then he glanced at his son Henry, standing by the door of the house, looking confused and a bit scared.

"What the devil are you talkin' about?" he asked at last.

"I'm talking about your communication with . . . well, you thought they were angels."

"You sayin' they ain't? What the hell do you know about it?" He reached a hand down toward the splitting maul he'd been using, but didn't touch it. He was getting too old to be splitting the damn firewood anyway.

"Mr. Blaisdell, we've learned the truth about those

angels," the man in the suit said. "They're quite real, you were right, but they aren't quite what you thought they were."

Oram considered this, threw Henry another glance, then asked, "You humorin' me, so you can get me to some doctor Henry called, or you serious?"

"I swear, Pa," Henry said, "I din't call nobody. He's got a badge 'n' all."

"Rose called, maybe?"

Henry shook his head. "I don't think so, Pa; she din't tell me a thing 'bout it if she did."

Oram studied his boy's face, then looked back at the government man.

"I can understand your doubts, sir," the government man said. "I'm sure you've had some people who thought you were imagining the whole thing, and you think your children might have been worried about you and tried to fool you for your own good, but I promise you, that's not the case. I'm really with the government." He flipped open a brown leather case and displayed a badge and document; Blaisdell didn't care to admit he couldn't read the damned thing without his glasses, and wasn't too sure he'd get it all even if he had them.

"We need your help," the man in gray said. "If you agree, we'll be driving you directly to Knoxville and putting you on a plane to Washington—a chartered plane. We'll provide accommodations at the other end, give you an expense account for meals; you'll be free to move about, to use the phone, call anyone you want, but we need to know if the . . . if these 'angels' contact you again."

"You think they will?"

The government man didn't answer that.

"You mind tellin' me what they *are*, if they ain't angels?"

"To be honest, sir, they didn't tell me that."

Blaisdell eyed him carefully. That sounded authentic and true, somehow.

Then he looked around, at the wood he'd been splitting, and at the house it was meant to heat.

"C'n I bring Henry, here? Or Rose?"

"I was told you could bring your family, yes, sir."

"How 'bout a lawyer?"

"If you want, yes—or you can call one locally after you reach Washington."

"C'n I bring a gun?"

"Yes, sir. You aren't under arrest; you can bring whatever you like."

That convinced him. "Gimme an hour to pack," he said.

An hour later he was in the back of the dark blue sedan, on his way to Knoxville, with his old leather suitcase in the trunk and a .357 Magnum in his lap.

At first Ray Aldridge thought he was being sued; it had happened before. Then he thought he was being arrested for fortune-telling; that had happened to a friend of his back in Massachusetts once.

Finally, though, he realized what was happening. He was being called in as a consultant. A psychic consultant.

He almost babbled with joy as he ran down the steps from his apartment to the waiting car. He was being hired as a psychic consultant to the *FBI*!

This was it. Even if he couldn't help, couldn't come up with a thing, just being called would be enough.

His career was made!

Margaret Thompson climbed aboard the plane with her head awhirl in confusion. Angela's invisible playmate was *real*? Her own little girl was getting mental messages from somewhere *real*? That silly made-up name, Basurpathork, was *real*?

Well, not quite—Angie had garbled it. Proserpine Thorpe—what kind of a name was that?

She looked down at her daughter. Angie was staring wide-eyed at the interior of the plane. "We're really gonna *fly*, Mommy? Up in the air?"

Margaret smiled, despite her confusion. "That's right, Angie, we'll fly right up into the air. All the way to Washington."

"If you guys are IRS, I swear I'll sue. It's unconstitutional," Carleton Miletti said, for the hundredth time.

"Yessir. We're not from the IRS, sir."

"You better not be." He sank back in the seat and watched the streets of Washington sliding past the car windows on either side.

He didn't understand this. He hadn't received any messages from anyone, didn't know what the hell these people were talking about. He didn't remember anything special this past spring—but then, he'd been busy.

Still, he thought he'd remember any mysterious messages, and he didn't.

It had to be a coincidence, or just his imagination, that the odd feeling of being watched was back.

CHAPTER 10

It was Nancy.

At least, Pel thought the woman he had created from hairs and nail clippings was truly Nancy.

She lay there, nude and lifeless, and Pel stared at her, looked over every inch of her, looking for any flaw, any sign that he had failed to perfectly re-create his wife's body in every detail.

Of course, he had only his memory to go on, and he was dismayed by how untrustworthy that was. The curl of the hair was right, the curve of the hip, but was that mole on her thigh in exactly the right spot? Had it maybe been a quarter-inch lower before?

He couldn't be sure.

There were photos back in the house, and he could send a fetch for them, but those wouldn't help—those were portraits and ordinary snapshots, no full-length nudes, nothing that could show him every single feature.

He couldn't be absolutely sure—but as far as he could see, this was Nancy, re-created and intact, just as she had been. Even the smell was right.

But she wasn't alive. Not yet.

He touched her, carefully.

Her skin was cold and dry, her eyes blank; he drew back, shuddering.

This was really creepy, he realized. He had been so intent on it that he hadn't really thought about what he was doing. This was like something out of a Stephen King novel, trying to bring back the dead—or really, maybe it was more like something from *Invasion of the Body Snatchers*, since this wasn't really Nancy's body at all. This was a copy, grown from tiny discarded bits, and the *real* Nancy was still lying dead and mutilated somewhere in the Galactic Empire.

He was back in Storyland, only this time it wasn't some great heroic adventure, it was a horror story. Something terrible was going to happen, he was meddling in things Man was not meant to know . . .

But he had *magic*, damn it. Nothing would go wrong. He could bring her back, safe and sound, in this re-created body. He could do *anything*—he held Shadow's matrix, controlled all the magic, all the creative energy, of this entire *universe*.

He knew he could.

He took a deep breath, clenched his fists, then unclenched them and let out his breath. He gathered in the magic, sucked in energy through the matrix—he didn't want to fail by not putting enough effort into it. He wanted to get it right the first time; he didn't want to go through this again. He had saved out part of the hair and a toenail clipping and some powdery residue he was fairly sure came from hair or skin, but he didn't want to have to use it.

Most especially, he didn't want to have to destroy a botched attempt.

For a moment he thought about calling Boudicca or Athelstan back into the room to advise him, or even just Susan, for moral support, but then he clenched his fists again and quashed the idea. He would do this *himself.* He didn't want anyone else seeing Nancy like this. He didn't want anyone else watching if something went wrong. He didn't want anyone else around, inhibiting him, if everything went right. He didn't want to worry about distractions or explanations or anything else.

He would do it alone.

He drew in the energy, filled the chamber with a thick roiling fog of magic, so dense that the colors seemed like liquid currents in the air, deep orange and blood red and seething molten gold.

He waded through them, feeling the viscous electric force prickling and oozing across his skin, and approached his re-created Nancy. He moved around to the foot of the table and stood there, looking down at her, at toes and legs and the tight curls of hair, and he wrapped the magic around her, felt it soak into her, permeate every part of her.

Pel wasn't just raising a fetch this time; he wound the pattern of energy in her spine and brain, but at the same time he drew the pattern from the flesh itself, and did something he couldn't describe in words, reaching out in one of those directions that wasn't really there, but to which magic gave him access. He somehow knew that he was reaching through the portals of death itself, to find Nancy's soul and draw it back.

He pulled and wove and pushed and embraced, all at once, all through the matrix—his own hands never touched her—until he felt the power flowing of its own accord, the heart beating strong and steady, the brain waking, the eyes seeing. The flesh warmed, blood surged, muscles tightened and relaxed.

She blinked, and turned her head, first to one side, then the other.

For a moment he held his breath; he let the magic pull away, let her life free itself from the matrix.

"Nancy?" he breathed at last.

She blinked, raised herself up on her elbows, and looked at him.

"Is that my name?" she asked.

"Shadow is *dead*?" Best asked, startled. "You're *sure*?"

"Man, where have you been these three days past, since the news first came?" The innkeeper set down the wooden mug of thick, foul-smelling beer. "Aye, Shadow is dead, destroyed at the hand of one Pelbrun, styled the Brown Magician—we've the word of half a dozen travelers on it, one of whom spoke to a man who had been in the very throne room of Shadow's fortress, and had spoken there with Lord Pelbrun."

Best picked up the mug warily, then glanced first at Begley, then at Poole, finally at Morcambe.

Morcambe shrugged.

"It's ... I mean, 'tis a hard thing to believe," Best said to the innkeeper.

"I'truth, it is!" the innkeeper agreed. "Yet all who come hither from the west attest it true, and it pleases me well to hear it. 'Tis to be a kinder reign, methinks, for Pelbrun's orders have come down to us, that there shall be no more hangings for aught but murther, and that we may serve the Goddess an we choose." He gestured toward the window; Best looked, and saw the gallows in the town square.

He had seen it before, when he and his men had arrived in the village—it seemed a perfectly ordinary gallows. Judging by the stains and general wear it had seen considerable use.

It was empty now, though, and perhaps that was what the innkeeper meant to point out. Presumably, when Shadow was running things, there was usually a criminal or two suspended there.

"What if it's trickery?" Best asked, doing his best to imitate the barbaric local accent, with its flat, harsh vowels and archaic phrasing. "What if Shadow still lives, and is only testing your loyalty?"

The innkeeper shrugged. "What would you have of us? What could *Shadow* have of us, an it yet lives and rules? We're but plain folk; if 'twould destroy us, it may, and what's to be done? Why strive to deceive, when 'twas long said that Shadow had the power to see within every heart, should it trouble itself to do so?"

"What if ..." Best paused, struggling to phrase his questions. This seemed too good to be true, that the superhuman enemy of the Empire had conveniently died, but he couldn't very well explain that to this brew-soaked barbarian. It seemed more likely that it was all part of some elaborate scheme, perhaps directed at the Empire.

And who was this Brown Magician?

"Enow, good sirs, I've others to tend to," the innkeeper said, after Best had groped unsuccessfully for words for a few seconds. " 'Tis a wonder indeed, that we should live to see this day, and I'll give you time to think upon it, and to resolve what you'd say. Drink heartily, and give voice an you'd have more." He turned away and stumped off.

Best looked at Begley. "What d'you think, Bill?" he asked.

"Sounds genuine to me," Begley answered.

"I don't know." He hesitated, then motioned to Morcambe. "Sid," he said, "you finish up, and then head back to the landing site—they're supposed to drop a ladder every four hours, but I wouldn't be surprised if they're off schedule. When they drop it, you climb back and tell them what we just heard."

"What about you?" Morcambe asked.

"I'm going on to Shadow's fortress," Best said. "I intend to see for myself, and get a look at this Brown Magician if I can."

Begley shifted uneasily.

"If you and Poole want to back out, we'll talk about it," Best said. "Chances are I'll send you back with reports before I get that far anyway."

"Yes, sir," Begley said, trying unsuccessfully not to look relieved.

Shock, Pel told himself. The shock of her death and resurrection had damaged her memory, but it would come back with time, he was sure.

"Yes," he said, "your name is Nancy Brown. You're my wife."

She sat up, legs still straight out in front of her, and stared at him.

"All right," she said.

"Don't you remember?" he asked.

She frowned slightly. "I'm not sure," she said. "I know things, I remember things, but it's all sort of vague."

"Do you know who *I* am?" he asked hopefully.

She squinted at him. "No," she said. "Except . . . you created me, didn't you? You're the magician who created me?"

Why would she think of magicians? That didn't sound right. Pel was suddenly afraid that something had gone very wrong. "I'm your husband, Pellinore Brown," he said, "and I didn't create you—I've brought you back from the dead."

"Was I dead?"

Pel nodded; his throat suddenly felt thick and clogged with emotion, and he couldn't speak.

"I don't remember that," she said. She cocked her head and looked at him, smiling sweetly, the movement and expression heart-wrenchingly familiar—though it was something Pel hadn't seen since a few days before Grummetty had walked out of the basement wall. His doubts vanished; that gesture was Nancy's.

"You were dead," he said. "You were killed by raiders on *Emerald Princess*, and I came here and killed Shadow so I could get you back, you and Rachel."

"I don't remember that," she said again—not smiling, this time.

"It's probably shock," Pel said. "Traumatic amnesia, or something, like on TV. It'll come back to you eventually, I think."

It struck him how bizarre this scene was—Nancy sitting calmly there on the table, stark naked, while the eerie, shifting patterns of the matrix flickered about her, filling the stone-walled, stone-floored chamber with vivid color.

She wasn't a screaming fury like the revenants in *Pet Sematary*, she wasn't possessed by demons—not visibly, anyway—but she wasn't frightened or upset, either, nor as confused as Pel thought she ought to be. She was just accepting it all—she hadn't asked about the matrix effects, or why he was wearing his present makeshift attire of loose black blouse and homespun trousers, or why she was nude, or, most important, where she was.

She hadn't asked *anything* except in response to his own words.

It had to be the shock, and the amnesia.

"What should I do now?" she asked, and he was unreasonably relieved to hear her ask it.

"Whatever you want," he said. "I'm so ... It's just ... I'm so glad to have you back!"

She turned and dangled her feet off the side of the table. "You missed me?" she asked.

"Of course!"

"How long was I dead?"

"I don't know, exactly—I've lost track of time. Weeks. Months." He watched as she slid off the table to stand on her own two feet.

"Ooh, the floor's cold!" she said. She looked down and danced from one foot to the other.

That was more than Pel could stand. He stepped around the table and swept her up in his arms.

At the feel of her warm, bare flesh, the weight of her in his arms after so long alone, his body responded instantly. He bent his neck and kissed her.

When their mouths parted he remembered himself enough to say, "There's a bedroom down the hall."

He hoped she would say no, or take the initiative wordlessly, or otherwise encourage him to take her here and now, on the rough wood of the table; he feared she would refuse, would draw back, either because she didn't remember him or because, after all, she had just awoken from the dead, she might need time to recover.

For a moment, he wasn't even certain she knew what he meant.

But she smiled and said, "All right."

"Ms. Jewell," Johnston said, "I had the impression there was something you wanted to tell me."

Amy Jewell shifted uneasily. "Well," she said, "It's just ... you said there wasn't any way we could get at the Empire."

"I guess I did, yes," Johnston agreed.

Jewell gestured helplessly.

"I take it you think there *is* a way, then?" Johnston asked. "I assure you, Ms. Jewell, we don't have any secret project that will open a path for us . . ."

"No, not that," she said, dismayed.

"What, then?"

"Well, you can send things through Pel, of course," Jewell explained. "He can open a portal to the Empire any time you want, and one to Earth, and you can send through whatever you want."

Johnston leaned back in his chair and stared at her. "That's obvious," he said slowly, "now that you've pointed it out. I'd thought of going through Faerie, of course, though it hadn't occurred to me that Mr. Brown would help us. But you know, he might. In fact, why shouldn't he?"

"I don't know," Amy replied.

She still looked uneasy, though—and she knew Brown better than Johnston did. "I think," he said, "that that's something we'll keep in mind, Ms. Jewell."

But he didn't think they'd be in any hurry to ask favors of Pel Brown.

The matrix flickered and dimmed as Pel lay back on the cool bedding. He felt a pool of sweat drying beneath him.

The re-created Nancy lay beside him, saying nothing, smiling blandly.

She had cooperated, had agreed to whatever he suggested—and had suggested nothing herself. She hadn't mentioned the weird pyrotechnics of the matrix, even though she had never seen any of it while she lived. She hadn't said *anything* unless he spoke first. She hadn't resisted when he had proposed things Nancy had always found disgusting; she'd cooperated. She hadn't commented on his endless matrix-supplied energy.

This wasn't Nancy.

Admitting that to himself caused a hard, sharp, physical pain in his belly, but he had to admit it. This wasn't Nancy.

He sat up again and looked down at the woman beside him in the bed, looked at her as only a matrix wizard could, using the magical network's power to see into her in a way that was more than physical.

This wasn't Nancy. It wasn't really human at all; the soul, if that was what it was, lacked the complexity of a living woman's.

This was an artificial being of his own creation.

He knew that she would do anything he told her to, without argument. She had no visible will or personality of her own. This wasn't Nancy. This wasn't a real woman at all. This was a homunculus, a *thing*, not a real person.

He hadn't raised the dead; instead, he had found the way Shadow had created those duplicates Raven and others had mentioned, her spies, her doppelgängers.

He supposed some men might even think that was enough—but he wanted *Nancy.*

He wept silently, and she smiled up at him uncomprehendingly.

"They've been collected, all of them, and brought to their capital city," Carrie Hall said. "All but Gwenyth, anyway."

"Why?" Secretary Markham demanded.

"To try to talk to us, I think," she answered uncertainly.

Markham's eyes narrowed. Telepaths weren't supposed to be uncertain. He had an idea, a pretty good one, that a telepath only showed uncertainty when lying—they were never uncertain about what they had read, nor afraid to admit when they didn't know something, but they could be uncertain, briefly, about how their lies were being received.

"It's a very difficult contact," Carrie said, as if answering his thoughts. She was probably doing exactly that—snooping inadvertently, maybe without even realizing she was doing it. Markham knew a lot about telepaths, had worked with them for twenty years, and while everyone knew that snooping without orders was a crime, he was aware that sometimes they couldn't help it.

"And the four of them haven't been *told* why they were

gathered," Carrie added. "They're guessing, and I'm working from their guesses."

Markham nodded. He turned to Carrie's brother.

"I've located a few possible contacts," Brian said, anticipating Markham's question—as Markham had expected him to. "I've found two of our own people. One is Samuel Best, the head of the intelligence squad Undersecretary Bascombe sent, and the other is a trooper named Ronald Wilkins, who accompanied Lord Raven for a time and then deserted the party. He suspects himself to be the only survivor of Colonel Carson's command."

"And what do they know about Shadow?"

"It's hard to read very much, sir—there are currents of energy that interfere. However, both our men have heard that Shadow is dead; Best has sent one of his men back for pickup, to tell us as much. Apparently Shadow has been replaced by someone or something called the Brown Magician."

"Brown?" Markham glanced at Carrie, then at Bascombe. "Pel Brown, perhaps?"

Pel debated whether or not he should destroy the false Nancy, and could reach no decision. He sat on Shadow's throne, considering, arguing with himself.

She was a mockery, a thing—but she was alive and she seemed so human, in her complacent and obedient way. She wasn't Nancy—but was she a person, all the same?

He had created her, but did that give him the right to destroy her?

Or the *obligation* to destroy her?

At least he hadn't re-created Rachel, he told himself. Destroying a grown woman would be bad enough, but a false child ...

But maybe he *should* re-create Rachel. Wasn't a simulacrum better than nothing? He had been so happy to have Nancy back, at first, until he had realized it wasn't her. He had so missed the warm companionship of a woman ...

But he didn't *want* an imitation, damn it! He wanted *Nancy*. And Rachel. Not just this Nancy puppet in his bed.

He looked up and saw Susan standing in the doorway, watching him. At least *she* was real, and not just a simulacrum, a magical imitation—she remembered her childhood in Southeast Asia, remembered how she had died here in Shadow's fortress. A simulacrum wouldn't have known any of that.

That was because he had simply repaired her dead body, forced life back into the corpse; he hadn't had to make a new body for her. He couldn't do that for Nancy or Rachel; he didn't have their bodies.

Red light surged up behind him and lit Susan's face a ghastly color. Pel blinked at her, and forgot all about the imitation of his wife.

He didn't have Nancy's body, or Rachel's.

But maybe he could *get* them.

CHAPTER 11

"*The general secretary has conferred with the Emperor*," the telepath said.

"And?" Albright demanded.

"The matter is being left to your discretion; His Imperial Majesty rests his full faith in your decision."

Albright swallowed, glanced at Markham, then nodded.

"All right, then," he said. "That gives us a free hand."

"Or enough rope," Markham replied.

"Or that," Albright agreed.

"I think, in that case, that our course is pretty clear."

Albright nodded. " 'The wise warrior does not fight two foes at once,' " he quoted. "Nicholson may be out of style, but it's still damn good advice."

"And, 'Know which enemies to fight, and which to appease,' " Markham replied.

"Right. And, 'Know who the true enemy is.' "

"Excuse me, sir," said Stuart, Albright's personal telepath. "Both of you find this exchange of aphorisms annoying."

Startled, Albright glanced up at the man behind his chair. "Right," he said. "We can both quote Nicholson and Majors, and appreciate their common sense—take that as given. And that probably means that we agree on what we want to do—get back Lieutenant Austin and his men, talk nicely to the Earthpeople, and then shut down the warp and forget Earth. They're not a threat."

"With one exception," Markham said. "If we could develop the space warp in response to Shadow's inroads, per-

118

haps they can develop something of their own, as well; the telepaths tell me that despite their apparently primitive science, they have their own areas of expertise in which they're very adept indeed. I'm given to understand that their mechanical communications devices are far better than ours, almost good enough to make up for their lack of telepaths."

Albright frowned. "But they don't have any such thing as a warp substitute *now*, do they?"

"No, but they might someday. Don't worry, Marshal, I'm not arguing with you—I agree, we should close off all direct contact with Earth until we've dealt with Shadow, or the Brown Magician, or whoever is running the opposition at present. I merely suggest that we delegate two telepaths, working in shifts, to maintain a watch on Earth."

Albright nodded. "Of course," he said.

"As for this Brown Magician—I think we want Imperial Intelligence to keep a very close watch there, indeed, and for you to keep your men alert to any threat he might pose, but we don't need to assume he's necessarily hostile. After all, we don't know whether he was Shadow's heir, or whether he overthrew it."

"In short, we may have had the interdimensional crisis resolved for us, without our having to fight."

"Exactly." Markham leaned back, smiling.

The Emperor and the general secretary had left this one to him and Albright, which meant their careers, and quite possibly their lives, were on the line—but he felt sure he was right in his actions. Earth was harmless unless they developed interdimensional travel, and this Brown Magician was a total unknown. No one could blame him for not attacking an unknown force immediately.

Furthermore, cutting off Earth, except for a telepathic watch, and transferring the combined attentions of the military and Imperial Intelligence to Shadow's realm, would leave that nuisance of a political appointee, John Bascombe, with nothing to do. It might keep him out of trouble.

And if not, Bascombe might make a convenient scapegoat, should one be needed.

Albright might still be nervous, but Markham was not. Markham was quite pleased.

"Hello, Angie," Prossie said, kneeling by the little girl's chair.

It was odd to see Angie's face as it really was, and not Angie's rather different self-image.

"Hello," Angie said politely.

Prossie smiled. "Do you know who I am?" she asked.

Angie shook her head.

"I'm Proserpine Thorpe."

Angie stared at her, and frowned. "*You're* not Basurpathork," she said. "That's Mr. Nobody's real name!"

"That's right," Prossie said, nodding. "I was Mr. Nobody. Sometimes. Sometimes it was one of my cousins."

"But Mr. Nobody was just inside my head," Angie objected.

"No, that's just how we talked to you."

"You aren't talking in my head *now*."

"No, I'm not," Prossie agreed. "I can't do it anymore—I forgot how. But my cousins still can. And we want you to tell us any time they say anything to you, even if they ask you not to tell. All right?"

Angie frowned.

Angie's mother leaned over. "Do what she says, Angie."

"But that's not nice," Angie protested. "That's telling secrets."

"I know," Prossie said. "It *isn't* nice. It's like spying, almost. But you see, that's what my cousins are doing— they're spying on *you*, and your mommy, and lots of other people."

"But Mr. Nobody's nice!"

Prossie nodded. "But there are bad people who are *making* my cousins do bad things. They can't help it." She waited for a moment, watching Angie's face.

"So," Prossie said, "will you tell us if they talk to you?"

Angie scuffed her toe on the blue hotel-room carpet. "I guess," she said.

Amy lay back in the bed and tried to be calm.

At least, with all the fuss about the Galactic Empire, Major Johnston hadn't interfered with her appointment. Walter's baby was gone, and Amy was rid of the man who had raped her. She wasn't about to forget what he'd done to her, he and Beth, but she didn't need any physical reminders. The bruises were healed, the baby was gone, and she could get on with her life.

She tried to tell herself that.

The abortion had been a nasty, intrusive, humiliating experience. The doctor and the nurses had been nice enough, but the procedure itself . . . well, it couldn't be helped, and it was over. The baby was gone.

She tried not to feel any twinge of regret. She didn't want children, she especially didn't want *Walter's* child, but still, the baby . . .

She shouldn't think of it as a baby, she told herself. The fetus. The tissue. Not the baby.

And it was too late to do anything about it now, anyway. She could get on with her life.

Of course, she wasn't sure just what sort of a life that was going to be, with her business ruined and her house under martial law and Major Johnston enlisting her as an adviser pretty much whether she wanted it or not. It wasn't as if she'd be going home from here; she'd be going to a fancy hotel in Crystal City, convenient to the Pentagon, at Air Force expense. She and Prossie had adjoining rooms.

That wasn't exactly her idea of a normal life.

One step at a time, she told herself, suppressing a shudder. One step at a time.

"I just don't want to talk about it," Ted Deranian insisted, for one final time.

"All right, that's fine," the woman in the blue Air Force captain's uniform said. "When you're ready, though, give us a call. Any time." She shook his hand and started to turn away.

"It wasn't ..." Ted began. She turned back. He hesitated.

"Was it really ... ?" he began again.

"Most of it, anyway," she said, understanding his incomplete question. "I don't know the details; maybe part of it was illusion. Most of it was real, though, yes; you've had an unprecedented experience, one you weren't prepared for, and you've been trying to handle it, trying to cope with things no one should ever have to cope with." She didn't mention that this was a modified version of the standard speech she gave to people who had cracked under the stress of combat or long imprisonment.

She'd never had to counsel anyone who'd fallen into another universe before.

"You go on home," she told him. "Take time off if you need it—we'll certify whatever you need, as far as that goes. You can tell people the truth, or tell them that you've been held hostage by terrorists—that's the easiest cover story, and we'll back you up. Or just tell them it's none of their business. And call any time—you've got the card." He patted his pocket and nodded. "And we'd like to see you again in a month or so."

"Thank you," Ted said.

He turned and left, closing the door carefully behind him.

"Who did you say this was?" Bob Heyworth leaned back in his chair. Tom Boyle glanced at him from the next desk, and Heyworth waved him away. Boyle went back to typing.

"My name's Ray Aldridge, I'm a professional psychic from California—maybe you've heard ... no, I guess you haven't."

"I'm not much into psychics, I'm afraid," Heyworth said. "You want me to connect you to someone a bit more in that line?"

"No, this isn't about me," the voice on the phone said. "I

mean, I hope you'll mention my name, but that's not why I'm calling."

"What is it, then?"

Heyworth could hear the hesitation before the voice said, "The government's in contact with aliens."

Heyworth grimaced, and asked, "How do you know?"

Tom Boyle glanced at him again, and Heyworth drew rings in the air by his ear to indicate that the caller was a nut.

That wasn't anything unusual; Boyle turned away.

"They told me," Aldridge answered. "They brought me here to see if I could help them."

Heyworth made a wordless noise that meant roughly, "Go on."

"See, they think that some psychic messages I reported back in the spring might have been a genuine contact with these people, who come from a galactic empire in another universe, so they brought me here to see if I'd get any more messages."

"And have you?"

"No, but ... listen, I know you think psychics are all fakes, and I'm not going to try to convince you of that part, because most of it *is* fake, but look, the FBI brought me here, to talk to people from Air Force Intelligence, and they've got people who came from this other universe, and they've been talking about how they have some kind of ship out in Maryland, in a place called Goshen—look, I'm afraid they might be trying to cover it all up, and I don't want that."

Heyworth blinked.

He had seen the phony spaceship in Goshen; the paper had been getting calls about it ever since someone had dumped it there months ago, back in April or May, and like most of the reporters he had eventually gotten curious enough to drive out and take a look at it.

And like all the others, he hadn't found anyone who knew anything about it. The lady who owned the place was never home, the government men who stopped by every so often to check on the place wouldn't talk—no one could make a story out of it. Jessie Wilber from Style had tried to do a sort of human-interest piece on the neighborhood reaction to this mysterious object, but it hadn't gone anywhere; most of the neighbors wouldn't talk about it, and the feds had given her a friendly warning that there were privacy considerations, that Ms. Jewell, the homeowner, was lawyer-happy.

So at first, when Heyworth made the connection, he thought this might be something interesting after all, that maybe somebody would finally explain that silly contraption and make it something more than a back-page filler.

Then he decided that no, this phony psychic had heard about the ship and had just figured it would be a good way to cash in; really, it was a wonder there weren't half a dozen cults popping up around it already.

But on the other hand—the psychic knew that the government agency watching the ship was Air Force, not one of the civilian outfits, even though the people who checked on it usually weren't in uniform. Heyworth only knew that himself because, in the proper reportorial manner, he had demanded to see ID before allowing himself to be chased away.

But he did know it. So this Aldridge had done his homework, that was all.

"We wouldn't want that either, Mr. Aldridge," Heyworth said. "I don't think we want to talk about it over the phone, though—you never know who could be listening. Is there somewhere I could meet you?"

The relief was plain in Aldridge's voice as he began babbling about a possible rendezvous.

Heyworth didn't know, when he hung up the phone, whether he would bother to show up. Standing a nuisance up was one of the best ways to get rid of him (or her)—but there was always a chance he might get something interesting out of this, and so far it had been a slow day.

He would call a couple of contacts, and see if the Air

Force might really have been talking to Aldridge, and if there was anything new on the Goshen spaceship.

"If your reports are accurate, and this isn't all an elaborate fraud," the man in the gray suit said, "then you're right. It's hardly just an intelligence matter anymore, and it certainly isn't just an *Air Force* matter."

"My reports are as accurate as I can make 'em," Johnston replied with a shrug. "And if it's a fraud, they've sure suckered *me*."

The man in the gray suit made it quite plain, without saying a word, that he didn't consider that to be evidence one way or the other. After a moment of silence, he added, "I'd heard rumors about this spaceship; we all took it for granted that it was a fake."

"So did I," Johnston said, as he pulled the car into Amy Jewell's driveway. He brought the vehicle to a stop inches from a previous arrival's bumper, shifted to park, set the brake, and turned off the engine. "If it were just the ship, I'd *still* think it was a fake, and I sure as hell wouldn't have called in the State Department."

"Just what was it that convinced you, then?" the man from the State Department asked as he opened the passenger door.

Johnston waited until they were both standing, then gestured at the rope ladder that dangled unsupported in the air.

"That, among other things," he said, as the State man gawked.

Ron Wilkins ambled slowly along the causeway across Shadowmarsh, considering the fortress that towered before him and trying to decide if this was really a smart move.

He sure as hell wouldn't have tried it if he thought Shadow was still alive and still in there.

All the reports, though, said that Shadow was dead, and the Brown Magician was in charge, and Wilkins could only figure that the Brown Magician was Pel Brown, which meant that somehow he and Raven and the rest had pulled it off, had defeated Shadow.

Which was pretty goddamned incredible.

Wilkins had noticed that nobody ever mentioned Raven, though, or any of the others. He figured that this probably meant one of two things: either all the others were dead, or some were dead and some had wound up in other universes.

Like back in the Galactic Empire.

Getting back to the Empire sounded like a pretty good idea.

Oh, he might be up for desertion, or something, but nobody over there could know exactly what had happened here, not even the bloody mind readers; the chain of command had been broken, Lieutenant Dibbs had told Wilkins and the others they could choose for themselves, and it couldn't very well be desertion to walk out on a bunch of crazies committing group suicide, could it? Raven wasn't an officer. Nobody in the whole bunch was, except Thorpe, and she was a Special, a mutant, not in the direct chain of command at all, not authorized to give orders.

So Wilkins didn't see that he'd broken any laws, and he didn't think he was important enough to be framed, so going home sounded *real* good.

Someplace with indoor plumbing, and decent food, and clean women who didn't scream if you so much as touched them . . .

Of course, if he was wrong about Brown being in charge, then he was walking right into Shadow's lap and was probably as good as dead—but hey, if he'd wanted to live forever, he would never have signed up to be a soldier.

But he wasn't in any hurry to be wrong. He was perfectly willing to take his time, just in case God decided to give him a sign or something. So he was walking down the causeway toward the fortress, but walking slowly.

He had the feeling that someone was watching him, as he strolled, and every so often he glimpsed *things* moving in the marsh to either side. The sky was gray and overcast.

Combine that with the heavy gravity, the low oxygen content of the air, and the off-color sunlight of this planet—if it really *was* a planet—and the whole place was about as oppressive and unpleasant as he ever cared to see. Leaving it would be a relief.

But he wasn't going to rush into anything.

Spaceman Second Class Thomas Sawyer, Imperial Military, paused for a moment in his work and leaned on his wooden shovel. Alison and Goody Fitzsimmons were gossiping again, exchanging the latest tales about the Brown Magician across the stableyard fence.

For a moment Sawyer once again considered trying to contact this legendary Pelbrun who had usurped Shadow's role. It almost had to be Mr. Brown.

But that would mean going into that fortress, and Sawyer couldn't bring himself to do that. He'd backed out at the very gate once before—and there was a good chance that Brown remembered and resented that. True, he'd apparently somehow won his battle against Shadow, but how many had died in the process? How many might have lived if there'd been another hand, such as Sawyer's, to help?

Better not to risk it. Life here wasn't all that bad. Rough, perhaps, but not too bad. Alison was a fine young woman, and he thought she was warming to him—that held some promise for the future, maybe more than he'd had in the Empire.

He stood, hefted the shovel, then scooped and lifted more manure into the oxcart.

Pel sat in his throne, physical eyes closed, and concentrated on the matrix, on bending his magical perceptions in a direction outside the three rational dimensions of normal space.

He had located the reality of the Galactic Empire, and found the place (place?) where the portal had been that allowed Shadow and her hundred fetches to step through.

He didn't want that, though; he wanted to find wherever Nancy and Rachel were.

Where their bodies were, rather.

Nancy had died aboard a spaceship, the *Emerald Princess*; Rachel had reportedly died on the rebel planet, Zeta Leo III. But Pel didn't know what had become of their remains. So far as he could recall, no one at Base One had told him, and he had been too distraught to ask.

He cursed himself for that now.

It seemed possible that both were on Zeta Leo III. Nancy's corpse might have been jettisoned somewhere in space, though.

Or both might have been brought to Base One. That seemed like the sort of thing the Empire would do.

He didn't know where to start; he had a whole galaxy to search. Admittedly, the galaxies of Imperial space appeared to be much smaller than those of Earth's universe, but still, there were thousands of worlds there.

As he groped about, in great sweeping arcs through nonspace, he felt odd little tugs and discontinuities, like snags in the fabric of space. At first he thought they were natural; then he thought he was doing something wrong; and then he realized that those were the places where Shadow had opened portals into the Empire.

He paused and considered.

It was interesting to see that portals left a permanent mark in what he could only think of as the shape of space itself. One might even think of it as permanent damage, and he wondered whether he might have hold of something that could destroy entire universes if misused, or even just overused.

He smiled wryly. Stand aside, atom bomb—magic could wreck universes, far beyond just a planet or two!

More importantly, as far as he was concerned, these snags were places Shadow had penetrated into the Empire, and while some of those penetrations had been botched scouting expeditions that had ended as a bunch of dead monsters, hadn't she managed to plant spies in the Imperial Military?

The Empire had certainly thought so.

A portal that had been used to plant a spy would presumably come out somewhere useful. Someone could step through and ask questions, maybe learn something useful. If he could make contact with the Imperial Military, get a message to General Hart at Base One, he could ask them to deliver the remains of his wife and daughter.

He had helped dispose of Shadow, after all, and after they had sent him here, to almost certain death, instead of just sending him home. They owed him one.

Of course, he couldn't go through such a portal himself—that was what had brought Shadow to ruin. He could send someone, though.

Fetches weren't very bright, and couldn't talk, and could hardly blend into a crowd if there was a problem; the locals here would he hopelessly out of place in a relatively civilized universe of spaceships and aircars.

He could wait for that Imperial spy, or whatever he was, to arrive—but Pel thought it would be better if one of his own people took care of things.

"Susan!" he called.

CHAPTER 12

*The State Department man and the deputy from the Imperial Department of Science were chatting quietly on one corner of Amy Jewell's patio, the Imperial's purple spacesuit an odd contrast with the Earthman's gray jacket. Major Johnston had been carefully not listening to them even before he got into the argument with the newly arrived FBI agent-in-charge, but he did wonder just what they were saying.

The first official contact between the governments of the United States of America and the Galactic Empire was taking place just a few feet away, and here he was in a stupid jurisdictional dispute.

"The Bureau dumped it on us back in April," Johnston pointed out.

"An error," the agent insisted. "We're correcting that."

"Seems to me that it's not really your concern any more than it's an Air Force matter, at this point. State and the CIA might have a claim, but why you? There's a spacecraft involved, which would mean either Air Force or NASA, but no one's committed any federal crimes. And we do have seniority here."

"Domestic espionage is a matter for the Bureau," the FBI man argued.

Johnston had been keeping half his attention on watching Lieutenant Austin and his two men climb the ladder; now he dropped the argument completely to watch as Spaceman Farmer—a name and rank combination that Earthpeople found funny, but the Imperials apparently didn't—vanished into thin air upon reaching the top. Farmer's bulky purple spacesuit just disappeared, as if erased.

Barrington followed, and Austin was nearing the top when an AP distracted Johnston.

"Sir, there's a reporter out front."

"What reporter?" Johnston asked, turning away.

"Heyworth, from the *Post*."

"Any video? Photographers?"

"Not that I saw, sir."

Johnston nodded.

He'd known it wouldn't stay quiet forever; *everything* leaked eventually. In this particular case he hadn't even tried for real secrecy; relying on normal discretion and the high unbelievability factor had seemed like a better idea. The nut theories that had been circulating for decades about a government cover-up of alien spaceships had been about the best protection he could have asked for, and classifying anything would only have made people suspect that there was something real this time.

But with the FBI and State involved, and the four psychic contacts, something had to leak, and he had known sooner or later someone would check it out. Johnston did wonder whether it had been the paranoid Miletti or the publicity-hungry Aldridge who called Heyworth—they seemed the most likely candidates.

If it was either of them, it was probably Aldridge; Miletti would more likely have just called more lawyers.

"Should I allow him back here, sir?"

Johnston glanced up in time to see Austin's purple-booted feet disappear. "I don't think we can legally stop him," he said. "You tell Heyworth that this is private property, and he's trespassing at his own risk, but if that doesn't keep him out, then let him past." He wished he'd brought Ms. Jewell along, so she could order the reporters away, but he hadn't thought of it; she was, as far as he knew, in the hotel in Crystal City, a good forty minutes away.

The AP turned and headed back around the side of the

house; Johnston watched him go, then glanced at the diplomats.

They were shaking hands; then the State Department man watched as the Imperial representative turned and trotted out toward the rope ladder, lifting his bubble helmet into place as he went.

Johnston blinked.

"If we had our men in place here," the FBI man said, "I think we could find a way to keep reporters out."

"Oh, I could find a way," Johnston answered. "For a while. If I told the APs to keep 'em out, they would, legal or not, but why antagonize the press? They'll find out sooner or later, and if we treat them nicely maybe they'll make us look good in their reports."

"We could order them not to interfere in an ongoing investigation."

"And you think that would *work*?"

The Imperial envoy was climbing the ladder, and Johnston was puzzled and uneasy. He had had the distinct impression, when he had ordered Austin and the others released, that this deputy was supposed to serve as the Imperial representative here until an ambassador could be sent—so why was the man climbing back up there?

"It's within the Bureau's authority," the FBI man said.

"Okay, fine," Johnston said; he could hear footsteps, and glanced over to see Heyworth coming around the corner, first staring up at the unsupported top of the dangling rope ladder, then at the spacesuited figure clambering upward. "Fine; you tell Mr. Heyworth that." He turned away and headed for the State Department man, leaving the FBI agent to deal with the reporter.

The man from State was calmly watching as the Imperial ascended. "What's going on?" Johnston asked.

"Hmm?" The man in the gray suit looked mildly startled.

"What's going on?" Johnston repeated. "Where's he going?"

"Oh, he's just going back to get his staff," the State Department rep replied. "He wasn't sure how many he could bring, what sort of facilities we would have."

"But he'll be back?"

"Oh, yes, of course. He'll be right back. Ten minutes, he said."

Johnston frowned, then turned to watch as the Imperial climbed. He was about fifty feet up now and climbing fast.

Heyworth was trying to shove past the FBI man to get closer to the ladder, and the FBI man was holding him back; the AP had followed Heyworth and was hanging back, standing by the back door of the house.

"You," Johnston called, "get me a radio."

"Yessir," the AP said, with a salute. He trotted away.

Johnston watched the Imperial climb.

He didn't like this; once that man was back through the warp the Empire would be free of any commitment to Earth. The hostages had been freed—Johnston didn't mind admitting to himself that Austin and the others had been hostages, though he would have vehemently denied any such thing if it had been suggested by anyone else. The crew of *Ruthless* was long gone. Prossie Thorpe was in exile.

Of course, the Empire was perfectly willing to abandon their people anyway; they'd demonstrated that before. Maybe it didn't mean anything that in a few moments they would have none of their people on Earth.

But Johnston didn't like it.

He couldn't *do* anything about it without possibly creating an international—*interdimensional*—incident, but he didn't like it.

Ten minutes, the State Department man had said.

The AP returned with the radio when the Department of Science deputy was a little over halfway up the long climb.

Johnston got through to the people he wanted at about the three-fourths point.

"Listen, that copter we had on standby," he said, "get it in the air and get it up here. Right now."

He didn't really listen to the acknowledgment.

Heyworth had stopped arguing; he was standing where he was, watching the diplomat climb, just as Johnston and the State rep were. The FBI man was watching Heyworth.

The Imperial reached the top and vanished; the State man clapped his hands together and said, "Well! He should be back in a moment; shall we have a drink while we wait? I'm sure there must be something around here." He seemed to notice Heyworth for the first time, and frowned slightly.

Johnston paid no attention; he was staring at the ladder.

Heyworth turned to answer the man in the gray suit, the FBI man turned to follow the reporter, the AP stationed by the ladder had glanced away, so only Johnston saw the first jerk as the ladder moved.

"Damn it," he exclaimed as he dashed across the patio. "Grab it!" he shouted at the AP.

The other three men turned and stared in astonishment as Johnston ran across Amy's back lawn and took a wild leap, trying to catch the bottom rung of the rapidly rising ladder. The AP had grabbed hold and was being yanked upward.

Johnston's own grab missed, and he barely kept himself from falling when he landed on the grass; by the time he could collect himself for another jump it was obviously far too late. The ladder was being hauled upward at a rapid rate, and the AP had lost his nerve and dived free, to land rolling on the grass.

"God *damn* it!" Johnston shouted as the ladder vanished upward into the space warp.

The State Department man stared at the empty air.

"But he said he'd be right back," he said. "Maybe it'll be right back!"

The FBI man didn't say anything; Johnston snorted.

"What the hell is going on?" Heyworth demanded.

Johnston looked around at the others, and a sudden silence fell.

Heyworth was still badgering them, trying to get a response, when the Air Force helicopter arrived a few minutes later, to fly aimlessly back and forth through empty air where the space warp had been.

Someone was entering the fortress; Pel could sense it, but right now he was too busy to care. Susan was ready, wearing a green dress that Pel hoped wouldn't stand out in the Empire—he had seen very few civilians at Base One, and didn't really remember what the women had worn on Psi Cassiopeia II or Zeta Leo III.

Not that he'd seen all that many women there, either.

He did remember the passengers on *Emerald Princess*, though, and he thought this green dress he'd magically created from fabric he'd found in one of Shadow's workshops was a reasonable approximation of the gowns they wore. Simpler, perhaps—he hadn't bothered with any sequins or lace—but along the same general lines, with its high waistline and long skirt.

Susan didn't argue about the dress—but then, Susan didn't seem to argue about anything anymore. After the one burst of uncharacteristic action that had gotten her killed she seemed to have become more passive and tolerant than ever.

She stood there in her seamless new dress, purse slung on her shoulder, a blaster tucked in the purse, and said nothing at all as Pel tried to locate the spot where he wanted to open a portal.

He was seated on the throne, the matrix seething about him; Susan stood before him, waiting, eyes closed against the glare. The fetch who had brought the hairbrushes from Earth stood by the back wall, motionless, dead eyes untroubled by the brilliance of the magical display.

Pel could sense the simulacrum of Nancy, still waiting in the bedroom down the stone corridor; he could sense the other fetches scattered about the fortress, and the hundreds of homunculi and other creatures with which Shadow had peopled the place. Boudicca and Athelstan were eating in a kitchen two levels below. Since Pel's takeover, a handful of the local peasants had also made themselves at home in the fortress; he could feel their presence, as well. The thousands of monster slugs in the surrounding marsh were also detectable, tiny dark sparks in the magical tracery.

The lone man who had just walked in through the front gate was no one Pel recognized from the pattern of magical energy; that meant it wasn't Taillefer or any other wizard, nor any of the peasants who had spoken to him before. It might, he supposed, be that Imperial spy, though he wouldn't have expected the spy to march in so openly.

Well, if it was the spy, then that was all the more reason to get on with it. The portal would form a few feet to Pel's left, Susan's right, and Susan could just walk right through.

Perhaps he should send the false Nancy, or Athelstan, or Boudicca, or one of the peasants—but he didn't trust any of them, really. And he had thought of Susan first, and here she was.

He twisted the matrix, poured energy through it, and felt reality give way as the portal opened. A cool breeze blew into the throne room from somewhere in the Galactic Empire, cutting through the thick, overheated air.

"It's open," Pel said. "Go ahead."

Susan straightened, adjusted her purse strap, stepped forward—and almost collided with the man stepping *out* of the portal.

Samuel Best stared at the fortress.

He hadn't expected it to be quite so ugly. And he hadn't expected it to be built on a sort of island at the center of a vast open marsh.

There were only two ways to approach the place, so far as he could see—openly, walking along the causeway, or by sneaking through the marsh.

He looked down and contemplated the mud, the sawgrass, and the likelihood that there were leeches, ticks, and assorted other vermin, quite aside from whatever defenses Shadow or its successor might have deliberately planted.

He sighed.

"Poole," he said, "it's your turn. Begley and I are going

to wait here for orders, because I'm not interested in either wading through a swamp or walking into somebody's gunsights. You go back for pickup and tell 'em what this place looks like, and that unless something unexpected turns up, we aren't going any farther without a direct order to do so." He glanced at Begley, and added, "If then."

"It's a long way back," Poole objected.

"But it's back home," Best pointed out. "If you'd rather stay, maybe Begley wants to go."

Begley smiled, and Poole shrugged. "I'll go," he said.

"Good," Best said.

"Best has hit a dead end," Brian Hall announced. "He's sending his man Poole back for orders."

Markham glanced at Hall in surprise. "What's the problem?" he asked.

"Shadow's fortress—or the Brown Magician's, whichever it is—is surrounded by marsh, sir. The only safe approach is by a completely unsheltered causeway several miles long."

"What about the other man, Wilkins? Has Best contacted him?"

"No, sir," Hall answered. "Wilkins went on into the fortress, by way of the causeway."

"Can you contact either man?"

"Not reliably, sir—neither one is *expecting* telepathic contact, you see, and they're both in the area where the interference is very strong. It's getting hard to read Best, and I can only perceive Wilkins intermittently now."

"It's very suspicious, that interference," Markham said. "Why is it there?"

"I don't know, sir. It may not be deliberate."

"Hmm." Markham frowned. "Well, keep me posted as best you can."

"Damn it," Pel said, "strangers aren't supposed to keep stepping out of these things!" He made no attempt to suppress the glare of the matrix as he glowered at the newcomer.

The man was squinting, shielding his face with a fore-arm, but he didn't look perturbed by the brightness, nor in any way confused or frightened. He wore a black jacket of a cut that seemed peculiar and slightly archaic to Pel, but which was not all that different from some he had seen in the Galactic Empire. Beneath the jacket was a purple silk vest, a pale pink cravat, and a white shirt with fancy white-on-white patterning to it—Pel couldn't make out the details of the design past the jacket, vest, tie, and shifting light. The man's pants were slightly flared black slacks with old-fashioned wide cuffs.

The overall effect was of a dandy from some alternate past, where fashion had followed a different route.

And in fact, that was probably just what the fellow was, Pel thought—some foppish Imperial who had wandered through the portal by accident. But why wasn't he dismayed by his sudden transition into another universe?

"Who the hell are you?" Pel asked. His anger filtered into the matrix, and his voice boomed from the walls while red light flickered overhead and a pale, insubstantial mist swirled coldly around the stranger's ankles.

The well-dressed man turned to face the throne directly, and Pel could see him blinking behind his shielding arm.

"I'm called Peter Gregory," he said. "I take it that you aren't Shadow, though you sit in its stead."

"No, I'm not," Pel said warily. "You knew Shadow?" He had his doubts about that, given Gregory's choice of pronoun.

"Shadow created me," Gregory said.

Pel blinked, and reached out into the magical web that surrounded him. He drew it down onto this Gregory, and really *looked* at him.

He looked human—but Pel could see that he wasn't quite. There were subtle differences, *extremely* subtle, detectable through magic, but probably by no other means. Pel stared intently.

Gregory's inner force, his magical essence, was smoother than a real human being's. It wasn't like the damaged magical core of a fetch, or the simplified one of a homunculus or monster, but it lacked the . . . the *texture* of a human's.

Just the way the artificial Nancy's essence did.

"You're a simulacrum," Pel guessed.

"Yes, sir," Gregory said.

"Was there a real Peter Gregory, then? What happened to him?"

"Shadow killed him, I believe; I'm not entirely sure."

The simulacrum seemed utterly undisturbed by the death of his original, and Pel shuddered; the matrix flickered eerily purple-white for a moment, reflecting his discomfort.

Pel looked away from the simulacrum for a moment and noticed Susan standing close by, waiting patiently. He also felt the stranger in the fortress, down in the gallery—whoever it was was moving slowly, clearly in no hurry to confront the Brown Magician.

"Go sit down somewhere," Pel told Susan. "It may take a while to straighten this out."

And he decided he didn't want the new arrival—the Imperial spy, if that's who it was—to come into the throne room just yet; the doors at the top of the stairs swung closed, and a tendril of the matrix sealed them shut.

Susan nodded and headed for one of the side doors.

"Where's Shadow?" Gregory asked as the Earthwoman departed. "Why are you in the matrix now?"

"Shadow's dead," Pel said, preparing to flash-fry the simulacrum if it proved necessary to stop an attack.

Gregory blinked, but did not question the pronouncement.

"You spied for her, didn't you?" Pel asked.

Gregory nodded.

"Did she tell you what to do if she died?"

"Of course not," Gregory answered. "She didn't think she could die."

That was probably true, Pel thought—but he couldn't be sure; Shadow had been clever.

"Will you obey me now, as you did her?"

"Of course, if you want me to," Gregory replied. "You

hold the power that made me, as Shadow did; you sit in her throne, the master of her fortress and her world. You are my god, as she was my goddess."

Pel smiled, and began to dim down the matrix glare.

"Good," he said. "You spied on the Galactic Empire for her?"

"Yes."

"You know your way around there?"

"Yes."

"Are there other spies, as well? Captain Cahn thought there were."

"Oh, yes, sir; I am simply the one who was waiting by the gateway when it opened. I was due to report some time ago, but the gateway did not open on schedule, so I waited. By the time the opening finally appeared there were three of us taking turns waiting, and there are many more of us, placed throughout the Empire. Some are probably still waiting at other gateways."

"Excellent!" Pel grinned broadly. "Then listen, Peter Gregory—I have a new job for all of you. I suppose Shadow wanted information, and was planning all sorts of elaborate schemes, and wanted to conquer the Empire, but all *I* want are two people . . . two . . . two bodies. There's a woman, medium height, dark hair, named Nancy Brown—she was killed aboard a ship, I.S.S. *Emerald Princess*. And the other's a little girl, Rachel Brown; she died on Zeta Leo Three. I want their bodies.

"You go back through that portal and tell the others—do whatever it takes to bring me those two.

"*Whatever* it takes."

Gregory nodded.

"Yes, sir," he said, as he turned back toward the portal.

CHAPTER 13

"*Do firearms work in Imperial space?*" *Johnston asked,* pacing. Amy watched his feet moving across the tile floor of his office.

She was tired, and she wasn't sure how much was the aftereffects of the abortion, how much was just weariness of this whole ongoing mess. She was back on Earth, and that was wonderful; Walter's child was gone, which was a relief; but was she *ever* going to get back to a normal life?

Beside her, Prossie frowned. "I'm not sure," she said. "I know that some tribes used projectile weapons before the invention of the blaster, but I don't know if they operated on the same principles as yours."

"Susan's gun worked in Faerie," Amy mentioned without looking up.

"*Magic* works in Faerie," Prossie pointed out. "Did Susan ever fire it in Imperial space?"

"I don't know," Amy said. "I don't think so."

"That copter—if it had got through . . ."

"Pel's digital watch didn't work in Imperial space, *or* in Faerie," Amy said. "I wouldn't want to be on the helicopter if it tried it, especially since the warp's out in the vacuum of space."

"It is?" Johnston was startled. "Is that why they wore the spacesuits?"

Amy looked up at him, equally startled. "Of course," she said. "Didn't we tell you that?"

"Not that I recall," Johnston said. "It doesn't matter, though. The warp's gone."

"You don't think they'll reopen it?"

"Frankly, Ms. Jewell—no, I don't. And neither do our psychics."

It took Amy a moment to realize who Johnston was referring to; she hadn't thought of that motley collection of people as "psychics." Little Angie Thompson was hardly a "psychic."

"How would they know?" Amy asked. "Did the Empire *tell* them?"

Johnston shook his head. "No, this is something Ms. Thorpe suggested. There's a good deal of . . . of leakage in telepathic communication, on an unconscious level. Telepaths know things without realizing it, and sometimes convey that information without meaning to. Ms. Thorpe suggested that our four contactees might have picked up such information, and with her help we've developed some techniques for getting at it—questions asked so quickly that the answerer has no time to think, oblique references, and so on."

Amy looked at Prossie, who shrugged. "Back home, we all knew about leakage," Prossie said. "It wasn't safe to mention it, though. It violated the secrecy rules—but the truth was that anything any of us knew, we all knew, on an unconscious level."

Johnston nodded. "Mr. Miletti's been the most useful in that regard. He remains completely unaware of any contact on the conscious level, but he's answered several questions for us by simply replying without thinking about it."

Prossie explained, "We could never establish any conscious contact with Mr. Miletti—but we *knew* he was receptive on some level. I think that when we tried to reach him he must have gotten linked into the unconscious network, just as if he were a part of my family—and since it's unconscious, with no voluntary control, they can't just cut him off or keep anything secret now."

Johnston nodded. "And it's not just Miletti on this particular point, in any case—all four of them agree that the Empire is done with Earth."

Prossie sighed, and Amy wasn't sure if her reaction was relief or disappointment. This meant that the Empire wasn't hunting their rogue telepath anymore—but it also meant that she was cut off from her family, from her entire home universe. At least, on a conscious level; Amy wondered whether that unconscious link might still be there, just as it was for Carleton Miletti.

Not that it mattered.

"Why are you worrying about guns, then?" she asked. "If the Empire's going to leave us alone, why don't we just forget about them? Besides, you can't get at them anyway, can you?"

"But *they* can get at *us*, Ms. Jewell," Johnston said, "and we have to be ready to deal with them if they ever decide to do that. By your own accounts, this Galactic Empire is a fairly aggressive imperial power, accustomed to doing pretty much whatever it pleases—there's no balance of power keeping it in check, is there?"

"Not that I ever heard of," Amy admitted.

"No, there isn't," Prossie said, very definitely. "The concept of a balance of power doesn't really even exist in the Empire anymore; they see themselves as the rightful rulers of the universe."

"But we aren't *in* their universe!" Amy protested.

"It wouldn't surprise me if they extended their doctrine, though," Johnston said. Prossie nodded.

"But you can't get *at* them," Amy repeated.

"Well, we weren't planning on a preemptive strike, in any case," Johnston said. "The United States does not operate that way—not as a general thing," he added hastily, as Amy prepared to provide counterexamples. "However, it seems prudent to consider our options, especially since this cutoff is a display of bad faith on the Empire's part—they lied to us. We'll definitely want to talk to Mr. Brown about this when we have a chance—he can provide access to the Empire, if necessary. You suggested that yourself, Ms. Jewell; we're just taking your own advice."

That was true enough, and Amy had to admit that she

didn't entirely trust the Empire. Back on Zeta Leo III those Imperial troops had seemed like the cavalry coming to the rescue, but where were they when the monsters attacked in Faerie? Where were they during the long march to Shadow's castle? And the fact that they had sent Amy and the others to Faerie in the first place, instead of safely home to Earth . . .

Susan Nguyen was dead because of that bit of Imperial arrogance. Not to mention that about a dozen of the Empire's own men had died, as well. But still, it seemed as if Johnston was going looking for trouble. The Empire was gone, Amy and Prossie and Ted were safe at home, Shadow was dead, and Pel had become a sort of demigod in Faerie—wasn't that a satisfactory solution?

It was good enough for Amy. If she could just get her home back and get Johnston and all these other people to stop bothering her, she'd be satisfied.

"Furthermore," Johnston was saying, "now that the press has gotten involved, even though they haven't gone public yet, we don't want to get caught unprepared . . ."

Amy scuffed her feet on the tiles and wished Johnston would shut up and send her home.

The Gregory simulacrum was gone, and the portal was closed; Susan and Pel were alone in the throne room, excluding the pair of fetches Pel had summoned.

And whoever it was outside the throne-room door was waiting patiently. He—or she, Pel couldn't be entirely certain from the perception through the matrix—seemed to be sitting quietly, not particularly concerned about anything.

That was interesting; all Pel's previous visitors had been very nervous indeed.

Pel opened the door.

A man rose quickly and smoothly to his feet and stood on the landing, shielding his eyes against the flickering glare of the matrix. "That you in there, Brown?" he asked.

Pel blinked in astonishment. He stared through the magical light show and fought down the emanations as quickly as he could.

The man wore peasant homespun and carried a rough sack with a drawstring—and his boots were black Imperial Military issue, dusty and worn, but recognizable even at this distance. Peasants didn't wear such boots here, and no nobleman would dress like that.

And the face . . .

"Wilkins!" Pel shouted, and the name rang eerily from the walls, carried by the matrix.

Wilkins smiled. "Guess it *is* you," he said.

"Come in!" Pel called, delighted to see a familiar face, pleased to know that Wilkins had survived. "Come in!"

Wilkins ambled into the room, his sack over his shoulder, and belatedly noticed Susan. "Good morning, Miss Goyen," he said.

"Nguyen," Pel corrected. Susan didn't respond. Wilkins glanced at her sharply.

Pel was annoyed with Susan; this man was a long-lost friend, and she was just standing there, silent as a fetch. "I'm glad to see you," he said, addressing Wilkins.

"And I'm relieved to see you, Mr. Brown—at least, as best I *can* see you. What's making all those lights?"

"That's the matrix," Pel explained. "Shadow's magic. It's mine now." He completed the suppression, and the last sparkles died away, leaving a slightly run-down colonnaded room of stone, wood, cloth, and gilt. He came forward, hand outstretched, and the two men shook hands.

Wilkins appeared wary of the contact, but Pel kept the matrix forcibly restrained, and only flesh touched the Imperial's hand.

"How'd *that* happen, if you don't mind me asking?" Wilkins said.

"It's a long story," Pel answered.

"I'll listen or not, whichever you like," Wilkins said. "I guessed that something like this had happened when I heard the stories about a Brown Magician, but I wasn't completely *sure* until I heard your voice call my name just now."

"It can wait, then," Pel said. "I mean, you can probably guess the basics. What about you, though?"

"Well, after I got separated from the rest of you . . ."

"After you deserted us, you mean," Pel said, and Wilkins hesitated uncomfortably. "Oh, don't worry—if any of us had had any sense we wouldn't have come here. You kept yourself alive, which is more than Raven or Singer or Valadrakul or even Susan here can say."

Wilkins glanced uneasily at Susan.

"I brought her back," Pel explained. "Shadow hadn't done anything terrible to her—the others were all burned, but Susan had just had her heart stopped. She was dead for a few days, though."

"Is that why she's so quiet?"

Pel frowned. "She was always quiet," he said.

Wilkins swallowed.

"You were saying what happened after you left," Pel reminded him, eager to get the conversation back on track, and onto more comfortable topics.

"Oh," Wilkins said. "Well, there wasn't much to it. I didn't see any point in going on to face Shadow alone, or in going back to the shipwreck, either, because if anyone was going to rescue Lieutenant Dibbs they'd probably done it days earlier, so I figured I was pretty much on my own. I just took odd jobs where I could, stole a few things when I couldn't see another way to manage—I was getting settled in, after a fashion, when the word came about Shadow being dead." He looked at Pel. "Is it really dead?"

Pel nodded. "She's dead, all right—Prossie Thorpe blasted her."

"Thorpe?" The expression on Wilkins' face was so odd that Pel wished he could read minds; it looked like a mix of startlement, fear, distaste, and other things, as well. "Thorpe? Not you, or that wizard?"

"Well, I set it up, but Thorpe pulled the trigger," Pel explained. "Valadrakul was already dead by then." He mentally upbraided himself for allowing the conversation to drift back to the subject of death. "So did you see any of the others anywhere? Sawyer, maybe?"

"Wasn't Sawyer with you?" Wilkins asked, surprised.

"He turned back at the gate," Pel said, "and I think there were some of Dibbs' bunch we never accounted for."

"Did you account for *any* of them?"

Pel nodded, reluctantly—here he was again. "Shadow killed most of them; we saw the bodies. I buried them myself, after Shadow was dead." Trying once more to turn the conversation cheerful, he asked, "So, why'd you come here? I mean, I'm glad to see you, but were you just curious to see what had happened, or was there something in particular you were after?"

"I was hoping you could send me home," Wilkins said.

That was so obvious Pel couldn't imagine why he hadn't guessed it without asking.

"I mean," Wilkins added, "I was doing all right here, but it's not exactly a life of luxury, and it's not my *home*. I'd like to get back to the Empire."

The Empire. Pel had just turned Shadow's entire network of spies loose on the Empire, trying to recover the remains of his wife and daughter.

Wilkins was not just Pel's old companion in adventure; he was an Imperial soldier. Pel could send him through to the Empire, but he could only be sure Wilkins would wind up somewhere civilized, and be reasonably certain of getting home intact, if he sent him to one of the points where Shadow's spies reported.

That wouldn't do. Pel didn't know just what was on the other sides of those closed portals, but he had visions of dropping an Imperial soldier into what amounted to an enemy headquarters.

Somebody would get hurt, and the body recovery might be hindered.

"I don't think I can do that," he said.

* * *

"We've lost Wilkins," Brian Hall reported.

"What do you mean, lost him?" Markham demanded. "Is he dead?"

"I don't know, sir, but he's in Shadow's fortress—or the Brown Magician's, whichever it is. We can't contact him at all anymore; the interference is much too strong."

Markham put down his pen. "Remind me," he said. "Why was Wilkins going into the fortress to begin with?"

"Because, sir, he believed that this Brown Magician was the same Pellinore Brown whom we had sent into Shadow's universe with Colonel Carson and Lord Raven and the others, and he wanted Brown to create a space warp, or a magical portal, or whatever you want to call it, back to the Empire, so that he, Wilkins, could return here and report in."

"And do you think he's right? That this Pellinore Brown has somehow usurped Shadow's rule?"

"Well, sir, that's what all the evidence indicates, both from Shadow's universe and from Brown's native universe."

Markham nodded. "True enough." He didn't say any more than that aloud, but Hall read the next question from his mind—Markham had authorized such minor intrusions, to increase efficiency.

"I have no idea how Mr. Brown could have accomplished it," Hall said. "But then, I don't understand Shadow's power, either. It really does seem to be a sort of magic."

"Magic is misunderstood science," Markham reminded him.

"In our reality, yes, sir," Hall said, "but in Faerie?"

"The laws of physics may change," Markham replied, "but the laws of logic don't, and science is applied logic. This 'magic' Shadow used, and that our Mr. Brown appears to have mastered, has to have rules and limits and all the rest, all subject to determination by the scientific method. And if he can learn and use them, anyone can."

Hall didn't argue.

"So Wilkins expects to be sent back to us?" Markham asked.

"Yes, sir."

"You think Brown can do it?"

"I don't know, sir. He did apparently send Prossie Thorpe and the others to Earth."

"True." Markham considered for a moment. "It seems to me," he said, "that we should expect Spaceman Wilkins to reappear somewhere in the Empire at any moment now. I want to know when it happens—I want to know *where* and when, and I want him brought here to Base One as fast as humanly possible. You broadcast that to your whole family, Hall—I want every telepath in the Empire to spread the word. I want Ronald Wilkins."

"Yes, sir," Hall said. He saluted sloppily and exchanged a glance with his second cousin, Markham's personal telepath.

"I'll tell George," that man said.

Markham wasn't sure who George was—some other telepath, presumably. "And inform Marshal Albright immediately," Markham said. "I don't want any problems with him."

"Yes, sir. I'll tell Stuart." Stuart was Albright's personal telepath. Hall hesitated. "What about Undersecretary Bascombe?"

"What *about* him? It's not his problem anymore."

"Yes, sir," Hall agreed.

John Bascombe drew a circle on the desktop with his finger. "So we've lost Wilkins," he said.

"We've lost contact," Carrie Hall agreed.

"What about Best?"

"Oh, he's fine; he's reached Shadowmarsh, and is waiting there for further orders."

Bascombe looked up. "And has anyone *given* him further orders?"

Carrie hesitated. "No, sir," she said. "Telepathic communication isn't reliable, so close to the fortress, and his messenger, Spaceman Poole, hasn't reached the rendezvous point yet."

"But we know he's coming?"

"Yes, sir."

Bascombe frowned.

He was out of the matter now, in bureaucratic limbo. He hadn't officially been reprimanded or removed, he was still Undersecretary for Interdimensional Affairs—but the telepaths and messengers all reported directly to Markham or Albright, and no one invited Bascombe to their conferences or meetings. He had been shunted aside.

And he bitterly resented it.

He had ordered Carrie Hall to bring him up to date. He had had to leave his office and track down an unassigned messenger to find her, and the embarrassment rankled. He had seen her hesitate when he first told her to report what was happening, and he had known that she was trying to decide whether he still had the authority to ask that.

The damnable mutant bitch had probably actually had to check with other telepaths to decide whether or not he, John Bascombe, an Imperial undersecretary, had the right to give orders to a stinking mind-reading freak!

He needed to get himself back into things, and this, he thought, might be the opportunity. No one had given Best his orders yet. It might be a simple oversight, or it might be an attempt by Markham and Albright to cut Imperial Intelligence out of the potential political profits in this operation, or it might be part of an arcane maneuver in a duel *between* Markham and Albright. Albright might be deliberately trying to sabotage Best's mission.

Bascombe thought that, in a way, he'd like to see Albright best Markham—it would be a pleasant petty revenge for the way Markham had treated Bascombe—but on the other hand, as a career move, it would be better to back Markham. Albright wasn't in a position to help Bascombe as much as Markham was.

And backing Imperial Intelligence against either or both of them was probably a smart move, in any case. Imperial

Intelligence was certainly more dangerous to an ambitious career than either the military or the Department of Science, and potentially more valuable. The Smarts could make or break anyone.

And if it was just an oversight—well, he didn't care to be the scapegoat if someone spotted it later.

"Send a messenger," he told Carrie. "Through the warp, I mean. I'll write up Best's orders immediately."

He opened a drawer and looked for paper.

The fact that he hadn't yet decided what orders to write, that he had given no thought to what orders would best serve the Empire's interests, troubled him not at all.

CHAPTER 14

"*It's* creepy," Carleton Miletti complained. "*I know all* this stuff, and I don't know how or why, or what half of it means."

"I don't *care* what any of it means," Margaret Thompson answered. "I just want to take Angie and go home."

"In that case, Ms. Thompson," Major Johnston said from the doorway, "I think we can oblige you."

The five looked up, startled.

"Are you giving up the project?" Aldridge asked.

"No, not at all," Johnston said. "We may want to call you back again, if anything develops. For now, though, events seem to be at a standstill, and there's no reason to inconvenience all of you."

"So you're sending us home?" Miletti asked.

Johnston hesitated; his mouth twisted wryly. "No, Mr. Miletti," he said. "We're saying that Ms. Thompson can take her daughter and go home, if she wants, and Mr. Aldridge and Mr. Blaisdell can go, as well, if they choose—we'll provide transportation right to their doors, and an escort if they want, as well as a lump-sum payment as compensation for the time and inconvenience we've put them to. But they don't *have* to go—we'd be just as pleased if they stayed here."

"They? What about *me*?" Miletti demanded.

"Well, Mr. Miletti," Johnston said, "we do want to keep one contact available at all times, just in case, and you've been so successful that we'd prefer it to be you." Before Miletti could protest, Johnston raised a hand. "We won't insist; you're a free citizen, and if you walk out that door right now I won't stop you. However I would advise against it."

"Why?"

"Because we would find it necessary to ask other governmental agencies to keep a *very* close eye on you, Mr. Miletti. The IRS, for example. And your local police. And of course, the FBI is already involved in this operation."

"You're threatening me with harassment, in front of witnesses!"

Johnston didn't answer that; instead, he went on, "I'm sure that we can come to some comfortable arrangement; we don't insist that you be *here*, only that you be available on a moment's notice, and that you talk regularly with one of our people. I understand you live not far from here; do you have a portable phone? If not, we'll provide one. And a pager. That should be more comfortable than wearing a wire at all times, don't you think?"

Miletti stared at him in horror.

"I still don't see why you won't send me home, Mr. Brown," Wilkins said.

"I told you, it's nothing personal," Brown answered edgily. "It's just that I've sent someone into the Empire to get something I want, and I don't want to risk you interfering."

"Why the hell would I interfere?"

"No reason," Pel admitted. "I'm just being cautious."

Wilkins thought he was being a good bit more than cautious, but decided it wouldn't do any good to say so again. They had been through this argument several times over the last few days, to no avail.

At least this time he'd gotten something vaguely resembling an explanation; up until now, Brown had refused to give any reason at all.

He'd been willing to talk about almost anything else— Wilkins had eventually got the whole story of how Pel Brown had defeated Shadow and become Pelbrun the Brown Magician, told piece by piece and gradually assembled into a fairly coherent whole—but this was the first time he'd said anything about sending someone else into the Empire.

What in all the worlds could the absolute ruler of an entire universe want from the Empire? Why from the *Empire*, and not from Earth? Pel was from Earth; wouldn't it be from there that he'd want something?

"I'm afraid I'll have to ask you to leave the room now, Wilkins," Brown said.

Wilkins stared at the polychrome glare for a moment, then shrugged. "Let me know when you can send me home, all right?" he said. Then he turned and walked out, not through the side door that led to the fortress living quarters, but through the big double door that led to the stairs and down to the grand entrance hall.

"I'm taking a walk," he announced. Not that Brown had asked.

Wilkins wanted a breath of fresh air. He'd have to settle for the nasty stuff that covered Shadowmarsh, which was foul even by the standards of this unpleasant world, but at least he'd be out-of-doors.

"It's honest work," Best said with a shrug. He dropped another handful of berries into his bucket.

"It may be honest, and it's certainly work, but that doesn't mean I have to like it," Begley replied, as he untangled his trousers from the thorns of a berry bush. "How long do we wait? What if Poole didn't make it back, or whoever's bringing our orders gets killed on the way here? What if he can't *find* us, because we're down here in the bogs picking berries?"

"I give it a month," Best replied. "If we haven't heard anything by then, we pack it in and go back to the rendezvous."

Begley looked at him silently for a moment, then announced, "I'm going back up to the highway, to see if I can see anything."

"Please yourself," Best said, plucking another handful.

* * *

For a moment, Pel considered opening a portal to Earth and sending a fetch, or maybe Susan, to bring back some clothes and toiletries. Getting a place ready for Nancy and Rachel, complete with familiar clothes and belongings, would keep him occupied, keep his mind off the delays. The simulacra in the Empire seemed to be taking a long time to deliver the bodies.

But then, he was impatient, he knew he was impatient, and after all, they weren't necessarily even on the right *planet*. The Galactic Empire had faster-than-light travel—in their universe there was apparently no reason not to—but it still wasn't anywhere near instantaneous, and each of the thousands of inhabited planets was, if not as big as all of Earth, at least the size of Mars.

It might be weeks, or months, before he had his wife's corpse available to resuscitate. Setting up a room for her now would just add to the frustration. And he'd have to resist the temptation to let the Nancy simulacrum use things—he was constantly fighting the urge to treat her as Nancy, or to try to turn her into a closer substitute for Nancy.

Besides, he reminded himself, he had an appointment. That was why he had sent Wilkins away—it was time to check on Peter Gregory, to see what progress was being made.

He worked quickly; the portal-opening procedure, which Shadow and the other wizards would have called a spell, had become very familiar in the last few days. He twisted his perceptions through the matrix, in a direction that wasn't conceivable to anyone but a matrix wizard, and found the weak spot between realities.

Gregory was waiting; the instant the portal opened, he stepped through.

He looked worried, and Pel felt suddenly nervous. Simulacra weren't prone to worry—generally, they just went along with whatever happened, untroubled by guilt, responsibility, or fear. Pel had noticed that behavior first in the imitation Nancy, who would agree to anything he proposed—he suspected that she would have smiled and nodded and obeyed if he ordered her to cut her own throat. Gregory and Shadow's other spies had all acted similarly, as if their lives, being artificial creations, had no real value.

Maybe it was because they'd had no childhoods. Maybe it was something inherent in the matrix magic. Pel didn't know, and didn't really care; he'd simply observed that the characteristic was there.

So how could Gregory be worried?

"Master," Gregory said, "Felton's been captured."

Pel blinked, then asked, "Who's Felton?"

"One of our agents," Gregory replied. "Augustus Felton. Shadow replaced him about two years ago. He's a military records clerk. Balding, mid-fifties, overweight ..."

"That's enough," Pel interrupted. "How'd it happen?"

"As nearly as we can determine," Gregory explained, "Felton was checking through the files, trying to find where your wife's remains were, and when he couldn't find what he wanted in the regular files he tried to get into the records of Imperial Intelligence, and got caught in a restricted area."

"He's in prison, then?"

"We don't know *where* he is—Imperial Intelligence operates very secretively."

"That figures." Pel stared at Gregory for a moment, trying to think, then he shrugged. Despite his two-week stay at Base One, he didn't know what the Empire was like, and Gregory did. "Now what?" he asked.

"I don't know," Gregory said. "Whatever you tell us to do. I'm sorry Felton failed you."

"Not *your* fault," Pel said. He didn't see where this was really a big problem, and he wondered why Gregory had looked so concerned. "You tell everyone to get on with it and get me those bodies, and to be more careful, that's all. And if you can find Felton and get him out, that's fine, but it isn't important. Finding the bodies, *that's* what's important!"

Gregory nodded, his expression again cheerful. "Yes, O Great One," he said with a bow.

He turned, and Pel watched him vanish back through the portal.

It occurred to Pel, a little belatedly, that perhaps he should have ordered Gregory, and through him the others, to keep the search for the bodies quiet. A simulacrum would gladly die rather than disobey orders, or at least so Gregory had assured him, so he assumed he wouldn't have had to worry about Felton breaking under interrogation.

But he hadn't given such orders.

Well, Felton would probably figure out for himself that he was supposed to keep quiet.

And if the Empire *did* find out that Pel wanted the bodies, so what?

Celia Howe was not stupid; quite the contrary. She could hardly have risen as far as she had in Imperial Intelligence if she were a fool. All the same, she came very close to making a serious error regarding the proper disposition of the information received from telepathic interrogation of the records clerk, Augustus Felton.

It would have been a natural mistake. After all, if Felton was working for the Brown Magician of Faerie, that made his apprehension an interdimensional affair, and reporting it to the Undersecretary for Interdimensional Affairs would appear to be the proper, sensible thing to do.

Howe trembled when she thought how close she had come to doing just that.

Fortunately for her career and her political ambitions, she had paused at the last minute—perhaps it was something in the telepath's expression, or perhaps the telepath was illegally projecting a bit, or perhaps Howe's well-developed sense of self-preservation had awakened a bit late—and had forced her to reconsider.

A check of recent reports and the whereabouts of various appointees made it clear that Undersecretary Bascombe was currently out of favor. He was still in office, and would have to be informed if he asked, but if Intelligence, in the form of Howe or her representative, could report directly to someone higher than Bascombe, that would be a better move in the continuing struggle for status and power.

Of course, Howe could have just passed the information to her own superior and let *him* worry about it, but that wouldn't do her any good, not really. She wasn't going to make a friend of Stanley Winter, and Stanley Winter wasn't going to help her advance in the service.

And jumping to the next level up, or straight to the director at the level above that, would make too many enemies—not just Stan Winter, but others as well. No, she was best served by passing along this information herself, while her written report wound its way through channels to the uppermost echelons.

But telling Bascombe was out.

Though Secretary Markham was the next obvious possibility, Howe hesitated. Marshal Albright was also at Base One, and the military had been active in Faerie. And there was always the possibility of going clear to the top, to the General Secretary or even the Emperor himself—though bothering His Imperial Majesty with something he considered beneath his notice was a good way to end a career completely. Howe, upon consideration, didn't think this little affair was worthy of the Imperial notice. That left three possibilities.

The General Secretary, of course, had his own ways of obtaining information; he would know soon enough, and he wasn't particularly pleased by attempts at ingratiation.

That left Markham or Albright.

She looked at the notes she had made of the telepath's oral report. Felton's assignment had been to locate and retrieve two corpses—he didn't know why anyone in Faerie wanted these particular bodies, only that he and his cell of Faerie's spy network were under orders to obtain them by any means available.

It was interesting to learn that Faerie's spy network still existed and functioned, despite Shadow's death, and despite

Operation Spotlight, which had rooted Shadow's agents out of the ruling circles of half a dozen rebel worlds—and a few Imperial ones as well. Howe had not been aware that other spies continued to operate, and she suspected that her superiors still didn't know it.

And they *were* active, and wanted these bodies, a woman and a child.

Well, who *had* the corpses?

Howe didn't know—but she would find out. If it was the military, she would report to Albright. If it was the Department of Science, she would report to Markham.

If neither organization had the corpses, or if each had one of the two, then she would tell Albright *and* Markham, she decided.

As for learning where the corpses were, she didn't worry about how she might do that. That was exactly the sort of thing Imperial Intelligence had always been best at, she thought with a wry smile—finding where the bodies were buried.

Sometimes Pel considered just sending a messenger to the clearing in the Sunderland woods, and through that warp the Empire kept opening there, to ask the Empire for the bodies. It surely wouldn't be a big deal for them to deliver Nancy and Rachel.

On the other hand, somehow he suspected that the Empire wouldn't cooperate with even so simple a request. He'd probably get caught up in the bureaucracy somehow, or they'd demand some absurd payment.

Better to get them on his own, if he could. He could always ask the Empire openly, if other methods didn't work.

It wasn't, after all, as if the Empire had openly sent their representatives into Faerie. No ambassadors had turned up at the fortress, asking for audience. Instead they were apparently sending spies.

Well, Pel had spies of his own, and Gregory and the others seemed fairly confident that they could, in time, locate Nancy and Rachel.

He sat on his throne, drumming his fingers, while magic and light played in shifting patterns through the air around him.

Begley looked eastward, toward the Sunderland forests—though of course he couldn't see that far, even on this over-sized planet with its distant horizons. He could see scattered houses, a few trees, thousands upon thousands of berry bushes and acres upon acres of bogland, and the narrow path the locals considered a highway cutting its way through half a mile or so of the countryside before it was lost in the background.

Nothing moved anywhere on the highway, so far as he could see.

He turned to the west, where Shadow's fortress thrust up from the horizon beyond a vast open marsh, at the end of a narrow causeway.

A man was walking on the causeway, a very long way off. "Someone's coming this way, from the fortress," he called down to Best. "Should we talk to him?"

Best looked up. "Couldn't hurt," he said. "At least, not if you're careful."

Begley nodded. "I'll be careful," he said.

Wilkins ambled along, bored and aggravated. He should have been back at Base One by now. If it weren't for this mysterious secret project Brown was working on, he *would* have been back.

If he had been stuck here for good, that would have been less than ideal, but he could have lived with it. If he got home, that would be fine. But this dismal *waiting*, caught in between, was annoying.

He scanned the horizon, planning to turn back—after all, he didn't have anywhere else to go, and the hot, swampy air out here wasn't much of an improvement over the dusty dimness of the fortress.

A movement caught his eye.

Someone was standing on the highway, off in the

distance—Wilkins couldn't tell whether the figure was man or woman, whether it stood inside or outside the boundary of Shadowmarsh, but someone was standing on the highway.

Wilkins paused, and thought for a moment.

Nothing was happening back at the fortress, so far as he could see. What harm would it do to walk on out and say hello to whoever that was? It would take time, of course—maybe an hour each way—but so what? It would relieve the boredom.

And that might be a woman—maybe one as bored and lonely as he was.

He turned eastward and trotted on.

The messenger crouched quickly and listened. Yes, those were footsteps, coming toward him through the forest.

He hated this. This was not what he had signed up for. Fighting was one thing; running messages around Base One was another; but neither of those had anything to do with sneaking through a huge alien forest, trying to find a couple of spies on a hostile planet where science was all cockeyed, aircars and blasters didn't work, and he didn't have any roads to follow or addresses to find.

Samuel Best was reportedly waiting at the east end of the causeway across Shadowmarsh—how was he supposed to find that in this wilderness? Was he supposed to ask the natives for directions, and hope they wouldn't put a bunch of arrows in him or tie him to a stake and burn him? It wasn't as if there were any maps—no one had done an orbital survey, or even brought back whatever crude doodles the locals used.

He wished that idiot Bascombe had picked someone else to carry his message. Wasn't this sort of thing what telepaths were for?

He brushed against a bush, then snatched his elbow away as the leaves rustled loudly.

The footsteps stopped. "Anyone there?" a voice called.

The messenger hesitated. The language was English, but

then the locals here supposedly spoke English, as well. The accent didn't seem exotic.

"My name's Poole," the voice said. "That looks like Imperial purple behind that thicket, assuming I'm not imagining things. If it is, I'm on your side."

The voice didn't *sound* hostile. Cautiously, the messenger stood up.

"Good morning," the man who called himself Poole said, smiling. "What brings you here? Are there others? You aren't one of Lieutenant Dibbs' men, are you?"

The man wasn't in uniform; he was wearing a baggy, ugly woolen outfit, brown and dark gray. His hair was blond and short, though, and how would a native know about a Lieutenant Dibbs?

If the truth be known, the messenger had never heard of Lieutenant Dibbs, but somehow that just made it all the more convincing. "I've got orders for Samuel Best," he said.

"No shit?" Poole grinned. "Well, I'll be damned. He sent me back to get further orders—you've saved me some hiking."

"You said your name was Poole . . ."

"Right—Abner Poole, Imperial Intelligence. I'm with Best. Come on, I'll take you to him."

For a moment the messenger hesitated anew; this was all almost *too* easy. But then, the man said he'd been on his way back for orders, and where did this miserable trail go other than the clearing where the space warp came out?

"Right," the messenger said. He stepped out from behind the bushes.

"So what are the orders?" Poole asked curiously, as the two set out westward.

"You'll have to wait," the messenger said. "They're for Best."

Poole shrugged. "Good enough," he said. He strolled on, leading the way toward Shadowmarsh.

It was simple enough to find the little girl; her body had been recovered in a pacification operation on a backwater planet called Zeta Leo III, at the start of the recent campaign to incorporate Shadow's puppet governments into the Empire. The corpse had been brought to Base One, and was in cold storage in the zero-gee lockers near the core of the hollowed-out asteroid headquarters.

The military had offered it to the Department of Science, in case someone wanted to dissect it and see if Earthpeople were different from normal humans, but so far no one in Science had shown an interest. After a moment's consideration, Howe removed a few records and made sure that no one ever would.

The other body was much harder to track down. Howe could find no records about it except the interviews with the Earthpeople, where Nancy Brown's death was reported.

Nancy Brown had died during the capture of *Emerald Princess*—but her body wasn't aboard when Zeta Leo III was taken and *Emerald Princess* recovered.

Well, why would the pirates have kept it? They had undoubtedly shoved it out the airlock and left it to drift in space. Celia Howe frowned. That might be difficult. Finding a floating corpse . . .

They did know the ship's course, and running a heavy gravity generator along the route might turn up something. The Department of Science had done a few fishing expeditions that way in the past.

The military had their own equipment, of course; gravity generators had plenty of uses in combat. There was no need to bring in Science.

It was time, though, to talk to Marshal Albright.

CHAPTER 15

"We know where one of them is," Gregory explained. "Rachel Brown's body is in cold storage at Base One. We haven't located Nancy Brown yet, though." He hesitated, then asked, "Do you want us to bring you Rachel?"

Pel thought about that, and felt tears welling up; the matrix swirled an uncomfortable shade of blue and splashed up the throne-room walls. His throat tightened, and for a moment he couldn't speak.

He missed Rachel so much—but bringing her back here, to a strange place where her father radiated color and light, where zombies walked the halls, and where her mother was dead . . .

And besides, if Gregory and the others were to steal Rachel back, it might alert the Empire and make it that much harder to recover Nancy.

He swallowed, and managed to speak.

"Not yet," he said. "But the minute you find Nancy, get them both."

Wilkins was disappointed; it wasn't a woman, or anyone interesting at all. It was just a couple of berry-pickers working unusually close to the edge of the marsh.

He'd come this far, though, so he figured he might as well go on. Especially since one of them, the one who'd been on the highway to begin with, had spotted him; now they were both standing there, talking quietly and watching him approach. Wilkins didn't really think there'd be any

164

trouble if he turned and headed back to the fortress, but he hated to think they might think they'd scared him off.

"Good morrow, gentlemen!" he called. The locals seemed to consider that a normal greeting.

"And to you, sir!" the taller one called back—not that either of them was particularly tall; the people of Faerie ran a bit short, by Imperial standards, and Wilkins wasn't sure if it was the gravity or the diet that was responsible.

Probably both, he decided.

These two weren't runts, though—just middling.

And they hadn't turned and run, or called any threats, or just stood there silently the way most peasants usually did. Maybe they'd be interesting after all.

"My name's Wilkins," Wilkins said—he was close enough now that shouting was unnecessary. A native—a human native, anyway, not the dwarfs or gnomes or whatever they were that he'd met once or twice—would probably have phrased it differently, getting "hight" or "yclept" in there, but Wilkins didn't feel like dealing with that just now, and these two looked bright enough to figure out what he meant even if he didn't talk like an old book.

For a moment, the pair of strangers seemed to take that in stride. Then the taller one's eyes widened.

"Wilkins, did you say?"

Wilkins stopped walking a few feet farther away than he had originally intended. Warily, he said, "Yes, sir—do I know you?" He didn't remember meeting this fellow anywhere, but he'd offended a few people, mostly women, and his name might have been spread around.

"Spaceman First Class Ronald Wilkins?"

Now Wilkins' own eyes widened; he stared.

He should have realized. These two were too clean, their blond hair too short, their beards still only half-grown. "Who're you?" he asked.

The taller one stepped forward and held out a hand. "Samuel Best, Imperial Intelligence," he said.

Wilkins hesitated for half a second. The man was Intelligence. That could mean a treason charge, a desertion charge—that could mean *anything*—shaking the fellow's hand might be his own death sentence, and in any case, to Wilkins, touching an Intelligence man would be like touching a rat.

On the other hand, *offending* an Intelligence man was a very bad idea, very bad indeed. Wilkins stepped forward and took the proffered hand.

"I hadn't expected to find you alive," Best said. "Are any of the others with you? Do you know what's happened to them?"

"Which others?" Wilkins asked. "Do you mean the Earthpeople?"

"The Earthpeople, or Lieutenant Dibbs, or anyone . . . Look, you have a lot to tell us. Have a seat, have some of these berries—sorry we don't have anything to drink." He gestured to the buckets and a hummock of dry grass. "Oh, this is Begley. He's in Intelligence, too," he added as an afterthought.

Together, the three men settled to the ground.

Howe's concern about which cabinet officer to tell had been irrelevant, she discovered; the first thing Marshal Albright had done was to call Secretary Markham in to hear the news.

"You know, at first glance," Markham remarked as he twiddled with a pen, "it would seem perfectly natural for this Pellinore Brown to want to recover the bodies of his wife and child."

Albright nodded. "I thought of that," he said. "It's the *method* that has me puzzled—and concerned. Why is he using Shadow's spies? For that matter, why are Shadow's spies still *here*? Shouldn't they all have been recalled? I suppose I should have known better than to have believed that Operation Spotlight had really broken the back of Shadow's whole espionage network, but this Brown Magician was supposed to be on our side—or at least, not hostile. It seems hostile to be sneaking around this way, though, instead of just asking for his family. He hasn't communicated openly with us at all—our only sources of information have been our own spies, both telepathic and normal. If it weren't for them, we wouldn't even know that Shadow is dead, or who had replaced it."

"And even there, he's deliberately blocked all telepathic contact," Markham pointed out. "No one in his fortress can be read."

"And our telepath on the spot, Proserpine Thorpe, went rogue," Albright agreed. "Probably subverted by this Brown. Hardly a friendly act."

"And Earth's government, the United States—they held our men hostage demanding recognition," Markham added. "Brown's an Earthman originally."

Howe didn't follow this; she wasn't familiar with the Thorpe case, or recent actions on Earth. She saw which way the wind was blowing, though.

"Shall I have Felton shot?" she asked.

Albright and Markham glanced quickly at each other; then Albright shook his head.

"Not yet," he said.

"I can just climb up a goddamned *ladder*?" Wilkins demanded. "Why in bloody hell didn't they lower one *sooner*, then, before Dibbs and the rest got butchered?"

Best shrugged. "They don't tell me everything," he said. "Hell, half the time they don't even tell me what I'm supposed to be doing, or provide half the information I need to do it."

Wilkins snorted. "I can believe it," he said. He looked back at the marsh for a moment, considering.

"Listen," he said, "I don't know what our Mr. Brown is up to out there in his castle, but it's taking too damn long to suit me. Maybe he'd send me home tomorrow—but for all I know, it'd be next year at Donalmas before he saw fit to do it, and if I walk back up to Sunderland I'll have sore feet, but I'll be back at Base One in a fortnight."

Best nodded. "They'll be glad to hear from you, if they have any sense."

"And if they *have* closed the fucking warp, I'll just come

back here, and my temper's going to be foul enough after that walk that Brown had damned well *better* send me home!"

Begley laughed nervously.

"Either of you care to join me?" Wilkins asked.

Begley's laughter died; he glanced warily sideways at Best.

Best shook his head. " 'Fraid not," he said. "We have our orders—such as they are—and I said I'd wait here until I got further instructions. So I wait here."

Wilkins shrugged. "Suit yourself," he said.

"Wilkins has emerged from the fortress," Brian Hall reported.

Markham leaned back in his chair and looked up at the telepath. He didn't need to say anything to convey his question.

"Pelbrun the Brown Magician, ruler of Faerie, is indeed the Earthman Pellinore Brown; Wilkins heard the entire story from Brown's own lips, though he didn't bother to remember most of it, and our link is sufficiently tenuous that we can't recover anything he's not consciously thinking about. Wilkins met our man Best on the road, and the two exchanged information, so we were able to pick up some of the details from that."

Markham nodded, and Hall knew that the details could wait.

"Wilkins is on his way back to our standing space warp."

"Good," Markham said. Then he frowned. "Wasn't he going to have Brown send him back?"

Hall nodded. "Yes, sir—but Brown refused. He told Wilkins that he had sent someone into the Empire to get something, and could not risk Wilkins interfering with that; he would only send Wilkins when he had obtained whatever it is he's after. Wilkins had no idea what that might be, or how long this might take, and finally left the fortress in disgust. It was sheer good luck that he encountered Best so quickly."

"Sent someone to get something?"

"Yes, sir. It might have been the bodies. It might have been something else."

"Have you been snooping, Hall?"

"Not intentionally, sir."

"But you know about the bodies. I suppose all you telepaths do."

"Not consciously, sir, but the information does tend to leak, and I *am* working on related matters."

Markham knew well that information leaked among telepaths; fortunately, most of them were very good at keeping their mouths shut around most *non*telepaths. Fear of summary execution could do that.

Of course, they would blab to anyone high enough in the Imperial government the minute someone asked the right question—fear of summary execution did that, too.

"What's Best doing now?" he asked. "Is he coming back with Wilkins?"

"No, sir; he's still awaiting orders. I believe they're on the way."

Markham nodded, leaning back still farther, hands folded across his belly.

Abruptly he sat up, startled, as the telepath's words registered. "Orders are on the way?" he demanded.

"Yes, sir."

"I didn't send any orders."

"A messenger went through the warp two or three days ago, I believe," the telepath said.

"At whose direction? Who wrote those orders?"

"It wasn't Marshal Albright," Hall assured him hastily, unable to ignore the suspicion of a political double-cross that suddenly dominated Markham's thoughts. "And it wasn't Intelligence, either; it was Undersecretary Bascombe."

"Bascombe?" Markham straightened further. "That idiot?"

"Yes, sir."

For a moment Markham stared at the telepath; then he glanced at the door.

"Bascombe sent Best in the first place," he said. "And Best's in Intelligence."

"Yes, sir."

"Does Albright know about this?"

"Not yet, sir—but I'm sure he'll find out. You know how it is."

"Yes, I know—you mutants can't keep a goddamn secret for five minutes." Markham knew that was unfair, that it usually took either Intelligence or someone of cabinet rank to pry secrets out of the telepaths, but he didn't care about being fair right now. "All right," he said, "call Albright's telepath for me, tell him I want to talk. And try not to mention this to Celia Howe—you or any of your family."

"Yes, sir," Hall said. "But . . ."

"I know," Markham said. "Intelligence will find out. But I'd like to talk to Albright first."

The purple uniform was a dead giveaway; Wilkins knew from half a mile away that he had spotted another friendly face. He assumed at first that the other man was a native guide, but there was never any question about the messenger. He *had* to be an Imperial.

Convincing them of his own identity was a bit trickier; the messenger was nervous and knew nothing at all about this world or who'd been there before him, and Poole, unlike Best, hadn't memorized the complete roster of Colonel Carson's ill-fated command.

Once he had convinced them, the conversation was much shorter than his talk with Best—Poole and Simons weren't interested in the details of how he'd survived or who was running things, and had little to add to what Best had already told him.

He gave them directions for finding Best and Begley, got directions to aid his own memory of where the wreck of I.S.S. *Christopher* lay, and then headed on eastward.

Albright and Markham stood side by side, watching as the research ship I.S.S. *Magnet* settled smoothly into her docking cradle. The telepaths had already assured them that the ship had found and collected a dead woman, but even so, Markham had some last-minute doubts. While space was immense, Nancy Brown hadn't been the only one to die aboard *Emerald Princess*; how sure were they that this was the right corpse?

And if it wasn't, was it because the Brown Magician's agents had already somehow recovered the one they wanted?

And what was Brown up to, anyway? Why were these corpses so important to him? Why hadn't he just *asked* for them?

The ship was down; the docking-bay doors were grinding slowly shut. Markham turned away from the thick glass of the window. "I want to see this for myself," he said. "You coming?"

"I'll watch from here," Albright said.

Markham shrugged. "Please yourself."

By the time he emerged from the stairwell the gauge by the door showed the docking bay at thirty-percent Terran sea-level air pressure and rising. Markham forced the latch and, with the help of the entry guard, heaved the door open.

Air whooshed past, almost sweeping him out into the bay; his ears popped. He let the wind carry him forward, across twenty feet of steel flooring, until he put up a hand and caught a fin to stop his progress.

The fin was hot steel—one of the guidance vanes for a collection bin on *Magnet*'s side, hot with waste heat from the ship's gravity generators. Markham snatched his fingers away.

He gasped for breath—the air was still thin in here—and glanced up, first at the side of the ship looming over him, then back at the observation area. Albright was shouting something, but Markham couldn't hear anything but roaring wind; he supposed the Imperial marshal was chastising him for hurrying out here before the pressure was equalized.

Markham didn't care about that; he looked up at the collection bin just above his head. It was tightly closed, the heavy shutter holding in whatever the gravity generators had drawn out of the void. There were other, identical bins elsewhere, a girdle of five of them encircling *Magnet*'s waist. The corpse could be in any of them, even the one on the underside that was only accessible from the service sump.

The rush of air was slowing, and a loud thump sounded; Markham looked for its source and saw that the ship's main hatch was opening.

"Come on," Markham shouted, "get on with it! I want to see her!"

A helmeted head appeared in the doorway. "She's not pretty, sir," the spaceman said.

"You think I give a tinker's damn what she looks like? Open those shutters!"

"You can get a look at her from in here, if you want."

"Can I?" Markham had never before had any use for the *Magnet*, and had little idea how she operated.

"Yes, sir."

"Show me." Markham hurried to the hatchway, where the spaceman reached down and caught his arm, boosting him up the yard or so between the floor of the docking bay and the floor of the air lock.

Together, the two men made their way into the ship's interior, through bare steel passages that gave no indication which of the curving surfaces were meant as walls, which as floors or ceilings. Markham remembered that when the massive gravity generators, capable of drawing in anything that would fit in the bins, were in use, they made it impossible to maintain ordinary shipboard artificial gravity. The crew had to tolerate the spillover, which would draw them toward the generators, so that "up" and "down" would be distorted all over the ship.

When that was happening, Markham judged that this straightforward corridor would become a slanting, treacherous tunnel. The grab bars along one side, he realized, would be rungs of a ladder.

"She's in Number Four," the spaceman said, pointing diagonally upward. He spun the wheel to undog the circular hatch at the end of the passage, swung the heavy portal open, and led the way into a peculiar space, a horizontal cylinder some thirty feet in diameter, webbed with catwalks and struts that were built at nightmarishly contradictory angles. The air here was thick and hot; Markham could sense the heat radiating from the far side.

The gravity generators were just beyond that bulkhead.

The spaceman wasn't giving any guided tours, though; he said, "This way," and pointed to a strangely angled staircase leading up and to the left.

Markham followed. The spaceman paused long enough at the next hatchway to unclip a handheld electric light from its bracket, and a moment later the two men were crawling through a narrow steel tube where that lamp's dim glow, largely blocked by the spaceman's body, was the only light. The air was hot and stank of sweat and machine oil.

Then the spaceman stopped and turned—Markham wasn't sure how he managed it in the confined space of what was really little more than a large pipe. He lifted the lamp almost in Markham's face.

"There she is," he said, gesturing.

Markham looked up in the direction indicated, and flinched.

A face was staring down at him through a window—or rather, a ruined red and black thing that had once been a face was pointed in his general direction.

He was a scientist, Markham reminded himself, and he stared calmly back, over his initial shock.

The window was a chunk of glass, or at any rate a clear substance, roughly six inches wide, a foot long, and four or five inches thick, set into the wall of the tube; it gave a view of the interior of one of the collection bins.

The woman's corpse had landed in the bin with the face pressed up against one end of the window; dark hair, gray dust, and a small pinkish something Markham didn't recognize at first covered the rest. More dust was smeared on her face; so was a dark powder that was probably dried blood.

The face had been battered even before she went out that airlock, and weeks drifting in hard vacuum had not been kind; the skin was flaked and torn, the flesh dehydrated and shrunken, bone protruding here and there. Markham looked at the pink thing for a moment, just to get away from that hideous visage, and then wished he hadn't.

The pink thing was the shriveled remains of a finger, one that was very clearly not attached to a hand.

"She landed a bit hard," the spaceman remarked. "Three fingers snapped right off and bounced around a bit—things get brittle when they've been out there in the cold for a while."

Markham swallowed bile.

"We got lucky," the spaceman added. "Never had one land with the face on the viewport like that before. Makes it a lot easier to get a look at her. So, that the right one?"

"Good God," Markham said, "you expect me to tell from *that*?"

The spaceman shrugged, and the little light wavered, sending eerie shadows dancing across the dead woman's face. "She's the only woman we found," he said. "We've got dead men in two of the other bins, five of them in all, a couple in *Emerald Princess* crew uniform, so we're pretty sure it's the right bunch, and she was the only woman."

Markham stared up at the corpse. Then he shook his head. "It's probably her," he said. "I was hoping I'd be able to tell from the descriptions I got, but I hadn't realized . . . well, I didn't account for her condition. We'll need to get Captain Cahn's men to identify her—they knew her when she was alive."

"Should've sent one with us," the spaceman said. "I'd hate to make another trip when we could've done it in one."

"I didn't think of it," Markham said. "I can't think of everything." He shuddered, all enthusiasm gone. "Let's get the hell out of here."

"After you," the spaceman said sardonically, and Markham began working his way back out of the observation tube.

CHAPTER 16

*B*est settled onto a patch of relatively dry ground and read the inscription on the little packet the messenger had handed him. The code, still legible despite the smearing, was correct—and really, there could be little doubt that the orders were genuine, under the circumstances.

Not that he was in any hurry to read them; they'd probably mean trouble, and he'd found berry picking to be fairly pleasant, low-stress work. It would have gotten intolerably dull eventually, but Best thought he could have handled a few more days of boredom.

"We didn't have any trouble," Poole said. "I just told anyone who asked that I was taking a man in purple to see Pelbrun." Best nodded in understanding, but the messenger looked puzzled; Poole explained, "They'd all heard about this proclamation he'd issued, that he wanted all the wizards and all the strangers in purple, and nobody was about to interfere with anyone following the Brown Magician's orders. A couple of centuries of Shadow's rule gave the locals a healthy respect for authority, and this Pelbrun is the man who *killed* Shadow. You're on his business, you're safe."

"Oh," the messenger said, comprehension dawning. "So *that's* why people fed us, even when we couldn't pay, but wouldn't talk to us. They were scared?"

Poole nodded. "You've got it exactly."

"Someone could run a pretty nice little scam that way," Begley remarked.

"You'd need an Imperial uniform," Best remarked, as he

reluctantly tugged at the seal on the envelope. "Not that easy to come by around here. And you'd have to be careful never to be seen heading away from the fortress."

"The direction isn't a big problem," Begley argued. "You could always double back cross-country. And how many of the natives know what a real Imperial uniform looks like?"

"Good point," Best conceded. The wax broke, and he opened the flap.

Before taking the folded paper out he looked up at the others. "Sit down, all of you," he said. "You make me nervous, standing around like that."

"I should be getting back . . ." the messenger muttered uneasily, glancing out across Shadowmarsh. He had obviously picked up a few stories about the place during his nine-day hike down from Sunderland—even if the natives wouldn't talk to him, Best was sure Poole had had a few things to say.

"Without waiting to see if I have a reply, or a report?" Best said mildly. "I don't think they'd like that back at Base One."

The messenger sat down, with an uncomfortable glance to the west.

Best unfolded the paper and read.

From Undersecretary Bascombe, with Bascombe's full title, official address, and all the other usual curlicues, while the "to" line read simply, "Samuel Best, in the field." No rank, no unit—everyone in the Empire knew that meant he was in Intelligence. And "in the field" was nicely vague, while being completely accurate—they were sitting on the edge of a blackberry field.

Best smiled to himself at the thought that, if he'd been working in the cranberry bog down the highway a bit, the address should say "in the bog." Maybe it should have read "in the rain"—but the rain had stopped.

He was putting it off, he realized. He forced himself to get past the salutations and authorizations and down to the actual orders.

They didn't take long to read; he stared at them in disbelief.

Was this some kind of joke? He glanced down at the bottom.

"John Bascombe, Undersecretary of Science for Interdimensional Affairs, by appointment, in service to His Imperial Majesty George VIII." And the Great Seal, embossed in light blue.

Nobody would put the Emperor's name and Imperial seal on a joke.

"That's insane," he said. He looked up at the messenger. "This is completely insane."

The messenger, perched uncomfortably on a hillock of wet sand, shrugged.

"Why?" Begley asked. "What do they want us to do?"

Best threw down the letter.

"That *idiot* Bascombe!" he said. "He's ordered us to arrest Pellinore Brown!"

There were two uniformed spacemen waiting in the clearing.

The last time Wilkins had seen the place, the dead body of Shadow's giant bat creature had lain across most of the opening, completely covering the useless hulk of I.S.S. *Christopher*; now much of the monster's substance had been cut away, or been eaten away by the local wildlife, or had simply rotted. What remained was a rather grisly maze of dried black hide and protruding white bone, with a clear path to *Christopher*'s main hatch and various other navigable routes in and out of the mass.

The two Imperials were standing near the center of this macabre tangle; one was leaning against a gigantic rib, while the other was fully upright.

Neither of them had noticed Wilkins yet; he had a habit of moving stealthily any time he walked alone across country, and he was good at it. He had seen men die because they'd made a wrong assumption about how dangerous the supposedly friendly terrain was, and he didn't intend to follow suit.

He didn't make reckless assumptions about supposedly friendly people, either. In theory, those two men should be his bosom buddies; in practice, he was out of uniform and they probably weren't expecting anyone, and might shoot first and ask questions later.

Not that they could shoot him, really. Their blasters wouldn't work here.

They probably weren't used to that yet—he noticed they both wore holstered blasters on their belts. And they were in those easy-to-spot bright purple uniforms, while he was in dull, hard-to-see brown. He had other advantages besides simple surprise.

That damned messenger Simons hadn't mentioned any guards, though. He probably had assumed Wilkins already knew about them; he hadn't seemed terribly bright. One didn't get a messenger job by graduating top of the class, after all.

And all this debate wasn't getting him anywhere.

He stepped forward, into a pool of sunlight, and called, "Hey!"

The two turned, startled; the one who had been leaning stood up, and the other's hand fell to his holster flap. Old habits die hard, Wilkins thought with a smile.

"Hey, yourself," the former leaner called, relaxing somewhat at the sight of him. "Are you Ron Wilkins, by any chance?"

Wilkins blinked, almost as startled by the question as the guards had been by his shout. "How the hell did you know that?" he called back.

"Telepath said you were coming," the guard said. "We were sent to escort you home."

"Telepath?" That made sense. And an escort? As far as he knew, there were two kinds of escorts—honor guards and jailers. Wilkins wondered which kind *his* escort was supposed to be.

Not that it really mattered; he figured he could manage

either way. The Empire knew he was alive now, and they had telepaths tracking him; he wouldn't be able to escape if they really wanted him. He didn't have much of a choice about going back.

He stepped forward into the clearing, and let the two soldiers lead him to the ladder.

The crew of I.S.S. *Ruthless* had been dispersed in the course of Operation Spotlight, and then again after Best had tracked them down and consulted them, but Albright had found that two of them, Elmer Soorn and Bill Mervyn, happened to be on Base One. He had the two of them detached from their regular duties and sent to the cold-storage lockers, without explanation—and without their sidearms.

Markham met them in the security room.

"You wait here," he ordered Mervyn. Then he crooked a finger at Soorn. "You come with me."

Together, the two men stepped past the guards, and Markham led the way through the vault door into the locker where the corpses lay.

"Recognize them?" he asked, pointing to the two bodies that sprawled stiffly on dissection tables.

"What's this about?" Soorn asked. He glanced at the cadavers—then stopped, and looked more closely. "Oh," he said.

"You know them?"

Soorn hesitated. "The little girl . . . I know who she was, yeah. That's Mr. Brown's little girl, from Earth. Rebecca, was it? Something like that."

"Rachel," Markham said, his breath puffing out in a cold little cloud. "What about the other?"

"Mister, whoever you are, be serious—look at her! She's been out in space, hasn't she? She's bloody well freeze-dried, barely looks human. And it looks as if her face was smashed in even before she went out the lock."

"You can't venture a guess?"

Soorn looked at the larger corpse again.

"I could guess," he said, "if you promise not to hold me to it."

"Guess, then."

"Well, since you've got her here with the little girl, I'd guess she might be the girl's mother, Mrs. Brown."

"You think she could be?"

Soorn shrugged. "The hair's right, what's left of it. If there were any clothing . . ."

"This is how we found her," Markham said.

"Last I saw," Soorn said, "Mrs. Brown was wearing a borrowed uniform—there were probably half a dozen other women who wore them just aboard *Princess*, though."

"This one wasn't wearing anything when she was recovered," Markham said. "What about the face?"

"The face . . ." Soorn shuddered. "There's nothing that makes it impossible, but who could tell?"

Markham nodded.

"I think that'll do," he said.

Ten minutes later Mervyn rather queasily confirmed Soorn's guess that the body was Nancy Brown's—though he, too, was reluctant to swear to it. He hadn't known Mrs. Brown well, he insisted, and he, too, pointed out the condition the corpse was in.

Secretary Markham had to admit the body was in bad shape, but he was reasonably certain now that it was the right one. He left the vaults feeling rather pleased with himself.

That lasted until he reached his office and found the telepath waiting to report.

"The Empire has recovered your wife's body," Gregory reported, "but they're keeping it, and Rachel's, under heavy guard; we can't get at them."

Pel frowned. "Have you tried bribery?" he said.

Gregory nodded.

This was very annoying. That simulacrum, Felton, must have talked; the Empire knew that he wanted the bodies.

Well, that wasn't really such a big deal. He'd just have to talk to the Empire and get them back openly.

He couldn't go there himself, of course—the matrix would collapse the instant he set foot through a portal, and then he'd never be able to resurrect Nancy and Rachel—but he could send an emissary.

He could send Gregory—but that seemed rather a waste. The Empire might hang him for espionage.

Or they might not believe him in the first place.

No, they had telepaths—they could check.

But could telepaths read the minds of simulacra? And the Empire didn't have all that many telepaths; they might not bother to check before consigning Gregory to the loony bin—or the noose.

This would require some thought.

He could, Pel supposed, send Wilkins as his emissary—that would be a nice little goodwill gesture, and would leave no doubt that the message really came from Faerie.

He cast about with the matrix, and discovered, to his surprise, that Wilkins wasn't in the fortress, or anywhere nearby.

That was puzzling.

Thinking back, he realized he hadn't seen Wilkins in days—not since he had announced that he was going out for a walk. Pel hoped nothing had happened to him; he sort of liked Wilkins.

Maybe he'd gone off somewhere; Pel looked farther out in the matrix. He couldn't really tell one person from another—reliably—when they were outside the fortress, and certainly not by the time they were outside Shadowmarsh, but if he saw anyone around who felt out of place . . .

He didn't notice anyone he could recognize as Wilkins.

There were three men coming up the causeway, though—presumably they were coming to see the Brown Magician.

Pel decided he could attend to whatever they wanted, then get back to worrying about the Empire.

"Go back and wait," he told Gregory. "I'll get back to you shortly."

The simulacrum bowed, and stepped through the waiting portal, out of the throne room and back to his little corner of the Galactic Empire.

"Bascombe ordered *what*?" Markham stared at the telepath in disbelief.

"He ordered Best to arrest Pellinore Brown on charges of subornation of treason," the telepath repeated, then added, "Specifically, coercing Proserpine Thorpe into going rogue."

"But he's a head of state!" Markham shouted. "He's a bloody dictator, for God's sake! You can't just walk in and arrest him!"

The telepath just stood there, staring straight ahead, and after a moment Markham calmed down enough to stare back.

"Pel Brown's a head of state, and John Bascombe's an idiot," he said.

The telepath didn't argue.

"All right," Markham said, "Best is in Intelligence, so I assume he's *not* an idiot. What's he doing about his orders?" Markham knew what he hoped Best was doing— sending back a request for confirmation and clarification. That would eat up two or three weeks of transit in both directions, and was the only legitimate stalling tactic Markham could think of.

Then the clarification would be to tell Best to ignore the directive, because Bascombe's an idiot.

Best would see that, surely. Markham's spirits rose.

"He's . . . well, he's more or less planning to attempt to carry them out, sir."

Markham's spirits plummeted again. "He's *what*?"

"I'm afraid his opinion of Undersecretary Bascombe matches your own, so he assumes that the orders meant just what they said, and any clarification would just confirm that. Furthermore, he and his men—especially his men—are tired of delay, and prefer not to wait around. Therefore, they're planning to enter the fortress and ask the Brown Magician to return to the Empire with them; in fact, they're already on the causeway across the marsh. Given Spaceman Wilkins' experience, they don't expect to be harmed outright. Best has no intention of mentioning anything about an arrest."

Markham stared. He considered. Then he shrugged. "What the hell," he said, "it can't hurt."

"You sound like an Imperial or an Earthman," Pel said, "but there aren't supposed to be any other Earthpeople around, and as far as Imperials go, you're not Ron Wilkins, or Tom Sawyer, either. What the hell are you doing here? Who are you?"

"No, sir, I'm not Wilkins or Sawyer or an Earthman," the man said, blinking and shading his eyes against the glare of the matrix. "My name's Samuel Best. And I'm here on behalf of the Galactic Empire."

Pel stared, drumming his fingers on his knee and letting the matrix swirl greenly. He glanced quickly at Susan, standing silently to one side, then back at his visitor. There was something familiar about the man—not his physical appearance, but his magical one. Pel placed it finally.

"You're the spy," he said. "One of them, anyway. The ones they sent through the portal in Sunderland's Low Forest. And those two are more of them."

He reached out with the matrix and drew Begley and Poole forward, from the landing into the throne room. Neither of them screamed, which was something of a relief. Peasants always screamed.

"Yes, sir, I am," Best admitted.

"I didn't expect you to just walk in here like this," Pel said. "I figured you'd be sneaking around causing trouble."

"My orders were changed," Best—if that was really his name—explained.

"They told you to come talk to me?"

Best nodded. "Yes, sir. And to respectfully request that you accompany me back to the Empire."

Pel stared. The matrix billowed up in a deep blue glow, wrapping around Best.

"Why?" Pel asked.

"They want to talk to you about what happened to their men here, and to the telepath, Proserpine Thorpe," Best said—and Pel knew he was lying; the matrix couldn't provide telepathy, but it could, he had discovered, read physiological signs, much as a polygraph could.

The matrix darkened.

Best could sense that the conversation had suddenly gone bad; the blinding waves of light and color shifted, and what had previously seemed like an outward manifestation of irritated curiosity was now on the verge of turning openly hostile. He tried desperately to recover.

"I don't really know what they want to talk to you about," he said hastily. "I'm just a spy; they sent me because I was handy, and told me to bring you back to the Empire with me. They didn't say why."

The seething cloud of color surged forward slightly, stopping just short of engulfing him. Was there really a human being behind that, controlling it? It hardly seemed possible. Best began to suspect that if it truly was Pellinore Brown in there, he was no longer entirely human.

"They think they can just order me around?" that thunderous voice roared.

"I don't know what they think!" Best protested. "I'm just the messenger!"

"Messenger?" The Brown Magician's voice boomed from the walls. "All right, messenger, I've got a message for you to carry!"

The sergeant stared. "Who the hell are you, and why are you dressed like that?" he demanded.

"My name is Samuel Best," the man in the primitive clothes replied. "I was just stranded here, wherever I am, and I need to get back to Base One immediately." He hesitated, then added, "I'm working for Imperial Intelligence."

The sergeant considered that. It wasn't a very likely story; it sounded like something out of the fiction magazines, really.

On the other hand, strangers in crude woolen tunics and baggy tights didn't generally walk in off the street here; the local government on Delta Scorpius IV was not known for its sense of humor. Still, ships were coming and going all the time; one of them could have dumped an unwanted passenger here easily enough.

Why anyone would bother to strand someone alive was another matter. If he had been a smuggler or pirate, the sergeant thought, he'd have just dumped the troublemaker out an air lock—but he supposed some outlaws might have scruples about such things.

It wasn't as if sending a man to Base One was a big deal; the regular supply run was headed out there in another two hours anyway. Passing the problem along would be the simplest solution, and if the fellow really *was* in Intelligence, the sergeant didn't want to interfere.

"I'll have to ask you to submit to a search," he said, "and from the look of that outfit, a delousing, too. Do you have any credentials?"

CHAPTER 17

"*He wants the bodies,*" Best said. "*He said I should* say that you'd know what he meant, but if you . . . well, in his words, if you try to play dumb, he means he wants the remains of his wife and daughter."

Markham drummed fingers on his desk. "Now he's asking," he said.

"Because we've got them secure and he can't get them any other way," Albright said.

"Or because he knows that we know he wants them," Howe suggested. "He wants us to think he's coming out in the open."

"You don't think he is?" Markham asked her, mildly startled.

Howe shrugged. "I never trust anyone a telepath can't read," she said.

"Sensible attitude," Albright agreed.

"I wonder if we shouldn't tell the general secretary about this," Markham said. "After all, this Brown is effectively a head of state—a real one, not some penny-ante rebel tyrant—and he's asking us to turn over what might be Imperial property. I don't see this as within the purview of the Department of Science. We were directed to investigate and contain Shadow, and to contact any other interdimensional civilizations we could locate. We've done that—Shadow is dead, and we've got this Brown ready to talk. So we're done."

"As long as the Empire's security is threatened, the military is still involved," Albright said, "but I don't see this as a military matter, either."

Albright and Markham turned to Howe, who shrugged. "I'm not authorized to say anything about Intelligence's opinion," she said.

"Neither am I," Best said. "I'm just a field agent on detached duty to the Department of Interdimensional Affairs."

Best had noticed that John Bascombe, head of that department, was not present. He didn't have to ask why, but he did wonder whether Bascombe was still alive and free. He hadn't heard Bascombe's name spoken since he had arrived at Base One; he'd been sent directly to Markham's office, where the current gathering had formed. It was quite clear that Bascombe was no longer in any position of authority.

Best was fairly sure that, initially, Markham would just have removed Bascombe from duty—that was easier to keep quiet. If Bascombe didn't *want* to keep quiet, though, if he protested—well, there were prisons where no word would get out. And if that was too much trouble, a blaster charge was cheaper and more permanent.

In any case, mentioning him did not seem like a good idea, and Best didn't.

This talk about the general secretary wasn't comforting, though. Any blame that Secretary Sheffield might want to hand out would be directed at higher levels than that of mere field agents, but Intelligence's internal attitude was another matter. Nothing official would be done, but agents who showed any signs of developing a high profile had a tendency to wind up either in obscure backwaters or on assignments with excessive casualty rates. Like one hundred percent.

Best hoped Bascombe, wherever he was, was proud of himself.

Miletti was slumped in the armchair, staring disinterestedly at the TV, when the daily knock came.

"Come in, it's open," he called.

The lieutenant crept in, tape recorder in hand and already running. He'd had practice. The questioning went better if Miletti wasn't paying attention—and both he and Miletti knew that. Miletti wasn't being rude by watching reruns of "$25,000 Pyramid," he was making it easier on everyone.

The lieutenant did wonder sometimes about what shape Miletti was in, physically and emotionally—he obviously didn't enjoy any of this.

That wasn't the lieutenant's department, though; he was just an interviewer. (That sounded much nicer than "interrogator.")

"Any attempts at contact?" he asked.

"They're listening," Miletti said, without looking up.

"Sending?"

"Not sending."

"Any mention of Earth?"

"Nothing new."

"Proserpine Thorpe?"

"Nothing new."

"Amy Jewell?"

"Nothing."

"Pel Brown?"

"Sent a message."

Miletti blinked, startled by his own words.

The lieutenant was almost equally startled—until now there had been no change for a couple of weeks. "What's the message?" he asked.

"He wants the bodies," Miletti answered without thinking. "His wife and daughter."

This was outside anything the lieutenant was prepared to deal with, but he could at least ask the obvious. "Why?"

"Don't know."

"Is the Empire going to deliver them?"

Miletti looked up at the lieutenant. "This is spooky, you know," he said. "I really hate this. And I can't believe it's real. How do you know I'm getting this right, and not just making it up?"

"Not my department," the lieutenant said. "Are they going to give Brown the bodies?"

"That's what's really spooky," Miletti said. "*They* think they don't know yet, but they do, and I know it." The lieutenant needed a second to puzzle that out, and had just got it straight when Miletti concluded, "They aren't going to."

"How do I report that?" Carrie Hall asked her brother.

He didn't need to ask what she meant.

"You don't," he said. "Bad enough they know we're leaking anything; if they find out we're leaking things that we aren't supposed to know, that *nobody* knows consciously . . . well, hell, maybe he's wrong, anyway. Maybe it's just an opinion he picked up somewhere. Just don't mention it."

Carrie nodded reluctantly.

She didn't like it, though. Telepaths weren't supposed to keep secrets like that—they had orders to report on Miletti, and they weren't supposed to leave out anything important. And there shouldn't be that sort of leakage. There never had been before they started getting involved with these other worlds. Telepaths all knew things they shouldn't, but nobody in the entire Empire had ever tapped into the group unconscious of the telepaths the way this Miletti had.

Earthpeople were apparently slightly different from Imperials, in some very subtle way—or at least, Miletti was. Maybe he was a mutant himself—maybe he would *be* a telepath in Imperial space, if he ever came through a space warp into the normal universe, and maybe that was why they couldn't shut him out.

They had tried. Miletti was the only psychic they'd found on Earth with whom they hadn't been able to make any conscious contact at all, even though they knew he ought to be receptive. Maybe it was because he'd had enough telepathic talent that he'd learned to shut them out.

But he couldn't shut out *their* unconscious transmissions—and neither could they. They'd been able to close off the others, but not Miletti.

So for the first time ever a nontelepath, someone who hadn't been brought up from infancy in the Special Branch, who hadn't been trained in keeping secrets, someone who hadn't sworn loyalty to the Emperor and the Empire, was linked into the telepathic network.

Nothing like that had ever happened before they'd begun messing around with other universes.

And Prossie hadn't been an outcast before they contacted Earth. She never would have gone rogue if she'd stayed in the Empire.

And if she had gone rogue anywhere in the Empire she would never have survived if she hadn't had Earth to escape to. Carrie suspected that infectious thoughts were leaking through from Prossie on some subconscious level, just as secrets were leaking through to Miletti, and that Prossie's horrible rebelliousness was affecting the entire family—everyone seemed to be thinking strangely lately.

Or maybe it wasn't Prossie, maybe it was just all those minds out there, on Earth and in Faerie, with their alien ways of thinking, subtly different from the ordinary thoughts of the Imperial citizenry.

Could Miletti know a decision that no one in the Empire had consciously reached yet? These Earth psychics were so odd, with their erratic, untrained receptiveness, each one a bit different—could he have really learned that from the telepaths? Did they all really know it? Had they suppressed it?

Could Miletti be precognitive? Imperial science said that was impossible, but reality was different on Earth. Maybe he was seeing the future with his own psychic talent, not reading the telepathic unconscious at all.

And *would* the Empire deliver the two corpses?

Maybe Miletti knew, but Carrie didn't, or at least didn't want to admit it if she did, and she didn't like that.

She didn't like any of this.

"How long should I give them?" Pel asked, without looking at Susan.

"However long seems reasonable," she replied.

"How long is that?" He glanced at her; as usual, she was standing by the side of the room, not doing much of anything.

That didn't seem right, somehow; shouldn't she be going about her own business, instead of just hanging around him all the time?

But then, what business did she have?

"I don't know," she said.

"Neither do I," Pel muttered. "I don't know how long it takes to get from Gregory's place to Base One, or who'll have to authorize the decision, or how long they'll need to argue about it." He sighed. "Maybe I shouldn't have sent those two away—Begley and Poole, I mean. I just sent them back out to the berry patches, but I could have sent them somewhere in the Empire, and maybe that would have sped things up. Or maybe I should have tried the weak spots until I found a portal that goes directly to Terra—there must be one. Then I could've sent someone straight to the Emperor; he'd have to listen, right? I mean, I'm ruler of an entire universe, right? Even if all I've seen of it is some woods and a marsh and a few villages and this damned depressing fortress." He slumped back in the throne, thinking.

What he had just said wasn't exactly true, Pel realized. That was all he had seen with his own eyes, but he could reach out through the matrix and touch almost any place in Faerie. The matrix distorted distances, and he couldn't sense all of it at once—probably, he thought, just because his brain couldn't handle anything so large—but he had a vague idea of just how huge Shadow's realm was. The space warp that the Empire maintained in West Sunderland was two hundred miles away—and that was right next door. Even assuming that the scale was constant, which he was fairly sure wasn't true, he could sense things dozens of times as distant as that, which would put them three thousand miles or more away.

And in fact, he believed the scale was logarithmic, which would make that distance tens of thousands of miles.

It still wasn't anything like the Galactic Empire, with its thousands of planets, but surely it deserved some respect, and surely, once his request worked its way far enough up the chain of command, someone over there would see how reasonable it was and would deliver Nancy and Rachel.

No one had come through the Empire's warp out in Sunderland lately, though; there had been that party of three outbound a while back, but no one coming in.

This would all be much simpler if the Galactic Empire had telephones.

Or maybe not; after all, how could you use telephones between planets? And radio wouldn't work, either; the planets might be closer together than they were in the *real* world, but the interstellar distances were still measured in light-years.

At least he could have run a phone line through that space warp, though, instead of running messengers back and forth. Not through one of his portals, because then he'd have had to keep it open constantly, and he couldn't do that, but the space warp . . .

Well, the space warp came and went, too, but it didn't *have* to, did it?

It all seemed very weird, that there could be a Galactic Empire with space warps and telepathy and antigravity, but no telephones. Movies and telegraphs, but no telephones or TV. The old science-fiction stories had never described anything like that. Maybe it had something to do with the different physics involved.

He looked around at the marble walls of the chamber he sat in; more different physics, he thought. If this room were in either the Empire or the real world he wouldn't be able to see a thing, because he'd be sitting in pitch darkness. The only light here came from the matrix he controlled.

Maybe he should do more with that magic. Maybe he should see more of this world he controlled. Maybe, just maybe, he and Nancy and Rachel wouldn't go straight back to Earth once he'd restored them to life. First, though, he had to get them back. The *real* ones, not cheap imitations like that thing waiting for him in the bedroom.

And she *was* still waiting for him in the bedroom; he had told her to, so she would. She wouldn't leave that room for anything, not even to eat . . .

Was there a chamber pot there? He hoped so. And there wasn't any food.

"Damn," he said. He twitched the matrix, summoning a nearby fetch.

Life aboard ship was usually boring, but Best thought he'd have preferred honest boredom to the endless games of stoking Markham wanted to play; playing cards with the secretary of science was wearing on his nerves. He was never sure whether to play his honest best, or to deliberately lose, and just how badly to lose. And stoking was never one of his favorite games in the first place.

He wished Albright or Howe or someone had come along, instead of staying at Base One; then he or she could play with Markham and give Best a break.

"Burn," he said, dropping the king of cups on the central pile.

"Damp," Markham replied, tossing the king of swords.

Best looked at the table, and drew three. "I don't know why you need me along, anyway," he said, in an unusual moment of honesty. "I can't tell Secretary Sheffield anything you can't. Hell, I can't tell him anything the telepaths haven't *already* told him; I'm not sure why we're making this trip at all."

"You were there," Markham said, looking at his hand. "The general secretary always likes to hear things firsthand, likes to talk it out before deciding. Without telepaths." He pulled out a card and threw the eight of diamonds. "Burn."

With a sigh, Best played the knave of sticks. "Damp," he said, and added three points to Markham's score. He glanced up from the scratch pad and happened to catch the secretary's personal telepath watching.

As if playing stoking wasn't bad enough, he had to

worry about the mutant reading his thoughts and telling Markham all the details of his aggravation.

And of his cards, for that matter. Not that Markham would bother to cheat, but he might find out that Best had deliberately overlooked the nine of swords in his own hand. Best didn't think Markham would like knowing that Best was losing intentionally.

But he didn't think Markham would like losing, either.

Well, it was only two more days to Terra.

"You don't know what this mysterious project of his was?" Albright asked.

"No, sir," Wilkins replied. He was already over his nervousness at finding himself questioned by the Imperial Space Marshal, and was now treating Albright as just another officer.

A good one, but just another officer.

And he was getting tired of repeating all this.

"It kept him from sending you home, though?"

"Yes, sir—that's what he said."

"D'you think it had anything to do with these bodies he wants?"

"I don't know, sir; he never mentioned them to me."

"But he could have just sent *you* to ask for them, at any time," Albright said. "Why did he wait until Best showed up?"

"I have no idea, sir."

Albright considered Wilkins silently for a moment, then turned to his telepath.

"I don't like the sound of it," he said. "Tell Secretary Sheffield and Secretary Markham about this."

"Yes, sir," the telepath said.

"I'm going to check," Pel said, already gathering the energies to open a portal.

Susan and the false Nancy didn't argue; Susan stood motionless, and Nancy smiled agreeably. And of course the fetch didn't respond.

Just having someone better to talk to would be a relief, Pel thought. Not that Gregory was much of an improvement.

He reached, and twisted, and the portal opened.

No one was there.

"Damn," Pel said. He picked a fetch.

"You," he said, "go find Peter Gregory."

CHAPTER 18

By the time Gregory emerged from the portal Pel was furious with impatience, his fingers striking blue sparks from the dark wood as he drummed on the arm of his throne. "Where the hell were you?" he demanded without preamble, his voice echoing unnaturally. Angry orange currents swirled through the air.

"Down at the port," Gregory replied, unfazed. "I was trying to get word of what's happening at Base One."

"Did you?"

"A little."

"And?"

"The bodies are still under heavy guard. The Secretary of Science is on his way to Terra to confer with the General Secretary."

"Is that it?"

"Yes, O Great One."

Pel glared at Gregory's bland face, infuriated by the simulacrum's calm.

"Get someone to Terra," he said. "Get a message to the General Secretary—or the Emperor, or whoever's in charge. Tell him I want those bodies *now*. Through that space warp out in Sunderland."

"Yes, O Great One."

"That's all. Go on, get out of here!" He gestured angrily, waving Gregory toward the portal.

Gregory bowed deeply, then stepped backward and vanished.

Pel stared at the slight shimmer in the air where the portal hung. To his eyes, it was virtually invisible—if he strained, he could see the very faintest distortion. To his internal vision through the matrix, though, the portal was a gaping hole in reality, an infinite tunnel of powerful blue-black magic that somehow had no length at all, ending in the utter impenetrable darkness of nonmagic space.

He knew it came out on some planet he'd never heard of, Delta something-or-other, roughly half a day's space-flight from Base One. He'd never found a weak spot that would open directly into Base One; apparently Shadow hadn't had any portals there. He could create new portals, of course, but he couldn't aim them all that well, and trying different places in the Empire at random could take forever. Not to mention that if he ever *did* open a path to Base One, it might come out in the middle of a firing range or something.

So he had no direct route, and the delays were infuriating.

Of course, the Empire's space warp connected Faerie to Base One, but that was out in Sunderland, ten days' march to the east, and he was stuck here in Shadow's fortress . . .

Wasn't he?

Pel blinked, and the matrix slowed into contemplative green spirals. *Was* he stuck here?

Why should he be?

Shadow had claimed this fortress and lived here because it was a natural focal point for the network of magical currents that permeated Faerie, so that it was easier to maintain and control the matrix here—but did that mean this was the *only* place the matrix could be used?

That was silly. Shadow had talked about the early matrix wizards roaming around, taking over each other's strongholds, absorbing each other's matrices. They hadn't all just sat at home like spiders in their webs.

Why *couldn't* Pel go up to Sunderland if he chose?

And that obnoxious coward Taillefer had been able to fly, probably at a pretty good speed—sixty, seventy, maybe as much as a hundred miles an hour, and *he* wasn't any

matrix wizard, he was just a little hedge magician, too feeble for Shadow to have bothered hunting him down and
killing him.

Anything Taillefer could do, the master of the great matrix should be able to do. If Pel could do *that*, if he could
fly, he could be in Sunderland in a matter of hours.

Of course, he couldn't take all his fetches and monsters
along, or Susan, or the false Nancy—but so what?

But *could* he go anywhere? Could he learn to fly, blown
on a magical wind the way Taillefer was?

He could damn well try. At the very least, it would give
him something to do while the Empire dawdled.

He stood up and marched for the stairs—not the huge
staircase down to that absurd entrance hall, but the narrow
steps up to the battlements.

"A message from the General Secretary," the telepath said
suddenly, startling Best so much he almost dropped his
cards.

"What is it?" Markham asked, looking up; at first he
seemed annoyed by the interruption, but by the time he finished raising his head and pronouncing those three simple
words he was calm again.

"He wants to know if you have anything to add to what's
already been relayed telepathically, regarding the Brown
Magician."

"Not that I know of," Markham replied. "Do I?"

The telepath's mouth quirked in a ghost of a smile. "Not
that I can see, sir," he said.

"So why is he asking? Can you tell me?"

The telepath nodded. "In light of the interview with
Spaceman Wilkins, regarding the Magician's secret project
that prevented him from sending Wilkins home, Secretary
Sheffield believes that we should cease any further delays
or stalling tactics and open direct negotiations with Brown.
Therefore, you're to turn around and return to Base One
forthwith; he'll be coming out as well, along with several
trained envoys."

"Envoys?" Best asked. "What envoys?"

"Well, obviously," the telepath explained, "the Empire hasn't needed actual ambassadors since the Unification, but there's apparently a staff of envoys on Terra, kept on hand in case of need. They've occasionally seen duty in negotiating terms of surrender with rebel worlds, and they're theoretically ready if we ever meet intelligent extraterrestrials."

"I didn't know that," Best marveled. "They think of everything, don't they?"

"They try," Markham said dryly. "Tell the captain of the change in plans."

As the telepath hurried out of the stateroom, Markham tossed the four of cups. "Burn," he said.

The wind whipped Pel's hair forward, slashing it back and forth across his face; it occurred to him that he hadn't had it cut in weeks, maybe months, not since he had left Base One. And he hadn't bothered shaving, hadn't had a chance, since then, either; he had a full beard for the first time in his life. He must be a mess.

He wondered if Nancy and Rachel would even recognize him like this. He hoped the beard wouldn't frighten Rachel. Of course, he could shave it off, once everything was back to normal, once he had Nancy and Rachel back.

But first he had to bring them back.

He stepped up on a merlon—at least, he thought that was what the stone blocks along the edge of the battlement were called. Maybe the right term was crenellation.

It didn't matter.

Below him the wall of the central tower formed a sheer drop of a hundred feet or more, down to the roofs and walls of the next layer of the fortress. Fifty feet farther out, that layer, in turn, fell away for another sixty or seventy feet, and then again and again the stone walls and slate roofs, squat ugly turrets and sinister battlements, until five hundred feet down and two hundred feet ahead lay the stagnant water and thick reeds of the surrounding marsh.

Above him was that single line of gargoyles, and a heavy, leaden overcast.

Around him seethed the light and shadow of the matrix.

He was standing on a stone fifty, maybe sixty stories up, unsheltered by anything but his magic. Nothing built without steel had any right to be this high, he thought. It must have used magic. Why hadn't it fallen down when Shadow died?

Because the matrix still held, of course. And he held it.

He reached out, down into the fortress; he couldn't sense any specific places where magic held the stone, but surely there were some.

The wind subsided slightly as his attention was distracted, and he shifted a foot to keep his balance.

The merlon was carved, the corners somewhat rounded, in what appeared to be a representation of leaves. It wasn't very well executed, and as he glanced at it through a purple swirl of magical energy Pel thought the result resembled a tooth more than anything else. The lines of the carving provided a bit of traction, but as Pel looked past the stone and past the haze of color at the drop below him he wished the corners were still solid and square.

What was he doing, standing here on top of a tower and deliberately summoning a wind that would blow him off?

This was insane. People couldn't fly.

Not on Earth, anyway, but this wasn't Earth. He'd seen Taillefer do it, and he had Shadow's entire matrix, where Taillefer had had only the leavings of it. Taillefer hadn't lived in a constant shifting mass of magic the way Pel did.

He wasn't going to jump. He wasn't going to step off. If he could conjure up a wind strong enough to *blow* him off, then he'd believe he could make one strong enough to carry him.

He felt the matrix, felt it moving the air, and he drew more power to that movement, summoned strength from earth and sky, and the wind hit him like a wall, sweeping him off the battlements, bearing him up and away into empty space.

* * *

"So how do we get a message to him?" Secretary Sheffield asked.

"Send a messenger through the space warp. It's about a ten-day hike from there to the fortress," Albright replied.

"There isn't anything faster?"

Albright shook his head. "We can't seem to relocate the warp to anywhere within five hundred miles or so of a previously used location, so we can't get it any closer to the fortress. Brown apparently has some way of contacting his network of spies, so he may well learn of our decision within a day or two, but we don't have any way of knowing that. We haven't been able to break the ring, or infiltrate, or even identify any members with certainty. We know Felton, and of course we know who Felton's contact was, but that was a woman named Fielding, and she committed suicide before we could capture and interrogate her. We're checking on her friends and associates, but so far we haven't found anything particularly suspicious."

"Felton didn't know any other names?"

"Not for certain. The telepaths are still digging."

"So our only way of contacting Brown is through our own space warps, and the only one we currently have is ten days' march from Brown's fortress—but can't we get some sort of vehicle through there?"

Albright shook his head. "Antigravity doesn't work in ... well, we call it Faerie. The telepaths picked up that name for it somewhere, and it seems to fit. Anyway, antigravity won't work—ships and aircars just fall to the ground and sit there."

"What about wheeled vehicles? Or is there a water route?"

Albright hesitated. "We don't *have* any wheeled vehicles," he pointed out. "And I suspect the roads aren't good enough. The warp comes out in a forest, and the pathway out is just that, a path. As for a water route, again, our entry point is in the middle of a forest, with no navigable rivers in the areas we've seen." He glanced at Best, who was

202 THE REIGN OF THE BROWN MAGICIAN

seated at one corner of the table, trying hard to be unobtrusive.

"No rivers," Best confirmed. "And there aren't any roads in the forest."

"What about opening a new warp over the sea somewhere?" Sheffield suggested. "It would have to be farther away, but it might be faster all the same. Is this fortress accessible by sea?"

Albright rubbed his nose thoughtfully. "I don't know," he said. "You understand, sir, I haven't seen it myself, and we haven't done any photoreconnaissance. I understand it's in the middle of a marsh, but I don't know any more than that—whether a small boat could get across the marsh is an excellent question." He turned to Best again. "You were there," he said.

"Yes, sir," Best admitted.

"You think a boat could reach this fortress?"

"I don't know much about boats," Best said, "but no, I don't think so. It's a pretty nasty marsh, and I didn't see where it connected to anything better. Besides, how would you power a boat? If you're rowing, that's no better than walking, is it?"

Sheffield acknowledged that with a nod.

"All right, then," he said, "we'll send an envoy to this forest and let him walk from there, and one of the demands will be to find a better way for future communications."

Demands?

This was the first mention Best had heard of demands. He tried to imagine what the Empire might be demanding of the Brown Magician.

And he tried to imagine how Brown would react to any such demands.

He didn't like what he came up with.

Riding the wind was a very strange sensation, something like swimming in a very strong current. And of course, he could steer the current by manipulating the matrix.

And the matrix added to the strangeness, because he

could feel that he was simultaneously riding and pulling it. It didn't *want* to have its center dragged away from the fortress.

Pel began to understand why Shadow had sat waiting in her fortress, rather than coming out to collect her visitors; it was uncomfortable being out here. He was stretching his web, forcing the patterns to shift and distort.

He rebelled at any thought of going back, though. He *could* operate out here, and he *would*—he wouldn't be held prisoner by his own power!

Besides, he could sense that the matrix would restructure itself with time; the patterns would slide and shift until they settled into new positions, and the discomfort would pass. It wasn't so much that he was restricted to one spot as that the matrix resisted moving about.

Of course, it would work best and be most comfortable in one of the natural places of power—Shadowmarsh was one, probably the strongest, but Castle Regisvert would work, too, or any number of other places.

He looked down.

He was not at airplane altitudes—he'd started at about five hundred feet, and hadn't risen much above that. He didn't see any need to go higher. From this height he could follow the road without difficulty, from the causeway across the marsh back past the berry fields and plains to the villages, one after another, strung out across the ridges and valleys of the Starlinshire Downs.

The roads branched, the towns held forks and crossroads, but Pel simply remembered that he and his party had traveled almost due west, so he kept his bearings and headed eastward.

From this altitude, low as it was, he could see far more of the countryside than he had from the ground. Farms and villages stretched off in all directions; castles were scattered about, but all of them looked abandoned, and most were outright ruins—Shadow had not been kind to the conquered nobility.

Some castles, of course, had belonged to wizards. To the

unassisted eye those were built in more or less random locations and were all no more than ruins—some, in fact, more nearly resembled craters than castles. Through the matrix, however, Pel could see that these locations weren't random at all, but carefully sited on the natural magical currents of earth and sky, currents that were now all diverted into the matrix itself, leaving shadowy ghosts of themselves in an odd sort of double image.

Other castles, the more intact ones, tended to be built on commanding hilltops or bends in rivers—defensible positions, in short, and ones that could control a respectable territory. Those, Pel assumed, had belonged to the mundane nobility.

Pel suspected that virtually all of the places of power had been occupied by matrix magicians at one time or another, before Shadow consolidated all the matrices into one. Certainly, every one he could see as he blew across the landscape seemed to have a ruin on it.

The matrix griped about leaving Shadow's fortress because that was where it had been centered for so long, but if another matrix magician had won out, it might just as well have been centered in one of the dozen or so other spots he passed—or in the hundreds or thousands of others he knew lay beyond the horizon. He couldn't see those, but he could sense them through the matrix.

If Pel wanted a castle other than the fortress, one where the matrix would be comfortable, he supposed he could rebuild Regisvert or one of the others. If he needed to relocate closer to the space warp, that might be a good idea; the matrix would shift itself to fit the new location, and the present discomfort would pass.

Or he could erect himself a new fortress out in Sunderland, if he chose, but there was little natural magic there; it wouldn't be as suitable as a power spot, and the matrix might never accommodate itself properly.

And it shouldn't be necessary, anyway—he should have the bodies as soon as the Empire could take care of the paperwork, and then he'd be able to take them anywhere, back to the fortress or anywhere he wanted.

The Low Forest was a dark green line on the horizon before him, and the overgrown ruin ahead and to the left, where the power flowed strongly just beneath the ground, was surely the ruins of Castle Regisvert. Pel adjusted his course, and blew onward.

Spaceman Thomas Sawyer looked up from the pigpen and saw the glowing, seething mass of color and light tear across the sky to the south, moving eastward. The flickering lit the mud and the hogs in quick flashes of color, like a fireworks display.

"What the hell is *that*?" he asked no one in particular.

It had to be magic, of course. They didn't have fireworks here in Faerie, did they?

It had to be magic. So even if Shadow was really dead, there was still magic running loose, and it didn't look like just the stuff people like Taillefer and Valadrakul did.

Sawyer had no intention of getting involved in anything like that. It looked like he'd be staying down on the farm for a while yet.

Lieutenant Sebastian Warner checked the seals on his spacesuit one final time, then cycled the air lock. He waited patiently while the pressure decreased, and when the signal light came on he undogged the outer door and stepped out into the vacuum of space.

Huge machinery surrounded him, but he closed his eyes and ignored it as he proceeded carefully toward the space warp, moving hand-over-hand along the rope ladder. Even with his eyes tightly shut the glare was painfully bright, forcing him to work entirely by touch.

This wasn't his first trip through, though; he was an old hand now, and could find his way easily. He had already made almost two dozen quick trips to see how things stood on the other side, and whether anyone interesting was in the area around the base of the ladder.

This time the job description was slightly different—he was supposed to prepare the site for an Imperial envoy, whatever that meant. As far as he was concerned, it was more of the same, and just as dull as ever.

He'd missed the assignment when Spaceman Wilkins had been picked up; dull as that was, it had been about the most excitement here since Warner had been given his current duty. James and Butler had got that one, had met Wilkins and brought him up the ladder; Warner had never encountered *anyone* on the other side.

Warner had hopes of spotting something interesting eventually. Even just one of the primitives finding the ladder while out hunting would do. If nothing else, it would give Warner a chance to see whether the stories were true, that blasters really didn't work on the other side. He hadn't wanted to test the theory without a valid reason, in case one of those damned spying mutants reported it.

He'd spent the first twenty years of his life without ever being on the same planet as a telepath, but lately it seemed as if he couldn't get away from the bloody freaks.

He was through the warp; he could tell because the gravity had shifted—the ladder now led down instead of forward—and because the intense glare of the warp had faded. Without thinking, he had gotten his feet securely onto a rung.

He opened his eyes on bright, cool sunlight, saw the green roof of the forest spread out below him, and began climbing down toward it.

He was just passing the highest branches when a bright flicker of movement attracted his attention. He turned his head, expecting to see a wild bird or other flying creature of some kind, hoping it wasn't even the most distant cousin of that dead giant bat-thing that lay in the clearing below.

Instead he saw, miles away but approaching rapidly, a thing like a cloud of polychrome light.

He froze, clinging to the ladder, and stared. He'd wished for something interesting, but this was a little more than he'd had in mind. And it was coming closer *fast*, at least as fast as an aircar at cruising speed.

He shouldn't stay here, exposed, he realized. He should either climb back up and give the alarm, or he should get down to the ground, take shelter, and watch, maybe wait until it had passed, and then get the hell back to Base One.

He had no idea what the thing was—some weird natural phenomenon peculiar to this strange world? Some sort of creature? A weapon, sent by the so-called Brown Magician, or maybe Shadow? They said Shadow was dead; he wasn't convinced. Maybe Shadow and the Magician were still fighting this out, and the thing coming toward him was involved in that.

Whatever it was, he had to *move*.

He looked up, at those long yards of ladder exposed in the open air, then down at the shelter of the trees, and he began descending as rapidly and silently as he could.

CHAPTER 19

Pel frowned as he looked down at the trees beneath. He remembered, a little belatedly, how Taillefer had landed at Regisvert, tumbling out of the sky onto half a dozen waiting helpers.

Pel didn't have any helpers. And tumbling down through the forest canopy looked scratchy.

On the other hand, he had access to more power than Taillefer could ever imagine.

But Taillefer was more experienced and skilled at using his power, and this particular area was one where there were no strong natural currents of magic, so that the matrix was relatively weak.

Relatively weak, but still vastly stronger than anything Taillefer could call upon. And even here, Valadrakul had been able to blast Shadow's creatures.

The power to do any sort of landing he wanted was unquestionably there, but Pel had to admit that he didn't really know *how* to land, other than to simply let himself fall. And here in the forest, that might mean breaking a leg or putting his eye out on a broken branch.

He supposed he could use the matrix to protect himself from damage; Shadow had certainly taken her personal invulnerability for granted, and with good reason. It might well be that the matrix would protect him even if he did nothing consciously at all. His instincts rebelled at the idea, though. Letting himself drop into the trees ...

He couldn't do it. At least, not from this height. Maybe, if he lowered himself gradually ...

He looked ahead, trying to judge distances, and spotted something strange, off to the left. Something was sticking up out of the forest.

He had glimpsed it before, from a distance, and had taken it for an odd branch, or a dead trunk, but now he saw he had badly misjudged its size and distance.

He turned and steered for it.

It rose straight up out of the forest, straighter than anything that could naturally grow there, taller and thinner, as well, and swaying slightly in the wind. Pel couldn't see the top. He could see above where it stopped, but somehow he couldn't see the exact point at which it ended; there was a blind spot.

And the matrix was kinked out of shape there, he realized.

This was the space warp. This was what he had intended to be aiming for all along, but he'd gotten so involved in the mechanics of flying, and the view of the landscape, that he had lost track of it.

He hadn't really expected anything visible, but there it was.

He'd never bothered to ask Best or his companions how they got through the warp, but now he saw. That thing was a *ladder*, a rope ladder that reached down into the forest somewhere from a space warp that was situated about five hundred feet up. It was swinging in gentle curves, swaying back and forth in a shallow sine wave.

That would be an uncomfortably long climb and a dizzy, seasick one, but obviously the Imperial spies had managed it.

And Pel could, too. He wasn't about to go up through the warp—he'd lose control of the matrix if he left Faerie for even a second—but he could grab the ladder and climb down to the ground.

That, at least, was the theory; steering himself through the air at perhaps forty miles an hour and boarding a stationary rope ladder turned out to be much more difficult than he had expected. Instead he smacked into it and then slid on past before he could grab hold, sending the ladder into violent, twisting oscillations and drawing a nasty rope burn across his right cheek.

He made a wide loop, rubbing his injured face and muttering obscenities, then came back for another pass, dropping so much speed that he began losing altitude rapidly.

He hit the ladder hard and barely managed to clamp his hands onto a rung about three steps lower than he intended. His arms jarred with the impact, and he wondered if he had injured his shoulder, but he kept his grip.

Sebastian Warner stared up at the glowing, seething *thing* that hung in the sky above him.

It had struck the ladder and then passed on through. Warner had seen that the ladder was still there and thought he was safe, but then the thing had looped around and hit the ladder again, and this time it *stayed* there.

It looked as if the ladder was being consumed by some sort of eldritch energy cloud. Since no severed end came tumbling to the ground, Warner assumed that it was not actually being consumed, but he was still cut off from the space warp. He wasn't about to try climbing through *that*.

In fact, as soon as he was safely off the ladder, he was hurrying to get away, behind a tree, where the thing might not spot him—assuming it could see. Once there, he turned and watched for a moment. If he hadn't still been suited up, he'd have drawn his blaster and found out once and for all whether the things really didn't work here.

Well, he'd wished for something interesting to happen. He should have known better. This was something interesting, all right, and it looked like very bad news indeed.

Of course, it could get worse—and as he watched, it *did* get worse.

The thing started moving downward.

Pel's shoulder ached, his back felt oddly scraped and raw from the now-vanished wind pressure, and the thick, damp, hot air above the forest made his skin itch and his head hurt, but at least he'd finally gotten both hands and both feet onto the ladder.

He began descending, carefully. The ladder swayed more than he would have liked, so he moved slowly.

As he neared the treetops he noticed the light and color of the matrix flitting across the leaves and decided he didn't like that. It might attract unwanted attention, and besides, it made it harder for him to see whatever there might be to see around here. Shadow had apparently been able to use the matrix to enhance her senses as a regular, permanent effect, but Pel's mastery of it wasn't anywhere near that complete; it took an effort of will to sense anything through the matrix unless whatever he was sensing was somehow *part* of the matrix.

The space warp was a part of the matrix, in a way, and any attempt to use magic was, too. Fetches and homunculi and the rest of Shadow's servants and creatures qualified, as well, and showed up without any special effort on his part.

Trees, however, didn't.

That was mildly interesting, actually; Pel had always thought of trees as rather magical things. Certainly they were magical in most of the fantasy stories he'd read.

Maybe some *were* magical, but the Low Forest wasn't, or at least the matrix didn't register anything special there, and the energy currents were weak. And Pel's eyes were having some trouble seeing through the magical haze.

So he suppressed it, forcing the magical radiation out of the visible spectrum, and then continued climbing.

The instant it had started downward, Warner had taken off his space helmet and begun opening his suit. He had dragged out his blaster, pointed it, and pressed the trigger.

They were right; nothing happened. It didn't so much as buzz. He shoved it back in the holster, and was debating whether to turn and run when the cloud-thing vanished, revealing a rather battered-looking man climbing slowly downward.

Was that the notorious Brown Magician, perhaps? Or one of his representatives?

He didn't look like much of a threat.

Warner backed off a few paces and found himself a hiding place in the underbrush, then he waited to see what the new arrival was up to.

Pel was about ten feet up when he spotted the man in the spacesuit. He smiled, and dropped to the ground, skipping the last few rungs. "Hey, you!" he called, the matrix amplifying his voice.

The man froze.

"Come on out where I can see you!" Pel beckoned.

The man hesitated, then stepped out of the concealing foliage. He had a bubble helmet under one arm, and his free hand was on the butt of a blaster that protruded through an open seam in his vacuum armor.

"The ray gun won't work here," Pel told him. "You can try it if you want."

The man's hand dropped away from the useless weapon.

"I'm Pel Brown," Pel said. "I run this place. Who're you?"

"Lieutenant Sebastian Warner, Imperial Fleet," the stranger replied.

"Good!" Pel said, smiling. This was just what he had hoped—and, from the instant he first saw Warner, expected; nobody but the Galactic Empire would have sent someone here in a purple outfit. "You're holding down the fort for your people, I take it?"

Warner blinked. "I'm sorry, I . . ."

"I mean, they left you in charge here? Or is there a whole installation in the next clearing? Maybe you're using the *Christopher* as your headquarters. If you're not in charge, can you take me to whoever is?"

"It's just . . . listen, whoever you are, I don't have to answer any questions!"

Pel abruptly dropped the suppression, and the matrix flared up around them both in red and orange swirls. "No," he said, "you don't have to answer any questions—but you might *want* to. My name's Pel Brown, as I said, but I'm better known here as Pelbrun, the Brown Magician."

Warner made a wordless noise and stared in horror at the surrounding colors.

"Now, I don't see anyone else here, so unless you tell me otherwise I'm going to assume you're it—in which case, Lieutenant Warner, I do have one question to ask you, and if you don't answer it, you're toast." Pel stopped, caught for a moment by the sudden image his own words conjured up—of Raven and Valadrakul and Singer incinerated by Shadow's power.

If Pel wanted it, in an instant this Warner really could be nothing but burnt toast—but the idea sickened Pel. Murder him for failing to answer a question?

He hadn't really meant the threat, Pel told himself. He just wanted his answer.

Then he admitted to himself that maybe he wanted it enough that he *had* meant the threat seriously, when he made it.

He didn't now, though; he had no intention of harming this poor jerk.

But he didn't want Warner to know that.

"Are they going to give me what I asked for?" Pel demanded.

"I . . . I don't know," Warner stammered. "What did you ask for?"

"*They* know," Pel said. "You don't? Okay, fine, you don't—then I want you to carry a message for me. You go back up that ladder and tell them I want those bodies *now*. They have . . ." He glanced at Faerie's pale sun. "They have until dawn. Maybe fifteen hours. I'm being generous."

Warner glanced up at the setting sun, as well, then swallowed.

"Now, you get back up that ladder and *tell* them!" Pel shouted.

Quickly, Warner started to set his helmet in place, then realized that the sealing buckles and latches along the side seam weren't closed. He dropped the helmet and began clamping them shut as quickly as he could, even as the apparition he had taken for an ordinary man stared at him from a boiling cloud of violet smoke.

A moment later he was suited up and climbing. Pel watched him ascend a few feet; then he sat down on the dirt of the forest floor and sighed.

Warner glanced down, but kept moving.

Pel watched Warner clamber up into the treetops, then out into the sky beyond.

He had given them until dawn, which meant he would be spending the night here, in the woods. He looked about.

The matrix would provide light and heat without any effort at all, but shelter . . . well, he could make it easily enough, but wasn't the wreck of the *Christopher* just over that way?

And seeing what remained of the giant bat-thing would be interesting, too.

Pel got up, dusted off the seat of his pants, and, after a final glance at Warner's distant form, he strolled off into the trees.

"It's all clear, I suppose?" Warner's captain said; then he got a look at the lieutenant's face as Warner stepped out of the air lock, his helmet already off and dangling from one hand, and the captain realized that something was wrong.

"He's down there!" Warner said, addressing his superior and ignoring the Imperial envoy who stood to one side, half-in and half-out of a spacesuit.

"Who is?" the captain asked, glancing at the array of Imperial brass up in the observation area.

"Pelbrun! The Brown Magician!" Warner answered, ignoring the glance.

"Where?" the envoy asked. "He's supposed to be in his fortress, I . . ."

"He's right there! At the foot of the ladder! He came out of a cloud and found me there!"

The captain looked up again, and caught Albright's signal.

"Wait here," he said.

"The telepaths say it's possible," Markham told the others. "Apparently they don't have a very good grasp of the geography there, especially now that both our contacts have returned to Imperial space, but Brown does appear to have moved out of his fortress somehow."

"So he's waiting for us to deliver the bodies," Sheffield said. "He said he wanted them *there, now*, and he's come to collect them."

"And he's given us a specific deadline this time," Albright commented.

"Which we don't know exactly, since your lieutenant neglected to check his watch," Markham pointed out.

"We wouldn't know it exactly in any case, since none of your people have ever bothered to calibrate the local cycles there," Albright retorted. "Besides, how does this Earthman define dawn? First light? Semicircle at true horizon? Sun clear of the visible horizon?"

"Not much of a horizon in the middle of a forest," Markham answered.

"I don't think we want to wait for his deadline in any case," Sheffield said. "I think we go ahead with our original plan, and send the envoy—the only difference is that he'll be negotiating right now, instead of days from now. Do either of you gentlemen see any reason we shouldn't proceed thus?"

Markham and Albright glanced quickly at one another, but neither spoke.

Pel had worked his way through the mummified remnants of Shadow's flying monster, studying the bones and skin with interest, puzzling out just why the Imperials had cut away the parts they did while leaving the rest, and was just starting a look through the wreck of I.S.S. *Christopher* when he heard a human voice calling.

He hesitated. It was obvious that the Imperials had used the ship and clearing as a temporary base during their ventures into Faerie, and he was curious about just how they had set it up, and how many of them had been here—and for that matter, whether anyone might still be here.

No, he could tell, magically, that no one was in the ship.

He did want to see the inside—he'd felt a twinge of nostalgia when he first saw the familiar purple paint, now somewhat marred by weather and abuse. He had only been on the ship for perhaps an hour, but it had, after all, been a fairly important hour, the one that brought him to Faerie, where he had found a chance to revive his family.

But that voice was probably one of the Empire's representatives, delivering the bodies, and if he had a choice between thinking about his wife and child as they were, or bringing them back from the dead, he'd be a fool to settle for memories.

Anyone who wanted to find him here could do so readily enough, since he hadn't bothered to suppress the matrix and the glow was probably visible for miles, but still, it wouldn't hurt to let whoever it was know that he was welcome.

"Hello!" Pel called, stepping out of the hatchway. "Over here!"

Perhaps two minutes later he and the Imperial envoy came face-to-face on the narrow track Imperial traffic had worn between ladder and clearing; Pel stopped dead at the sight of him.

The man was wearing the most outlandish outfit Pel had encountered since leaving Earth, somewhat the worse for having been stuffed inside a spacesuit for the climb through the warp. The pants were black velvet with broad purple silk stripes down either side, stuffed into shiny black jackboots; the shirt was white silk with elaborate lace ruffles down the front, artfully fluffed up around a diagonal purple silk sash that combined with a purple silk cummerbund to make a bizarre imitation of a Sam Browne belt. Over this, the stranger wore a bright red cutaway jacket with gold braid on the cuffs and shoulders, and the Imperial seal on the breast—a lion and unicorn rampant against a sunburst, a seal that Pel had first seen on the door of an aircar on Psi Cassiopeia II.

Pel couldn't tell whether the gold-and-white ruffled lace collar that flared out from the man's neck was part of the shirt, the jacket, or neither.

The crowning glory of this comic-opera outfit was undoubtedly the hat, a curling, almost brimless, vaguely conical thing of red velvet and white and purple ostrich plumes.

That the sunlight was gone and the only illumination came from the shifting colors of the matrix made this costume all the more bizarre. Pel tried to shift the light toward white, so as to see this thing better, and belatedly thought to make sure that the matrix was transparent, so that this character could see him, as well.

Why on Earth had they sent this person to deliver the bodies, instead of just assigning a soldier or two?

"My Lord Pelbrun?" the man asked, standing straight and snapping his heels together.

"Yeah," Pel managed.

The apparition took off his hat and bowed, with a flourish. After a moment of frozen formal subordination, he rose, reached into an inside pocket, and pulled out a packet roughly the size of a business envelope, which he proffered to Pel. "My credentials, sir."

Too dazed to even laugh, and feeling a twinge of dread, Pel reached out with a tendril of magic and took the packet; it felt like parchment, and was sealed with gold leaf and purple sealing wax. He pulled it open and tugged out a large sheet, which he unfolded and glanced at.

It was in elaborate old-fashioned script, and Pel didn't care to bother reading it by matrixlight, but he did notice the signature and elaborate blue seal at the bottom.

Georgius VIII Imperator et Rex.

That sounded pretty official.

"Okay," Pel said, "the Emperor sent you. Who the hell *are* you?"

"My name is Ambrose Curran, my lord, and I am an accredited Imperial envoy. His Imperial Majesty has sent me to negotiate the terms under which he will yield to you the mortal remains of Nancy and Rachel Brown."

"Terms?" Pel needed a second or two to absorb that; he was still bemused by Curran's appearance.

Then it sank in, and the matrix turned angry red as he repeated, *"Terms?"* His voice rang and echoed, and tree branches creaked warningly.

CHAPTER 20

Ambrose Curran stepped back involuntarily and threw up an arm to shield his eyes as the ragged man vanished behind a blazing, surging cloud of scarlet energy. White and red light flashed across the forest, interspersed with sharp-edged stripes of black shadow where the trees blocked the furious brilliance.

"Yes, my lord," Curran said, "but I assure you, the terms are not onerous in the least. As His Imperial Majesty's representative, I promise you we seek only the friendship natural between two great and puissant lords and their respective realms."

According to accepted protocol that was a proper way to phrase it, but Curran had some doubts as to whether this Brown would like it. From his speech and appearance the man seemed to be rather a rough and ready sort, not a traditional aristocrat at all—and that was hardly surprising, since he was, after all, a usurper.

"I don't want your fucking emperor's *friendship*," said the roaring voice from the glowing cloud, "I want my wife and child!"

"Of course," Curran said, just managing to keep his voice steady. He wished he knew whether this obscenity was an indication of the Brown Magician's fury, or simply a lower-class usurper's natural style. "And we intend to deliver them, just as soon as we have your assurance that you will cease your interference in Imperial affairs."

"I don't give a shit about Imperial affairs!" the voice screamed, and Curran heard branches crack and fall. The cloud was showing several colors now, changing too fast for Curran to name them all. "'I want Nancy and Rachel, I want them lowered down a rope from that fucking hole in the sky you've got up there, and I want it done *now*, or you can kiss your whole fucking Galactic Empire goodbye!"

"My lord . . ."

"Just shut up with that 'lord' crap while you're at it, and get your ass back up that ladder!"

"I have my orders, Mr. Brown . . ."

"Then they've ordered you to die, you stupid son of a bitch! Last chance!"

"And you think they'll deliver if you kill me?" Curran shouted, backing away another step.

The air suddenly stilled, and for a moment an unnatural silence fell. Then the voice spoke again, and to Curran it sounded more like growling machinery than like anything human.

"State your terms, then, errand boy."

Curran did not think this was the time for formality or protocol; he gave his position in the simplest, most direct way he could. "We want your spies withdrawn, that's all. We know we didn't get them all. We want them out of the Empire, and your word that you won't send more. As soon as they're gone, we deliver the bodies."

Again there was a moment of eerie stillness. Then the voice, once again sounding human, said, "That's all?"

"That's all."

"You really want them withdrawn, or would you rather they turned themselves in? You could question them about whatever they did for Shadow before I took over; might be interesting for your cops."

Curran hesitated. That hadn't been covered in his instructions; no one had considered the possibility that Brown could be so ruthless as to turn his own people over to Imperial Intelligence.

It seemed an irresistible opportunity, and after all, if Secretary Sheffield decided it was a mistake, he could just have them all sent through the warp. Or killed.

"Either one would be satisfactory," he said.

"They'll turn themselves in, then," the voice said. "Easier for me—I don't have any use for them here."

"As you please."

"It may take a few days for word to reach 'em all."

"Of course."

"If you get back up that ladder and get the gears turning on your end, I'll get started on mine. I want those corpses *soon*—you tell your people that. No more stupid delays; as soon as my people start surrendering, you get those bodies here."

"I'll deliver your terms, of course." Curran bowed again.

"Go on, then!"

Curran turned and walked off with as much dignity as he could muster, hoping he wouldn't have any difficulty finding the ladder and donning his spacesuit in the dark.

He was not looking forward to that long climb.

The welcome at the top should be pleasant enough, though; Brown had, after all, agreed.

Pel didn't bother to watch as the Imperial geek put his spacesuit on and started up the ladder; despite his shouting, he knew it would be hours before Curran could get his message through and the bureaucracy could process it. He didn't really expect the bodies to be delivered for a day or so.

Pel shook his head as he trudged back toward I.S.S. *Christopher*.

That outfit Curran wore was really amazing; now that Pel was over his initial surprise and subsequent fury, he could marvel at its absurdity. The Galactic Empire really did have some odd quirks. *Why* would they dress their ambassadors, or whatever they were, like that?

It certainly made them distinctive, anyway.

Which was probably the point.

If that regalia was what ambassadors wore, what did the Emperor wear for formal occasions?

It didn't matter, of course. What mattered was getting

Nancy and Rachel back. And that would be easy enough; all he had to do was order Gregory to spread the word— everyone was to pass the message on, then surrender to the Imperial authorities.

That was really reasonable enough. When Pel had first heard that the Empire had terms he had expected something difficult or unpleasant. Once he had his family back, though, what did he need spies for?

He wondered what the Empire would do with them all; Pel didn't know himself how extensive Shadow's network of spies actually was, but he was fairly sure there were at least a couple of dozen. He supposed they'd wind up serving time in prison for espionage.

If they had been real people, Pel might have felt guilty about that, but surely they were all simulacra or fetches or other Shadow creatures, and from everything he'd seen of those, they had such a flattened emotional response that prison probably wouldn't bother them much.

And maybe he could work some sort of trade later on, buy them free somehow.

Maybe he should have said that he'd withdraw them, rather than suggesting that they turn themselves in—but what would he have done with them all, here in Faerie? They'd have just been in the way.

And it would have taken ages to round them all up.

He stumbled over a broken branch, and, annoyed, vaporized it in a shower of emerald green sparks.

Then he was in the clearing, the bat-thing's remains rearing up before him in an eerie maze of black flesh and white bone; he marched past without paying much attention, up to the hatchway of *Christopher*.

He'd open his portal to Gregory's place, whatever it was, aboard the ship; he didn't want to do it out here in the open, where stray birds or chipmunks or something might wander through it. He wondered if birds ever flew into the Empire's space warp up there, to emerge into vacuum and die.

That was a nasty thought.

For that matter, he wondered why air didn't flow constantly through the opening into the space beyond. Did the warp create some sort of static field, perhaps, that held it back?

He didn't know—and it didn't matter.

The interior of the ship wasn't quite as he remembered it; there were dead leaves here and there, a few seats had been removed, and it appeared that something had chewed at some of the maroon leatherette upholstery. Squirrels, probably.

The lights didn't work, of course, but the matrix made them superfluous in any case.

He settled in one of the aisle seats that was still clean and intact, and began concentrating on opening a portal.

It was much more difficult than he had expected. The nearness of the space warp created a fierce counterpressure that he had to struggle against, and the relative weakness of the matrix, so far from any power spot, left him with far less energy than he had ever had available before when attempting such a task.

Nonetheless, after about half an hour of effort that left him sweating and trembling, he forced open the portal.

Nothing happened. No one stepped out.

"God *damn* it!" Pel shouted. Fighting to maintain the spell, he reached a magical tendril back into the aft storeroom and swept out everything he could reach.

Steel bottles of oxygen, purple cotton packs and bedrolls, black folding shovels, pieces of spacesuits, and a great pile of unidentifiable equipment came tumbling through the hatchway into the passenger compartment; Pel let most of it drop as he snatched up an oxygen cylinder and heaved it through the portal.

It vanished, instantly and silently, but Pel was sure it made a suitable clatter on the other side.

He waited.

The portal refused to stabilize completely; keeping it open took a constant effort, and after five more minutes Pel wasn't sure how long he could hold it. The matrix seemed to be fighting him, rather than cooperating.

He found a piece of equipment with glass parts—he had no idea what it was, some sort of scientific apparatus by the look of it—and heaved *that* through the opening.

Then he waited again.

Finally, Gregory's head appeared, and a moment later Pel's chief spy stood aboard the ship, looking around with mild interest.

"Yes, Master?" he asked.

Pel cleared his throat, and began explaining.

When he got to the main point, that everyone was to surrender, Gregory's usual bland expression turned uneasy.

"O Great One, are you sure that . . ."

"Sure enough. Do it."

"Yes, Master," Gregory said unhappily.

It was the first time Pel had seen such unhappiness on a simulacrum's face, and he felt a twinge of guilt.

"Listen, if you think they'll mistreat you . . ."

"No, O Great One, it's not that," Gregory explained. "It's that we'll no longer be able to serve you. We won't have a master to tell us what to do."

Pel blinked. Shadow had obviously done a thorough job of indoctrinating her creations—or maybe it was something in the nature of simulacra.

"All right, then," he said, "if you want, and they allow it, you can swear fealty or whatever to the Emperor, and make *him* your new master."

Gregory's relief was evident. "Thank you," he said.

"Now, get back there and get it started!"

Curran was startled to not see any officials in the prep room when he emerged from the air lock. He had expected Markham and Albright and Secretary Sheffield to be waiting impatiently, had thought they would reprimand him for taking the time to remove his spacesuit.

Instead there was just an ordinary soldier standing there, ready to welcome him back.

"This way, sir," the young man said, gesturing.

Curran followed, puzzled, as he was led out of the warp facility and into the main working area of Base One, down corridors and up lifts until he arrived at the door of a conference room.

Two guards stood at the door. After an exchange of salutes and whispers, one of the guards opened the door and ushered Curran in.

Sheffield stood at the head of a long table, presiding over the meeting; along the sides were Markham, Albright, and Howe, as Curran might have expected—but also John Bascombe, Samuel Best, Sebastian Warner, Ron Wilkins, Brian Hall, Carrie Hall, General Hart, Major Cochran, and at least a dozen others Curran didn't immediately recognize.

Everyone who had attended *any* of Curran's briefings for this assignment appeared to be present. All of them glanced up as the door opened.

"Ah, Curran," Secretary Sheffield said, "come in! We've saved you a seat." He pointed.

Curran took the chair indicated, between Best and Warner, and whispered to Best, "What's happened?"

Best leaned over and whispered back, "One of Brown's agents threatened the Emperor. In person. In the Imperial Palace itself."

"He *what*?" Curran blinked.

"She. We got word telepathically just after you went through the warp—even thought about calling you back, but by the time we could have suited someone else up . . ."

"How'd this person . . . what did she . . ."

"No one knows how she got in, but she was waiting in the Emperor's private apartments when he prepared to retire, and she told him that the Brown Magician wants the bodies *now*."

"Oh, my God."

"But what's *really* frightening," Best said, "is that she *got away*."

"*How?*"

"We don't know."

"I take it, Mr. Curran," Sheffield's voice said, overriding the private exchange, "that Mr. Best has filled you in on the situation."

Curran looked up, startled. "Yes, sir," he said.

"I believe you've just spoken with the Brown Magician—and after this latest stunt, I begin to think he deserves to be called a magician."

"Yes, sir."

"Did he say anything that might shed light on this situation?"

Curran hesitated, swallowed, then stood up and reported the conversation. He was still answering questions about the details when the telepaths began delivering the first reports of surrendering agents.

"So what's the general attitude over there?" the lieutenant asked casually.

"Scared shitless," Carleton Miletti replied.

That was different; the lieutenant struggled not to show any interest, since that might break Milettti's semi-trance. "Why's that?" he asked.

"Oh, Brown did something they didn't think was possible, something to do with their emperor," Miletti explained.

"What did he do?"

Miletti shrugged. "No idea," he said. "I didn't catch that."

"Was he trying to scare them into turning over the remains?" the lieutenant asked.

"Probably. They don't know."

"Didn't work, of course."

"Of course not."

Pel stretched and yawned as he stood in the open hatchway. He'd slept away most of the morning, he was sure. The sunlight spattered across the clearing was not at a particularly low angle.

Leaves rustled overhead, and branches sighed in the

breeze, but other than that all was quiet. There was no Imperial deputation waiting to deliver the bodies.

He supposed they might be huddling at the foot of the ladder, but he doubted it. More likely they were signing receipts and filling out forms before releasing anything. Either that, or they were waiting to see how many spies they collected before they paid for them.

After a good night's sleep, Pel was in a far better temper than he had been; he was willing to be magnanimous and patient. The Empire had agreed to deliver the corpses, he had met their terms—it was just a matter of time.

He hopped down from the ship and ambled toward the ladder, smiling.

The first surrenders were on Delta Scorpius IV; from there, they radiated out into the Empire at slightly less than the speed a courier ship could travel.

Word of the initial round reached Base One almost instantly; when Samuel Best had turned up on Delta Scorpius IV, Albright had made sure that the local government there had a telepath on hand at all times. He'd also had men search the area where Best said he had appeared, and had had a guard posted, but had not located any sort of space warp. Best's description wasn't sufficient to pinpoint the exact spot, but at least they knew which building it was—Best said he had found himself in the office area of an old warehouse.

When the surrenders began, Albright sent for a report from those guards.

There had been a small disturbance a day or so before the first surrender—objects had appeared loudly from nowhere. A civilian who had been hanging around, one of the people who worked there, had argued with the guards, slipped out of sight for a time, then returned.

They hadn't held him. Albright cursed them all for idiots when he heard that.

They had checked his identity, though—his name was Peter Gregory. Albright ordered an immediate search.

It was two days later that Gregory was found—or rather, that he turned himself in at the local constabulary, announcing that he was the ringleader of the Brown Magician's espionage network.

By then, however, Albright hardly cared. The surrenders had spread as far as Base One, and shock after shock was registering as one trusted person after another announced that he or she was actually one of Shadow's spies, now working for the Brown Magician. The telepaths were constantly busy, interrogating the captured spies—or trying to; many, it turned out, were impervious to telepathy, which explained how they had survived for so long.

No one had expected that.

And no one had expected how *many* spies would turn themselves in. The official count made Peter Gregory number 113, and Marshal Albright was certain that there were others whose capture had not yet been reported—that there were many more yet to come.

After all, these were just from a two-day radius around Delta Scorpius IV, and the Empire's full expanse required thirty days to cross.

And while no one in the Emperor's cabinet had surrendered, nor anyone in Intelligence, nor any telepaths—*that* was a terrifying thought!—still, it was a shock when General Hart's aide confessed to deliberately arranging for the inept Colonel Carson to command the expedition to Faerie, instead of the competent Captain Haggerty, to insure the mission's failure; when an engineer confessed to unsuccessfully attempting to sabotage the entire space-warp program; when Major Harrison acknowledged doing everything he could to insure hostility between the Empire and Earth . . .

How could there be so many infiltrators?

Why hadn't the telepaths long ago spotted them and reported them?

And the most frightening question of all—if Pel Brown was giving all these agents up, *what was he holding back?*

CHAPTER 21

*P*el sat cross-legged on the veranda of his tree house and glared angrily up the dangling rope ladder.

A little time for paperwork and general dithering was one thing, but this was getting ridiculous. He had been hanging around here for *days*, waiting for the Empire to make good on its promise.

He had kept himself busy. He had constructed the elaborate four-room tree house, growing some parts and building others, and then furnishing it to suit himself, using pieces of the dead bat-thing and I.S.S. *Christopher* for some of his raw materials. He had sent messages written on tree bark and shaped into gliders, rather like paper airplanes, back to the fortress, to keep Susan and the imitation Nancy apprised of his whereabouts. He had created a few monstrous little servants for himself from bits of tissue he found in the forest—tufts of fur, lost feathers, and the like.

He'd done all that, made himself this cozy little nest, and all the time, what the hell had the Empire done?

Nothing, so far as he could see! No one had emerged from the warp since that popinjay Curran had departed.

And nobody responded when he opened the portal to Gregory's place and threw things in—presumably Gregory had, as ordered, turned himself in to the Imperial police.

Well, they'd had quite long enough.

Without looking, he sent an arm of the matrix back to the clearing, a hundred yards away—he'd done this often enough while working on the house that he hardly needed to think about it any more.

The magic touched *Christopher*. Rivets flashed red and parted, as purple paint blackened and flaked away; a moment later a hull plate, about four feet by eight, popped out of the wrecked ship's hull and floated gently upward.

Black letters etched themselves into the metal surface, spelling out Pel's message: YOU HAVE ONE HOUR TO CONTACT ME AND EXPLAIN THE DELAY.

Then the curved steel sheet sailed up through the treetops, and on through the space warp at the top of the ladder.

How many more were there?

Secretary Sheffield's hands trembled as he stared at the latest list. Terra itself appeared to be complete now, as Base One had been for days; the woman who had appeared in the Emperor's own bedroom was secure, under heavy guard. Surrenders had ceased throughout most of the inner Empire, though more of Shadow's agents continued to trickle in elsewhere.

The count was over four hundred in all.

Four hundred, including generals, technicians, records clerks, confidential secretaries, and assorted others in sensitive positions.

And they had thought that after Operation Spotlight, with its haul of almost a hundred, there might still be as many as twenty left.

How had Shadow done it? She must have spent all her free time for seven years infiltrating her agents into the Empire! And some of these agents were people who had well-documented histories going back to childhood, thirty, forty, fifty years ago, but the telepaths were now saying that some of them weren't even truly human. How had Shadow managed that? Had she corrupted records? Had she somehow created false memories in friends and family members? Had she substituted her imitations for the real people?

If so, how had she done it without their closest friends noticing any change?

Had she actually been working her agents into the Empire for decades, not just the seven years everyone had assumed?

And what was Pel Brown holding in reserve? Surely, he

wouldn't give up this network for next to nothing. Were these four hundred just the tip of the iceberg?

It was a nightmare.

The list was still clutched in his hand when someone knocked on the door.

"Come in," he called.

The door opened, and a messenger saluted nervously.

"A message has been received, Your Excellency," he said, "from the Brown Magician."

Sheffield looked up, cold dread clutching his heart.

The messenger cleared his throat, and continued, "It was etched into a plate from a spaceship's outer hull. The complete text read, 'You have one hour to contact me and explain the delay.' It came through the warp . . ." He glanced at his watch. ". . . twenty-three minutes ago."

"Good God," Sheffield said, struggling to his feet.

His legs didn't want to support him; he leaned heavily on the table.

They had to keep Brown talking.

"Send a messenger through immediately," he said, "before the hour is up. The messenger is to say that an explanation will be along within another hour. Use a telepath to get that to the warp crew, if it's fastest—do whatever it takes. Go! Get going!"

The messenger saluted, and turned away.

"Run!" Sheffield shouted after him. "Run, damn you!"

The messenger ran.

Pel wished he had a watch.

Electronics didn't work in Faerie, though, so his old digital watch would have been useless even if he still had it. Spring-driven watches probably worked well enough, but they didn't appear to have been invented here—at any rate, Pel hadn't seen any.

He hadn't bothered to make a sundial, either.

An hourglass would be in keeping with the local technology, but he didn't have one, and he had no idea how he could calibrate the thing if he created one.

It made it hard to tell how much of the hour had passed. It *felt* as if it had been an hour or more since he had sent that chunk of steel through the warp, but he couldn't really tell for sure.

Just then he felt the kinking of the matrix as something came through the warp. He looked up, blinking against the sun, and tried to focus on the top of the ladder.

Leaves were in the way, but that was easily fixed; a brief flare in the matrix and nothing blocked his view, not even the drifting wisp of smoke that was all that remained of the branches that had obtruded.

The spacesuited figure was moving slowly and carefully down the ladder, and Pel didn't want to wait; he reached a magical something up and snatched the person off the ladder, swept him spiraling down through the treetops and deposited him with a bump on Pel's own veranda, in the very midst of the glare of the matrix.

"Maybe you should just give him the damn bodies," Markham suggested.

Albright turned, shocked. "Give up our only bargaining chip?"

Markham shrugged.

"Why the hell not?" he asked.

But he knew he was outvoted.

Pel kept the first messenger on the veranda while they waited for the second.

The man was terrified. At first Pel didn't much care; he let the fellow sit there in his spacesuit with the helmet off, trembling, looking around at the trees, at the twenty-foot drop to the ground, at the shifting polychrome of the matrix.

But it was probably going to be an hour before the next guy appeared, and it wasn't the poor messenger's fault he'd been sent. This wasn't anyone Pel had seen before, not Curran or any of the soldiers.

"You been here before?" Pel asked at last.

"No," the messenger said, shaking his head violently. "I haven't even been in a suit since basic training."

"Why'd they send you, then?"

"I was handy. I'm just a base messenger. Secretary Sheffield was in private, no telepath, so they sent me to give him your message, and he sent me back, and they suited me up and put me through. All the regulars, Lieutenant Warner and Lieutenant James and Lieutenant Butler, were in conference somewhere."

"What about Best, or Wilkins?"

The messenger looked up into the glare, then blinked quickly and turned away. "Who?" he asked.

"Never mind." Pel considered telling the poor bastard to suit up and go home, but just then, as he glanced thoughtfully up the ladder, he saw something glitter in the sun.

The second messenger was arriving.

Again, he reached up and plucked the suited figure off the ladder, and swept it down to the veranda. As he lowered the newcomer to the wooden beams, Pel smiled.

It was Curran, and his absurd hat was squeezed into the helmet of his spacesuit, looking rather like an unborn chick inside its egg in one of those grade-school science books. Pel was tempted to shatter or dissolve the helmet to free the poor thing, but he resisted—that would have meant stranding the man here until a replacement helmet could be sent. Or made; Pel supposed he could make one almost as easily as he could shatter one.

Instead, he waited while Curran undogged the thing and lifted it off.

He then doffed his hat, and while still wearing his spacesuit he bowed dramatically, surreptitiously shaking the feathers back into shape as he did; Pel watched with amusement.

For one thing, Curran had misjudged Pel's position within the glowing haze of the matrix, and was bowing elegantly to a tree branch.

"All right, Curran," Pel said, "what's the story? Why aren't the bodies here? I had my people turn themselves in; what's the delay?"

"Your pardon, my lord," Curran said. "We just need some surety, some guarantee, that in fact *all* your agents have surrendered."

"Why? Do you have any evidence that some are missing?"

"No, my lord; we just need proof that you've held nothing back. We were, we confess, rather shaken by how high some of them had penetrated in the Imperial government, and we need to know that there are no more."

"There are no more. I give you my word on it," Pel said. "I ordered *all* of them to surrender." He hesitated. "I suppose it's possible a couple didn't get the word, but if so, they're people I've lost contact with myself, so they're harmless." He waved the possibility aside. "In any case, I've lived up to my side of the bargain—I've turned the lot of them over. Now it's the Empire's turn to deliver."

"The bodies of your wife and child, you mean."

"Right. I want them. Now."

"My lord, if you could give us some *proof* that no spies remain . . ."

"How the hell am I supposed to *prove* it?" Pel shouted. "I gave you my word I ordered them all to surrender; what the hell else can I do?"

"I'm afraid I don't know what would satisfy my superiors, my lord; perhaps they don't know themselves."

"Well, you better go back and bloody well find out!" Pel shouted, lifting Curran into the air. "Or better yet, tell them to go fuck themselves—if those bodies aren't here in . . . in two hours, I'll make the Empire regret it!" He tried to force himself to calm down, and partially managed it. "Look, Curran," he said, "all I'm asking is this one simple thing—two corpses that I know you people already have, stored away in a freezer somewhere on Base One. All you have to do is haul 'em through the space warp and lower them down on a rope—what's the big deal? *You* don't care about them! And *I* don't care about your stupid Galactic Empire—I just want my wife and daughter back. You people have set me conditions, you've put me off, you've lied and procrastinated, and I've done nothing but go along with it. I've acted in good faith, I've had dozens of my servants give themselves up, and God only knows what you're doing with them all. And what have I got to show for it?" His temper snapped again. *"Nothing!"* he shouted. *"That's* what I've got to show for it! Well, to hell with you and your damn empire, Mr. Curran—I want those bodies *now*, within *two hours*, or the Empire's going to be very sorry! You go back and you tell them that!"

Curran might have been trying to say something, but whatever it was, Pel didn't wait to hear it; he sent Curran soaring upward on an arc of raw magical energy, toward and through the space warp.

Curran was still trying to dog down his helmet seals when he vanished.

"It's an empty threat," Albright said. "It has to be. What can he possibly do to us? After all, this psionic superscience of his, his so-called magic, can't operate in normal space, can it?"

"Not that we know of," Markham agreed.

"We've broken his spy ring, haven't we? Four or five hundred of them—he *can't* have any more."

"Then if he hasn't got any more, why don't we just give him the damned corpses?" Markham demanded.

"Because we don't *know*. He's making threats—what's he got to back them up with? We need to know."

"It seems to me that we're antagonizing him for no good reason," Markham insisted. "We're treating him as an enemy, and he isn't one." He paused, then corrected himself, "At least, he *wasn't* one. By now, who knows?"

"Of course he's an enemy," Albright said. "How could he be anything else? He's ruler of a world—of a universe! Naturally, he'll want to expand his power, and that means taking from the Empire."

"Does it?" Markham asked.

"If we give in to his demands," Secretary Sheffield said,

"then what's to keep him from making further demands, indefinitely?"

Markham looked at him, startled. "Nothing," he said, "but isn't that just what *we're* doing?"

Pel watched as the sun sank in the west. The two hours were up, obviously; they must have been up long ago.

And there had been nothing. No one had emerged from the warp.

The messenger was asleep on the veranda; Pel walked over and stared down at him for a moment.

He looked young and innocent, asleep there on the wooden platform, with his short blond hair and clean-shaven features, his uniform hidden by the bulky spacesuit.

Pel kicked him in the back of the head—not particularly hard, but more than a mere prodding. The messenger's eyes snapped open, and a hand flew up to the injured spot.

"Get your helmet on," Pel ordered. "You're going home, and I've got a message for you to take."

The messenger scrambled to his feet, and groped for his helmet.

"It's a very simple message," Pel said. "It's this: It'll stop when I have the bodies."

"What will?"

"You don't need to know that. You just tell them, it'll stop when I have the bodies, and not a moment sooner. Got that?"

"Yessir."

"Good. Here you go."

And the messenger was airborne, heading for the warp.

"Get your helmet on!" Pel shouted after him.

He slowed the ascent, and watched as the kid got his helmet in place; then the matrix flung him upward and out through the warp.

That done, the next step, Pel knew, was to attack the Empire. They'd asked for it, and they were going to get it; no more Mr. Nice Guy.

The only question was how.

CHAPTER 22

He didn't like it, but returning to Shadow's fortress was the fastest way to acquire an army. There weren't any people in the Low Forest; there weren't even a lot of animals to work with. He'd grown himself a few furry little servants, but they were hardly suitable for what he had in mind.

He had an entire world to draw on, of course, but the fortress still seemed like the place to start.

The stone halls were cold and gloomy, and Pel wondered why it had taken him so long to get the hell out of this damn tomb, into the wide green world—the sunlight might be the wrong color, the air strange, and the gravity harsh, but it was better than these dank corridors. He certainly didn't want to stay back here any longer than necessary.

He wished there were some sort of rapid transit possible between the fortress and the vicinity of the space warp; his wind-riding took between three and four hours by his best estimate. The sort of lifting and tossing he'd been doing with Curran and that poor twit of an Imperial messenger was severely limited in range—he couldn't use the pure magic of the matrix to move things much beyond what he could see, and he had trouble moving himself at all; the winds were faster and safer.

Even a phone line would be helpful, or a telepathic link like the ones in the Empire, but he didn't have one. He was fairly sure that magic could be used to communicate over long distances—he'd seen Valadrakul summon Taillefer from afar, and everyone seemed to think that Shadow had spied on people all over the world—but Pel didn't know how it had been done. Once or twice he had thought he was on the verge of using Shadow's trick of seeing through other people's eyes, but he had never quite managed it, and had no idea what he was doing wrong.

He could, he supposed, round up the wizards again and ask them—in fact, it might be a good idea. Not that he liked them much, or thought he could trust them. That could wait, though; first he needed to assemble his attack force.

He swept into the throne room, the matrix flaring up more brightly than it ever had in the wilds of Sunderland, and sent out the magical summons—*every* living thing in the fortress was to come to him.

They came—fetches, homunculi, simulacra, monsters, peasants, dogs, cats, everything. The monsters ranged from little buglike flying things the size of his finger up to a creature resembling a rhinoceros that struggled mightily to mount the steps from the entry, and from the sluglike marsh monsters with their simple tubular bodies to a thing that looked like a hundred-pound cross between a spider and an octopus, with additions—it had stalked eyes, tentacles, jointed legs, rudimentary wings, and mandibles like giant pliers.

The dragon, alas, was long dead, its head blown off by Pel's own magic and the remains incinerated. The gigantic bat-things were far too large to ever enter any building, and the great burrowers were not nearby—but that didn't matter, because Pel didn't think he could create a portal that anything that size could fit through.

Within moments the throne room was jammed full, and more were still arriving. The humanoids had clustered closest around the throne, arms or hands flung up to shield eyes from the glare; there was the false Nancy, and the real Susan, and any number of fetches and peasants.

Pel thought for a moment, then began giving orders.

Shelton Grigsby had always had mixed feelings about his post as governor-general of Beckett. Beckett was a pleasant enough place to live—the gravity was light, the air sweet, the sunlight rich, if a trifle unpleasantly reddish, and the locals were friendly and peaceful. The local flora was plentiful and only rarely toxic, the local fauna generally harmless. Of the three thousand worlds in the Empire, this was definitely one of the mildest environments.

The planet was, however, something of a backwater, well out of the political mainstream, and he sometimes regretted giving up the opportunities for advancement he'd have had if he'd held a post back on Terra or one of the other innermost worlds. A governor-general out here could expect to serve until retirement or death; a peerage, or promotion to the Imperial Council or the Emperor's cabinet, was unlikely in the extreme.

He had always consoled himself with the thought that he'd probably live longer without the stress and strain of political intrigue, that he'd given up his ambitions but found peace. He'd certainly never expected any trouble on Beckett, with its placid population of a hundred million or so, spread over four small continents and a score of moderately large cities.

He should have known better, he thought wryly.

But he had certainly never expected any trouble out of Blessingbury. The town was a resort in the foothills of the Darlington Mountains, small but reasonably modern, and well supplied with all the essentials and a good many luxuries—a place for the moderately well-off to spend their annual vacations hiking, riding, or swimming.

Now, though, Blessingbury seemed to be attracting trouble, rather than tourists.

First there were those mysterious sword-wielding corpses that had been shipped off to Base One and got the Empire to station a squad of soldiers and even a telepath in town.

Now he had a report of monsters.

He glanced out the window of the limousine; they had bypassed the town itself and headed for the meadows to the northeast, where the corpses had been found and where the monsters, or rather, monster, had been reported.

From up here everything looked ordinary enough.

The car was descending; the chauffeur had his orders, and was following them. A moment later, Grigsby stepped out and clapped his hat on his head—this was official business, and he had to look the part.

A lieutenant in full uniform stepped up to greet him; Grigsby snapped off a salute, then turned toward the meadow.

It wasn't hard to find the monster; the thing was lying dead, half a dozen soldiers standing in a ring around it.

It was black and hideous, with fangs and tentacles, and Grigsby had no doubt what it was—he'd read all those briefing papers, like a good little official.

It was a Shadow beast.

But wasn't Shadow supposed to be dead?

"What killed it?" he asked.

"We don't know," the lieutenant replied. "It was still alive and moving when it was first spotted, but it apparently keeled over shortly after, and by the time anyone dared get close it was definitely dead."

"Where'd it come from?"

The lieutenant shrugged. "Who knows? There was a trail in the grass, but it appeared out of nowhere a few feet back."

Grigsby turned to look at the place the soldier indicated—and at that moment, three pale, black-garbed men stepped out of thin air in that exact spot, ray guns ready in their hands.

One of the soldiers reached for his blaster, and an invader blew his head off before the weapon cleared its holster.

Even to the governor's untrained eye, though, the attacker's hand seemed unsteady, his aim poor; only the very short range allowed him to hit his target.

"Down!" the lieutenant shouted, tugging at Grigsby's arm, and Grigsby dropped, stunned by what he had just seen.

That first shot was followed by more; Grigsby heard the

electric crackle of blaster discharge and the dull explosions of superheated tissue where the bolts struck but didn't see any of what was happening as he dropped and huddled in the tall grass, the lieutenant's arm flung protectively across his shoulders.

Then, cautiously, he looked up from behind the carcass of the dead monster.

The grass surrounded them in broken disarray; to one side was the slick black hide of the Shadow beast. Overhead was the familiar purple sky of Beckett, but the blue-white discharges of blasters discolored it in streaks and flashes.

He couldn't see, from here, who was firing at what.

"What's going on?" he shouted.

The lieutenant lifted up on one elbow. "There are more of them," he said, "but I don't see . . ."

Another blaster crackled, and the lieutenant dove again. He groped at his belt for his own weapon. "Stay down, Your Excellency," he said. Then he was up on his knees, crouching behind the dead Shadow beast, using it for shelter as he snapped off three quick shots.

Then blue-white electric fire tore through the air and the lieutenant dropped his blaster and fell, clutching at the bloody ruin of his left ear.

"Drop your weapons!" someone shouted—a woman's voice. "If you don't shoot at us, we won't hurt you!"

Grigsby looked at the wounded lieutenant, at the blaster flashes, and shouted, "Cease fire!" He tugged at the lieutenant's sleeve and told him, "Order them! Cease fire!"

The lieutenant winced, hesitated, then called, "Cease fire!"

The louder discharges stopped almost immediately; the enemy, whoever they were, took two more shots before they, too, stopped firing.

Cautiously, Grigsby pushed himself up on all fours, then rose to a kneeling position and peered over the dead monster's back.

There were eight or nine of the strangers now—eight or

nine still standing, at any rate, and others lying on the ground, dead or wounded. Most of them were men wearing odd, primitive clothing—the same sort of clothing, Grigsby realized, as those mysterious corpses that had appeared in this same meadow some weeks back.

Behind the others, though, was a woman—a woman wearing a heavy black jacket but little or nothing else; her legs were completely bare.

What the hell was a half-naked woman doing on a battlefield?

Of the six soldiers who had surrounded the dead monster, three lay unmoving, two of them visibly missing pieces and obviously dead, the third perhaps only wounded; another sat clutching a blackened arm that hung limp; and the other two, who had taken shelter behind the monster, appeared unhurt.

A stray bolt had hit Grigsby's official aircar, and a corner of the roof was now torn, blackened, twisted metal instead of sleek purple lacquer. The chauffeur, Ben Miller, had dived out the other side and now crouched behind the vehicle.

At least, Grigsby thought, Miller hadn't simply flown off and left the others to die.

On the other hand, if he *had* flown off, and hadn't been shot down, he might have summoned aid.

"Who are you? What do you want?" Grigsby shouted.

And where the devil did they come from, he wondered silently. He had seen the first three appear as if out of nowhere, and these others had presumably arrived during the fighting, but there were no tracks, there had been no sound to indicate their arrival.

"If you'll step this way, we'll explain everything," the woman answered, gesturing. Grigsby noticed for the first time that her hands were empty. In fact, he realized, most of the attackers appeared to be unarmed; he only counted three blasters.

Maybe ceasing fire had been a mistake; if those were the

same three blasters that the first arrivals had had, they couldn't have very much charge left.

It was too late now, though; he would play along for the moment.

"You, the driver," the woman called, "and you in the fancy suit—you two go first, the wounded go last."

Grigsby had serious misgivings about this, but he reluctantly emerged from what little shelter he had and stepped up to where the woman indicated.

"Here?" he said.

"One more step," she replied.

He obligingly took one more step . . .

And Beckett vanished.

"So what's the total?" Pel asked, looking up from the unconscious lieutenant.

"We now have nine blasters," Susan replied. "However, two of them appear to be low on charge. Eight fetches were destroyed. Nancy and the other fetches are unhurt."

"Fetches are no great loss," Pel said. "Was anyone on their side hurt?"

"Three men dead," the false Nancy reported. "Six captured."

"I can count the captured for myself." Pel, still on his knees, looked around.

There were four soldiers, counting the lieutenant; he had already repaired an injured arm on one before attending to the lieutenant's ruined ear. There was a dignified elderly man in a fancy suit—nothing as elaborate as that man Curran's rig, but this fellow was obviously someone important. And the last man wore a black-and-maroon uniform that Pel had never seen before.

"Someone go get the dead ones," Pel said. He picked two of the fetches and pointed them out by surrounding them in a golden glow. "You and you—bring the three dead men." He glanced at the Nancy simulacrum. "Were they all soldiers?"

"Yes."

"Just the ones in purple uniforms, then—don't bother with the ones in black."

The fetches disappeared into the portal.

Pel stood up, stretched his back, and crossed to his throne. He settled in, got himself comfortable, then largely suppressed the visible manifestations of the matrix, allowing the Imperials to see him.

"All right," he said, "who are you all?" He pointed at the man in the fancy suit. "You first."

"My name is Shelton Grigsby," that gentleman said. "I'm a representative of His Imperial Majesty's government on Beckett."

"What sort of a representative?" Pel asked, curious.

Grigsby didn't answer. Pel shrugged, and pointed to the man in the black uniform. "What about you?"

The man glanced at Grigsby, then said, "I'm Gov ... I'm Mr. Grigsby's driver."

"What's your name?"

"Ben Miller."

"You're a chauffeur?"

Miller nodded.

"You drive aircars?"

Miller nodded again.

"Good!" Pel said. "That's perfect. You tell me what kind of a representative your Mr. Grigsby is, then, and I'll let you go home."

Miller glanced at his superior, who said nothing, whose expression gave nothing away. The soldiers shifted about uneasily; the lieutenant, no longer under Pel's sleep spell, stirred uneasily.

"Okay, don't tell me," Pel said with a shrug. "I'd think, after seeing me grow that man a new ear and put the other's arm back together, you'd have a bit more appreciation of me than that, but what the hell. Susan, get a blaster."

Susan took a ray gun from a nearby fetch.

"Now, unless someone tells me just who this Mr. Grigsby is, what his job is, and what an Imperial representative is doing on your little backwater planet," Pel said,

"I'm going to tell this woman to put that blaster to Mr. Miller's ear and pull the trigger." He grinned broadly as he spoke.

It was, he supposed, a pretty cruel joke; these people didn't know that the blaster wouldn't work here. Frankly, though, he didn't much care; he was fed up with Imperial uncooperativeness. He wanted to show he could be ruthless—and he had to do it before they saw him bring their dead companions back to life, or the effect would be ruined.

Of course, he could threaten to fry them all magically, which would be a more *honest* threat, but somehow Pel suspected the blaster would be a more *effective* threat. These people undoubtedly believed in blasters, while they probably didn't believe in magic.

It was Grigsby who spoke up, which obscurely pleased Pel.

"Don't shoot him," he said. "I'm the governor-general of Beckett."

Pel's nasty grin turned into a pleased smile. "Governor-general? Is that what it sounds like?"

"I couldn't say," Grigsby answered. "I've no idea what it sounds like to a barbarian such as yourself. And just who, might I ask, *are* you? You know who we are; who are you? Are you Shadow?"

"No, I'm . . ." Pel hesitated, then gave the name he was known by here—maybe back on Earth he was Pellinore Brown, but not here. "I'm Pelbrun, the Brown Magician. And to me, 'governor-general' sounds like the highest office on the . . . the planet? Is Beckett the name of the planet? Or is it just an island or a continent or something?"

"Beckett is the planet," Grigsby admitted.

"That's great!" Pel was absolutely delighted; this was a real stroke of luck. This first raid in his planned campaign of terror had just been intended to add to his armory; he hadn't hoped for so valuable a hostage.

He had figured that in any sort of open combat, soldiers from Faerie would get cut to pieces if they didn't have any better weapons than swords and spears, and he didn't have the patience to infiltrate an entire new network of spies and saboteurs. He did have three blasters—the one Prossie had used to kill Shadow, and two others that had belonged to Lieutenant Dibbs' men when Shadow slaughtered them. What he needed was to get more.

So he had sent the monster through, knowing it would die, so that soldiers would come and look at it, maybe post a guard; then the fetches were sent through, three at a time, to kill or capture the soldiers in order to get more blasters.

The first three had gotten killed, but another threesome had been close behind, ready to snatch up the blasters the first set dropped and continue the fight; and then, after a dozen had gone through, he had sent the false Nancy to assess the situation and either sound the retreat or call for the enemy's surrender, whichever seemed appropriate.

And it seemed to have worked. They had more blasters.

The fetches reappeared and lowered a purple-uniformed corpse to the floor. That was something to practice resurrection on, Pel thought, smiling.

The fetches vanished back through the portal.

"All right, Mr. Miller," he said, "you can go—just step back through that portal, the way those two just did. Then get in your aircar and go—but I want you to take a message back to your bosses for me."

"What message?" Miller said warily.

"Simple enough—you tell those fools at Base One that I'll trade your governor-general here, and these fine soldiers, for the bodies of my wife and daughter. I get the bodies, I let everyone go. But if I don't get them soon, I start killing hostages. And if I run out of hostages, I'll stage another raid—and probably not on Beckett. My men could pop up anywhere in the whole fuckin' Galactic Empire, Mr. Miller—you tell those bastards that!"

Miller hesitated, unsure what to say; he stared at Pel for a few seconds, glanced at Grigsby, then back at Pel.

"Go on," Pel said, with an impatient gesture.

Miller stepped forward, groping for the opening—and then he was gone.

Pel nodded with satisfaction. It would take time for Miller to get back to wherever he came from and pass the word; it would take time for the message to reach Base One, and for the brass there to decide what to do.

They might well decide the wrong thing; the Empire had demonstrated before just how pigheaded and stupid it could be. Pel told himself that he had to be ready if the idiots said no again.

And he only had nine blasters so far.

"Another report," the telepath said. "This one's from my cousin Sharon—I mean, from Gamma Trianguli II. A party of armed men appeared from nowhere, took hostages, broke into the local constabulary's armory, then vanished, taking the hostages with them. They left a note demanding the bodies."

"God," Albright said, resting his head in his hands and staring down at the desk.

"We should have just delivered them in the first place," Markham said. "All the raids have been new arrivals, there haven't been any signs that he left spies or saboteurs in place; we should have believed him and given him the damn bodies."

"That's as may be," Sheffield replied. "We didn't, and we can't now."

"Why not?" Albright asked, lifting his head. "Why the hell not?"

"Because we can't give in to terrorism. We mustn't let ourselves be blackmailed, or he'll have won, we'll have to do whatever he demands. I have His Majesty's backing on this—we will *not* give in."

Albright stared silently at his superior for a long moment, then glanced at Markham.

Markham shrugged.

"For God's sake," Albright said. "He wants something

that's his by right, that we *should* have given him long ago, and now you say that we *can't?*"

"Not while he's attacking us. If he returns all our hostages, then maybe we can negotiate. If we choose."

"We *did* negotiate," Markham pointed out. "He agreed to our terms, and did what he said he would, and then we changed the rules."

"We asked for proof, that's all."

"Proof—how the hell was he supposed to prove a negative?"

"Look, it *doesn't matter*," Sheffield insisted. "The Emperor says we don't give him anything. We don't even talk until he stops the attacks."

"And if he *never* stops the attacks?"

"We're going to *make* him stop the attacks."

"How?" Albright demanded. "We don't have any way of locating or blocking the space warps he's using; they don't produce the same radiation ours do. They don't produce *any* radiation we can detect. As far as we can tell, they can pop up *anywhere*."

Sheffield shook his head. "I don't think so," he said. He turned to Celia Howe, who had sat silently throughout the debate. "What's the latest report?"

"We've been interviewing all the captured subjects, of course," Howe replied. "It's been assigned our highest priority. Most of them know very little about Brown, or for that matter Shadow, but they seem willing to tell us what they do know, even those immune to telepathy, though of course we can't be sure those aren't lying. We've resorted to unpleasant methods with some of them . . ."

"Torture," Albright muttered. Howe ignored him.

". . . and we've been collecting and collating the data as fast as we can. So far, we have not learned of any enemy personnel who have not surrendered to us—each subject has listed all agents known to him, and so far every single one is accounted for. This tends to support Brown's claim that he gave up his entire network, however irrational such an action may appear to us—it may be that we're dealing with a lunatic."

"What about these space warps?" Sheffield asked. "Have we learned anything more about them?"

Howe shook her head. "There are indications that the portals, as they call them, always manifested themselves in exactly the same place in the Empire, though the location of the opening on the other end might vary somewhat. However, we have been unable to establish whether this was merely a matter of convenience, or whether it's inherent in the system."

Markham and Albright looked at each other. Markham volunteered, "We've been forced to open space warps in exactly the same spot—we can't get them anywhere within about five hundred miles of where one previously occurred without using exactly the same place. Maybe Shadow's method, whatever it is, has the same limitation."

"If we put all known warp locations under heavy guard," Albright suggested, "perhaps we could stop any further raiding."

"Or perhaps," Markham added reluctantly, "we'd just force Brown to move to someplace five hundred miles away. The Empire's a big place; we can't guard *all* of it."

"At the very least, we should guard every known location on Terra," Albright said. "Are any known here on Base One?"

Howe shook her head. "So far, we know of none on either Terra or on Base One. The Terran cell of Shadow's network received its orders from off-world."

"Then how'd that woman get into the Emperor's bedroom?" Albright asked.

Howe frowned. "I'm afraid I can't answer that; it's a top-security matter." She pointed at the telepath. "I *certainly* can't say anything with him in the room. But it doesn't appear to have involved a space-warp portal."

"None of this is important," Sheffield said, cutting off the discussion. "When I said we were going to stop the attacks I wasn't talking about some feeble blockade."

Markham grimaced. "Somehow, I didn't think you meant blockading the portals. So what *did* you mean?"

"I thought it was obvious," Sheffield said.

"So I'm stupid," Markham replied. "Humor me."

"The Galactic Empire is the natural end of political evolution," Sheffield said. "Everyone knows that. It's our destiny to rule the entire human species, and I see no reason that should be limited to our own universe, now that we know others exist. Shadow was an unknown quantity, but Brown—we know about Brown. We don't know *everything*, but enough. He's just a man—and an amateur, at that. It's inevitable that we'll add his kingdom to the Empire, and these raids he's making just mean we need to do it now." He smiled grimly. "We're going to counterattack, of course. The Imperial Army is going to flatten this upstart once and for all."

CHAPTER 23

The abrupt twist in the matrix startled Pel out of a light doze. He sat up and looked around.

He was in his bed, safe in Shadow's fortress; the light of the matrix blazed gold and crimson from the bare stone walls. The false Nancy lay naked beside him, sound asleep.

What had roused him? There wasn't anything out of place in the bedchamber. Had he heard something?

Not through the foot-thick walls, certainly; he reached out with the matrix and opened the door, while sensing everything that lay in the corridor beyond.

Except there wasn't anything in the corridor.

He reached out farther.

There were fetches and monsters and people going about their business, there were his dozens of hostages all secure in the dungeons and towers; all was as it should be, throughout the fortress.

The weather above was a normal, if unpleasant, drizzle; the marsh was quiet.

Then, finally, he noticed the kink.

The Imperial space warp had opened again. It had been closed for some time; in fact, he hadn't noticed it open since he had begun his little attempts at convincing the Empire to cooperate. He had flown out to the familiar spot by his tree house in the Low Forest of West Sunderland a few days before to see if the Empire had come to its collective senses, if the bodies had been delivered before the warp had been closed, or at some time while he was asleep or distracted, and he'd found nothing but empty air and woods.

Now it was back—but the space warp had moved; instead of being in Sunderland it was somewhere far off in the other direction.

And it seemed *larger*.

Pel was now fully awake, and angry. What the hell was the Empire up to?

He would just have to go and see.

Captain Hamilton Puckett took a deep breath, tightened his grip on his sword, and jumped, his eyes still firmly closed. His left hand was on the hilt of his blaster—he knew all the experts said it wouldn't work, but he couldn't help it, he still wanted that familiar reassurance, and he'd made sure his holster was slung on the outside of his spacesuit.

The glare of the warp abruptly vanished, and the red glow it made on the inside of his eyelids disappeared; he opened his eyes, and managed to catch himself just short of falling on his armored face. The drop seemed longer than it should have; he hoped that was just an illusion caused by the transition to higher gravity.

He got himself upright, released his blaster, wiped dust from the front of his helmet, and looked around.

People were staring at him—*strange* people, all of them terribly tall and thin, with pale narrow faces and long black hair, wearing flowing green and white clothes. He was standing on bare dirt; in fact, his landing had stirred up a cloud of dust. Around him were crude huts made of some sort of reeds or grasses, and all in all about a dozen faces peered at him from the doorways of the huts or the spaces between them. Their expressions were odd—not fear or anger or anything he could read plainly.

They didn't look happy, though.

Well, why should they? He'd just popped out of thin air in the middle of their village.

"Damn," he said.

The word was oddly muffled by the helmet he wore.

He turned and groped for the warp—the scientists had said they were going to bring it in right at ground level.

They hadn't; it was a good four feet off the ground. He had to back up and take his best running leap in order to get through it, and he imagined he looked like a particularly ridiculous sort of monster as he galloped through the middle of the village in his spacesuit, waving his sword about.

His jump turned into an exceptionally awkward dive—he'd misjudged either the suit's mass or the local gravity—but he did sail back through into the blinding white light of the space warp. His landing knocked the wind out of him, and for a moment he lay motionless on the steel walkway.

When he raised his head at last, he saw people signaling wildly to him from the observation area.

He sighed and clambered to his feet; he'd have to go up and report.

They probably weren't going to like this. They'd wanted someplace near human habitation, to avoid impassable wilderness and make foraging easier, but no one had wanted to come out smack in some primitive village. And they'd wanted ground level, where they could just step through, not a four-foot drop.

Well, it wasn't *his* fault; they could shout at the scientists.

But they'd probably want to try again, which would mean someone would have to make another leap into the unknown, and Hamilton Puckett had a pretty good idea who'd be making that leap.

After all, he had experience now. And if he wanted to command the first assault, he needed to scout the terrain—that was the deal the brass had offered.

And it was a deal he intended to keep.

"It's getting bad," Miletti said. "They're escalating, turning it into a war."

Major Johnston considered this for a moment, then turned to Prossie Thorpe. "Ms. Thorpe," he said, "if you don't want to answer I won't press it, but you know more about this than any of the rest of us. In your opinion, is a war between Faerie and the Empire good or bad for us here on Earth?"

"I don't know," Thorpe said.

"How can any war be good?" Amy Jewell asked. She seemed uncomfortable, here in Miletti's living room—and that was, Johnston thought, reasonable enough; after all, Miletti hadn't invited her, and didn't particularly want any of them here. It had been Johnston who had brought them along, in an effort to speed up the process of questioning Miletti and interpreting the data he provided.

If Miletti had been willing to come down to the Pentagon, or Crystal City . . .

But he wasn't. He insisted he could provide more information if he stayed safely in his suburban home, with familiar surroundings and sixty-eight channels of cable TV, and Johnston had decided that there might be enough truth in that to make it a mistake to argue with him, or to order him anywhere.

"If it removes them both as threats," Johnston answered Amy's question. "I'd consider that a good war, for us."

"I don't think Pel was ever a threat to anybody," Thorpe replied.

"He is now," Miletti said, looking up from his television.

"Secure the village," they said. Just what the devil did they think that meant?

Captain Puckett only knew one way to make sure a village was secure, and he didn't like it much. He was fairly certain that Marshal Albright knew what was involved, but Secretary Markham and Secretary Sheffield might not. Someone might get softhearted later, and if that happened Puckett supposed he'd take the blame for the massacre and probably spend the rest of his days on a pension somewhere like old man Blackburn, with parents warning their children away from him.

But if he didn't do it, he'd catch hell right now.

He looked over his men once again. In their spacesuits

they all looked alike, faceless gleaming automatons—but the swords they held looked weirdly out of place, throwbacks to some earlier century, as if they were knights in distorted armor rather than Imperial troopers.

He chalked a final warning on the board—REMEMBER! FOUR-FOOT DROP, HIGH GRAVITY! Naturally, the scientists hadn't fixed that—they claimed they couldn't. Puckett had his own opinion on that, but knew better than to say it aloud.

He put down the chalk and signaled the door crew. The big panel slid open, admitting the blinding glare of the space warp, and Puckett waved his men forward.

He wondered if any of them were yelling as they charged across the open, airless expanse and into the light.

Pel had never seen this part of his new world before—but that was hardly surprising, since he had never seen most of the place.

He estimated that he had covered at least two hundred miles so far, probably more, and the twist in the matrix was still far ahead of him, somewhere to the southwest. The terrain below was not as lush as the Starlinshire Downs, by any means—there were occasional open areas that looked like little more than bare sand, while trees were few and far between.

Far off to his right, almost on the horizon, he could make out a distant ocean, glittering in the afternoon sun. Behind and to his left were green hills. Ahead, he saw mostly flat scrubland.

There weren't any roads or villages along this stretch; there had been, closer in toward Shadowmarsh, but he had passed them all.

What the hell was the Empire doing, opening a warp out here?

And using it, too; he'd sensed people coming through the warp for some time.

And there had been people around the warp before the Empire's people started arriving. Had the Empire found local allies? Maybe some part of the resistance movement that Raven and Valadrakul had belonged to still survived, and wanted to see Shadow's matrix destroyed, rather than passed on.

Well, once he had his family back, Pel wouldn't have any great objection to that. If the matrix exploded and wild magic wrecked what little civilization Faerie possessed, it wasn't *his* problem.

He glimpsed something moving in the air ahead, and almost fell off the wind he was riding before he recognized it as just distant smoke.

It seemed like rather a *lot* of smoke, though.

He reached out through the matrix.

Shadow had had some way to see far-off places magically, through the eyes of the people or animals there, but Pel had never managed it, and he still couldn't contrive to get a look at whatever was happening there—it didn't help any that he was whipping through the air several hundred feet up at about fifty miles an hour.

Sometimes, when he used the matrix, he felt as if he were one of those poor fools with a big fancy computer loaded with expensive software that he only used for balancing his checkbook because he didn't know how to access anything else. Shadow had only taught him to open interdimensional portals; she hadn't intended to turn the matrix over to him permanently. He had picked up a few other things from the other wizards, there were a few things that simply *feeling* the matrix made obvious, and every so often he would stumble across something else the matrix could do—such as enable him to fly—but he still had the tantalizing feeling that there were a thousand other wonderful things just out of reach.

And some way of seeing what was making that smoke was probably—almost certainly!—one of them. He could sense the shape of the matrix. He could sense people, usually. But he couldn't *see* anything, or *hear* anything.

The matrix was bent out of shape by the intruding space warp, and Pel could tell that this warp was bigger than the old one in Sunderland—but why? That one had been big enough to fit a spaceship; what more would they need?

And there were people there. There were a *lot* of people there. Two different kinds . . .

That was strange; he hadn't usually been able to use the matrix to tell people apart before, and certainly not at so great a distance. Fetches felt different from natural people; so, much more subtly, did simulacra, and wizards. But other than that, people were people; he hadn't noticed any difference between natives, Earthpeople, or Imperials.

So why did some of the people ahead feel different?

They seemed *brighter* somehow, as if they held more of that trace of magic that people had, as if they were more nearly linked to the matrix.

The new space warp had come through at the center of a magical power spot, he noticed. Did that have anything to do with it? Had these people absorbed some of the world's magic by living there?

More and more Imperials were arriving, or at least more and more people were coming through the warp, and he assumed they were Imperials. The others, the strange-feeling ones, were scattering in all directions, moving away from the warp.

What the hell was going on? There were *dozens* of Imperials there, a whole *army* of . . .

An army.

There was an entire Imperial army coming through the warp.

An invasion!

The Empire was invading! They were actually invading Faerie!

How could they be so stupid?

And that explained the smoke . . . or did it? Blasters didn't work here, and the Empire had no conventional firearms, so far as he knew; what weapons would they be using that might start fires?

Angry and worried, he gathered more of the energy of the matrix into the wind that carried him.

* * *

These funny-looking natives were deucedly hard to kill. Puckett's troops were not particularly skilled swordsmen, and their spacesuits had gotten in the way at first, but all the same, Puckett thought they ought to have been able to handle a bunch of mostly unarmed wogs, regardless of what sort of wogs they were.

Maybe half a dozen of the natives had turned up with ornately carved spears, but the others had had only bare hands. Slaughtering the lot of them should have been easy.

But they *dodged*. And they hid. And they ran, without ever seeming to hurry, and those abnormally long legs of theirs could really cover territory.

None of them had said a word, none had shouted or screamed, even when Puckett's swordsmen surrounded them and hacked them to pieces. It wasn't natural.

And there must have been a hundred or more in the village originally, but Puckett could only confirm four killed—and he'd lost five of his own men to those spears.

Now, though, the natives had been driven away, their huts burned, and the village was, he could say with some confidence, secured.

And it hadn't been a slaughter at all, really. That was almost a relief. Puckett didn't need to worry about being another Major Blackburn.

Of course, with so many wogs still out there, they'd need to be constantly on guard for counterattacks, snipers, and the like, since they hadn't killed the villagers. That wasn't in accordance with doctrine; Colonel Scarborough and the rest of the brass might not like it.

Puckett scanned the situation from his position at one end of the wide steel steps leading up to the warp. The Colonel and the others could just stuff it, he thought—it wasn't his fault that the natives had fled and faded away, or that his men had to arrive in those bulky, awkward suits that were never meant for use on a planetary surface, or that they had to use archaic, unfamiliar weapons.

At least matches worked here. And dropping the steps

through the warp at the very first had made transit easy enough.

The supply dumps were arriving now, and the men were clearing away the last burning wreckage of the crude native huts; they would have some tents and probably a few more substantial shelters up well before sunset. Swordsmen were patrolling the perimeter, ready to fend off any wog counter-attack. Order and organization were arising out of chaos.

If this campaign was going to last long, though, Puckett hoped the brass would see about getting some different armament. These swords they'd been issued were a bit flimsy—they weren't serious fighting blades, they were just ceremonial swords that had been sharpened, since that was all that had been available in quantity on short notice. Some of the men were using their standard-issue knives, instead, and it wasn't just because the knives were more familiar.

Some sort of missile weapons—bows, crossbows, powder firearms, something like that—would help considerably. Even some decent spears or pikes would be useful.

"Captain!" someone shouted.

Puckett turned, and saw men pointing skyward. He shaded his eyes and looked up to the northeast.

"Damn," he muttered.

The brass had assured him that aircars didn't work here, any more than blasters did—and of course, any number of his men had tested blasters; he had, himself. No, blasters didn't work, so the assumption had been that aircars didn't, either.

But something did, because that wasn't any bird or bat or airfish or pterosaur approaching. For that matter, it wasn't any sort of aircar Puckett had ever seen before, either. Puckett didn't know *what* it was—it blazed almost as brightly as the afternoon sun, but in a thousand changing colors. Tendrils of light and smoke trailed out in all directions, shifting constantly.

Was it a weapon?

The glare dimmed momentarily, and Puckett thought he

glimpsed something at the thing's center—something that looked like a man.

Not a man in an aircar or any other sort of machine, just a man, flying unsupported through the air like a leaf in the wind, in the middle of that great insubstantial thing.

And flying *fast*, too.

Puckett wished more than ever for a squad of crossbow-men. Or rocketeers; would rockets work here? He couldn't see how they wouldn't, but he wasn't a scientist. When he sent his next report he'd suggest bringing rockets. Why hadn't anyone thought of that sooner?

But right now he didn't have rockets, or anything else that could shoot that thing down. "Maintain your positions," he called. "It may be a diversion—keep alert!"

He hoped it wasn't a serious attack—after all, there was only the one man in there. Maybe someone was coming to parley.

But how would the enemy have known they were there? Had the displaced villagers gotten word back that fast? Base One had said the enemy's central fortress was over three hundred miles up the coast; did the enemy have tele-paths, or some equivalent?

Maybe this thing was from a local garrison somewhere.

The flying thing was coming closer; it was crossing the perimeter. Puckett cursed under his breath; he supposed no one at Base One had even *thought* about air cover.

But after all, it was just one man in there.

The ground looked as if it had measles—purple measles. The whole area was speckled with the purple spots of Im-perial uniforms. Pel stared down at them in annoyed amazement.

The Empire could organize an entire invasion, but they couldn't turn over two bodies.

The invaders were interestingly arranged, Pel thought; al-most in a target. The thickest concentration was right in the center, where he knew the warp was, where dozens of uni-formed men were hauling boxes and beams about; then there was a broad ring where they were relatively scarce. Outside that was a ring of men, and then another clear area, with only a few advance scouts moving quickly at angles through the scrub.

The warp made a perfect bull's-eye.

He passed directly over it, and saw faces turned upward, watching him—but no one was shooting at him. They probably didn't have anything that *could* shoot at him.

Now, what had this place been before the Imperials arrived? Where were those strange people he had sensed? What had made all the smoke he had seen?

The smoke he could partially explain, at any rate—there were heaps of ash still smoldering. But what had they been originally?

And the people were mostly still alive, but not in the circle the Imperials had established as their beachhead—he could sense them on all sides, a few hundred yards away, as inexplicable as ever.

That was reassuring—at least the Imperials hadn't butchered them all.

He looked at the piles of ash, at how they were arranged, and suddenly Pel realized what they were.

They had been houses. This had been a village of those strange people, and the Imperials had come in and burned it all.

They had just marched in and burned people's homes.

What *right* did they have?

Those people weren't Imperial citizens. They weren't rebel slavers, like the ones on Zeta Leo III. They were Faerie folk, going about their own business.

They were Shadow's subjects, not the Empire's—except Shadow was dead.

So they were *Pel's* subjects.

And they'd been attacked because Pel had attacked the Empire. Not because they'd done anything, but because *Pel* had attacked the Empire to try to get his family back.

Damn the Empire!

Magic flowed thick and strong here; the matrix hummed

through Pel almost as strongly as back in his fortress, and he could sense half a dozen currents of natural energy intersecting just where that Imperial space warp had come out.

It couldn't be a coincidence, but how could the Empire have known? It had to be something in the nature of interdimensional travel, Pel thought. The warp over the Low Forest hadn't been near any power spots, but the Empire had been aiming that one for a particular place, safely away from Shadow's stronghold; this new one had probably been allowed to come out wherever it was easy.

Maybe it had some connection with why it was impossible to open two portals near one another. Whatever the reason, the result was that Pel had all the power he could ask for here, enough to dispose of the Imperial intrusion if he wanted to.

He wondered whether the power spot had any connection with the strange people, then upbraided himself. Of *course* it did! They were more attuned to magic, he could sense that—not as much as the wizards were, their auras or whatever they were weren't patterned and formed like that, but these people definitely had something magical about them. They must have sited their village here deliberately, to take advantage of it.

Were they all some sort of low-level wizards, then? That was something to investigate.

Right now, though, what they all *were* was refugees, the Empire was occupying their village, and it was Pel's job, as their ruler and protector, to do something about it.

While he was observing and thinking through this much, he had passed completely over the Imperial perimeter; now he wheeled back for another pass.

He had to do something about the invasion—but what?

The simplest thing would be to just unleash some of that magic and flash-fry the Imperials, as Shadow had flash-fried Raven and the others in her fortress, but Pel hesitated. That seemed unnecessarily ruthless.

He could twist the warp into nonexistence, he mused—he wasn't certain, but he thought that it would be possible. That would cut off these soldiers, several hundred of them by the look of it, with nowhere to go, nothing to do but make trouble . . . not a good idea.

He wanted the Empire to hand over the bodies. He wanted them to see that they didn't stand a chance. Cutting off the warp and leaving their men alive wouldn't do that. Simply obliterating the expeditionary force would be more effective—but not quite right, either.

He wanted survivors who would tell the Empire what had happened.

He turned again, this time moving himself toward the rim of the Imperial circle, and began to bend the matrix into the shape he wanted.

"What the devil is it?" Lieutenant Miles asked.

"Haven't the faintest notion," Puckett replied. The glowing thing had passed directly over the camp, swooped back across, then veered off to one side; now it seemed to be circling their perimeter.

But it wasn't *doing* anything, so far as Puckett could see; it flew along at a steady altitude, a few hundred feet up, with all those patterns of light and color and shadow spraying every which way, but doing nothing.

Then something flashed, and someone screamed; Puckett drew his blaster without thinking, swore, and flung it aside, reaching for his sword instead.

Another flash, more screams, and wild shouting, but Puckett still couldn't see what was happening.

Another flash, and another, and another, moving along below the flying thing, in a great sweeping curve just beyond the Imperial perimeter.

And there were men running, falling back from the perimeter, some retreating in good order, others screaming and running, as the flashes blended into a solid ring of fire.

"What's happening?" Puckett snapped.

A sergeant saluted from the foot of the steps. "Sir, explosions all along the perimeter! We're losing men, burned alive—can't see what's causing it, there're no bombs falling, just bang, and some poor fellow goes up in flames."

"Damn," Puckett said. "All right, fall back—everyone fall back. Noncombatants to suit up and get back through the warp immediately; combat troops to stand ready. Miles, Sergeant, spread the word!"

Puckett watched as his men gathered inward, contracting toward the warp. The flames had closed the circle now, and were beginning to spiral inward—that flying thing was *fast*.

Another supply team stepped out of the warp just then, their load slung from poles on their shoulders, and stood, staring in astonishment at the surrounding chaos. Puckett grabbed them, turned them around, and shoved them back toward the warp.

"Get back through there!" he shouted. Then he grabbed a man who was about to put on his space helmet, and told him, "Pass the word—no more traffic outbound! Tell them on the other side—we're doing at least a partial withdrawal! Understand?"

"Yes, sir!" the soldier barked, saluting. Puckett noticed that he wore an engineer's insignia—that was good; engineers could follow orders.

"Good! Now, get that helmet on and get back there!" He slapped the engineer on the back and turned his attention to the ring of fire.

This looked very bad. Somehow, he didn't think a partial withdrawal was going to be enough.

Pel watched as the last survivors vanished through the warp mere inches ahead of the magical flames, still trying to pull on spacesuits and helmets; he wondered whether they'd make it to safety across the airless expanse between the warp and the rest of Base One.

Plenty of their comrades hadn't even made it that far, of course; the broad burned-over expanse outside the contracting circle of flame was covered with drifting black dust, much of which had been Imperial troops. And their equipment, of course, as well as some of the native plants and a few structures left from the native village.

Now, everything was gone except the warp itself and the steps leading up to it, there in the heart of the flame.

The steel steps melted and sagged, as Pel reached out for the warp itself, and twisted hard, pouring magical force into it, trying to straighten the shape of space itself.

It resisted for several seconds, then gave, and the warp was gone. He had done it; he had closed it. He wondered what effect that would have on their machinery, back on Base One.

He hoped it wasn't damaged; then they wouldn't be able to deliver the bodies until it was repaired.

CHAPTER 24

*P*el stood in the center of the blasted clearing and looked around.

This had been a village once, but between the Imperial invasion and his own magical destruction of the invaders, there wasn't much left—just sand and ash.

He wondered what the villagers would do now.

He was tempted to just leave and let them do it—he had his own problems. He would want to retaliate for the invasion, send a message to the Empire.

But on the other hand, it was his fault the Empire had destroyed their village, and he was their ruler and protector; he should do something to help.

With the matrix, he had the power to help.

And he was curious about who these strange people were, why and how they were linked to the matrix.

He considered what he could do.

He considered building them a new village, the way he had built his tree house in the Low Forest—but this wasn't a forest; there were no raw materials to work with here.

Or were there? He looked down.

There was plenty of sand and ash, and the matrix would provide all the heat he could want. What more did he need to make glass?

Half an hour later he knew what else he needed—knowledge. And maybe practice. The ugly brownish green stuff he had produced probably qualified as glass, but it wasn't very *good* glass, and his fanciful notion of raising a fairy city of glittering glass spires was obviously not going to work unless he spent a lot longer at it than he had intended.

On the other hand, he had attracted an audience; a ring of people had formed around the edge of the blasted area, all of them watching him solemnly. These were the strange people, the ones who were linked to the matrix. There were perhaps sixty or seventy of them, men and women, but no children that Pel could see. They were all thin, with long white faces and straight black hair worn long, wearing peculiar green and white robes.

Pel tossed aside his latest unsatisfactory lump of glass and beckoned. "Come here," he called, using the matrix to amplify his voice. "I want to talk to you."

A man stepped forward, and strode calmly up, to stand a few feet away. He seemed untroubled by the light of the matrix; in fact, the way he stared impassively straight ahead, Pel wondered for a moment if he might be blind.

He was taller than Pel had realized, and paler—and he had pointed ears. It dawned on Pel that these people weren't exactly *people*, and it struck him what they must be.

They were elves.

Well, why not? This was Faerie, wasn't it? And Pel had met gnomes, and been told that they weren't elves, that elves were something else.

Well, these were elves—weren't they?

"You're an elf," Pel said.

"And you are a human," the man replied, speaking English with an accent Pel couldn't place, but which sounded somehow Asian.

"You're really an elf?"

The other nodded. "And you are called Pelbrun, the Brown Magician."

"Well, I'll be damned."

"As to that, I could not say," the elf replied.

"I never met an elf before," Pel said.

"I never met *you* before."

There was something unsatisfactory about this conversation, Pel thought. The elf's voice was musical and pleasant enough, but shouldn't he be saying things that were deep and meaningful?

Well, Pel's own words hadn't exactly been brilliant.

"Listen," he said, "I'm sorry about the village. I'd hoped I could help rebuild it, but I don't know how. I'm not really a very good magician yet."

"We can rebuild it to our own liking."

Pel looked around. He had no idea what the elf intended to rebuild *with*, but if he said they could . . .

"Don't elves traditionally live in forests?" he asked.

"This is the place Shadow allowed us," the elf replied.

Pel bit his lip and looked around. That explained it. This place was a reservation. Shadow must have put the elves here to keep them out of the way, just the way whites had put Indians on various badlands back on Earth.

"Listen," he said, "I could move you to the Low Forest of West Sunderland, if you want, above the Starlinshire Downs. Nobody lives there."

"We would starve," the elf replied.

Pel blinked. "You aren't starving here, but you would there?"

The elf nodded.

It seemed to Pel that this fellow was playing the strong silent type a bit more than was entirely wise. "*Why* would you starve there? What do you eat?"

"The earth itself sustains us, magician; we do not eat crude matter as humans do."

For a moment Pel stared blankly at him; then comprehension dawned. *That* was why these people were linked to the matrix! That was what they lived on; they consumed raw magical energy.

No wonder they wouldn't want to live in the Low Forest.

"Oh," Pel said.

And that, he realized, might even explain some of the old folktales about fairy feasts, about how insubstantial fairy food was.

That also eliminated any possibility of sending elves into the Empire, for any purpose at all—they'd undoubtedly die there, just as the monsters did, or as Alella and Grummetty had.

Not that Pel had seriously been thinking about it, but the idea that they might want to avenge the destruction of their village had occurred to him.

Well, that idea was out.

"Okay, well," Pel said, "I don't know where else I could send you; I haven't learned the local geography yet."

"We are content here," the elf answered.

Pel shrugged. "Suit yourself, then," he said. He looked around at the circle of elves and the sandy wasteland, and decided that he'd tried, and if they weren't going to ask for any help, he wasn't going to give it. Let them rebuild their own damn village. "Stand back," he said.

The elf began retreating.

Pel had never tried taking off from flat ground before—at the fortress he'd launched himself off the tower, and in the Low Forest he had jumped from a treetop, but there wasn't any handy tower or tree to climb, and this desolate circle didn't have anything that would block the wind. Taillefer had taken off from Castle Regisvert; Pelbrun, Pel thought, ought to be able to take off here.

And the elves could take care of themselves.

He took a deep breath and summoned the wind.

"One hundred and eight dead or missing," Albright said, tossing the report onto the table in front of Sheffield.

"For nothing," he added a second later, as he settled into his chair.

"Hardly for nothing," Sheffield said. "We know now that this Pelbrun either has some way of detecting intrusions into his universe, or that he has some form of high-speed communication that allowed the villagers to warn him. We also know that he has extremely effective weaponry using his 'magical' superscience. We've gained some important knowledge—that's hardly nothing."

"What good is it going to do us?" Albright argued.

"You tell me," Sheffield replied. "Now that you know that, what would you do differently?"

"Me? Colonel Scarborough handled this."

"Colonel Scarborough is out of the picture now; what would *you* do?"

Albright stared at Sheffield for a moment, thinking.

"Well, to begin with," he said, "I'd make everything fire-proof . . ."

Pel made his counterraid through the same spot Peter Gregory had used—nine fetches under the false Nancy's direction burst through, shot everyone in sight with their blasters, collected three more blasters from the bodies, then left Pel's prepared message, painted on a nonflammable stone slab, prominently on display.

YOU CAN'T HURT ME, it read, BUT I CAN HURT YOU. DELIVER THE BODIES.

By the time the reports reached Base One, however, Operation Brown-Out was under way. The message was ignored.

"I think they know on both sides that it won't work," Miletti said. "They just aren't ready to admit it."

Prossie looked up at this oracular pronouncement, made not in response to any question, but out of the blue.

She glanced at the lieutenant; he looked back at her and shrugged, then turned away again.

Prossie looked at Miletti, then at the lieutenant, then back down at her book.

Miletti was behaving strangely, she thought—but what did she know of what was normal for these people? She wished she could read his mind, to see whether the strain and isolation were getting to him, or whether it was something else—but she couldn't.

And it wasn't really any of her business anyway. She was supposed to be studying this planet's history, as part of her assimilation, not worrying about Miletti's mental health. They were keeping her here, letting her sleep in Miletti's guest room, in case one of Miletti's reports needed explanation, but it wasn't really her problem anymore.

For her, the Empire and Faerie were the past; Earth was the future.

Pel stared at the plateful of corned beef and cabbage.

He wasn't really hungry—but when had he last eaten?

He didn't know. It had occurred to him that he ought to eat, so he had had this dinner prepared and served, but he wasn't hungry.

And he couldn't remember the last time he had eaten anything.

It was obvious what was happening, of course; he was drawing energy directly from the matrix, feeding off pure magic, the way the elves did.

He remembered what was supposed to happen to people who ate of fairy feasts, though—they were trapped in Faerie forever, unable to return to Earth.

That was just an old story, of course, a folktale for children ... but he had been living a storybook existence for months now, ever since poor little Grummetty had stepped out of the basement wall. He had fought monsters, been captured by space pirates, been rescued by a Galactic Empire, defeated an evil wizard, become a wizard himself ... if all *that* could happen in real life, if he could be sitting here in a magical stone fortress, in a room lit by his own raw magical energy, staring at a meal prepared by zombies, how could he possibly say that the old fairy tales were nonsense?

He picked up a forkful of meat and chewed.

His stomach protested with a sudden cramp.

He knew why, and he felt a tremor of terror at the realization. He had gone so long without food that his digestive processes were not up to handling anything this rich; he should be starting off with a thin broth, or even just water, as if he had been on the verge of starvation.

But he felt fine and healthy—other than the nausea, anyway.

Maybe he *couldn't* go back to ordinary food, he thought. Maybe it *was* too late. Maybe it would just sit, undigested, in his gut.

Maybe he wasn't really human anymore; maybe he was becoming an elf, or something else native to this other cosmos. Maybe all those stories about Shadow being an elemental force, rather than a human being, had been true, in a way. Maybe Susan's bullets wouldn't have killed Shadow even if they had hit her.

Maybe she could *only* be killed when she had become human again by leaving Faerie. And maybe he, too, was changing into something else.

But then, how could he ever go home again? How could he return to Earth once Nancy and Rachel were restored to life?

Shadow had been able to leave, to go to the Galactic Empire—but she had died there. Could she have survived even if Prossie hadn't shot her, or would she have died the way Grummetty and Alella did?

He swallowed.

He would, he thought, just have to wait and see.

He loaded his fork again.

Then he stopped, fork halfway to his mouth.

The matrix had just twisted again. The Empire had opened a new space warp.

He put the fork down, telling himself that he had to investigate, that doing so was more important than eating this meal.

He wished he really believed it.

Fifteen minutes later the taste of corned beef still lingered in his mouth as he leapt from the fortress tower into the waiting winds.

Captain Puckett eyed the horizon warily as his men hauled equipment through the warp.

This time the damned thing had come out a full eight feet up, and it had taken most of an hour to locate something better than a ladder to compensate for the drop. Some clever fellow had finally located a set of folding bleachers—Puckett had no idea what such a thing was doing anywhere on Base One, but there it was, and it worked fine.

And they hadn't come out in the middle of a village this time; instead the warp hung invisibly above a field of barley. A special squad had captured the farmer and his family—they hadn't resisted, so no one had been killed. The residents of the neighboring farms had either surrendered or fled.

These weren't any pale, skinny freaks this time, just ordinary people—though they had an odd accent and an old-fashioned way of speaking. They had been terrified at the sight of the Imperial troopers in their bulky purple spacesuits—after the previous massacre, no one had opposed the suggestion that the troops keep their suits on, despite the inconvenience and discomfort. Helmets could be loosened to save on bottled air, or even removed, but the main suit, which was fireproof, stayed on.

Puckett was happy with that—not that his opinion mattered anymore. No one had openly blamed him for the disaster, but he wasn't even nominally in command this time; he was a "special adviser" to Colonel Bender, along to provide whatever expertise he might have acquired in the course of utter defeat.

He wasn't sure just how much of that expertise applied here. They were some six hundred miles southeast of the site of the previous landing, and the terrain was totally different. Where the other site was barren, this one was lush; instead of whitish sand, the earth was rich black loam producing a variety of crops, while any place in sight that wasn't under cultivation was either forest or rapidly returning to forest. Instead of grass huts, the natives had sturdy, well-weathered homes of stone and timber, with intricately carved lintels and shutters and generously stocked with good-quality crockery.

And of course, there was the castle.

Puckett raised his binoculars and took another look at the

thing, perched perhaps five miles to the southeast, atop the highest of the surrounding hills. Stone walls, watchtowers, overhanging parapets—that was a serious fortification there. It wouldn't have stood half a day against blasters and aircars, but against the improvised armaments of this particular Imperial expedition . . .

Well, the Empire's officers still knew how to besiege a fortress, even if they hadn't ever actually done it.

So far, the castle's occupants had shown no signs of making a sortie against the invaders. The scouts had reported that faces could sometimes be glimpsed on the battlements, watching the Imperial forces as they made camp, but the heavy gates had shut within two hours of the warp's first appearance and had remained closed ever since.

A crow cawed somewhere.

The castle was daunting, in its way, but it wasn't what worried Puckett, not really. Anyone who needed those massive defensive walls . . . well, somehow Puckett didn't think the thing that had slaughtered his men lived in a place like that.

If it had really been the Brown Magician, as Imperial Intelligence believed, then it didn't live anywhere near here; his place, their eventual target, was supposed to be somewhere hundreds of miles to the north, according to the space warp scientists.

At that thought, Puckett turned his glasses northward and scanned the treetops and the sky above.

And there it was.

At first he thought he'd imagined it, but then he found it again, and focused the binoculars on it, and there wasn't any doubt.

"Colonel!" he shouted. "Colonel Bender!"

The expedition's commander looked up from some papers a clerk was showing him.

"Sir, there it is!" Puckett shouted. "It's coming!"

Bender turned, and by then it was visible even without the binoculars, a seething, constantly changing mass of light and color swooping toward them out of the northern sky.

Bender began shouting, but Puckett didn't wait for his own orders; he clapped his helmet in place and began dogging it down tight.

Pel didn't bother reconnoitering; it was obvious that the Empire was trying again. This wasn't a power spot, but it was near one, and a strong current of magic flowed through the earth here; Pel reached down and pulled that current upward, then turned it loose.

Fire burst up from the ground, and men screamed—but at first they simply retreated, with their faces scorched, but still alive, protected by their spacesuits.

Pel couldn't allow that. He couldn't just use flame to hem them in or drive them back; since they had worn those protective suits he had to make it plain that there was no defense against the Brown Magician's power.

He reached down to the magical flow again, and brought it up, and this time an Imperial soldier became a walking torch, collapsing into nothing an instant later. He didn't even have time to scream before his suit held nothing but ash.

Then another went, and a third.

The suits made it slower, though; Pel had to manifest the flames inside the men's bodies, and the lack of air made it necessary to use more magic.

Then, as he concentrated on his fourth victim, something whizzed past him, through the matrix. An entire barrage tore through the air toward him, and he recognized them—arrows!

He turned them all aside easily, but it distracted him for a moment.

The Empire was getting more inventive, it seemed; Pel decided that he had best be more cautious. He twisted the light, to insure that he would be completely invisible behind the cloud of color and shadow, and thickened the air below and before himself, forming a protective barrier.

More arrows flew up at him, and were diverted.

Something made a cracking sound, and something smaller and faster than an arrow tore past—a bullet.

He hadn't known the Empire had guns, and for a moment he was on the verge of panic.

Then he remembered who and what he was. He thickened his barrier once again and looped back for another pass over the Imperials—he had overshot their entire installation while they were shooting at him.

There were the bowmen, he saw—or rather, the crossbowmen. And there was someone with a muzzle-loading pistol, stuffing a wad down the barrel—was *that* the best the Galactic Empire could do?

That was nothing. Pel carefully targeted the pistolier as his next incendiary victim, then began on the archers.

By the time he had incinerated a dozen men the Imperials appeared to be in full retreat, most of them running for their precious escape route, and Pel decided that he had made his point; he didn't have to kill anyone else.

"Deliver the bodies!" he shouted, using the matrix to amplify his voice so that everyone could hear it.

Most of them probably didn't have any idea what he was talking about, but word would reach those who did.

"I can close the warp, you know," he called. "I'm letting you go. All I want is the bodies."

One of the Imperials raised a megaphone—it figured that they wouldn't even have a proper bullhorn; their technology was really pretty primitive, outside of the blasters and antigravity. Mostly equivalent to the early nineteenth century, Pel estimated—they weren't very advanced at all, Galactic Empire or not.

"If you continue, we'll destroy the bodies!" the man bellowed.

For a moment, Pel was shocked into silence; he flew on past the Imperials and wheeled about before replying.

"You do that," Pel shouted back, trembling with anger, "and your fucking Empire will never know a minute's peace as long as I live! You think I've given you trouble before, you're fooling yourselves! I haven't *begun*! I can make your lives hell!" He turned again. "You tell your masters that! You go home now, or you die—and you tell your masters that if they damage those bodies they're all dead meat!"

He gestured, and fire burst up in walls around the Imperials, flames roaring twenty feet into the air, driving them back toward the space warp.

"You tell them that!" he shrieked. *"Tell them!"*

"How marvelous," Markham muttered, reading the reports. "Now we've made him mad."

"You think he's serious?" Sheffield asked quietly.

Markham looked up in astonishment. "Of *course* he's serious!"

"You think he can make good on his threat?"

"I don't have any idea," Markham said, "but it wouldn't surprise me a bit."

Pel didn't go back to Shadowmarsh after the warp collapsed into nonexistence, leaving ash and debris scattered across some poor farmer's fields. He needed to think.

His fit of temper had subsided, but he was still in no mood to see anyone else just now. The flight to the fortress would take hours, and night was approaching, but he still didn't want to head back yet.

Instead he sailed over the castle, waving to the tiny figures on the battlements; a few waved back, while most ran to hide. Then he let the wind blow him onward, across unfamiliar terrain; he knew that he could always find his way back, thanks to the matrix that had become a part of him.

And it didn't matter anyway. He had the matrix with him wherever he went, anywhere in Faerie—but he didn't have Nancy and Rachel.

He had to convince the Empire to give him the bodies. Asking politely hadn't worked. Making token raids hadn't worked. Fighting off their counterattacks hadn't worked. What could he do that would convince them?

What could he offer them?

Conversely, what could he threaten them with?

He had an entire world he could give them—he didn't care what happened to Faerie, so long as he got his family back and could go safely home to Earth. But how could he insure that they would deliver the bodies? They didn't trust him, and he didn't trust them; how could they work an exchange safely, when he couldn't go into the Empire, and they couldn't come here without his permission? Why should they believe that he wouldn't just fry them all and take Faerie back once he had what he wanted?

They wouldn't. Bribes wouldn't work. It would have to be threats.

But what could he threaten them with? He had *already* threatened them with raids and sabotage and the like. What could he say that would scare them ...

"Them."

Just who were they, anyway? Who did he have to scare?

He didn't know; he had talked to a bunch of different officers and civilian officials, but none of them had been very high in the Imperial hierarchy. Somehow, he doubted Major Southern was running things at Base One. There was that General Hart people had talked about—Pel wasn't sure whether he had ever met him.

But they weren't all that important, Pel was sure. They weren't making policy.

Pel didn't know who was making Imperial policy.

He did know who the nominal head of state was, though, and he suddenly thought of what threat he could make, even if he didn't know who he was threatening.

Whether His Imperial Majesty George VIII was a figurehead or an actual monarch Pel didn't know, and somehow he suspected it didn't matter, because in neither case could the Empire's rulers sit by and let him be assassinated.

Pel let the wind lower him gently, and landed in a forest, where magic flowed strongly in intricate patterns through the trees. Cutting wooden slabs was easy, and using his finger as a focal point it was easy to cut letters into them with his magic. The light of the matrix made the gathering gloom of evening irrelevant.

He would not settle for one. He could not risk anything going wrong, and one board might get lost, might be ignored, might land someplace too far from wherever the bodies were kept, someplace that didn't have one of the Empire's four hundred telepaths close at hand.

And he'd send these to places he'd hit before, and places he hadn't—let them know that they couldn't stop him.

He cut slab after slab, and wrote the same message into each of them.

IF THE BODIES ARE NOT DELIVERED WITHIN TWENTY-FOUR HOURS OF THE APPEARANCE OF THIS MESSAGE, YOUR EMPEROR WILL DIE.

CHAPTER 25

"He can't mean it," Sheffield said.

"Why the hell not?" Albright demanded.

"I wish we knew more about him," Markham said. "If we knew why he wanted the corpses . . . maybe we should send someone to Earth, to talk to people who knew him."

Albright snorted. "Not that easy. We cut Earth off; they've no reason to cooperate, and they've got a guard on our warp site. We'd have to open a new one, and then our men would have to find some way to cross hundreds of miles of unfamiliar terrain without being noticed, find the right people to talk to without alerting the local government . . ."

"You don't think they'd cooperate?" Markham asked.

"Why should they?" Albright said with a shrug.

"Given time, we might manage a mission such as you describe," Celia Howe said. "But what good would it do? We couldn't possibly get anything useful done before that twenty-four-hour deadline."

The telepath in the corner cleared his throat, and all four faces turned toward him.

"His Imperial Majesty informs me," the telepath said, "that we are to return this man's family forthwith."

"Well, that's it, then," Markham said, with visible relief.

"But does His Majesty understand that we cannot be sure what Brown intends . . ." Sheffield began.

"His Majesty understands quite enough," the telepath said, cutting him off. "He also desires that we proffer a formal apology, and Secretary Sheffield is hereby recalled to Terra immediately."

The others glanced at one another; they knew what this meant. George VIII let his governments operate independently up to a point—but when his personal safety was threatened, that point had been passed.

Sheffield was ruined, at least temporarily; the Emperor would undoubtedly convene the Council and the Peerage and ask them to appoint a new government. And until they came up with one he liked, he would run the Empire himself.

Whether Albright and Markham retained their posts . . . well, the Emperor hated doing the work of running the Empire himself. He would want a new government installed quickly. That meant as few cabinet changes as possible, and His Imperial Majesty might well instruct the legislature accordingly.

But on the other hand, Albright and Markham were involved in this interdimensional debacle, just as much as Sheffield was.

It was up to the Imperial whim.

Meanwhile, they had little choice but to obey orders as quickly and efficiently as possible. Albright stood up.

"Get me a messenger," he said.

The matrix twisted, and Pel almost fell. A space warp had opened, one that was fairly close, and big enough to disturb the matrix noticeably.

It was, he quickly realized, in the same place as the second invasion.

He looked down at the forest below with something like regret; he had been enjoying his scenic tour of Faerie. The mountains ahead looked quite spectacular, and he was sure there was plenty more to be seen. He hadn't yet come across more elves, nor any of the little people, the gnomes, as they were called, let alone their homeland of Hrumph.

Of course, Grummetty's comments all those months ago had implied that Shadow had driven the gnomes out of

Hrumph—they might have wound up on a reservation somewhere, the way the elves had.

There was so much Pel didn't know.

For some time he had thought of Faerie as a narrow strip stretching from Shadowmarsh to the Low Forest, but now it had finally sunk in that it was an entire *world*.

Perhaps he and Nancy and Rachel could take a vacation here before returning to Earth, take a flying tour of the countryside. They couldn't see all of it, of course—there was far too much, a world larger than the whole Earth—but they could roam about a bit.

For now, though, it was time to see whether the Empire had finally seen reason, or whether he would have to find a way to kill George VIII and hope that George IX, or whoever the next Emperor was, would be more sensible.

He wheeled about and headed back across the wooded hills, accelerating as he went.

Moments later he stumbled to a stop on the charred remains of a barley field, where two steel cylinders lay side by side, a sheet of paper atop one of them.

He picked up the paper and read, "With Our apologies for the delay, and hopes for cordial relations hereafter." A blue seal adorned one corner. The signature was done with something like a rubber stamp and was slightly blurred, but still decipherable—*Georgius VIII Imperator et Rex*. An illegible scribble next to it was presumably the mark of the secretary who had stamped the document in accordance with Imperial instructions.

"Well, that's more like it," Pel said to no one, dropping the paper and turning to the cylinders.

His stomach was suddenly trembling inside him, his knees unsteady.

The cylinders were cold to the touch. Each was held closed by two complex screwed-down latches of some sort; Pel spun the flywheel of each latch on the nearer container and pried open the complicated hooks.

He felt as if he might faint, and his hands were cold, and

not just from the cold metal. He was sweating. At last, at long last, he had his wife and daughter back.

Either that, or the Empire was in for unrelieved hell, if this should prove to be some other stupid delay.

He lifted the lid, not breathing, and looked inside.

For a moment he thought that it *was* some sort of trick, that they had substituted some ghastly thing for his wife; then he realized he was wrong.

This thing was Nancy.

She was naked, but so battered and horrific that that hardly mattered. Her skin was pale and discolored, a sickly grayish hue, and large areas were flaking or peeling, as if her skin were badly weathered paint. Her belly was a ruin of blackened, torn meat—the pirates had shot her in the gut with a blaster at point-blank range. She was half-frozen, still stiff, lying in a puddle of condensation.

One of her legs was *cracked*, exposing bone and flesh; Pel supposed it had happened while she was frozen.

And three fingers were gone from her right hand, but a moment later Pel spotted them, little shriveled pink things lying by her hip.

And her face . . . part of the skin was gone from around her left eye, and her right cheekbone was caved in; a huge purple bruise had apparently formed before death. Her eyes were wide open and staring.

But it was Nancy.

Pel stepped back and sat down abruptly to keep from falling. He felt sick and faint.

He had never thought about what she would look like. He had thought of her looking as if she were asleep.

He should have known better. Especially after some of the things he had seen since—the disemboweled bodies hanging from gibbets in Shadow's empire, the blackened remnants of Shadow's enemies, the corpses he had resurrected himself, the Imperial troops he had killed himself—he should certainly have known better.

He put his head down and took deep, slow breaths, and tried not to think about her appearance.

After a minute or two he felt better—still sick, but fairly sure he wouldn't faint or vomit.

He didn't look at Nancy again; instead he went to the other cylinder and opened the latches.

He hesitated, however, before lifting the lid.

No one had said how Rachel had died. He knew she had died on Zeta Leo III, at the hands of the slave-owners there, but only that. Nancy had been beaten, raped, and murdered by the pirates on *Emerald Princess*; Rachel's death was a mystery.

He had to be prepared for the worst.

He took a deep breath, then opened the cylinder and looked in.

It wasn't as bad.

She was wrapped in dirty white cloth from her shoulders to her knees, and whatever might be hidden by the cloth, Pel wasn't interested in seeing. There were no bloodstains, nothing obviously broken or missing; her eyes were closed. Although she was plainly dead, so pale and lifeless that no one would ever mistake her for a living child, she showed no signs of whatever had killed her. There were a few bruises, though, and her face was smudged with dirt. Bits of dirt clung to her hair, as well, and more dirt was smeared across the cloth . . .

She had been buried, Pel realized. That was why it had taken the Imperial task force so long to find her. They had found her and dug her up and brought her back to Base One after someone, probably her killer, had buried her.

Buried her without a coffin, obviously—just wrapped in an improvised shroud.

Had whoever it was been trying to do the right thing? Or had the killer just been disposing of the evidence? It didn't matter; all that mattered was that Pel had her back.

He reached down and touched her. Her skin was cold and dead—*very* cold. Like Nancy, she had apparently been frozen, or at least refrigerated.

Pel shuddered and withdrew his hand, and the motion jarred the corpse; Rachel's head rolled slightly to one side, and Pel saw the purple finger marks on her neck and knew how she had died.

But that was past. She was here now, in a world where magic worked, and her father, who had done nothing to save her when she was alive, would bring her back to life.

He closed the lid and screwed down the latches, then did the same for the other cylinder. A moment later he was airborne, the cylinders following him northward through the sky, toward Shadowmarsh and Shadow's fortress, where Shadow's magic would restore them all.

John Bascombe leaned back and smiled. The news had spread like wildfire, like the shock wave of a supernova—the Empire had yielded to the Brown Magician's demands. The war was over, and the Empire had come out second-best. Sheffield had been recalled to Terra. A new government would be formed.

And John Bascombe, Undersecretary for Interdimensional Affairs, was pretty sure that Sheffield would take the others down with him—Markham and Albright and Hart and all the rest of them.

But not him. Not John Bascombe. Because he'd been cut out of everything, shunted off to the side; none of what had happened was *his* fault.

Or at least, none of it could be pinned on him, and that was what counted.

And with Markham and the rest surely doomed, that would mean opportunities for advancement. He might not be the new Secretary of Science, but he thought he ought to be able to move up a notch or two. Perhaps General Undersecretary of Science? Imperial Adviser on Science?

He was musing pleasantly on the various possibilities when the door of his office burst open and two men stepped in, blasters drawn. They wore the purple and gold of the Imperial Guard. Bascombe sat up suddenly and stared.

"John Bascombe?" one of them asked.

"Uh," Bascombe said.

"John Bascombe, you are under arrest, by order of His Imperial Majesty, George the Eighth."

"Uh," Bascombe said again, staring.

How could he be under arrest? And it wasn't just Sheffield or the others taking a last-minute revenge—the Imperial Guard didn't take orders from anyone but the Emperor and their own officers.

They didn't ordinarily leave Terra at all—the Emperor must have sent them here especially. It must be a full-scale purge, Bascombe realized.

But he hadn't done anything wrong! Oh, he had intrigued a little, hidden a few little mishaps, but he hadn't done anything *wrong*, he hadn't been one of Sheffield's people . . .

"What . . ." he said, mouth dry. "What charge?"

"Treason," the guardsman said.

And Bascombe knew that whatever happened, whether he lived or died, was acquitted or convicted, with a treason charge on his record, even if it was dismissed as a mistake, he was never, ever going to be Secretary of Science.

Pel brought the cylinders through the front gate, up the great staircase to the throne room, where some of the inhabitants of the fortress were awaiting his return.

He didn't pay much attention.

He knew, in a vague, detached sort of way, that he had been awake and active for far too long. He had spent most of the day in the air, riding the winds hither and yon; he had spent the night before carving wooden message boards and sending them through portals into the Empire. And that had followed the day in which he located and destroyed the Empire's second attempted invasion.

He hadn't slept in thirty-six hours or more.

He hadn't eaten anything but a bite or two of corned beef in weeks. He was letting the matrix support him—and it was doing so, so that he still wasn't physically tired, but he knew he ought to sleep, he knew that he wasn't thinking clearly anymore. It wasn't healthy. It wasn't safe.

But he had the bodies, at last. He had the bodies. He had his family back.

He looked up and saw Susan Nguyen standing in the doorway, and he smiled. There she was, the proof that he could restore the dead.

But of course, he would have to repair the bodies first, Nancy's especially.

And there was the false Nancy now, standing at Susan's side, and she could serve him as a model.

"Come here," he called, "both of you!"

"Did you, or did you not, order an officer of the Imperial Intelligence Service to arrest one Pellinore Brown, also known as Pelbrun the Brown Magician?" the presiding officer of the court—Bascombe wasn't sure just what the correct title was, or for that matter what the exact nature of this hearing was—demanded.

No one worried about telling the accused such unnecessary details in an affair like this.

"I don't know," Bascombe said. "Did I? Why does it matter?"

The judge, if that was what he was, sat back in his chair. "Pellinore Brown," he said, "is a reigning head of state. To order his arrest is an act of war. To commit an act of war against a friendly nation in the Empire's name is an act of treason. Now, do you deny issuing that order?"

Bascombe glanced at the silent young woman sitting in the corner of the room. "What difference does it make? You've got a telepath there; you know whether I did it better than I know myself."

"We would prefer to have your own words on the record."

"I don't remember whether I issued such an order," Bascombe said, truthfully. "I may have. I wasn't aware that the Empire had recognized Pellinore Brown as a head of state, or that his nation was a friendly one. I didn't know there *was* such a thing as a friendly nation."

The judge glanced at the woman, who nodded.

Bascombe watched the judge's face, and thought he saw something there, something that might have been a trace of disappointment.

And John Bascombe suppressed a sigh of relief; he was fairly sure that that disappointment meant that at least so far, his answers had not condemned him to death.

At last, when he had been unable to organize the matrix currents properly in order to repair Nancy's intestines, despite three attempts, Pel gave up and found a bed.

He awoke with no idea how long he had slept, and no interest in finding out; he returned immediately to the throne room, to resume work on the bodies.

It took hours; the damage to Nancy's body was extensive, severe, and often subtle. Tissues had been burned, frozen, dehydrated, attacked in dozens of ways, and everything had to be *perfect*.

He took a break every so often; he didn't want to risk screwing anything up through fatigue.

At last, though, he had them both ready, the bodies repaired but lifeless.

They weren't going to *stay* lifeless, though; at long last, he was about to raise them both from the dead.

And Nancy would be first.

"They're in chaos," Miletti said. "The Emperor's royally pissed off by the whole affair. He's convinced the whole thing should have been turned over to the spies right from the start, that the military and the scientists had no business keeping it to themselves, and that his prime minister or general secretary or whatever he's called should have known better."

"And how's this affect us?" Johnston asked.

Miletti shrugged.

"They don't care about us," Miletti said.

Then he added as an afterthought, "At least, not yet they don't."

* * *

Nancy's eyes opened, and she stared upward for a fraction of a second; then she closed them, tight, and flung an arm across them protectively.

"The matrix," Susan suggested. "She's never seen it before."

Pel had forgotten that; he quickly fought down the glow, reduced it to a dim flickering, no brighter than a few candles. He was relieved that he had allowed Susan to stay when he had sent all the others away; he had become so accustomed to the matrix, and to his own immunity to its brilliance, that he might not have identified the problem for a minute or two, and he didn't want to waste even a second.

He remembered how the simulacrum had reacted when she first awoke; if this one did the same thing then he would know he had failed, and it would all be over.

"Nancy?" he said.

The eyes opened again, the arm lifted, and she looked up at his worried face. She looked at the beard, at the unkempt long hair, and then at his eyes.

She blinked, and stared into his eyes for a long moment.

"Pel?" she said at last, and the Brown Magician smiled the most wonderful smile of his life.

CHAPTER 26

It was perfect. It was, Pel thought, really almost perfect.
It wasn't at all like that first night with the simulacrum of
Nancy. It wasn't like any night ever before, not even their
honeymoon.

At first Nancy had asked about Rachel—Pel hadn't told
her where Rachel was, or that she was dead; he had merely
told her that their daughter was safe, that he would explain
everything later.

He knew she had still wondered, in a halfhearted way,
but she hadn't argued too strenuously.

And she had asked where they were, and Pel had told her
they were in Faerie, but it was all right, Shadow was dead
and they were safe, he would explain it all later.

And she had asked about the glow, the strange colors
flickering around him, and he had told her that it was
magic, but it was under control, he would explain later.

And she had asked about his beard and hair, and he told
her he'd been too busy to shave lately, but he'd clean himself up when he had a moment.

And she had asked how she got there, and he said she
had been unconscious for a long time, but she was all right
now.

And then she had run out of questions and he had taken
her in his arms, and it had been damn near perfect.

At first.

But then he woke up beside her, and looked at her sleep-
ing there, and he thought it over.

She shouldn't have been aware of any long separation.

She had died just a dozen yards away from him, aboard that ship; they had been together until just hours before. Yet she had acted as if they were reunited after months apart.

They *were*, but how would she know?

Was it just his own altered appearance that had let her know? That shouldn't have been enough, he thought—it wouldn't have had the emotional impact she seemed to have felt. Had she been somehow aware while she was dead? Had he snatched her back from Heaven, perhaps?

Pel had never really believed in Heaven, and he still didn't—but he had never believed in a lot of things he had seen for himself of late.

And she hadn't argued with him about anything, not really. She hadn't insisted on knowing where Rachel was, or who was looking after her.

Well, there must have been something of a shock, going from being raped aboard a spaceship to waking up in a magician's castle.

And she hadn't mentioned being raped, but all the survivors of *Emerald Princess* had said she was raped before the pirates killed her.

There hadn't been any physical evidence that Pel could see, but after all, the body had been in such terrible condition that he wouldn't have been able to tell anything for certain whether it had been there or not, and why would the others have lied?

So she had been raped—and how could she go so willingly from that to her husband's bed? It didn't seem right, somehow. That fetch he had restored had screamed at the memory of what had happened to him; Nancy hadn't. Why not?

Pel frowned, and told himself that he was worrying about nothing, trying to ruin his own happiness with all these niggling little worries. Maybe years spent as Shadow's fetch were far more horrible than what Nancy had lived through. Maybe she didn't remember being raped; he hadn't asked her about it, so he didn't really know. Maybe she had blocked out those last few minutes. Or maybe that was why she *had* been eager enough to not ask more about Rachel, maybe she had wanted something clean and good to wipe away the memory.

This was Nancy. She had known his name when she first woke up. She had asked about Rachel, even if she hadn't insisted. She had responded just about the way Nancy always had, nothing had seemed wrong or strange—until now, until he sat here thinking too much.

Had she been a little slow to react to things, a little detached?

Well, she had been *dead*.

He got up and had the matrix drape a robe about him, leaving Nancy undisturbed.

There wasn't anything wrong with her.

There wasn't, he told himself as he walked down the stone corridor, finding his way in his own light, anything wrong with her.

But somewhere in the back of his head he remembered something Shadow had said before she died.

The exact words were hard to recall, given her archaic phrasing, but he thought he had it. "I can instill therein a semblance of life, indistinguishable by any normal means from any mortal born," she had said, "yet some certain spark is lacking."

She had been referring to the ability of a resurrected person to use magic, to hold a matrix, Pel reminded himself. Nancy could never be a magician—but who cared?

That was all Shadow had meant, Pel told himself.

It was still Nancy. She was alive again.

And in an hour or so, Rachel would be, too.

His Imperial Majesty George VIII drummed his fingers on a six-hundred-year-old table and considered his disgraced general secretary, delivered directly from the spaceport to the palace and rushed hastily through security.

"Bucky, whatever were you thinking of?" he asked.

"I don't know what you mean, Your Majesty," Sheffield replied uneasily.

"We mean why did you persist in antagonizing this Brown person? You know better than that."

"I'm not sure I do, Your Majesty," Sheffield said. "I did what seemed best to me."

"We're disappointed, then. Why in the world didn't you just give him his dead wife back? What possible harm could that have done?"

"I am not quite sure, Your Majesty, and I preferred to err on the side of caution. Secretary Markham seemed to believe that the so-called magic at Mr. Brown's disposal might be able to make some use of the woman's remains."

"And what possible use could be worse for us than getting Brown furiously angry?" the Emperor asked. "And not only that, Bucky, but you *lied* to the man—you promised delivery, then balked. He did everything you asked—do you realize he ordered his entire network of spies to swear loyalty to us? To us, personally? That was more than anyone asked, and entirely his own idea, and he didn't even bother to mention it. The man was being as friendly as he could be, and how did we respond?"

"Um," Sheffield said. "But Your Majesty, he . . . the Empire cannot afford to appear weak."

"Oh, nonsense. The Empire *isn't* weak, so it doesn't really matter how we appear. Except that it's much easier to stab someone from behind, and an enemy will never turn his back, while a friend won't give it a second thought, so we *should* have done all we could to appear friendly. We should have turned over the bodies immediately."

Sheffield swallowed. "So Secretary Markham came to believe," he said.

After all, just because his own career was ruined, that didn't mean that he had to drag innocents down with him.

"And what did Albright, your other partner in crime, think?"

"I'm not sure he voiced an opinion, Your Majesty. Marshal Albright quite properly thinks in terms of means, rather than ends, as a military man should."

"A good soldier knows when to offer suggestions, Bucky, even if he doesn't try to force them on anyone," the Emperor said gently. "It may be time for Marshal Albright to retire honorably."

That wasn't so bad, really, Sheffield thought.

"General Hart will be court-martialed," the Emperor said. "John Bascombe's already up on a charge of treason, and he's guilty, but I don't think we'll hang him, as he's not so much dangerous as he is stupid. The telepaths identify those two as responsible for a great deal of the bumbling prior to Mr. Brown's ascension, and some of the mishaps afterward." He smiled. "The rest, we're afraid, was largely your own doing—well-intentioned, but wrong."

"The telepaths, Your Majesty?"

"Oh, yes, Bucky—there's nothing in the world more useful in untangling a mess like this than the network of telepaths. We wish we had a million of them, not just a few hundred."

Sheffield shifted uneasily. He wanted to say something about the untrustworthiness of the mutants for anything beyond interrogation and long-distance communication, but he couldn't think how to phrase it properly.

"You don't like them, do you?" the Emperor asked. "The greater fool you, then. Don't you know they're just people? They want to be liked and appreciated, and most people hate their guts—they must be miserable. All you have to do is like them a little, and they'll love you in return. And we *do* like them." He grinned. "They could tell if we were faking, after all." The smile faded.

"And right now," he said, "we can't think of anyone better to run things until they're straightened out than the telepaths."

He paused, then added, "Under our own direction, of course."

Rachel sat up and blinked.

This time Pel had suppressed the visible portion of the matrix in advance; he sat there looking as ordinary as he could contrive to look. He'd combed out his hair and trimmed both his hair and his beard somewhat, but he hadn't managed to shave.

He hadn't shaved for several days before he and Rachel were separated, so that shouldn't be *too* strange, and otherwise he thought he looked pretty much as Rachel would remember him.

Except for the robe, anyway; he hadn't bothered to find any Earth-style clothing. And they were in a bare, candlelit stone chamber that wasn't terribly friendly looking.

"Where am I, Daddy?" Rachel said.

"You're in a place called Faerie, honey," Pel replied.

"You're dressed funny," she said. Then she looked down and squealed, "And I'm not dressed *at all!*"

"You've been sick, Rachel, very sick," Pel said. He hesitated, then asked, "What's the last thing you remember?"

Rachel looked up at him, thought for a moment, then said solemnly, "The bad man squeezing my neck." She added, "It hurt a lot."

Pel swallowed. "The bad man is gone," he said. "The soldiers in the purple uniforms came and took him away, and he's gone forever. But he'd hurt you so bad it took magic to fix it, so I came here and learned to do magic, and here you are, all better."

"Do I have to stay here?"

"No," Pel said, smiling as he tried to keep his eyes from tearing, "no, you can go home if you want."

"What about you and Mommy? Will you go home? Is Mommy all right?"

"We're both fine, honey," Pel said.

"She isn't dead?"

"No, she isn't dead," Pel said. He managed to keep himself from adding, "Not anymore." Rachel wouldn't have understood.

"Can I see her?"

"Sure," Pel said. "Come on."

* * *

"So he's got the bodies back," Johnston remarked as he led Amy and Prossie down the front walk of Miletti's suburban home. "Think he can really resurrect them?"

"Shadow said she could raise the dead," Amy replied.

"But Pel isn't Shadow," Prossie pointed out. "He's got the power, but does he know how to use it?"

"You sound like someone in a bad movie, saying that," Johnston said. He hastily added, "No offense meant."

"Pel obviously *thinks* he can do it," Amy said.

"Or at least hopes he can," Prossie corrected her. "And for all we know, Shadow was lying in the first place."

Johnston opened the car door for the women.

"I don't think she was lying," Amy said, as Prossie climbed in. "But I think she said something about the resurrected people not being quite the same."

"Like in *Pet Sematary*?" Johnston asked. "They come back evil, or something?"

Amy shook her head, then seated herself. "I don't think it was anything like that; just they're a bit less lively, or something."

Johnston shrugged. "Well, it still sounds like a happy ending to me, then," he said.

He slammed the car door and circled around to the driver's side.

Pel watched as Nancy and Rachel embraced. He had wiped away his tears, but was still grinning so broadly that his jaws hurt.

They didn't cry, he noticed. Neither of them did. They smiled, but that was all.

But then, he reminded himself, they didn't know they'd been dead. Nancy had seen Rachel alive and well just minutes before the pirates hauled Nancy out of the storage locker and raped her; Rachel had been safe with her father the whole time, for all Nancy knew.

And Rachel didn't really understand what had happened to her, or to her mother.

Still, he had somehow expected weeping.

Nancy looked up, and asked, "Pel? Are you ready to explain what's going on?"

Pel hesitated.

"I'd rather not, just yet," he said.

"If Rachel weren't here?"

Reluctantly, Pel nodded.

"I'll get Susan to keep an eye on her," he said.

"Susan? Susan Nguyen?"

Pel nodded again.

"She's here?"

"Yes."

"What about the others? Ted and Raven and Amy and the rest?"

"Ted and Amy are back home on Earth," Pel said. "Raven is dead. Most of them are dead, and the rest have gone home; it's just Susan and I who are still here."

"Why?" Nancy asked.

"Why what?"

"Why are the two of you still here?"

"I had to get you two fixed up," Pel said. "And Susan stayed to help, I guess. I offered to send her home, but she didn't want to go."

"That's odd," Nancy said. "*You* offered to send her home? What about Elani?"

"Elani's dead," Pel said. "I'm a wizard now."

Nancy stared at him. "Go get Susan," she said. "You have a *lot* of explaining to do, Pel Brown."

Pel stepped to the doorway, but that was just for appearance's sake; he used the matrix to summon Susan with a gentle tug.

She had been waiting down the hall, as he had told her to do; she was there within seconds.

"Go with Susan, Rachel," Pel said, giving his daughter a gentle shove. "She'll try to find you some proper clothes."

Rachel looked up and said nothing. She was still wrapped in the crude shroud she had been buried in.

Together, silently, Susan and Rachel left the room, and

Pel turned to his wife, who sat up in bed, wrapped in a sheet.

"I was dead, wasn't I?" Nancy said. "I remember that man pointing that ray gun at me and pulling the trigger, and I remember this incredible pain. I wasn't just unconscious, was I?"

"You were dead," Pel admitted. "For months."

"And Rachel?"

Pel nodded. "She was killed a few weeks later. Strangled."

"And Susan?"

"Susan, too. Shadow stopped her heart."

"The others?"

Pel shook his head. "Nobody else who's still alive."

"So if we died . . . well, what about you? Are you dead, too? Is this some sort of afterlife?"

"No, I didn't die," he said. "There were a couple of times I wanted to die, or was certain I was about to, but I never did."

"So what happened? How can you be a wizard? Did you make a deal with the devil, or something? Or with Shadow?"

"I'll explain," Pel said. He took a deep breath, and began.

He told her how *Emerald Princess* had been captured by pirates under the direction of one of Shadow's agents, how the passengers and crew had been sold as slaves on Zeta Leo III, how he had worked in the mines until the Imperial task force came and liberated them all—and found Rachel dead.

He explained how the Empire had sent the survivors back into Shadow's world on a suicide mission to get rid of them, how some of them had made their way cross-country to Shadow's fortress, gradually realizing that that was what Shadow had wanted them to do, because she wanted someone to serve as a placeholder, keeping her magic for her, while she explored the Galactic Empire.

He told Nancy how Shadow had casually killed anyone

who displeased her, reducing Raven and Singer and Valadrakul to ash, and had settled on Pel as, as he bitterly put it, "her human bookmark."

And he described how Prossie had taken a blaster from one of the dead soldiers and had followed Shadow into the Empire and shot her dead.

He didn't mention that it had been his idea.

"Shadow was just an old woman?" Nancy asked.

"As human as I am," Pel replied.

He went on to explain that he had sent Amy, Ted, and Prossie to Earth, because Prossie had broken some law and couldn't go back to the Empire. He had stayed in Faerie to see if he could restore Nancy and Rachel to life, and after various difficulties, he had managed it.

He didn't mention his abortive attempts to introduce democracy and social justice to Shadow's world; he only told her he had wanted to resurrect her—and, of course, Rachel.

Susan, he explained, had been for practice.

"And here we are," he said.

"What about Raven?" she asked. "Are you going to bring him back next?"

"I wasn't planning to," Pel said. "I don't think there's enough left."

"What about any of the others?"

Pel shook his head. "I'm not God," he said.

"But you brought *me* back, and Rachel, and Susan . . ."

"Susan was right there, and I needed to try, to see if I could do it," Pel said. "And you and Rachel—I *love* you. I had to bring you back."

"Oh," she said.

Just that, flatly, and Pel felt slightly sick at the sound of it. "What do you want me to do?" he asked. "Bring back everyone who dies? I'd never have time for anything else, and I'd never keep up, anyway. It's not my responsibility."

"I guess not," she said. "So, what happens now?"

"Whatever you want," Pel said. "We can go home to Earth, if you like, and just forget any of this ever happened—but if we do, we can't ever come back here.

When I leave Faerie, the matrix will come apart, and I'd never be able to restore it, and there won't be anyone here to open portals for us."

"Is that what you want to do?"

"I don't know," Pel said. "Maybe not right away. I mean, there's a lot we could do here first—we could see the world. It's a big world, and I don't know much about it."

She nodded.

"Listen, do you want to get some clothes?" Pel asked. "I can open a portal back to Earth, and you could go get stuff for Rachel and yourself while I wait here."

Nancy glanced down at herself. "That might be a good idea," she said.

"Oh," Pel said, remembering, "but you'd want to wear something—there's this Air Force Intelligence officer camped out in our basement."

"Would he let me go upstairs?" Nancy asked.

"He ought to," Pel said.

Nancy considered, then said, "I guess I won't bother, yet."

"All right."

The conversation was becoming uncomfortable, and Pel wasn't sure why. It didn't feel right.

But why not? They were just talking, calmly discussing the situation . . .

And that was it. How could they be so calm? He had just brought Nancy back from the *dead*, turned a mutilated, months-old corpse back into his living, breathing wife—shouldn't they both be laughing and crying and screaming?

And Nancy's last memories . . .

"You said you remember dying? Being shot?"

Nancy nodded.

"Do you remember what happened . . . just before that?" Pel asked nervously.

"You mean being raped?"

Pel nodded silently.

"I remember," she said quietly.

"Do you . . . do you want to talk about it?"

She shook her head. "It's over."

"They're dead," Pel said suddenly, the words rushing from his mouth unwanted. "The Empire tracked them down and hanged them, hanged everyone involved, all the pirates, they've been dead for months."

"It doesn't matter," Nancy said.

And that, Pel knew, just wasn't right.

He didn't say anything then. He still tried to tell himself he was imagining it.

But half an hour later the real Nancy encountered her simulacrum in the passage.

She didn't scream, or even start; she simply turned to Pel and asked, "Who's this?"

"I tried several ways to bring you back before I got it right," Pel said.

"Oh. Is that really what I look like?" She eyed the duplicate with mild interest.

The duplicate looked back, complacent and smiling.

Pel looked back and forth between the two of them.

The real Nancy hadn't screamed, hadn't shouted at him, hadn't shuddered. She didn't even ask if he had bedded the simulacrum, either directly or by merely hinting.

Something was very, very wrong.

CHAPTER 27

"*Why don't you run and play?*" Pel asked.

"Don't want to," Rachel said.

"Do you want to go home? Back to Earth?"

"Don't care."

"Don't you miss Harvey, and all your friends?"

Rachel shrugged.

He turned to Susan. "Damn it, what's *wrong* with her?"

"She was dead," Susan said.

"She was dead too long, that's what it is," Pel said, turning back to stare at Rachel.

She was sitting cross-legged on the floor of the throne room, watching the changing colors of the matrix, and seemed quite content to do so indefinitely.

"They were *both* dead too long," Pel said angrily. "It's all because the goddamned Empire had to play their stupid games, and wouldn't just hand them over! I mean, what the hell is wrong with them? *You* aren't any different!"

"You didn't know me back on Earth," Susan said, but Pel didn't notice; he was working himself into a rage. Rachel watched quietly as the matrix became saturated with angry reds and began to seethe in tight little claw-shaped curls.

"The Empire had to play their fucking little power games," Pel said through gritted teeth. He turned to Susan. "I want fetches," he said. "With blasters."

"Fifteen dead," the telepath said. "That's not counting the attackers."

302

The Emperor drummed his fingers on the arm of his chair. "Three of them, we believe?"

"Yes, Your Majesty," the telepath replied.

The Emperor shot a quick glance at Sheffield, who said nothing; the telepath said, "Yes, Your Majesty, he is thinking that he told you so, that he warned you this would happen. He is also remembering that we haven't gotten back the hostages the Brown Magician claimed to have—roughly a hundred and fifty in all, he believes there were—but at least we've presumably recovered three blasters, and the others must be running low on charge, which will make it impossible for these raids to continue indefinitely."

Sheffield's expression was resigned, with no trace of self-righteousness that the Emperor could see. "He can always get more blasters," the Emperor said. "He started out with just three or four, didn't he, Bucky?"

"Yes, Your Majesty," Sheffield admitted.

"We wish we knew what he wants," the Emperor said, drumming his fingers again. "We gave him the bodies, and he hasn't *made* any other demands." He gazed thoughtfully at Sheffield, then at the telepath, and at last he shrugged.

"The simplest way is probably the best," he said. "Send that envoy, Curran, through the warp, and have him *ask* Brown what he wants."

"Yes, Your Majesty," the telepath said, bowing.

The matrix kinked suddenly, startling Pel so that he almost dropped Rachel.

He was lifting her over his head, bouncing her up and down, trying to make her laugh—and failing. He was trying to keep a smile and a good attitude, to have fun, but Rachel's solemn little face wasn't helping at all.

And now the Empire had opened another warp.

"Screw 'em," Pel said to Rachel. "Let 'em burn villages if they want to. I don't care anymore."

He didn't mean to pay any attention, but as he lowered Rachel to the floor he couldn't help noticing that the warp was in the Low Forest, in Sunderland.

They probably wanted to talk, then.

Screw 'em.

Curran explored the tree house thoroughly, evicting a squirrel and several birds in the process; the strange little servants, creatures like furry, misshapen dwarves, stood aside and let him search. None of them could speak—or at least, none of them *did* speak, so they could not tell him anything.

It was quite clear, even without confirmation from the servants, that the Brown Magician was not here, and had not been here in some time. He did not appear to have been near the shipwreck, either.

That left Curran in something of a quandary. How could he negotiate with someone who wasn't there?

The only solution seemed to be to go where Brown was, and while he didn't know for certain, the best guess was that fortress, in the place called Shadowmarsh—two hundred miles to the west.

And the only way to get there was by walking.

Curran sighed. He really didn't have any choice; his orders had come directly from the Emperor himself.

He started walking.

"Where do you want to live?" Pel bellowed.

"I don't care," Nancy repeated.

"You *have* to care!" Pel shouted at her. "*Think* about it, for God's sake! You can live here, where I have all the magic in the world and we can probably use it to live forever, or you can go back to Earth, where we can go back to a normal life, see your folks, all your friends, where I can talk to my mother and my sisters on the phone—where you'd *have* phones, and indoor plumbing, and books and TV and radio and we have a goddamn *VCR*, instead of magic! How can you not care?"

She shrugged. "It just doesn't matter to me."

Pel stared at her, frustrated beyond all control.

She had been alive again for a week, and all the initial euphoria was gone.

She didn't argue. She didn't complain. She didn't laugh. She never seemed to do anything on the spur of the moment, or show any real enthusiasm for anything.

She wasn't as obedient and agreeable as the simulacra; this was a different thing altogether. Instead, Nancy and Rachel seemed as closed and impervious as Susan.

But it had seemed *natural* in Susan, because she had always been quiet and reserved and calm, all the time Pel had known her.

Nancy hadn't. Nancy had had spirit.

But she didn't now.

And worse, neither did Rachel.

Pel couldn't stand it.

He raised both arms over his head and blasted a hole in the ceiling. It didn't matter; he could repair it later. But the boom and the shower of dust and debris were oddly satisfying.

For a moment.

Curran staggered along the causeway, hoping that he could make it to the fortress before he collapsed.

His fancy coat was long gone, stolen in the first village he had passed through; the cummerbund had been traded for a meal, the silk sash for a night's lodging. The hat had fallen off in a storm, and never been recovered.

The soles of his shiny black boots were worn paper-thin, but still intact, though one of the nails holding the right heel had worked its way up through the sole and was now poking into his foot, so that he limped slightly.

The ruffles on his white shirt were stained, torn, and flattened; the shirt itself was more brown than white now. His velvet pants had shredded, and been replaced with a stolen pair of soft leather breeches.

He hadn't shaved in almost a fortnight, his hair was shaggy and uncombed, and he had developed a nasty cough that he hoped wasn't anything serious.

Mostly, though, he was simply exhausted. A two-hundred-mile walk through a hostile country was no joke, and this country had definitely turned out to be hostile.

In fact, it had appeared to be on the verge of anarchy. His clothing had marked him as a figure of fun, not someone to be taken seriously as a threat, which had probably saved his life, as several groups he had encountered had seemed prone to strike first and ask questions later.

The Brown Magician did not appear to be a strong ruler. There were apparently several factions claiming to act in his name, and he had done nothing to settle the disputes.

As several people mentioned, Shadow had never allowed this sort of thing.

All the same, the Brown Magician was the ruler, as everyone agreed, and he was undoubtedly the one behind the raids into Imperial space, so he, and no one else, was who Curran had to speak to.

The causeway really seemed unreasonably long; why had Shadow, or whoever it was, built that fortress so far out in the marsh?

Curran staggered again, and decided he really needed to just sit down for a moment and rest, he wouldn't go to sleep or anything, he would just sit down, maybe close his eyes for a second . . .

At first, Pel didn't recognize the bedraggled figure the fetches held upright before him. Then the ruffled shirt caught his attention, and something clicked.

"Ambrose Curran?" he asked. "The Imperial envoy?"

Curran, still not entirely conscious, nodded weakly.

"Good heavens," Pel said, "what happened to *you*?"

Curran managed to mutter, "It's a long walk."

"So it is," Pel agreed, amused. "You came through the warp in the Low Forest? That was almost two weeks ago!"

Curran nodded again.

"Here, take him somewhere and feed him and get him rested up," Pel ordered the fetches. "Mr. Curran, you take your time, and come back when you feel up to talking. And don't worry, I haven't been launching any more raids lately."

He watched as the fetches dragged the semiconscious envoy away, and shook his head in amazement.

Were all those *other* warps delivering envoys and ambassadors? The Empire had been opening space warps every day or two, in various places, and then shutting them down again after one or two people had come through; Pel had assumed that they were all spies.

But maybe not.

He hadn't worried about it in any case; he hadn't *cared*. If the Empire wanted to subvert and conquer Faerie, it wasn't any skin off *his* nose—he still controlled all the magic, so they couldn't touch him or his, and he could leave and go home to Earth any time he wanted.

At least, he could if he could get Rachel and Nancy to agree.

And Susan, too, he supposed. So far, though, the three revenants had not expressed any interest in returning to Earth. They hadn't voiced any objections, either; they were frankly disinterested.

It was really very depressing. Pel no longer blamed the Empire; Susan assured him that she was just as changed as the others, so the delay couldn't have been all that important.

The change was just that extra spark Shadow had referred to. Whatever it was, it was gone, irretrievably.

Pel had talked to the revenants, argued with them, studied them with all the magical resources at his disposal, and still hadn't found anything broken that he could fix, anything missing that he could replace. All of them readily acknowledged that they were changed; they could remember thinking that things were important, they could remember laughing and crying and caring, but all that was gone. When they had first come back there'd been something, all three agreed on that, but it had faded and vanished, like a pleasant dream upon waking. It might have just been a lingering habit of caring, rather than the emotions themselves, but whatever it had been, even that was gone now.

And it didn't matter to them. That was the worst part, Pel thought—that they didn't *care* that they'd lost something. That they didn't care about *anything*.

Including him.

He had asked Nancy, one night, if she still loved him. He had expected her to either say, "Yes, of course," or to say something about how he had let her be killed, how he had let her down.

But she hadn't said anything like that.

She had shrugged.

"Not really," she had said.

"Not really."

What was he supposed to do now?

How could he make her love him again?

He didn't know; it had been eating at him for days.

So Curran's arrival was a welcome distraction. He hoped the little diplomat would recover quickly.

"Miletti still says there's nothing new," Major Johnston said, and Amy guessed what was coming.

She'd been anticipating it for the last few days, really; things had been so quiet since that one final raid, and the Empire sending an envoy.

"There's absolutely no sign that the Empire's taking any interest in Earth anymore," Johnston continued. "They're still involved with Faerie, more or less, but the situation has lost its criticality; Mr. Brown is no longer counterattacking, or resisting minor Imperial incursions. Miletti says they even sent another telepath into Faerie the day before yesterday, the first one since Ms. Thorpe—they'd never have risked that when Brown was taking active countermeasures. And apparently Brown isn't really running Faerie, anyway; he's holed up in that fortress of his, ignoring everything."

Amy nodded.

"My point, Ms. Jewell, Ms. Thorpe, is that there's no longer any perceptible threat to the national security here—

and it's damned hard to convince most people that there ever was one; nobody wants to believe in invaders from another dimension, even if they've seen the evidence. I can't justify my requests for funding any more consultations. I've managed to get Miletti into the budget as an ongoing special surveillance, which means I've got at least six months before they review what he's costing us and eliminate it, but you two were outside consultants, and orders are to end the project, which means paying you your expenses and per diem to date and saying goodbye."

"I understand, Major," Amy said.

"We'd hoped that Miletti might want to keep Ms. Thorpe on as his guest," Johnston added, "but he says he prefers to have her leave."

"I'd rather stay with Amy, anyway," Prossie said.

"If it's any comfort, the cuts also mean pulling out our observation post at your house," Johnston said. "We'll be paying you a lump-sum compensation for that. It won't be very much, but maybe it'll tide you over for a while."

"Thank you," Amy said.

For a moment, she and Johnston looked at each other, not saying anything; it had really all been said, but neither was in a hurry to cut the conversation short.

At last, Amy stood up.

"I guess that's it, then," she said. "Thank you for your consideration, Major."

"You're very welcome, Ms. Jewell, and I'm very sorry for all the inconvenience. Feel free to call me if there's anything you need to discuss—you have the number." He hesitated, then added, "And if we've misjudged, and the Galactic Empire starts dropping paratroopers in your backyard, you call me right away, any time, day or night, and then you get out of there—you've done more than your share."

"Thank you," Amy said again.

"So what brings you here?" Pel asked, looking Curran over as he stood there in his ragged shirt and leather pants, squinting against the glare of the matrix.

The last time Pel had seen the Imperial diplomat had been out in the Low Forest, in his tree house, and it occurred to Pel that Nancy and Rachel might like that tree house. Especially Rachel.

Or at least, they would have before they died; now they probably wouldn't care.

"I was sent in response to your raid on the guildhall on Iota Cephus Four," Curran said. "His Imperial Majesty wishes me—or *wished* me, at any rate—to extend his fondest greetings, and to inquire what prompted this unwarranted attack on his people. He believes—believed—that this must be the result of a misunderstanding, and asked what could be done to rectify the situation." He cleared his throat. "I feel constrained to use the past tense, because of the long delay in my arrival. We regret that we have no faster way of reaching your capital."

"My capital?" Pel looked around at the white stone columns and walls. "It's not a capital, it's a goddamn fortress. As for that raid, if it's the one I think it was, it wasn't a misunderstanding, I was just royally pissed off—*imperially* pissed off, in fact." He smiled bitterly at his feeble joke.

Curran hesitated. "I'm afraid I don't recognize the idiom, but I take it to mean you were angry about something. Was it something that the Empire was responsible for?"

"No, no." Pel waved a hand in dismissal. "Nothing like that. A personal matter. At the time I thought it was the Empire's fault, but it wasn't."

"Then all is well between yourself and His Imperial Majesty, and His Majesty's servants?"

"As far as I'm concerned, sure. I'm still pissed ... still annoyed that you people took *so* damn long to deliver what you'd promised, but that's all."

"Then may I convey to His Imperial Majesty your assurances that there will be no further attacks on his dominions?"

"No," Pel said, "because I haven't decided about that. I may just attack again, if I feel like it. But I'm not currently planning anything."

Curran hesitated. "His Imperial Majesty may not find that entirely reassuring."

"Fuck His Imperial Majesty, then," Pel said. "It's the best answer he's going to get."

Curran swallowed uneasily. "There are two other matters," he said.

"What?" Pel asked. He was getting tired of this. Curran wasn't anywhere near as funny without his fancy costume.

Of course, not much was really funny anymore, with Nancy and Rachel the way they were.

"The lesser is to ask, on my own behalf as much as my government's, if it would be possible for you to transport me back to the Empire magically, to save me the journey back to the forests of Sunderland."

"Sure," Pel agreed. "I can't guarantee where in the Empire you'll come out, though; I never learned all the place names."

"Thank you, sir." Curran bowed.

"What's the other?"

"Please remember, sir, that I have been out of touch for almost a fortnight, so this may no longer be relevant, but part of my original charge was to request the return of the hostages you took in the course of the prolonged misunderstanding between yourself and certain former ministers of His Imperial Majesty's government. It was His Imperial Majesty's understanding, perhaps faulty, that they were to be returned when the bodies of your wife and daughter had been delivered. That was done some time ago."

"The hostages," Pel said. His last trace of good humor vanished. Curran was no longer funny at all.

Pel had completely forgotten about the hostages. They were undoubtedly still somewhere in the dungeons beneath the fortress—Shadow had burrowed out miles of dreary passages, lined with cells and chambers, and Pel had ordered the prisoners taken there and looked after . . .

And then he'd forgotten all about them.

"Yes, sir," Curran said. "I was told that there were over

a hundred, including His Excellency Shelton Grigsby, governor-general of Beckett."

"No," Pel said, "you can't have them. I'm keeping them."

"But, sir . . ."

"You tell His Imperial Flatulence that I'm keeping them until he gives back all my spies, *and* gets all his spies out of Faerie, and *proves* it. He expected me to prove it when my people turned themselves in, let's see how *he* does it!"

"Sir, His Imperial Majesty had no part in that unfortunate . . ."

"It's his fucking empire, isn't it?" Pel demanded.

Curran struggled for words.

"Then it's his goddamn responsibility." He shifted in his throne. "I've had enough of this. Just shut up for a few minutes, Curran, and I'll open a portal for you—but I'll send the hostages back when I'm good and ready, and not a moment before."

Curran hesitated, opened his mouth, closed it—then bowed, and stepped back.

Pel reached out into the matrix and began preparing a portal into the Empire. As he did, he tried not to think about those neglected and forgotten hostages.

He wondered where they all were, and whether they were still alive.

"I hate to pull it," Johnston said, looking over the latest budget statement. "We don't have anyone who can watch Faerie for us the way Miletti watches the Empire. And Brown might turn up at any time."

"Well, sir, what if he does?" the lieutenant asked. "Won't that mean it's all over?"

"Except for the lawsuits," Johnston agreed. "His sisters are trying to have him declared legally dead, and they're fighting his mortgage company, which wants to foreclose, and he's got some problems with unfinished business from his consulting firm."

"None of that's really any of our concern, though, is it, sir?"

"The mortgage might be, but no, not really," Johnston admitted, putting down the clipboard. "All right, we pull out, and his sisters can have the house."

Pel sat on his throne and stared for a long, long moment at the empty air where Curran had stepped through the portal to the Empire—to somewhere in the Empire, Pel didn't know where. He hadn't worried about which portal he had opened.

All those hostages . . . He still had all those people down in the dungeons, and he'd completely forgotten about them.

But what did it really matter? What did anything matter, if his wife and daughter didn't love him anymore?

He looked up at the hole in the throne-room ceiling, raised a hand—then lowered it again.

What did *any* of it matter?

CHAPTER 28

"*He didn't say what he wanted from us?*" the Emperor asked, baffled.

The telepath replied, "Mr. Curran says it was his impression that Mr. Brown didn't really want anything. It was his impression that Mr. Brown was depressed about something, and simply didn't want to deal with us."

"We don't understand," the Emperor said. "Ask Mr. Curran if he thinks further approaches might be more productive."

The telepath did not reply for several seconds, as the question and answer were relayed. Then he said, "It's Mr. Curran's belief that further approaches by representatives of the Empire might be productive, but might equally well be disastrous—Mr. Brown is, Mr. Curran judges, in a state of extreme whimsicality, liable to do anything at all, for no reason whatsoever."

"And he might launch another raid at any time?"

"So he said, Your Majesty."

"And he's not returning the hostages?"

"He is not, Your Majesty."

"That's intolerable. Really."

"Yes, Your Majesty."

His Imperial Majesty George VIII marched back and forth along the antique carpet, thinking hard. "We don't understand this man," he muttered. "And we can't send one of you to read his mind, because you can't. And those spies of his that we spoke to knew nothing about him. He's an enigma, an alien ..."

314

He stopped pacing and looked up.

"What about his family?" he asked.

"His wife and daughter . . ." the telepath began.

"No, no, we know about them," the Emperor said, dismissing Nancy and Rachel with a wave of his hand. "Does he have no brothers or sisters, no close friends we might interview?"

"I don't know, Your Majesty. There were the other Earthpeople who traveled with him . . ."

"Yes, there were!" the Emperor said, raising a finger triumphantly. "Yes, exactly! There were those women, what were the names . . ."

"Amy Jewell, Your Majesty, and Susan Nguyen, and there was the madman, Ted Deranian."

"Yes, well, a madman won't do us any good, but what about the others?"

"Susan Nguyen appears to be living in the fortress in Faerie, Your Majesty, and Amy Jewell has returned to her home on Earth."

"Has she?"

"Yes, Your Majesty."

"And is she, by any chance, the one whose home lies almost directly below our arrival point on Earth?"

"Yes, Your Majesty, she is."

"Oh, that's excellent, then! Fetch her immediately!"

The telepath blinked. "Your Majesty?"

"Oh, read our bloody mind, will you? It's so much quicker."

"Yes, Your Majesty," the telepath agreed.

"They want the Jewell woman to talk to Brown," Miletti said, between gulps of bourbon.

"What for?" the lieutenant asked, startled.

"How the bloody hell should I know?" Miletti shouted at him. He threw the glass of bourbon on the rocks at the lieutenant's head, but missed. He glared angrily, then realized his drink was gone and snatched up the half-empty bottle, cuddling it close.

"How should I know?" he repeated. "How do I know any of this?"

He swigged bourbon.

The lieutenant watched him warily for a moment, then went to call the major.

Amy marveled at her kitchen.

When the Air Force men had pulled out they had cleaned up, and had done, she had to admit, a better job on the kitchen than Amy had ever done herself. The place was spotless.

The rest of the house wasn't quite so good—there was a cigarette burn on her couch, and some sort of brown stain on the carpet in the upstairs hall, though mostly it was all right.

The kitchen was wonderful, though; it shone, from the chrome faucets to the brass-plated doorknobs. They had even scrubbed the windows.

She looked out through the sparkling-clean glass at the remains of I.S.S. *Ruthless*, still lying out there in her yard.

She remembered someone saying that some of the machinery aboard was partly made of platinum; maybe she could salvage that and sell it to a jeweler?

Or maybe she could sell the whole thing to an amusement park somewhere—she ought to be able to get at least the cost of hauling it away.

"It's still there," Prossie said, as she leaned over Amy's shoulder.

"A little bit of home, huh?" Amy asked.

Prossie shook her head. "Maybe," she said, "but it's not anything I'm nostalgic about."

"No?"

"No. I miss my family, and I miss my talent, but I don't miss being in the military. And actually, even though I miss being able to read minds, it's nice to be alone sometimes, too, to know that my thoughts are my own." She stepped back, away from Amy. "I don't suppose that's anything you'd understand—your thoughts have *always* been your own."

"Well, the way you mean, yes," Amy agreed, "but there were certainly times when I paid too much attention to what other people thought." She hesitated, and asked, "Have you settled on what you want to do yet?"

"I want to study psychology," Prossie said, "and probably become a therapist—that's the right word?"

Amy nodded.

Prossie smiled wryly. "After all, I'm the only person on this planet who's ever *really* known what other people are thinking." She sighed. "But it's going to be expensive, isn't it? I'm still not used to worrying about money like this; back home . . . I mean, back in the Empire, I was government property, and everything I wanted was either provided for me or forbidden."

"Maybe we can find you a scholarship somewhere."

"I wouldn't know how to begin," Prossie said. "And after all, I don't even have a . . . a diploma?"

"That's the word," Amy agreed. "But we can get you a GED easily enough, I'm sure."

"I hope . . ."

Prossie stopped in midsentence, her mouth falling open.

Amy whirled, guessing even before she looked out the window what had so surprised Prossie.

The ladder that had unrolled out of thin air was still dancing and swinging, not yet settled into place.

Pel stared moodily at the two Nancys as they sat talking over their dinner.

He hadn't bothered to eat lately; somehow, it didn't seem to matter. All the others had to eat, though.

Usually he didn't watch, but he had happened along the corridor as the Nancys and Rachel and Susan were dining, and had looked in, and there they were.

He wondered what they talked about. Neither of them showed any interest in talking to *him*. The simulacrum was always ready and eager to do what he told her, but she wasn't much of a conversationalist, in his experience.

And the revenant—he no longer thought of her as "the real Nancy"—was always polite, but disinterested.

Rachel was listening solemnly to both women. Pel had noticed that she seemed unable to tell them apart, and called them both "Mommy."

Pel had no trouble distinguishing between them, so long as they were awake—their manner was sufficiently different that he could tell which was which the moment a word was said or an expression displayed.

But he wasn't sure he cared anymore.

He wasn't sure he cared about *anything*.

He had planned to go down to the dungeons and find the hostages, something he'd been meaning to do for a couple of days now, but now he reconsidered.

What did he care where they were, or what shape they were in?

What did it matter?

He was the Brown Magician; he could do anything he wanted, could have anything he wanted.

But he didn't know what he wanted.

No one answered at the number Major Johnston had given her; Amy slammed the phone down angrily, then picked it up and dialed again.

It rang and rang, without response.

So much for all his fine assurances!

She turned back to the window, bent down, and looked up.

A spacesuited figure was climbing slowly down the ladder, with a white flag clutched in one gauntlet and an immense pack on his back.

That flag was promising; they weren't coming in with drawn weapons. Amy still wasn't inclined to trust them.

Major Johnston had told her to flee if any Imperials showed up, but he had also told her to call first, and she hadn't gotten through. Didn't the man have phone mail, or an answering machine, or something? It was incredibly inconsiderate of him to have stranded her like this.

She heard a car on the road out front, which was nothing

unusual, and she would not ordinarily have even noticed it consciously—except this one stopped. She heard tires on gravel, and then the engine died.

She looked, but couldn't see anything from her post in the kitchen.

"Here, you watch out back," she told Prossie, handing her the phone. "If anyone answers the damn phone, tell them what's happening."

Prossie silently accepted the receiver as if she expected it to explode at any second, and Amy marched through the archway to the living room, where she looked out the front window.

The car out front was dark blue, with U.S. AIR FORCE stenciled on the door, and a familiar figure was climbing out. No wonder she hadn't been able to reach him at his office! He must have been on his way even before the ladder appeared. Miletti must have delivered a warning.

Why the hell hadn't Johnston called ahead, to tell her he was coming?

She strode to the front door and flung it open, but before she could say a word, Johnston called, "Ms. Jewell! Are you all right?"

"I'm fine," she called back.

She started to gesture and say more, but Johnston called, "We saw the ladder as we drove up—is someone coming down?"

"Yes," she called.

Johnston turned and nodded to the uniformed man who had just climbed out the other side of the car. "Come on," he said.

Side by side, the two men trotted around the house.

Annoyed, Amy stepped in and closed the door, then marched back through to the kitchen.

"He's just reaching the ground," Prossie announced.

She was still holding the phone; Amy took it from her and hung it up. Then she looked out the window over the sink.

Sure enough, the Imperial was on the ground and undogging his helmet, the white flag still in his hand.

Johnston and the other man—a lieutenant, was he?—were coming into sight around the corner of the house.

The man lifted his helmet off and said something, but Amy couldn't hear it.

Johnston answered, and she couldn't make that out, either.

Damn it, she thought, this was *her yard*, and if people were going to talk here she wanted to hear what was said. The man looked harmless, and there weren't any more coming down the ladder, she could see that for herself.

She opened the back door and stepped out before Prossie could say a single word in protest.

The man in the spacesuit turned to her the moment she emerged and said, "Miss Jewell?"

"*Ms.* Jewell," she corrected him.

"You don't have to talk to him, Ms. Jewell," Johnston called.

"But *I* must talk to *Mrs.* Jewell," the Imperial said. "That's my assignment."

Amy blinked in surprise. "What?" she said.

"You don't have to be involved, Amy," Johnston said.

"That's all right, Major," she said, "I want to hear this."

The Imperial smiled, glanced at Major Johnston, then took a step toward Amy and began his explanation.

"We could just leave him alone and hope for the best," Sheffield suggested.

The Emperor nodded. "We could, Bucky," he said, "but hoping for the best generally isn't the best way to get it."

"You think *I* can talk sense into him?" Amy said, a hand to her chest.

"We think you have a better chance than anyone else," the Imperial envoy said. "If you're willing, I have a spacesuit in my pack that we think will fit you."

"What about his . . ."

Amy stopped.

She had never met Pel's mother or sisters, but she had heard him talk about them. His mother was not a well woman, and Amy couldn't imagine how she would cope with finding out that not only were there other universes, but her son was now the absolute ruler of one.

And besides, that would take so long—locating them, and explaining everything, and talking them into it.

And she was curious—what had happened, all these weeks since she had returned to Earth? Miletti's reports had given her a vague idea, but she didn't really *know*, and she was curious. Why was Pel behaving so unpleasantly? What horrible things had the Empire done to him? What had really happened to Nancy and Rachel—had Pel been able to resurrect them?

And there was another point. "Will you pay me?" she asked. "In gold?"

Johnston shifted his weight uneasily. The Imperial blinked in surprise.

"I'm sure that could be arranged," he said.

"Good," Amy replied. She started to say, "Let's go," and then remembered something.

Prossie was watching from the house. "Can you get an Imperial pardon for Proserpine Thorpe?" Amy asked.

The Imperial frowned. "That's the rogue telepath?"

Amy nodded, waiting.

"I don't know," the Imperial said. "I wasn't authorized to say anything about that." He looked unhappy. "Will you wait while I report in and ask?"

Amy looked at him, then at Prossie's face in the kitchen window, then at Johnston and the lieutenant.

"No," she said, "let's go. Major, would you please see that Prossie's all right till I get back?"

Then she stepped forward, reaching for the Imperial's pack.

Pel was sprawled across his throne, staring up at the still-unrepaired hole in the ceiling, when he felt the space warp in the Low Forest reopen.

Another spy, he supposed. He wondered idly what the spies were finding out that was worth reporting back.

Maybe he should go see for himself. Back before he had

resurrected Rachel and the second Nancy, he had been thinking about touring Faerie; maybe he should do that. Nancy and Rachel weren't interested, but who cared what they thought?

Maybe he should just kill everybody. Reduce the Nancys and Susan and Rachel to ash, and then go flying about frying anyone he came across.

There was the spy, coming through the warp. He could feel it.

He thought about going back to Earth, but if he didn't bring Nancy and Rachel he would have to explain what had happened to them, and he might well wind up either in the loony bin or on trial for murder.

And if he did bring them, he would have to explain why they were so ... so ... so *dead*.

And he would have to live with them, and that house in Germantown was a lot smaller than Shadow's fortress.

And his business must have collapsed into utter ruin long ago. If any of his clients still remembered him, it was probably as someone who had skipped out on a breach-of-contract suit.

Poor Silly Cat must surely be dead.

What was there to go back to? Here he was immortal and all-powerful ...

A second person had come through the warp; that was a trifle out of the ordinary. The Empire had mostly sent singles, not pairs.

If he went back, and took Nancy and Rachel, and no one noticed how their personalities had changed, there were other differences that someone would notice eventually. It had taken Pel some time to realize, himself.

As far as he could see, their hair and fingernails no longer grew. Nancy hadn't had her period since she died— Pel suspected that neither had Susan, but he hadn't yet asked her outright.

He suspected that Rachel wasn't growing, that she would remain six, physiologically, for the rest of her life.

Or maybe all of that had something to do with the magic

here in Faerie, and would reverse itself back on Earth—but if it didn't, how could he explain it?

A *third* person through the warp—how odd!

And if it did reverse . . . did that mean that they were immortal here in Faerie, but mortal on Earth? Could he ask them to give up eternal life?

He didn't know what he could ask. They owed him their lives, after all.

And he didn't *know* what would happen back on Earth.

And they wouldn't give any opinion on the subject, they both insisted they didn't care.

A fourth?

Pel blinked and sat up.

Maybe this wasn't just another spy mission. He waited.

A fifth. Then a sixth. Then a seventh.

Then nothing; he waited, but no more emerged.

Still, seven people—that was really a bit much.

He decided to go see what they wanted.

The Empire had obviously learned a few tricks, Amy thought as she looked at her escort.

Five of them still wore their gaudy purple uniforms and blond crew cuts, but there wasn't a blaster in sight; instead, they carried swords. Very practical-looking swords. And they wore daggers on their belts. Two of them had crossbows slung on their backs, with bandoliers of quarrels.

The sixth man had the appearance of a native guide; he wore a gray woolen tunic with a purple armband on each sleeve. He had a dagger, as well, but no sword; he had been introduced back at Base One as Samuel Best, and although no one had mentioned a rank, and there was no sign that he was an officer, he was clearly in charge of the expedition.

One of the uniformed troopers was Ronnie Wilkins; it was a relief to know he had somehow survived and made it back to the Empire.

The other four she didn't recognize; she had been given their names, but hadn't remembered them.

Amy herself was wearing a sort of modified hiking outfit

that the Empire had provided—purple T-shirt, leather walking shorts, black army boots. They'd offered her weapons, but she had declined.

Best and three of the others were sorting supplies in the clearing beside the mummified remains of Shadow's bat-monster, while Wilkins and the last stood guard, blades drawn, at either side. The spacesuits were all safely stowed in the wreck of I.S.S. *Christopher*, and stocks of food and clothing were being distributed and bundled for carrying.

"Too bad we couldn't get horses," one of the men muttered as he hoisted an immense pack.

"They're working on it," Best replied. "They've got a carrier now, they just don't have anywhere to stable them at Base One. You need a lot of fodder."

"Well, if they'd just brought them straight through, they wouldn't need to feed them," the other argued.

"Oh, yes, they would," Best said. "You see any grass around here? We're in the middle of a forest."

"You could get out to the Downs before the horses'd starve."

"Well, they didn't do it," Best said. "So we'll just have to walk—assuming that Brown doesn't come to us." He turned and motioned to Amy. "Come on, Mrs. Jewell," he said. "I've got the lead, then Howard, then you."

"Which pack is mine?" she asked.

"None of them," Best replied. "Orders—you travel light, in case you have to run for it. We take care of you."

"That doesn't seem fair."

Best shrugged. "It's our job," he said. He trudged toward the trail to the west; a trooper fell in behind him.

The others waited, and Amy reluctantly followed. The others fell in behind her, and the party of seven marched into the woods.

Seven of them, and then the warp had closed again; Pel was baffled. What could a group of seven be doing? It was too many for spies, too few for an invasion.

Well, he would know soon; he could sense them in the

forest below. He let the wind slacken, and descended slowly toward them.

The trees were in the way; he couldn't see anything. Annoyed, he blasted a clearing ahead of the Imperial party, and dropped down into it.

The light ahead seemed odd, Amy thought; there was a sort of sparkliness to it, something strange about the colors that filtered through the trees. She didn't *think* it was just the unfamiliar sunlight of Faerie.

She had forgotten how uncomfortable Faerie was, with its pale light and heavy gravity and thick, moist air. Going to talk to Pel had seemed exciting and noble back on Earth, or at Base One, but now it was beginning to seem stupid. She had made this two-hundred-mile walk once, and it had been hellish; so why had she volunteered to do it again?

At least she didn't have morning sickness this time.

She was about to remark on the colors when flame erupted ahead of her, like a bomb-burst; she flung an arm up to shield her face as heat and light blasted at her. The ground shook, and a deafening roar rolled through the forest; the compression of the air washed over her like a great ocean wave, forcing her back. Her hair whipped out behind her, dragging her head back painfully.

"Oh, hell," Best said, barely audible over the ringing in her ears.

Amy lowered her arm, expecting to see a blazing forest fire ahead. Instead she saw a flickering, shifting mass of color, cloud, light, and shadow, like a Hollywood special-effects light show run amok. She felt a tightening in her chest.

"Shadow," she said.

But Shadow was dead, she remembered.

"Pel," she said.

And a voice spoke from the matrix.

"Amy?" it said, in a sound of thunder. "Amy Jewell?"

CHAPTER 29

*A*my *didn't care very much for flying even with a plane,* and after the initial thrill wore off, this magical wind-riding of Pel's was far worse. The wind was a constant, unpleasant pressure; she couldn't speak over it. There was a constant sensation of falling, which she found slightly nauseating.

And it was cold, too.

And frightening.

And it went on and on; they had been airborne for hours. The sun had long since passed its zenith and was moving down the sky ahead of them.

Amy had also looked down at some of the villages they passed over, and been depressed to see that they looked dirtier and less pleasant than she had remembered.

At least all those dead bodies hanging on gallows were gone; she didn't see a gallows or gibbet anywhere. That was certainly an improvement.

She glanced sideways, first at Wilkins, to her right, then at Best, to her left. Pel had decided to bring them along, but none of the others, and hadn't bothered listening to any argument, he had just snatched the three of them up.

She wondered how Pel knew Best.

They were above the marsh now, and there was the fortress ahead of them, drawing quickly nearer; they were flying lower, and slowing down . . .

A moment later they landed, hard, on the causeway outside the gate. Pel stayed on his feet, but the others tumbled to the ground. Best landed rolling, and got quickly to his feet, dusty but unhurt. Wilkins hadn't done quite so well; he'd scraped one palm trying to catch himself, and seemed to have hurt his shoulder.

And Amy herself stretched full-length in the dirt, painfully bruising herself several places, scraping skin from her chin and hands and forearms.

She got slowly to her hands and knees, wincing as she put weight on her palms, and cursing herself for not remembering how roughly Taillefer had landed at Castle Regisvert.

The gate was standing open, and Pel was standing in the opening, his glow suppressed enough that he was visible as a vaguely human outline. "Come on in," he said.

Amy got stiffly to her feet, and followed Pel and Best. Wilkins brought up the rear.

The matrix lit the entry hall, and Amy looked about in mild surprise.

The hall was empty. The monsters were gone from the ledges on either side. Odd bits of debris were scattered about, mostly what appeared to be ash, and the entire place had a dusty, unkempt air, exaggerated, perhaps, by the weird, unsteady, colorful light.

The little party made their way the length of the hall, past a blackened, scorched-looking area and a few smudges that Amy hoped weren't bloodstains, onto the great staircase.

The great tube of light was gone completely. Pel noticed Amy looking at the hole where it had emerged, and said, "That was one of the magical currents turned visible—I don't know why Shadow bothered. I don't."

He marched on ahead, seemingly unwearied by the long flight, up the stairs and across the landing into the throne room. The matrix glow lingered sufficiently for the others, rather more worn, to make their way up the steps at their own pace.

Amy's legs ached by the time she stepped into the throne room, arm raised to fend off the glare.

"Pel?" she called, as she advanced cautiously into the light. "Could you turn it down?"

"Sure."

And the glow was gone—or rather, reduced to insignificance, to just enough to light the throne room pleasantly. Amy could see Pel's face.

His hair was fairly long and hung in graying tangles around his head; his beard was shaggy and uneven as well. Both appeared to have been cut at least once since she had last seen him—but it hadn't been very recently. He had obviously not concerned himself with his appearance lately.

She moved cautiously nearer. Best and Wilkins stepped to the doorway, but waited there as Amy walked warily into the room to talk to Pel.

They'd done their job; they'd gotten her to Pel safely. The rest was up to her. This was what the Empire was paying her a small fortune in gold for; this was what she had agreed to when she had coaxed from the Imperials a promise to commute Prossie's treason sentence from death to exile.

Amy looked around the room, trying to collect her thoughts.

She didn't remember that hole in the ceiling. She didn't remember the litter along the sides of the room, or the thin layer of ash that she scuffed through as she approached Pel's throne. She didn't remember the damp, faintly musty odor.

It reminded her of a preteenager's bedroom—the sort of kid who never cleaned up, and screamed if his parents dared move a single candy wrapper.

"So, how's it going?" she asked.

Pel shrugged. "Hard to say; how've you been doing? I guess the Empire sent you to talk to me about something?"

"I'm fine, thanks—the Air Force people have been very nice about everything. And yes, they tell me that the Emperor himself suggested I come talk to you."

"Really? Wow." Pel sprawled comfortably on his throne;

Amy looked around for somewhere she might sit, but found nothing.

After all, this was a ruler's throne room, she realized; she wasn't supposed to sit in the presence of royalty, or wizardry, or whatever Pel was.

"So here you are," Pel said, "and it's good to see a familiar face, and I hope we can talk awhile before I send you home again, but what was it the Emperor wanted you to say?"

Amy hesitated; she hardly knew where to begin. This wasn't going the way she had pictured it.

"Come on, let's get the business out of the way," Pel urged.

"He thinks you're upset about something," Amy said. "Or his advisers do, or the telepaths, or someone; I never talked to the Emperor, of course, just a bunch of officers and bureaucrats, but they seemed nicer than the ones we dealt with before."

"Maybe you're just more used to them now."

"Maybe," Amy agreed. "Or maybe I'm not so scared. They weren't trying to send me off to fight Shadow, after all, they just wanted me to talk to you."

"I'm as powerful as Shadow was," Pel remarked. "Or pretty nearly, anyway. I can't do a lot of the stuff she did, but I can do plenty."

"So I've heard." She hesitated, then asked, "*Are* you upset about something?"

Pel looked away, at a door in a side wall that had stood slightly ajar; now it slammed shut, though no one had touched it.

He looked back at Amy.

"Yeah, I guess I am," he said.

Amy glanced back at Best and Wilkins, who stepped back discreetly.

"What is it?" she asked.

Pel swallowed, and looked entirely human for a moment.

"It's Nancy," he said.

"Isn't Nancy dead?" Amy asked.

She wasn't sure just what had happened to Nancy. She knew that the Empire had delivered her corpse to Pel, she knew that Shadow had claimed to be able to raise the dead, and Pel claimed to have all Shadow's power, but had Pel really brought Nancy back to life?

"Yeah," Pel said, and Amy could hear the pain in his voice, "she's dead. She's up and walking, but she's still dead, as far as I'm concerned."

"You're sure?"

Pel slammed a fist into the back of his chair, and plumes of golden flame flared momentarily into existence on all sides, then vanished.

"Of *course* I'm sure, damn it!"

Amy took a step back, but then Pel burst into tears.

"Oh, God, Amy," he said, "of course I'm sure!"

It didn't really matter what she said, Pel thought; it was just good to have someone he could talk to, someone he could explain it all to, someone from Earth, someone *real*, someone who would understand.

He hadn't known Amy back on Earth, he had only met her at that first gathering in his house, when Raven of Stormcrack Keep and his little band of resistance fighters had led Captain Cahn and his crew, and Amy and her lawyer, and Pel and his wife and daughter and *their* lawyer, into Faerie.

For five minutes, Raven had said. Just to see. Just so they would know it was real.

How long had it been? Pel had lost track of time; here in the windowless depths of Shadow's fortress, where he didn't need to eat or sleep, he had let days slip by uncounted. The seasons were different here, the year longer than Earth's—it was autumn here, wasn't it? Back in Maryland, winter had probably come and gone.

Five minutes, Raven had said.

And Pel and Amy and the others had been trapped in this adventure, this long storybook saga that should have ended with Shadow's destruction and Pel's ascension, when everyone was supposed to live happily ever after.

Or with Nancy and Rachel's resurrection, when Pel had regained what he had lost, and once again, should have lived happily ever after.

Happily?

He wept openly; he sat on the floor with Amy's arms around him and cried miserably.

Best and Wilkins retreated to the stairs, embarrassed, and Pel had started to shut the doors, until Amy had reminded him that if he did that, the two Imperials would be in the dark.

So he had left the doors open, and he didn't care if they heard him crying. He was the goddamned Brown Magician, he could reduce them to ash with a thought, and he would cry if he wanted.

His wife and daughter were dead to him, and there was nothing he could do about it.

Amy held Pel and let him cry; she had to keep her eyes closed, and even so they stung with the glare of the matrix, because Pel's control of its brilliance had slipped with his loss of control of his emotions, but she didn't turn away or let him go. She held him and let him cry.

At last he stopped, and fought the matrix down, and she opened her eyes to find him looking up at her, his own eyes red and weary.

"Thanks," he said. "You look awful."

"So do you," she said, repressing a sudden urge to giggle. It was all so ridiculous, him lying there in her arms as if he were her lover, but with his hair and beard going every which way and his silly black robe like some comic-book wizard's cloak making him look like an ancient lunatic.

"Sorry."

"It's okay."

Pel sat up, and Amy released him.

"So what are you going to do?" Amy asked.

"About what?"

"Well, I meant about Nancy, but as long as you're asking, what about the Empire? I mean, they sent me here to ask if you'd send home their hostages, and promise not to attack them again, and all that. Normalize relations, I guess you'd say."

Pel shook his head. "I don't want to normalize relations. I want to be left alone. As long as they do that, I won't bother anyone. And they can have the hostages back; I don't even remember where I put them. They're somewhere in the fortress dungeons, I guess; I'll let them go, and they can go back to the space warp with Best and Wilkins."

"You won't open a portal for them?"

"No." Pel shifted around to face Amy properly. "No, I'm not going to do that. I wouldn't know where to send them; I don't know where any of the openings into the Empire come out." Amy doubted that that was true, but she didn't want to argue it. "And besides," Pel continued, "it's too much contact with the Empire; every time I've dealt with them it's been trouble. Let them take care of their own."

Amy shrugged. "I guess that'll have to do, then."

"It ought to."

"I think it will."

For a moment the two of them sat silently; then Amy looked around, before the silence became awkward, and remarked, "It's gotten a bit dusty in here; you've been letting the housekeeping go, I guess."

Pel looked up at the hole in the ceiling. "I always was a bit of a slob," he said.

Amy hesitated, then asked, "So what are you going to do about Nancy?"

Pel shrugged. "What *can* I do? She's my wife—my responsibility. I was the one who brought her here and brought her back to life. I have to stay with her and try to go on loving her." He sighed heavily. "I suggested that she go back to Earth without me, but she didn't want to. She didn't really *mind*, but . . . and besides, after what happened to Grummetty and Alella, I wasn't sure it was a good idea."

"So why don't *you* go back to Earth?"

"Leave her?" Pel looked at Amy, startled.

"You said she was dead, Pel; if she's dead, let her go."

"But she's alive, really, she's just different."

"If she's not the woman you married, let her go; if Rachel's not your daughter anymore, let Nancy have her."

Pel turned away. "That's easy for you to say."

"Pel," Amy said, "have I ever talked to you about my ex-husband, Stan?"

Pel didn't answer, and Amy continued, "One day I saw that he wasn't the man I'd thought I'd married, that I didn't know him and didn't love him, and I divorced him—and it was the smartest thing I could have done. Staying in a bad relationship isn't a good thing to do."

"This is different," Pel said.

"Yeah, I suppose it is—but is it *that* different?"

Pel got up and began brushing dust and ash from his black magician's robe. "I can't go back to Earth," he said, not looking at Amy. "I'm the Brown Magician, the ruler here. I control all the magic. If I leave, the matrix will come apart and all the magic will run wild."

"If you're happy here," Amy said, "then stay."

"It's not . . . I mean, I'm *needed*. Without me there'd be chaos."

"So you're running everything, the way Shadow did?"

"Not the way Shadow did," Pel replied. "No hangings—I've outlawed the death penalty for anything short of murder. And no eviscerations even for that. And I don't keep a close watch on everything the way she tried to do; I never learned how she did all that stuff."

"So what *do* you do?"

"I . . . well, I stopped the Empire from invading."

"They said *you* raided *them* first, and your men killed innocent people."

"Well, they'd lied to me! They cheated me!" The matrix flared up redly for a moment, and Amy decided not to argue with that.

Instead, she said, "So you attacked them?"

"Just some little raids."

"And they counterattacked, but you stopped them?"

He nodded. "That was easy. I just let some of the magic turn to flame, and burned them up, drove them back into the space warps."

"Same as Shadow would have done."

Pel nodded again, not looking at her. He had closed himself off again, Amy thought; that moment of emotional release, when he had wept in her arms, was past.

The matrix was flickering in and out of visibility around him, like spreading multicolored flames; a swirl of fine black ash rose up for a second in a gust of magical wind.

Amy wondered where that ash had come from. What had Pel burned here?

Had he burned people?

He had admitted burning those Imperial soldiers. He had committed murder, had taken human lives—and he didn't seem to think it was important.

She took a step back, suddenly frightened.

"Pel, I think I'd like to go home now," she said.

He turned to face her.

"I've said what the Empire wanted me to say," she said, "and I've given you my opinion about what you should do about Nancy and Rachel, and that's all I came to do. So could you send me home?"

For a moment he didn't answer.

"All right," he said finally. "Give me a minute."

Just before she stepped into the portal, Amy turned to face him for a final word.

"Be careful, Pel," she said. "The way you killed those soldiers, and everything, the way you've let yourself go—be careful you don't turn out like Shadow."

Then she was gone, back to Earth, to the basement of his own house, in Germantown, Maryland.

Angrily, he dropped the portal, let it collapse into nothingness as the matrix resumed its proper shape.

He wasn't like Shadow. He was a caring, considerate person. He wouldn't hurt anyone.

He'd killed those soldiers, but they weren't *real*, they were just Imperials . . .

And why weren't they real?

And he'd killed Shadow herself, of course, or at least set her up, and he'd destroyed all those fetches, but they weren't really *alive*, were they?

He'd killed a lot of Shadow's monsters, by sending them into the Empire to die, but they weren't people.

He had an excuse for everything—but he had an awful lot to excuse, didn't he?

Why hadn't he just gone back to Earth in the first place? Everyone would have been better off.

He tried to tell himself that no, the people of Faerie wouldn't have been better off, they wouldn't have had him there to protect them—but how much protection had he actually provided? Would the Empire have attacked the elves, or those farms, if Pel hadn't goaded them into it?

And most of the time he had just shut himself up here in this fortress, brooding over his own concerns, driving himself to distraction with his problems and ignoring everyone else. He didn't know a thing about Faerie, really. Had he ever talked to the people here? Did he know what they wanted?

He shook his head.

He really didn't. He'd made a halfhearted attempt, back at the beginning, to be the good ruler, but instead of listening to what his people wanted he had told them what *he* wanted, an end to executions and an attempt at democracy.

That was hardly anything to be proud of.

He wasn't doing anyone any good here—least of all himself, trapping himself here, surrounded by his own failures and by a world that he couldn't help seeing as somehow unreal, no matter how solid the stone walls might be.

The door at the side of the throne room opened, and Susan Nguyen—or at least, the thing that used her body and shared her memories—looked in.

"Go get Nancy and Rachel," Pel barked. "Both Nancys."

If he was going to do something irrevocable, if he was going to leave her, he had to let her know. If she asked him to stay, or asked him to take her with him, he would do it, he knew that.

But if she didn't, if she said she didn't care, what would he do?

Amy was right, he had to be free of Nancy. Nancy was dead and holding on to her wouldn't help. And the longer he stayed here in this fortress, in this world, the more like Shadow he became.

Maybe it was something in the matrix; maybe it was something in human nature. He didn't know, and it didn't matter. Having that power always there, straining to be free, waiting to be used, was changing him for the worse.

He had to leave Faerie. He didn't know how to release the matrix completely any other way.

And he couldn't pass it on; there was no one in Faerie who had the talent. Shadow had said so; that was why she had chosen him in the first place. The talent for matrix wizardry had been bred out of the inhabitants of Faerie, and among the Imperials she had only found it in the telepaths; only among Earthpeople was it reasonably common. And the only Earthpeople still here in Faerie were revenants or simulacra, who could never hold magic.

So he would release it, and the matrix would come apart, and wild magic would be loose in the world—and would that really be so bad?

Shadow had said it would, but Shadow could have been wrong, could have lied.

Pel couldn't see how it could be so bad. It would be wild and free, and Shadow would have seen that as bad, but was it really?

No new matrix wizards would arise, to gather the power together again—the talent had been bred out. The magic would *stay* free. Pel almost wished he could be here to see it.

But he couldn't; he had to go. Back home to Earth, to Maryland . . .

To Maryland?

Well, to Earth, certainly; he had no desire to live in the Galactic Empire, under the absolute rule of His Imperial Majesty George VIII.

But Maryland?

Back there where his business was ruined, and there were probably a hundred lawsuits and legal complications to deal with. because of his sudden disappearance?

Back to that house full of memories of Nancy and Rachel?

Why?

"You wanted us?" Nancy's voice called from the door.

"No," Pel said. "I mean, yes. Come here, all of you." He sat up in his throne and watched as the three women and the girl approached.

"If I were to leave," he asked, watching the passive faces, "permanently, would you prefer to come with me, or stay here?"

"It doesn't matter," Susan said.

"Whichever you like," the simulacrum said.

"I don't really care," the Nancy revenant said.

"I don't care a whole lot either," Rachel said.

And that, Pel thought, settled it.

"You're all free," he said, already feeling for the shape of the matrix and the links to Earth. "All of you, do whatever you want from now on. And everyone else in the fortress is free. My last command to you four—or request—is to make sure that the Imperials in the dungeons are all free to go, and that Best and Wilkins can find them."

The four just stared at him.

"They're on the stairs," Pel said, with a wave of his hand. "Best and Wilkins, I mean. Go tell them the hostages are free."

Susan glanced at the others, then turned and headed for the big double doors.

The others just stood there, watching him.

Pel stared back for a moment, then decided that he'd had enough of them. He would make his departure from atop the tower, where any discharge from the disintegrating matrix would dissipate harmlessly into the open air.

And he wouldn't want to go empty-handed, he realized; there was no telling where he might wind up.

He didn't have to rush off this very minute . . .

But soon.

CHAPTER 30

It was raining, and the water was spilling from the hole where the broken gargoyle had been, spattering across the battlements. Pel remembered the sound of Rachel's running footsteps, and smiled a wistful smile.

The tiny revenant downstairs didn't run and play. Rachel was gone.

He took a final look out at the gloomy countryside, at the gray marsh and the distant hills, at the long line of freed hostages marching away down the causeway, then reached out and twisted the matrix in an impossible direction, reaching for the opening to Earth, but turning aside from it, veering away to somewhere else on the planet.

Then the portal was there. He hefted the bag of gold coins in one hand, the pack of clothing and toiletries in the other, and stepped through.

And with a horrible wrenching the matrix came free, tore itself from his mind and shattered, and he staggered forward into total darkness, dazed, wondering if he had gone blind; he staggered, and fell, and landed on sand.

For a moment he lay there, face down, gathering his wits. It was strange to be in darkness; he hadn't seen true darkness in months, not since he first accepted the matrix from Shadow.

The possibility that he might be dead occurred to him, but the sand beneath him was cool and solid, and he heard a soft whispering that didn't sound like anything he would expect in the afterlife.

It sounded like the sea.

He rolled over, the gold coins clinking as he shifted them, and looked up at stars, millions of stars, twinkling white above him.

He wasn't blind; he'd arrived at night.

He sat up, and saw pale bands moving; he blinked, and saw that it was surf, phosphorescent surf rolling in to the beach on which he had arrived.

"And just wot didjer think you were doin' there?" a voice demanded from behind him. "This beach is closed to the public!"

The accent was Australian.

Pel smiled.

He'd always wanted to visit Australia.

"Sorry," he called, getting to his feet. "Which way out?"

Best looked up at the warning rumble, shielding his eyes with his hand to keep the rain out.

The matrix was a shimmering mass that completely surrounded the top twenty feet or more of the central tower; now, as he and the others looked up at it, it expanded, like impossibly fast-rising dough, seething rapidly outward ...

And then it exploded, not with a bang, but with a scream, and colors and patterns scattered wildly across the overcast sky; for a moment a cloud bank flickered red, another was crisscrossed with green tracery like the veins of a leaf, purple fire dripped sizzling down the tower, carrying molten stone with it. Creatures flapped and scrambled in the clouds.

Then it was gone, and the broken stump of the tower ended in a jagged line of blackened stone.

But the raindrops were faintly glowing and slightly iridescent, and somehow Best knew that magic was raining onto Shadowmarsh and all of Faerie.

He shuddered. He didn't like magic.

"Come on," he said. "Two hundred miles to Sunderland and Base One—let's go!"

"Brown's really gone?" the Emperor asked.

The telepath answered, "Yes, Your Majesty."

"Who's in charge, then?"

"The local governments appear to be reasserting themselves," the telepath replied. "The surviving remnants of the old nobility, Shadow's councils of elders, and the like. There's no central government; apparently, there never really was much of one. Either that, or it disintegrated upon Shadow's death."

The Emperor nodded, considering.

"We think," he said, staring at the rug, "that we will find it entertaining and profitable to pick up territories piecemeal in Faerie. An attempt to conquer it all at once would be impractical, and to risk a new Brown Magician arising would be foolish. Better to involve ourselves in it little by little, and stop any potential threat before it looms too large."

"Your Majesty's plan is, of course, wise," the telepath said.

George VIII looked up, pleased. "You really think so?" he said. "All of you?"

"Brown's gone," Miletti repeated. "Faerie's doing a planetary imitation of Yugoslavia."

"You're sure of that?"

"I'm not fucking sure of *anything*," Miletti said, "but it's my honest report."

The lieutenant nodded. He turned off the tape recorder and put it away.

"In that case, Mr. Miletti," he said. "I have good news. Our budget's been cut, and if there's no longer any plausible threat from either the Empire or Faerie, we don't need to monitor the telepaths anymore. That means we don't need you; the major says you're free to do as you please, and we'll be removing our equipment and ending the regular visits. We'll be mailing your check out on Monday."

Miletti stared at him for a long moment, then looked down at the bourbon bottle in his own right hand.

He dropped it to the carpet.

"About time," he said. "Thank you!"

* * *

"He's gone somewhere," Johnston's voice said, "but we don't know where; he never appeared at his house."

Amy looked out her back window at the spaceship in her yard.

"I don't blame him," she said. "Thank you, Major."

She hung up the phone, and realized that she was smiling. And why shouldn't she? The Empire's payment had plummeted out of the sky half an hour ago, enough gold to get her decorating business off the ground again. Prossie was in the other room, studying American history for her GED, and no longer had to worry about the Empire. Everything wasn't what it had been before *Ruthless* appeared, but it was good enough; all the complicated and nasty adventures in other worlds were over, and it was time to get on with her life.

She was happy with the situation.

She hoped Pel Brown was as happy, wherever he was.

She thought he might be.

And in a small town on the Australian coast, a barefoot, strangely dressed man with an American accent wandered down the village high street with a bag of gold coins in his pack—Faerie gold, to be sure, but he was reasonably certain that it wasn't going to disappear or turn to offal.

Of course, he wouldn't be able to sell any until the town's only jeweler opened his shop in the morning, so he had decided to walk the night away.

The air was warm, and rich with the smell of the sea; the stars of the southern hemisphere were bright and strange overhead. It was a beautiful night for a stroll, and the world was rich with possibilities.

He walked on, whistling.

A world of fantasy and adventure in the novels of

LAWRENCE WATT-EVANS

Published by Del Rey Books.
Available in your local bookstore.

DEL REY ONLINE!

The Del Rey Internet Newsletter...

A monthly electronic publication, posted on the Internet, GEnie, CompuServe, BIX, various BBSs, and the Panix gopher (gopher.panix.com). It features hype-free descriptions of books that are new in the stores, a list of our upcoming books, special announcements, a signing/reading/convention-attendance schedule for Del Rey authors, "In Depth" essays in which professionals in the field (authors, artists, designers, sales people, etc.) talk about their jobs in science fiction, a question-and-answer section, behind-the-scenes looks at sf publishing, and more!

Online editorial presence: Many of the Del Rey editors are online, on the Internet, GEnie, CompuServe, America Online, and Delphi. There is a Del Rey topic on GEnie and a Del Rey folder on America Online.

Our official e-mail address for Del Rey Books is delrey@randomhouse.com

Internet information source!

A lot of Del Rey material is available to the Internet on a gopher server: all back issues and the current issue of the Del Rey Internet Newsletter, a description of the DRIN and summaries of all the issues' contents, sample chapters of upcoming or current books (readable or downloadable for free), submission requirements, mail-order information, and much more. We will be adding more items of all sorts (mostly new DRINs and sample chapters) regularly. The address of the gopher is gopher.panix.com

Why? We at Del Rey realize that the networks are the medium of the future. That's where you'll find us promoting our books, socializing with others in the sf field, and—most importantly—making contact and sharing information with sf readers.

For more information, e-mail delrey@randomhouse.com